Isle of Joy

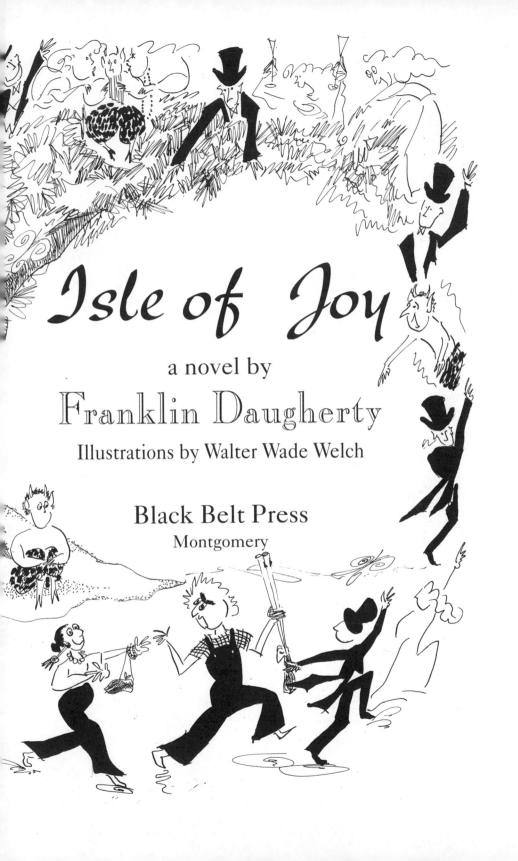

Isle of Joy

a novel by

Franklin Daugherty

Illustrations by Walter Wade Welch

Black Belt Press

Montgomery

The Black Belt Press

P.O. Box 551

Montgomery, AL 36101

Copyright © 1997 by Franklin Daugherty.
All rights reserved under International and Pan-American Copyright
Conventions. Published in the United States by the Black Belt Press, a
division of the Black Belt Communications Group, Inc., Montgomery,
Alabama.

Library of Congress Cataloging-in-Publication Data
Daugherty, Franklin.
    Isle of Joy : a novel / by Franklin Daugherty.
    p. cm.
    ISBN 1-881320-78-2
    1. Title.
    PS3554.A845I8 1996
    813'.54—dc20   96-30795
                                      CIP

DESIGN BY RANDALL WILLIAMS
Illustrations by Walter Wade Welch
Printed in the United States of America
96 97 98   5 4 3 2 1

*The Black Belt, defined by its dark, rich soil, stretches across central Alabama. It
was the heart of the cotton belt. It was and is a place of great beauty, of extreme
wealth and grinding poverty, of pain and joy. Here we take our stand, listening to
the past, looking to the future.*

Acknowledgments

The author wishes to express his gratitude to Erin Kellen, his editor, for her painstaking review of the text, her many astute suggestions, and her encouragement. He would also like to thank Randall Williams, publisher of Black Belt Press, for taking chances.

Special thanks are due to Dr. Michael Thomason and Elisa Baldwin of the University of South Alabama Archives. Dr. Thomason has shown great imagination and distinction as a historian by creating these extraordinary photo archives.

The author would furthermore like to express his appreciation to the following individuals and institutions: artist Walter Wade Welch of New Orleans; Palmer C. Hamilton and Amy St. John Hamilton; T. J. Potts, Jr., and Jane Potts; Rebecca Paul Florence; Tom Mason; Benjamin Trimmier; Robinson McClure, Jr.; Lucy Beaven Cope; Charles John Torrey III and the Museum of the City of Mobile; George Ewert, Director of the Local History and Genealogy Division of the Mobile Public Library; Christopher Ward of New Orleans; and the National Willoughby Institute.

Contents

PART THREE:
THE WINTER SOCIAL SEASON 287

EPILOGUE 300

Isle of Joy

Concise Guide to the Mobile Accent

By George Belzagui
Linguist (part-time)

When southbound travelers cross the live oak / gumbo line, so close to the Gulf of Mexico, and arrive in Mobile, they may notice that the accent changes, too, into deliquescent vowels and convolute sounds totally different from the upstate twang. It was probably influenced by the many Irish and German immigrants in the nineteenth century, and no doubt by black English as well. The true Mobile accent is spoken in full feather mainly by older people these days, alas, but once you hear it you will not mistake it for any other, north or south.

After many years of research according to strict scientific methodologies, I have ascertained that no one speaks a purer version of this accent than myself. And in a relentless quest for exact observation, I have spent many years—indeed, decades—listening to myself talk, often standing for hours on end in front of the mirror watching my lips, tongue, teeth, and gums articulate these mellifluous and well-crafted phonemes. An exhausting project, yes, but not without its pleasures.

Here are some of the highlights of my research:

THE MOBILE "UI": Most "er," "ur," and "ir" sounds are pronounced "ui." For example: "What on uith did Cuitus luin in chuich?" This is *quite* different, I assure you, from the New Orleans or New York "oi," as in "New Joisey." The first sound of the diphthong is a short "u."

THE SHORT "A" sounds like long "I" of "night," especially, for some reason, when ladies are talking. Thus "half" rhymes with "life," "pass" rhymes with "ice," "grand" with (standard English, not Southern) "grind." This is why, when clarity permits, in some of the dialogue in this epic "after" is spelled "ife-ter," "asked" is spelled "iced," "aunt" is spelled "inet," "last": "lyest," etc. To wit: "I had simply a *grind* time at the Grind Hotel."

"AR" AND SOME "AL" SOUNDS sound like "au" or "aw," as in

11

"Paul" or "saw": "Jimmy Cawter tawked about the waw."

THE MOBILE GLIDE: Long "A's" and long "O's" die a lingering death, so that "blame" becomes "blayim," or "suppose" becomes "suppo-uhs." Not two separate sounds, but a long Louis Armstrong shift in the back of the throat. "Felix ro-uhs from his thro-un."

THE WORDS "ON" AND "WANT" are pronounced "oin" and "woint," especially, for some reason, by younger people: "I cain't believe that about Carol Ortega! You're putting me *oin*!"

The true old-fashioned Old Mobilian speaks in a deep, low, rich, vibrating, throaty voice, and emphasizes every word slowly and carefully as though he or she were issuing the most important pronouncement ever uttered on the face of the earth.

After seeing these few examples, you will probably feel eager to hear many more of my observations about the way I talk. These are available in my recent work: *Complete Guide to the Mobile Accent*, by George Belzagui. Published by Kahlil Q. Belzagui Memorial Library, c/o George Belzagui, New Hamilton Street, 3839 pages. $499.99.

Supplies of the book depend on the availability of the Xerox machines at the Commerce National Bank, but chances are good that it will not yet be sold out when you write.

Handy Pronouncing Lexicon

Also by George Belzagui
Historian (part-time)

Readers in California and Vladisvostok and other such far-off places may wonder how to pronounce some of the names that figure prominently in this chronicle, in which, as the author has informed me, I was honored to play a small part. As president of the Iberville Historical Society (the esteemed Mrs. Odilia Belzagui, née de la Rochefoucauld, formerly Mrs. O. d.l.R. Chighizola, and myself constitute the bulk of the regular membership), I am in a position to shed some light on the matter.

DE LA ROCHEFOUCAULD: The purist pronunciation, *Rosh-foo-COLE*, has lately been preferred by Mrs. Odilia and her distinguished niece McCorquodale, the only remaining members of this genteel and refined, though strangely forgotten, French colonial family of Mobile. Despite many hours of research in the genealogical division of the Mobile Public Library, we have been unable to find a connection with the seventeenth-century philosopher, but a breakthrough is expected any day.

The more common pronunciation, however, is *ROSHfookle*, which has been used for many generations here, and indeed until recently the name was written "Roshfookle." Since "Beroujon" became *BERRY-john* locally, "Roche" became *Roach*, and "Huger" became *YOO-jee*, *ROSH-fookle*, too, can be said without fear of stigma.

CHIGHIZOLA: *Chig-i-ZOE-luh*. Mrs. Odilia's first husband, the late Joe Chighizola, the bookie at McAlpin's Pool Hall on St. Francis Street (now a parking lot), exemplified all the hard-working virtues of this proud Iberian line.

ODILIA: *O-DEEL-yuh*. Rhymes with "camellia."

BALLERIEL: *Buh-LAYR-i-el*. As in Fred "Astaire-i-el," as it were. No introduction is needed to this wealthy and prominent family. Now my grandfather, Raphael Belzagui, remembered Mrs. Harmsworth

Balleriel's great-grandfather, old Mr. Theo Parkhurst, when he had nothing but a fruit stand on Front Street.

BELZAGUI: *BEL-za-gooey*. Until my father retired in 1952 to gather the laurels of a long career in well-deserved repose, Belzagui's Shoeteria on St. Emanuel Street was a Mobile landmark. Wealth has unfortunately eluded us, but the Belzagui men became most prominent in the Knights of Columbus after arriving in Mobile from Lebanon (they were Maronite Catholics!) in the 1880s.

The pronunciation of other names, Anglo-Saxon and Celtic, we trust to the erudition of the reader.

Part One

The Winter Social Season

Rose Parkhurst Jamieson Balleriol

HUBBA HUBBA CLUB

U.S.S. Alabama

JUNIOR LEAGUE

Santa Claus Society

"Miss Brick House"

The Avant-garde

Tonya de Luxe

POSTMODERNISM

CHAPTER 1

Hot Day in November

What were you supposed to do if you didn't have a car? McCorquodale pondered the question on one of those occasional hot days in November as she carefully stepped in her red patent leather spike heels through the parking lot and minced gracefully onto a strip of grass by Airport Boulevard in suburban west Mobile. Motorists gawked at the extraordinary sight of someone walking, and speculated about her morality. A policeman on a motorcycle stopped to ask if something was wrong.

McCorquodale had caught a bus downtown on her way out, but had just missed the returning one and felt too annoyed to wait an hour for another. The day had started dreadfully. She had gotten up early at ten to contact the editor of *Interview* magazine in New York and debate an article about New Age music and postmodernism while she took her morning coffee with chicory. No dial tone. Then Aunt Odilia knocked on her door and showed her the cutoff notice from the telephone company. There were other threatening bills, too: a vulgar note from the gas company, and robber barons in Birmingham were getting nasty about the electric bill. "They'll never understand us down here," McCorquodale exclaimed scornfully.

The little wench with the Dolly Parton hairdo at the telephone service center had called her "mayum" and contorted her mouth into a smile—all the time eyeing her suspiciously—and asked for cash on the barrel. McCorquodale had painfully unrolled the twenties from her red silk handbag. That left exactly fifteen dollars, enough maybe for her and Aunt Odilia to eat for, what, two days?

Something would have to be done soon about the problem of money. McCorquodale was accustomed to certain creature comforts. Others might drink orange juice, but McCorquodale liked a nice glass of claret and imported kippers with her morning eggs and toast. Yet precisely four weeks ago she had quit a very unfulfilling position at AAA Superior Wallcoverings ("It left so many corners of my soul unlit"). She had also canceled all after-hours appointments. Generous young men in hot chase after her discerning spirit—that had been nice, but when you are born to greatness, you must begin to prepare for your moment of destiny.

A Chevrolet went by, and the man at the wheel seemed to be trying to pop his eyeballs out of his head right at her. McCorquodale looked away blankly.

If people stared, it was not just because she was walking. Margaret Constance Roshfookle was the fateful nexus of two candescent, if somewhat dimming, family lines. Her father's side, as represented by Aunt Odilia, a widow immersed in genealogical sleuthing, had inspired a regal bearing and way of dealing with people that could have sent foreign ambassadors bowing backwards out of the room. Her pale blond hair, however, her bitingly blue eyes, her taut and dewy skin came, along with her nickname, from the McCorquodales, one of the "premier families," at least chronologically, of Chunchula in the hilly piney woods in the north of the county. Even in her ultra-chic New Wave dress, divided into a red and a white patch from her right hip to her bared left shoulder, she retained something of the curvaceous and sassy charm of an unhoped-for Daisy Mae in overalls pumping gas at a Highway 45 Kayo filling station.

McCorquodale stopped walking for a moment and looked, really looked, at the suburban scene around her, something she generally tried to avoid. Cars as far as the eye could see whipping up the dust and a noxious haze. Hundreds of signs in screaming plastic colors. On the other side of the street, Alabama Power Company crews were busy whacking the tops off of some pine trees growing near the power lines, and hacking an ugly V into an old live oak.

"Where's my machine gun when I really need it?" McCorquodale wondered.

Behind the tree butchers, on the far side of a vast parking lot, a plastic

Swiss chalet pancake house glimmered like a mirage in the heat waves. McCorquodale could feel perspiration trickling down the stockings on her unusually well-turned and velvety calves.

"All that asphalt."

A flock of seagulls turned and circled and swooped above the asphalt, giving off sad, plangent cries. Why did they always come to these parking lots? What were they looking for? Did they find insects there? Could they possibly remember Wragg Swamp, filled in and paved over twenty-five years ago? Gulls had been coming to the swamps for centuries, probably millennia. There was nothing for them there now.

A wave of misgivings overpowered her. "Could it be I'm just deceiving myself?" she wondered. Maybe she should go to New York, start an avant-garde magazine like *Interview*, open a postmodern disco in Soho. For a moment she pictured what would happen if she took that road in the wood. She saw herself grabbing taxies in snowy winds, sparkling at cocktail parties. The excited talk-of-the-town articles about her activities, whatever those might be. The buzz and chatter and people looking her way. The boring fact that she had no money and did not know a soul up there hovered almost entirely out of sight on the dark edge of the picture.

But then her great dream came to mind, formed on occasional slow nights when her date's conversation was not quite up to her intellectual standards and her mind wandered: her own twenty-first century, brilliantly postmodern sidewalk café. And a swank avant-garde art gallery, and a cabaret, too, right downtown on Conti Street. Out in front, in bright lighting, she would be sitting at a table while Oriana Fallaci taped an interview with her for the *Paris Review*. Crowds would watch admiringly from a distance, including many blurred but familiar faces. They were standing in the dim street. Probably some clients from the interior decorating shop, some old dates. The Spanish film director Pedro Almodóvar would catch her eye and toast her from his table with his sherry.

"Of course," McCorquodale thought, "It's quite true that I could go to Manhattan and have them all at my feet overnight, but wouldn't that be just the easy way out? I have a duty right here. I can feel it in my bones that we're going postmodern. It's so curious that no one has spotted it yet, but that's my big chance. Gulf Coast postmodernism, darlings, *that* will be the cutting edge!"

But looking at the plastic chalet, the tree assassins, the endless swarm of cars, the asphalt all around, she suddenly felt as though it was all so much bigger than she was. "But it's all so dead. There must be more than this," she whispered.

The fact was, McCorquodale had come to a crisis in her life, and her spike heels were killing her. She stopped by a patch of bamboo, slipped them off and stared blankly at the traffic. "My Lord, fifteen dollars in my pocketbook. Can't start a sidewalk café on that."

Would it all end with her crawling back to Mrs. Watkins next week and begging for her old job back?

"Oh, NOOO!!"

H. Sloane Wolfe, president and chairman of the board of the Commerce National Bank, had left the chauffeur at home with the limousine at his mansion in Spring Hill so that he could drive into town himself in his silver BMW. He liked the feeling of sleek power it gave him, cruising down Airport Boulevard, accelerating, abruptly weaving in and out of the traffic on his way from the new branch bank in the western suburbs to a meeting of the United Fund. He liked to imagine that he was a tiger shark darting in front of a school of frightened redfish.

He smiled at the thought of his visit at the branch bank. No one had known he was coming and a complete hush fell upon the place when he walked through the door. Employees scurried right and left, and the branch manager, who had just returned from the dreaded tour-of-duty in a remote branch near the Mississippi state line, sweated visibly when Wolfe asked him to show him around the new place. Wolfe affected not to notice. "Scare the hell out of em and keep em wondering what you're really thinking," he chuckled.

Alas, these interludes of amusement were rare. He was a tycoon, a pillar of the city, and he had expansion plans that would soon strike terror into his competitors at the Prudential National Bank; yet Wolfe felt a certain unfilled space in his limited private life. Roberta was going crazy at home again redecorating the house; this time it was Pennsylvania Dutch. An evening spree during last Saturday's "business trip" to the French Quarter had fizzled when he got indigestion from the Oysters Rockefeller at that mafioso restaurant on Bourbon Street that provided the high-class escort service.

A vista of board meetings, work, and Roberta stretched out before him. "Even magnates," he reflected sadly, "need a little adventure now and then."

It was then that he saw a voluptuous blonde in a freaky red and white dress standing by the side of the road rubbing her feet. "Good God amighty," he murmured. The car horns blared furiously when the silver BMW streaked across three lanes of traffic and stopped by the side of the road.

What is life without balconies and galleries?

CHAPTER 2

That Royal Blood

H. Sloane Wolfe seemed astonished when he dropped McCorquodale off at the address on St. Anthony Street. "*This* is where she lives?" he wondered, but before he could say a word, the racy blonde, moving in her high heels now like a well-fed mink, slipped out of the car, blew him a kiss, and vanished through a gate in a brick wall.

One hundred years before it had been a choice residential neighborhood, and even in the youth of Aunt Odilia, it was full of somewhat dingy nineteenth-century houses inhabited by big families. But to H. Sloane Wolfe, it was a no-man's-land. All one could see of McCorquodale's house from the street was a narrow pink-plastered addition with an old slate roof in a single sideways slope, and two tall floor-length windows on the second floor opening onto a little balcony with cast iron railings. That was McCorquodale's bedroom. Everything else was hidden by the brick wall along the sidewalk covered with coral vine in full autumn bloom.

On one side of the house, at the corner of the block, stood Sam's Body Shop, a rundown automobile repair joint surrounded by cracked pavement covered with oil slicks. Rusting, partially stripped cars and pickup trucks were parked everywhere. On the other side were two vacant lots full of stacks of old tires. Across the street the kudzu was growing over the vacant lots and up the telephone poles, but somebody had planted zinnias in front of a little white Creole cottage with green shutters and new aluminum windows.

The gate through which McCorquodale disappeared concealed a shady courtyard that could hardly have been suspected from the street. Several huge camellias, small trees really, and azalea bushes of more than a human lifetime spared only a few small patches for a tangle of lilies and

ferns. The damp smell of thick humus, of rich black soil spaded for many
years, mingling with the medicinal odor of a hidden camphor tree, lent
an aura of haven to the place, and of an antiquity far beyond the actual
dates. It was an 1830s wooden house constructed in the shape of an L and
raised on piers almost eight feet off the ground. Every room, except for
those in the later brick wing facing the street, where McCorquodale
lived, opened onto a long, wide gallery badly in need of a paint job.

McCorquodale found Aunt Odilia walking around the parlor in a
festive mood with a tea glass of Mogen David. It never crossed her mind
that Aunt Odilia had made a stupendous discovery that would deflect
McCorquodale's new path, sending her straight down a noble *camino
real*. McCorquodale just thought that there must have been a sale on
pork loin at the grocery store.

Ever since the death of her noted husband, Joe Chighizola, once
known all over town as the bookie at McAlpin's Pool Hall on St. Francis
Street, Aunt Odilia had devoted herself to two great passions. The first
was clipping coupons from the grocery store ads in the *Mobile Herald-
Item*, and reporting her discoveries to a whole network of telephone
friends.

Every evening after supper she would start preparing. She would
spread the morning and evening editions out on the crocheted tablecloth
of the dining room table and clip. "Tuinip greens at Food Wuild, sixty-
nine cents a pound!" she would exclaim, or "The Baldwin County
potatuhs are in at Naman's, muicy!" Since McCorquodale had banished
the television set from the house because it was "the tentacle of mindless
mass society reaching for us, right down the chimney," Odilia had plenty
of time for very drawn-out nighttime conversations.

Aunt Odilia, like H. Sloane Wolfe, like nearly all native Mobilians
of a certain age, had the unmistakable, stagy Mobile accent, which was
studded with Baroque curlicues created when the English language
reached the Gulf of Mexico. In appearance she was in some ways a
vanishing type of Mobile matron. She always wore her dyed blue-black
hair pulled back in a bun, and always wore an impressive assortment of
earrings, beads, and brooches from the late and much regretted Kress's

five and ten cents store. This elegance was undermined somewhat by the very practical transition she had made some years back to white tennis shoes, and slacks that called attention to a prominent midriff bulge. An unsuspecting visitor to St. Joseph's Saturday afternoon vigil mass, spotting Aunt Odilia saying the Hail Mary with a large cluster of her friends and regular telephone interlocutors, all of them wearing an array of striped and spotted polyester stretch knit pants, might have thought they were a new missionary order created to minister to K-Mart shoppers.

Aunt Odilia's days were devoted to her second great passion, genealogy. The family was not in any way prominent, or even particularly known around town, even though the Roshfookles had been around for generations. Society people would have pegged them for impoverished lower middle class. "Roshfookle? Didn't they have that little ice house on Canal Street?" they might wonder. Or, "Didn't they use to replate silverware down at Five Points?"

Still, Mrs. Odilia Roshfookle Chighizola was convinced that glory lurked in the family tree. Early every morning she rose and walked to St. Joseph's for six-thirty mass, then pursued her research at the genealogical division of the Mobile Public Library. The afternoons were spent at the Canonical Archives on Government Street. After that she sometimes went shopping with money McCorquodale had given her, often with her friends Miss Alice and Miss Hattie Robinson, who had a car. These two sisters were a familiar sight to people all over town, even complete strangers, because they invariably drove their old 1950s Studebaker at fifteen miles per hour, followed everywhere they went by a long line of cars, like a diplomatic cortège, frantically looking for a chance to pass.

Aunt Odilia had raised McCorquodale since the tragic death of her parents when she was a child. It happened in 1965 when Hurricane Betsy hit New Orleans. Odilia's younger brother by twenty years, Red Roshfookle, was a jitterbug instructor at Arthur Murray Dance Studios. He met Betty Sue McCorquodale in the early fifties soon after she had moved to town from Chunchula to tend bar and dance with the guests at the Silver Lining Social Club near the river at the foot of Government Street.

After their marriage they lived to burn the candle at both ends. Year in, year out, it was cocktails at the downtown hotels and lounges, jitterbug at Fort Whiting Armory Auditorium Mardi Gras balls. All that the mad and giddy local nightlife had to offer they quaffed to the last drop. Everyone tried to keep them from going to New Orleans, but the prospect of a hurricane party at a friend's house near the levee was too tempting. A survivor reported that it was over in a flash. While the winds were howling outside, Red and Betty Sue executed a particularly difficult rock and roll step to a song by Mitch Rider and the Detroit Wheels. Red had just swung Betty Sue over his head from behind and caught her in midair. Without even pausing, they both squatted down and were swinging their behinds in a sassy swish to the words "Bend over, let me see you shake your tail feathers," when a coal barge came crashing into the room. They never knew what hit them.

After the accident, Aunt Odilia and McCorquodale lived on the insurance money and a small inheritance Aunt Odilia had saved. At first she sent McCorquodale to Bishop Toolen, the Catholic high school for girls, but later transferred her to the public Murphy High School because "Mawgret Constance liked to be around the little boys." McCorquodale had excelled at "Muiphy," and Aunt Odilia still kept her framed certificate of admission to the National Honor Society hanging in the front parlor and showed it to all her guests.

Like many a local parent, Aunt Odilia carefully instructed her niece in the glories of the family history. So when McCorquodale entered the room after being dropped off by H. Sloane Wolfe, Odilia calmed herself and began to go over the facts again, her powdered cheeks burning from the Mogen David sugar rush. Something was up, McCorquodale realized. She sat down and lit a Gauloise in her mother-of-pearl cigarette holder, listening approvingly. Even in the postmodern age, she reflected, one must not forget one's social standing.

The Roshfookles, Odilia reminded, had come over at the beginning of the eighteenth century with Bienville on the *Renommée*, the first ship of French colonists to arrive in Mobile. This assertion was based on her discovery one red-letter morning of the name "Gil de la Rochefoucauld" glimmering at her from a typed list of the ship's crew in a compilation of colonial documents. Obviously this very fragrant appellation was the original version of "Roshfookle." Did the "de" mean that they were noble? No doubt. At any rate, it completely disproved two vague family traditions, one that the Roshfookles had wandered down from the Carolinas to homestead, ridiculous thought. The other was that they had come by boat from Slovenia, an argument which to an outside observer might carry very strong weight from the fact that the Roshfookles had even heard the word "Slovenia" on these shores.

After this colonial arrival, the name seemed to vanish from all records and documents without a trace until reappearing without further explanation some one hundred and fifty years later with the mention of Jesse Elijah Roshfookle, married to one Carrie, in a county census. Evidently their grasp of French spelling had weakened in the interim.

Nothing was very certain about the family before they bought the house on St. Anthony Street in the 1890s. It was pure gall to remember that as a giddy young girl Odilia had passed up many priceless opportunities to ask older relatives about the family history. Family tradition had it that at one time way back before the War Between the States, the Roshfookles had owned a lot of land in the area. Aunt Odilia's father, Alois Roshfookle, principal desk clerk at the old Battle House Hotel, now closed, also used to say that around the 1840s a Roshfookle woman named Camille or something like that had been "the talk of the town" one carnival.

What had happened to the family prominence? Who was the exquisite Camille? Why was she so celebrated? For years Aunt Odilia had done research on the antebellum carnival groups which never seemed to lead anywhere. But today her good friend and fellow historian George Belzagui, mailroom supervisor at the Commerce National Bank, had reported finding a document of the Tea Drinkers Society, an early carnival mystic society, in which the name "Camille" was mentioned!

Odilia's black eyes sparkled and her dime store earrings trembled as she raised her short figure to its full height and laid a hand on her ample bosom. She had never told McCorquodale the goal of all her long days of

"resuich," but today, she said, "Jawage Belzagui confuimed my intui-
tions." Odilia was going to prove that Camille de la Rochefoucauld had
been crowned the first queen of Mardi Gras! McCorquodale, as the last
of the line, was her *only legitimate heir*.

Never mind that the telephone had been shut off. Never mind the
gas bill and the power bill. "In your veins, shuguh, you've got that royal
red." She took an excited swig from the tea glass, and a trickle of Mogen
David from the corner of her mouth left some doubt as to what liquid
was meant. But the suspense was soon cleared.

"The blood of the Rochefoucaulds!"

CHAPTER 3

Busy Day at the Bank

At least once every day Ce Ce Anne Stanton would come down to the mailroom of the Commerce National Bank to report the latest business tidings and affairs of state to Aunt Odilia's friend George Belzagui, mailroom supervisor, and Eddie the mailboy. Generally it was around four in the afternoon toward the end of her busy day.

Ce Ce Anne spent her mornings reconnoitering and gathering intelligence about events in town the night before. From noon to one-thirty she would have a leisurely lunch in the employees' cafeteria with a select group of up-and-coming young officers and socially notable tellers and secretaries. She usually began her rounds to all the departments around two, after lingering for half an hour in the employee library (in the same large room as the cafeteria) leafing through the *Wall Street Journal* (got to stay on top of things!) and keeping a sharp eye out for stragglers who might be returning with news from missions out in the business world.

Ce Ce Anne's talents were so wide-ranging that the bank had found it advisable to create the special position of "Liaison for Commercial Loan and Investment Concepts" for her. In the five years since her graduation from the University of Alabama, her rise through the bank hierarchy had been meteoric, a fact which particularly gladdened the heart of her father, Wallace Wade Stanton, a member of the board of directors and president of the Stanton Steamship Corporation.

After about a quarter till four Mr. Belzagui would put away his writings in a desk drawer and make a pot of coffee. Eddie always made a point of coming back to the mailroom before making his final collection of outgoing mail to take to the post office in big canvas bags.

Ce Ce Anne's dispatches on developments in the business community were generally considered to be authoritative. Her reconnaissance network had worked especially well the night before, and she walked into the mailroom, slim and elegant, cropped black hair gleaming in a fashionable "Betty Boop" cut, waving both her arms about her head so that her gold bracelets jingled.

"Just call me a liar; y'all are gonna tell me I'm *lyne*. Quick, get me a cup of coffee, Eddie, before I pice out." It was the sort of story that was always circulating downtown. Ce Ce Anne had heard it from a friend at Newhouse Imports, Inc., who had picked it up while exercising at the Athelstan Club the night before.

A rising "loung yawyer," as Ce Ce Anne called them, from a prominent law firm was defending a local plumber's union, but had been apprehended by the union president paying court to the president's wife at their home near Dauphin Island Parkway on the south side. Not pausing to hear lengthy forensic discussion, the plumber rushed for his gun, but the lawyer escaped through the second-story window, coming to work the next day with a distinct limp.

The members of the "A-Club" were delighted by the fact that the lawyer was scheduled to make a talk to the bar association the next week on the topic, "Outside the Courtroom: Extra Responsibilities in the Attorney-Client Relationship." The waggish word about town was that the law firm had adopted the slogan, "We make house calls."

It took Ce Ce Anne a long time to finish her business news, but she was not interrupted by a single person. Visitors rarely came there. In fact, the mailroom was virtually a forgotten department, located in the basement of the twenty-five-story building next to the storage room for old bank records.

Mr. Belzagui had entered the services of the Commerce National Bank fresh out of the army after World War II with the highest hopes for a brilliant business career. He did not have big family connections like Ce Ce Anne—he had grown up in a big Lebanese family on New Hamilton Street in one of those little white "California bungalows" with green awnings across the front gable and a plaster statue of the Virgin Mary in the front yard—but he started as mailroom supervisor expecting rapid promotion. Yet unlike Ce Ce Anne, he had lingered year after year thinking advancement was just around the corner.

In the first decade he had fired out ideas which the bank hierarchy considered far too unstable. He suggested starting branch banks and investing in television network stock. He wanted to distribute Commerce National Bank calendars. His idea for having pretty young bank tellers work for a week as train hostesses on lines to Chicago and New York—the slogan: "Let a Mobile bank bring you a world of *Commerce*"—would have been a sensational publicity stunt. But all fell on deaf ears. Even in later years, as the circle of his business ideas grew more restricted, the compilation of his monumental *Mailroom Regulations* had no effect.

Eventually Mr. Belzagui began to grow used to the security of his basement fiefdom. He suspended his Knights of Columbus sword from a ganglion of pipes above his desk and resigned himself to the solitary pleasures of a confirmed old bachelor. On his desk he kept a framed photo of the cedars of Lebanon growing on Mt. Hermon. He hung the memorabilia of his historical research on the mailroom walls, for he had begun to seek consolation in the enticing green labyrinths of local history, and found a kindred spirit in the magnetic and impressive Mrs. Odilia Chighizola.

All of Mr. Belzagui's remaining career hopes now were pinned on the completion of his opus, *Mailroom Regulations, Revised Edition*. When Ce Ce Anne had finished, he told her and Eddie about his most recent thoughts on "The Correct Procedure for Opening European Aerograms," a chapter of vital relevance to the International Department.

Ce Ce Anne was filled with genuine admiration for the project. "Mr. Belzagui, you're so smawt to be writing a book. One of these days I'm going to icek you to come and speak to my committee in the Junior League." Like many in that exclusive service organization of public-minded young women, Ce Ce Anne had been a Kappa at Alabama and still had the nasal Kappa twang, clamping her mouth shut when she talked. "You know I really have to go," she said. "It's not easy being a liaison and I only have hife an ouwuh to finish my work. I'm just *exhawsted* at the end of the day. But first, Eddie, show me your buttons."

Eddie sidled up beside Ce Ce Anne, leaned backward over the mail counter, and flashed his coat open with a practiced hand. On his shirt he wore his usual "Gay Power" button and the button of the day, "Wild in the Streets."

"I'm going to pice *out!*" Ce Ce Anne shrieked. Eddie was known among all the younger bank secretaries for his shocking buttons, which he changed every day and flashed discreetly with a quick gesture when he leaned over the desk to pick up the mail. Eddie considered himself something of a free spirit and saboteur within the bank. His real energies went into the productions of the Port City Players, where he had become one of the stars. His last role in *Brigadoon* had been a triumph, and he knew that the steady success on the Mobile stage he had found since leaving his native Lucedale, Mississippi, would soon launch him into national prominence.

He was proud of his piercing blue eyes, pointy black elven eyebrows, and blond hair which he knew flew out boyishly when he danced his quick steps on the stage. Sometimes he worried that his height (five feet six inches) might be a handicap in the career of stage and screen that awaited him, but in his earnest moments he would tell his friends, mixing his metaphors with nineteen-year-old enthusiasm, "I just know the arts here is fixen to bust into bloom. I can feel that excitement in the air. And when it comes, I'm gonna be rightchere ridin the crest of the wave."

At first Mr. Belzagui had been rather worried by Eddie's buttons and a certain tendency toward flamboyance that did not fit the general tone of the Commerce National Bank, but after considering what to do, he hit upon the solution of adding a revision to his *Mailroom Regulations*: "Metallic buttons with political, social and miscellaneous messages are strictly forbidden to mailroom employees on bank premises unless worn under a coat." Eddie always wore them under a coat anyway, and thus the matter was regulated.

It was a quarter till five when Ce Ce Anne finally left to spread her news to the bookkeeping department. Eddie went to pick up the mail, and Mr. Belzagui reread the day's writings. Then he took out the document he was to give Mrs. Chighizola, and repictured how excited she had been over the phone. His thoughts began to wander for no telling how long, woolgathering.

It had been a perfectly normal day in the basement of the Commerce National Bank, but in the offices of H. Sloane Wolfe on the twenty-fifth floor, earthshaking plans were being hatched.

CHAPTER 4

Progress At Last

For the philosophically minded, the Tennessee-Tombigbee Waterway, a massive Federal canal project which would connect Alabama rivers with Northern ports on the Mississippi River system, posed thorny questions. How was one to recognize those far-flung cities and streams, those rudely striving peoples with whom they were soon to have such intimate contact? For generations everybody had known within their heart of hearts that reality did not exist beyond the vast ring of forests stretching out to the north, east and west. To the south was the Gulf of Mexico. Mobile and the Eastern Shore of the bay lay sheltered at the center like an island. For the more practically minded, however, expectations began to reach a fever pitch, even among the most diverse groups. After more than two decades of local economic slump, a boom was expected like never before. The boosters were saying that Mobile would become the new Houston, sprawling out into Florida and Mississippi. Old-fashioned entrepreneurs had visions of smokestacks smoking in gigantic industrial plants while air, ship and rail connections rushed in and out of the city. Even political liberals who had moved here from out of town would say, "Just wait till the Tenn-Tom is finished, it's going to blow this town wide open."

If a street was widened, it was to get ready for the Tenn-Tom traffic. If Crispy Chick added special hot formula barbeque beans to the menu, it was because the anticipated population increase called for more variety. Eddie the mailboy had begun learning songs from *Evita* and *One Mo' Time* so that he would be ready to audition in the new theaters that would pop up in town. Even Sam at Sam's Body Shop was thinking of expanding and acquiring one of the vacant lots across the street from Aunt Odilia to stack their abandoned cars in.

No one waited for the Tenn-Tom Waterway with more anticipation than McCorquodale. Perhaps it was the energetic Scottish blood from her Chunchula side, for she liked to make use of every second of her time. On the morning after meeting H. Sloane Wolfe, she decided to spend the whole day at home and wait conveniently in bed. Propped up against the silk pillows, she sipped alternately from her coffee with chicory and a glass of claret, which was running dangerously short, and penned a few of her thoughts in a letter to the editor of *Interview* magazine in New York on a little black lacquer writing board given her last year by a foreign dignitary from a Russian ship. It was irksome that lately the editor had been refusing to come to the phone when she made her thought-provoking calls, and that hateful secretary recognized her voice now and had started saying that he was not in, except for once or twice when McCorquodale disguised her voice and made up a name. He really must be very busy these days, poor child, but anyway the letter was certain to elicit a delighted response. Occasionally she stretched in the pink satin sheets and purred softly.

Editor Darling,

I have spent most of the morning meditating on industrial expansion and I feel positively exhilarated. I am certain that as soon as the Tenn-Tom Waterway is finished, I will be able to have Jorge Amado and Lawrence Durrell and all my very favorite intellectual lights over for the opening of my new sidewalk café and gallery.

Yes, to be sure, there are those moments when I have my doubts and tell myself that all this canal dredging is dreadfully *modern* and not *postmodern* at all. It's then that I think the retirees and Yankee snowbirds will take over the way they did in Florida—there will be *angst* all over the place, and local TV commentators with doctorates in ethics. There will be psychological counseling for losing wrestlers on "Wrestling Live on Channel Five," and swapping of Julia Child recipes from the Sunday *New York Times* at smoked mullet parties on Dog River (I know I can say this to *you*, editor).

Oh, but it will all work out somehow. We'll put them in suburbs in

Mississippi. Progress, dear sir, progress. Think of the commerce, the
trade, the sailors! And that 55-foot ship channel. I must admit, the
prospect of deep-draft vessels has always excited me. We will soon glow
with a postmodernism that will make your friends at MOMA and the
Russian Tea Room gaga with envy. Tell them Soho and the Village will
have to wait for me. Remember, you maybe "bi-coastal," but we're *Gulf-
Coastal.*

    Grosses bises,

                              McC. R.

When she had finished this missive, McCorquodale lay back under
the plush burgundy eiderdown and slumbered through the afternoon. A
runner from the Commerce National Bank had arrived with a note
inviting her to a discreet evening rendezvous at Le Louis XIV with H.
Sloane Wolfe, and she needed to be at her very freshest. Something told
her that her bleak financial picture was about to improve dramatically.

    The light began changing early in the fall afternoons, and from his
office high, high, at the pinnacle of the Commerce National bank, H.
Sloane Wolfe could see the harbor and the bayous in the marshy land
north of the city begin to glow in the sinking sun. But Wolfe's thoughts
were not on the beauty of nature, and his cold stare was far removed from
the tender glances he had lavished upon McCorquodale the previous
afternoon in the silver BMW. It was the well-known steely look that
struck deep uneasiness into the hearts of his competitors, in particular
that of Hearn Moseley, president of the Prudential National Bank, who
even now might well be sitting in his board room at the top of his own
office tower staring at the same harbor scene.

    "We'll rip em, Uinest, we'll whip their fannies," he said of his
colleagues in the other tower. "Five years from now and they ain't gonna
be much more than a pawn shop in Vinegar Bend." Wolfe turned his
gaze indifferently to his young vice president, Ernest Balleriel, like a tiger
glancing away for a moment from a fat rabbit. Wolfe had a craggy face,
rough but distinguished by his graying temples. In his youth Wolfe had
been a high school football star, and he still considered himself a fighter

and a lady's man. "There's gonna be a whole new ball game in town," he added.

Involuntarily Balleriel glanced at the harbor as though thousands of Tenn-Tom tugboats and grain barges were already parading into the bay. Wolfe began to explain the necessity for expansion and for alertness and predatory readiness. "We're goin after the big game now." A new breed of investors was coming to town and "they ain't playing tiddly winks. This is gone be a big city now, they're gone be like foxes in the in the chicken coop." But Wolfe, turning his ire on the coming invaders, would "take them smart-ass sapsuckers and beat em at their own game."

Wolfe liked to affect plain country ways in private with business associates and friends, though the closest he had ever come to the country was the Mobile Country Club. He had, in fact, grown up in extremely comfortable circumstances and had gone to college. The Jekyll-and-Hyde ease with which he shifted tone was very disconcerting to strangers. Bank employees had identified two basic varieties, "Shoot-em-up Dude" and "Elder Statesman."

Ernest Balleriel, though only in his early thirties, was generally considered to be the heir apparent to the throne of the Commerce National Bank. He *looked* the part so well, every inch the young businessman, serious, professional, on the way up. A scion of a Mobile family of the very highest echelon and former king of Mardi Gras, he was known for his dapper good looks and poise, was always immaculately dressed and manicured, wore every lustrous auburn hair in the right place, was never at a loss for words, and cut a fine figure every spring as head of the Jaycees "Azalea Trail" campaign to attract tourists and flower-loving pilgrims. One Mardi Gras season the festive Spinsters Society, a select group of boisterous and sometimes roisterous unmarried post-debs and other young women, had named him their "Bachelor of the Year" dreamboat, but for the last several years he had appeared at all the balls and other social occasions with Ce Ce Anne Stanton, and a happy announcement was rumored to be in the works.

Balleriel identified completely with the goals of the Commerce National Bank and revered Wolfe as commander-in-chief, but he never felt comfortable with the familiarity of calling him "H. Sloane." No one would have suspected it, but Balleriel's fastidious facade was in part the product of secret inner doubts. Years ago, in a fit of youthful impetuosity, he had gone off to Sewanee and pledged Phi Delta Theta instead of becoming a Deke at Alabama. Now he sometimes worried that this faintest trace of non-predictability, ever so respectable though it was, might be a bit Bohemian for the bank.

"But now look here, son, I called you up here for a special reason . . ." Wolfe was shifting moods for a moment. No one else had been told, but H. Sloane was already formulating expansion plans. The Commerce National Bank would soon go statewide as the Wolfe Alabama Bancorporation (the name was suggested by the Chase Manhattan). They would start gobbling up small banks, then go after Birmingham and Montgomery. With statewide assets, a superbank, they would be ready for the big deals, the giant corporations. "Just bring on the big uns," he said broodingly. Then Wolfe rose and went to a small table. Balleriel wondered about the tall shape under white drapery. "This is a very solemn moment, Uinest," Wolfe intoned, "and you are the fuist to see it." He yanked the cord and the cloth fell off. It was a model of downtown, with tiny replicas of all the buildings, but near the waterfront there was an enormous pyramidal skyscraper soaring to a needle point far above the rest of the downtown skyline. It was at least three times as tall as the Prudential Bank Building, and made it look like a shriveled prune. "Wolfe Alabama corporate headquarters," he cried triumphantly, and pointed to the tip of the tower. "This is where I'll be."

They discussed the new strategy for several hours, and it was pitch black outside when Balleriel left. Wolfe chuckled at the thought of the coming evening with McCorquodale. Before he left he looked one more time at the lights in the Prudential Tower. "We'll whup em," he thought. "Whup em and the hoss they rode in on."

CHAPTER 5

A Night in the Subtropics

H. Sloane Wolfe was brimming with confidence after his conversation with young Balleriel about bank expansion, and he hummed a little tune of devilish anticipation as he entered the rear door of Le Louis XIV Restaurant. It was one of those exclusive new restaurants that marked the revival of Old South refinement in town after the bleak sixties and seventies, decades of gum-chewing waitresses in aprons, and saltine crackers served with every dish. Wolfe was a regular patron, and he could count on the utmost discretion from the restaurant staff whenever he took those special guests to the private chambers on the second floor. He had arranged for the chauffeur to pick up McCorquodale on St. Anthony Street. "You sly dog," he chuckled to himself. It would be a quiet evening just for the two of them, sheltered from prying eyes. And a night to follow.

McCorquodale, after a month of financial drought, was also feeling particularly gala. She lingered long in her extensive wardrobe before deciding that it would take an ensemble of the New Romanticism to match the magnificence of the occasion. It would be the Cossack Chieftainess look, so lately celebrated, she had read, among the Milanese *couturiers*.

Aunt Odilia was rapturous when McCorquodale appeared in her baggy, crude silk trousers stuffed into spike heel boots, her sweeping linen burlap cape tied with an amber clasp: "You suitainly look sweet, deuh. Makes me think of when you wuh a young guil going to those sockhops." And indeed, even in those pioneer days McCorquodale had stood leagues ahead of her young classmates in making haute couture fashion statements. Aunt Odilia was delighted that McCorquodale had found a nice young man to get her out of the house.

39

Le Louis XIV was only about ten blocks from McCorquodale's house, but when the chauffeur arrived—Grover Pippin, who doubled as H. Sloane Wolfe's boatman at the hunting lodge in the delta—McCorquodale made him drive the limousine up and down Government Street, and she waved graciously to the bag boys in the parking lot of Delchamps grocery store as they went by. Mr. Pippin had to help McCorquodale put on her enormous kolbek, the Russian fur cap, when they arrived at the restaurant, but she ignored his frantic attempts to go through the rear entrance. She was as inconspicuous in the entrance foyer, open to the main dining room, as Jacqueline Onassis might be strolling into Greek-American Night at the Municipal Auditorium.

"How very much like Baden-Baden before the war," she observed, looking around at her ease.

"Do you have a reservation?" asked the startled maitre d'.

"Princess Tatiana Troubetzkoy."

He showed an unfortunate inclination to check the reservation book, right saucy in McCorquodale's eyes.

"You may show me upstairs, darling," she announced firmly. "Forthwith."

In her tall kolbek, boots, and cape over the wide padded shoulders of her billowy white blouse, McCorquodale looked like a seven-foot Slavic, or perhaps Martian, goddess walking up the grand staircase. A roar of excited speculation rose from the tables below about whom she was meeting.

H. Sloane Wolfe was mollified somewhat when McCorquodale took off her huge Russian cap—releasing a luxuriant blond fall to cascade about her shoulders—but not until they were halfway through the truffled terrine did he begin to regain his composure from the shock of McCorquodale's grand entrance. The doors were firmly shut, however. No one had seen them, the Mumm's Cordon Rouge was soothing, and the hot blonde, so different from others he had known, was soon making flowing conversation.

That seemed to pose little problem for her, and indeed, Wolfe rarely had the opportunity to interpose a word. The menu was written in garbled French, and when the waiter came she insisted on ordering for herself.

"It's such a thoroughly postmodern tongue, don't you find? My aunt says we're French colonial. I suspect some *coureur de bois*, fur trapper offshoot of the Bourbons."

"Good idea, babe," said Wolfe, too titillated to absorb every word. "Waiter, that'll be two Jack Daniels and Coke."

"'La Lobsteur vivant au butteur blanche'?" McCorqudale was taken aback at what she read. "What is this obscure pidgin dialect?"

The waiter looked at her blankly for a minute, then brightened. "Oh, you mean number eight. Hi! My name is Calvert." He was a burly, red-bearded school of education grad student from the University of South Alabama, carefully trained by the restaurant in the fine points of French service. He smiled pleasantly and leaned with both hands on one of the chairs as he began explaining his master's thesis. "It's all about the cognitive domain, and how high school teachers oughtta be required to fill out a form showin they think about the cognitive domain every time they're writin out a test. It's real holistic." At length, H. Sloane Wolfe, registering with astonishment that the person was actually speaking to *him*, focused a cold stare on Calvert that sent him scurrying out of the room.

Calvert had to be told to clear the plates after each course, but Wolfe was savoring the evening. "Tell me, little lady," he said, cutting into his sirloin Bordelaise and admiring the delicate line of McCorquodale's Evening in Bali green eye shadow, "don't you need a big papa bear to shelter you from the cold, cold winds?"

"Bears are nice," McCorquodale answered, "though I do like Russian sables."

By the time the third bottle of Mumm's came, neither of them minded that Calvert sent the champagne cork ricocheting from the ceiling. Wolfe was beginning to give off heat like a radiator, but it was curious how she did not seem to catch his drift. When he let drop that he had a summer cottage over the bay, she said that the area was rich in ecological significance. Only when he talked about the trials of being a great tycoon, and the ambitious plans he had that people scarcely suspected, did McCorquodale follow him with pellucid attentiveness.

For dessert Calvert prepared the Bananas Foster on a gueridon right next to the table: "Y'all'll get a real charge out of this, my customers always love it." After the brown sugar had melted, he tilted the pan and let it heat until it smoked ominously, then poured on the rum with a grand flourish. A great cloud of flames came boiling out of the pan across the table, sending McCorquodale shrieking into the arms of a badly shaken Wolfe.

"Ask me anything and I'll give you the wuild," Wolfe said after Calvert had been banished in disgrace.

"Use of the chauffeur, a six-month's supply of *Chateau Margaux*, and a little allowance," McCorquodale whispered on the spur of the moment.

Meanwhile, only blocks away from Le Louis XIV, Ernest Balleriel was at the city jail and fit to be tied. The evening had started out quietly when he accompanied Ce Ce Anne on a ride down dark and dead streets to the Hubba Hubba Club on Conti Street. Ce Ce Anne was euphoric because her secret boyfriend Helmut, a sailor on the German merchant marine ship *Deutsche Freude*, was back in port and waiting for her to pick him up. "I know *they* would say it's beneath me but he's really *so* cosmopolitan," Ce Ce Anne had mused in the car. Hardly had Balleriel gotten back home when a call came from Eddie, bank mailboy and star of the Mobile stage, asking him to come bail him out.

Eddie had been arrested for making a footprint and signing his autograph in the wet cement in front of a new restaurant on Dauphin Street. "People don't appreciate me here worth doodly-squat. They don't know a star when they see one," Eddie protested on the way to the car.

"Are you nuts?" Balleriel screeched. "You've got to be more careful! This is like a small town. What if people saw us together? What do you suppose H. Sloane would make of it?"

Ernest's life had changed so much since Eddie began working at the bank. At the very first glimpse of the foxy eighteen-year-old in his tight little jeans, the young executive had felt something rising quickly within him. A little partition had gone up in flames, revealing previously shut-off rooms. But what a headache Eddie could be!

"It's O.K. for you to tap dance out of the closet, but I've got a very prestigious image to think about."

Even as he spoke, Wolfe's limousine passed carrying McCorquodale—alone, on her way back to St. Anthony Street, and deep in thought. Wolfe had looked like a deflated balloon when McCorquodale departed early, pretending that she had to telephone Rome early in the morning to answer pressing queries from Umberto Eco about the theory of esthetics. "Whew, that was close," she reflected, "but if I can just hold him off, I know my sidewalk café will soon be abuilding."

CHAPTER 6

'Tis The Season

Christmas was coming, but the predicted cold front failed to materialize, the days were warm, and mild mists rolled in from the river every night. After McCorquodale's portentous tryst with H. Sloane Wolfe at Le Louis XIV, the days filled up rapidly with assignations, dinner dates, and dances. Sometimes McCorquodale, putting on her tiara or spraying herself from head to toe with *Volcan d'amour* after bathing in fragrant oils and coconut milk, had to pause and try to remember exactly what she was getting ready for.

On one warm and breezy afternoon the week before Christmas, H. Sloane Wolfe had his pilot take him and McCorquodale up in his personal helicopter. Wolfe had never been so expansive. On that very morning, in a burst of generosity, he had issued a Christmas bonus that sent shock waves among bank employees from Bayou la Batre to Prattville (the Farmers and Mechanics Bank of Prattville was one of the first to fall to Wolfe's new empire). Twenty dollars for every man, woman, and teenager, twice the usual bonus!

For several hours they circled near the river eating fruitcake cookies McCorquodale had brought along and silverbells, scattering the red and green foil wrappers to the winds. When they reached the spot high in the clouds above the city where Wolfe calculated his office would be in the future Wolfe Alabama Tower, they stopped and hovered. Wolfe described the invisible building all around them, to be constructed on Tenn-Tom prosperity. "White marble floors, lovely lady. The cuitains roll back at the push of a button." But McCorquodale was secretly looking for the tiny spot on Conti Street where Almodóvar, direct from Madrid, would be toasting her in front of her future postmodern gallery, accompanied by Antonio Banderas, her favorite film star. "Should I include the Photo Realists and the Neo-Expressionists in the show?" she wondered aloud. Wolfe thought she was more mysterious than ever, but once again she failed to comprehend his hints about a visit to his hunting lodge in the tangle of bayous they could see glinting to the north. "Must get back," McCorquodale declared, "got to rest for the ball tonight. Are you sure you don't want to come?"

'Twas the "winter social season" in Mobile, and McCorquodale, now more confident than ever that the postmodern revolution was in the offing, took up once again the responsibility of her many social obligations. At the first ball of carnival in mid-November, the Thalians, at the Harlequins, the Camellia Ball, the notorious young lawyers' Christmas party, McCorquodale was greeted with yells and big kisses by some, notably the men who had provided her with invitations to the balls, and with curious stares by many. It was a face that people had seen and had not seen. Who was this sunburst blonde radiating such cloudless assurance?

Insiders dispensed information to small clusters of people who gazed appraisingly over the rim of their cocktail glasses at McCorquodale. A happy few were young men who could brag about a very close acquaintance in recent years. In their descriptions, an uncertain image emerged of a very opulent bunny with a puzzling interest in "some kind of art or something." The fact that the bunny had been in control every step of their acquaintance was generally omitted from their reports of conquest. Eventually these dates had gotten a little too rich for their blood, for these young businessmen, doctors, entrepreneurs. For a pearl of great price it seemed only natural to lavish jeweled watches, expensive dinners, orchids, and occasional discreet direct cash advances. Their evocations of McCorquodale were oddly distant, but judging from their nostalgic and often wistful expressions, the experience had been well worth it as long as their pocketbooks had held out.

A number of peering young matrons who had decorated new homes and bayside cottages were titillated to recognize the rather difficult sales assistant at AAA Superior Wallcoverings. She had never been observed to wear the same outfit twice! With her dazzling combinations, her torero

jackets and linen skirts, her very dernier cri oversize gabardine and
Donegal tweed suits, her endlessly varied jewelry, she had lent an
immediate air of expensive gentility to the store, but she could also
completely unnerve Mrs. Clarisse Watkins, the proprietress, with a
single word, so that her hands shook all afternoon. She was capable of
announcing right out loud, just as Mrs. Watkins was making her closing
sales pitch to a moneyed client, that there was "no such thing as Givenchy
Chippendale Colonial." Upon glimpsing house plans for a New England
saltbox house with widow's walk, she had tried to liberate an enthusiastic
young bride from "the karmic slavery of the suburban mind-set." Once,
when Mrs. Watkins sent her to a coffee klatsch held by a neighborhood
women's club, the blond woman had announced to the whole group that
their plans for a subdivision-wide Christmas at Williamsburg were "an
abomination unto God."

But very special insiders were those who remembered her from high
school; who could say, with sudden elation, "Oh is *that* who she is?!"
When they talked, heads huddled; silks rustled; gloved hands let their
cigarettes burn down to a stub; arms in black tailcoat sleeves rested across
bare young shoulders.

It seemed that for a whole year after she transferred to the public high
school from the Catholic girls' school, the blond woman, who at that
time was known as "Margaret Constance" (she started using her uncommon and stylish nickname only after graduating), was one of those
skinny girls standing in the background of group photos in the club
section of the school yearbook, but otherwise unknown. Something of
an outsider. Then right before her senior year she underwent a sudden
spurt of growth and a dramatic change in anatomy.

She appeared on campus that September like fireworks on a dark
night. The football team was the first to observe the transition, closely
followed by the Key Club and certain boys on the student council. Soon
McCorquodale was being asked to every school dance and high school
fraternity party of any significance. The girls were slower to come to grips
with her change in status, but were eager for more information. Dark
rumors began to circulate. It was said that McCorquodale never watched

television, and listened to classical music at home, and that she had read extra passages of John Milton for English class. The afternoon of tryouts for a vacancy on the cheerleader squad she ignored the whole event and went downtown to see a visiting troupe of Nigerian Folk Dancers. Despite these flaws, public opinion was on the verge of assigning her a place in the most ethereal heights of the popular in-groups, and the earth trembled with the rumor that she might be getting a midterm senior bid to the most exclusive high school sorority.

Unfortunately, that was the moment that McCorquodale, a leading light and, in fact, secretary of the French Club, chose to organize a hunger strike demanding bottled mineral water and—backward Puritan Anglo-Saxon liquor laws be deuced!—*vin rouge ordinaire* in the high school cafeteria. McCorquodale revealed uncommon leadership capabilities and unflinching resolve under fire, not to mention a precocious palate for noble causes. One tense afternoon the lunchroom rang with militant renditions of "Sur le pont d'Avignon" and "Parlez-moi d'amour." The principal was a no-nonsense former football coach, and upon being furnished with translations of their protest posters, he was not slow in instituting ruthless purges. The French Club was banned from campus for the rest of the year as the "mouthpiece of teenage hooliganism"; schoolwide assemblies were held on the dangers of teenage alcoholism; the ranks of the Spanish, German, and Latin clubs swelled suddenly with curious teenage thrill-seekers; and McCorquodale was suspended for a week. She never did get that sorority bid.

After high school, people were surprised that Margaret Constance did not go to college, despite her good grades, not even to one of the local colleges. She seemed to drop completely out of circulation. It was only in the last couple of years that her face had begun to appear at the Mardi Gras balls, and occasionally other events, always with some new, free-spending and very attentive date.

This year, as Wolfe adamantly refused to accompany her in public, McCorquodale decided to go *solitaire* to every Mardi Gras ball without exception. The idea of carnival enjoyed a central place in her postmodern ideology, merging in her mind with images of Venetian masked balls.

"Yes, the season," she would enthuse to Wolfe, who would listen to her detailed reports of these evenings with a little smile playing about his lips, and wonder if perhaps he should be jealous. "How I adore it. We must imagine we are wealthy cotton planters descending on the river packets to our opulent town houses in order to partake of the winter festivities. For months on end nothing but fine Southern breeding, *savoir vivre*, elegance, the cream of society."

A very gratifying tribute was paid McCorquodale at the exclusive Santa Claus Society ball the Friday before Christmas when she was proclaimed "Miss Brick House." The SCS was a Mardi Gras mystic society founded in 1886, and consisted mainly of young buck business-men in their twenties and early thirties who wandered about the cavern-ous Municipal Auditorium, which had hosted such scintillating events as the Harlem Globetrotters and the Gulf Coast Auto Show, dressed in Santa Claus suits.

It was an occasion when the Young Set turned out in force, *costume de rigueur* to the teeth. Eschewing for the nonce her usual New Wave apparel, McCorquodale was all belle, going as a "ruby snow queen," crimson *peau de soie* against rime-white skin, tiny red camellias in her blond hair.

As the ball warmed up, the debonair Santa Clauses began to stagger and grab in unguarded places. The band switched to sixties soul music, and a group of energetic Santa Claus dancers gathered in front doing the Deke Sway, leaning imperceptibly back and forth with their arms around their dates. Ce Ce Anne Stanton and even the staid Ernest Balleriel, dream couple of the Young Set, jitterbugged with Yuletide merriment. Balleriel was meeting Eddie the mailboy after the ball, and Helmut was waiting for Ce Ce Anne with hot grog on board the *Deutsche Freude*.

Ce Ce Anne got her entire Junior League Committee on Urban Affairs to come in red and green plaid taffeta, and the crowd went wild when they went up on stage to perform their celebrated Supremes imitation. While the row of Junior Leaguers jumped about in their long gowns and fancy-stepped and turned in unison, rolling their hands and wagging their fingers in mock-threatening gestures, Ce Ce Anne stood out in front and lip-synched her interpretation of "You Can Have My Husband But Please Don't Monk With My Man."

Everyone began to scream for the Miss Brick House contest. At first McCorquodale was reluctant to enter, feeling her unfair advantage over the other contestants, but the moderator of the contest, lead singer Maskman Mongo of the Biloxi band *Maskman Mongo and the Tabulations*, kept calling to her over the microphone until she gave in. "Would that red stone fox in the high-heeled sneakers *please* step up on this stage?"

When a bevy of twenty beauties was clustered on stage, the *Tabulations* struck up "She's a Brick House" and one by one the budding graces stepped forward to swing and gyrate for the appreciative crowd. A tense moment came when it appeared that Lou Ethyl Strovers—a majestic brunette with three-and-a-half-foot measurements who was in town from Demopolis making her debut—might actually win. Lou Ethyl bumped and ground down the little path that Maskman Mongo had set aside like a B-52 taking off. People threw their plastic champagne cups in the air and college boys home on vacation swallowed in their white ties. Maskman Mongo provided a running commentary: "Do the monkey jump, now!" "Tallyho!" "Aw shucks now, lookin good!"

McCorquodale, who was to follow Lou Ethyl and end the contest, allowed a mild flicker of interest to pass over her face. She undid the flowers in her hair and turned to Regina Hammerstein next to her. "Hold my camellias, honey."

McCorquodale's dancing tended to bring out the prominent S-architecture formed by jutting components of her anatomy. With a far-away look on her face, she barely swung her upraised forearms and rolled her body from side to side in time with the beat, like the massive inventory of a heavily-loaded clipper ship shifting in the breeze. Several tottery and thrashing Santa Clauses passed out on their dates in the front row, and the elegant crowd roared as Maskman Mongo gave McCorquodale the silver cup, proclaiming, "She a Mojo Mama and a Body Shaker!"

"If you've got it, you've got it," McCorquodale thought, but she was

careful to flatter Lou Ethyl: "Surely you studied at the Vaganova
Choreographic Institute in Leningrad?"

Money was flowing in again on St. Anthony Street, to Aunt Odilia's
enormous relief. McCorquodale, careful to keep her in the dark about H.
Sloane Wolfe, had told her that the unpaid bills were just a matter of
forgetfulness and that Odilia had misunderstood the situation. Her
savings from the AAA Superior Wallcoverings job (she did not mention
the thoughtful, and perhaps hard-earned, contributions from previous
male escorts) would be more than enough for them to live on for years to
come. Odilia's notions of financial realities had always been rather vague,
despite her daily dragnets for grocery store mark-downs.

To celebrate, Aunt Odilia decided to give a little Christmas Eve
party at home before midnight mass. Camellias from the courtyard were
festooned everywhere, not only because of the December warm spell, but
also because of the important evidence unearthed by her ally George
Belzagui in the two-front war of research to prove the extreme but
forgotten aristocracy of the Roshfookles or "Rochefoucaulds." One day
Mr. Belzagui had stopped by after work with another tremendous
breakthrough, a handwritten copy of a terse 1840s newspaper notice he
said he had found in a bank storage room. "Among the guests, Camille
Roshfookle," it noted, "luminary belle of the Southern sky, appeared in
a diadem of white camellias at a reception given by the Good Fellows
Volunteer Fire Company Saturday night." Aunt Odilia was overwhelmed.
"Diadems, yase, I was *suitain* we had wawn them," she repeated to all and
sundry, including the floor and ceiling, as Christmas spirits flowed freely.

Present at Aunt Odilia's party were her friends Miss Alice and Miss
Hattie Robinson, McCorquodale, in a black mantilla, and George
Belzagui, resplendent in the *chapeau*, baldric, tails and red-lined cape of
a Knight of Columbus of the fourth degree.

Odilia served her remarkable eggnog. The secret ingredient was
what she called a liqueur supplied by McCorquodale's grandfather
Hiram McCorquodale. Over the years a trade route had developed
between the two households, barter of diplomacy: pepper jelly, bottled
chow-chow, amaryllis lilies, prize camellias tied up wet in plastic bags to

keep them fresh. Old Mr. McCorquodale had stopped by from Chunchula that afternoon to remind McCorquodale of the service at the Mt. Pisgah Baptist Church Christmas morning and drop off several bottles of his renowned holiday home brew, which he liked to call "Spirits of Cats A'Fussin.'" "Take jest a smidgen now," he had warned Aunt Odilia, "hit'll hitcha betwixt the eyes."

After several cups the Misses Robinson, members of the august Government Street Baptist Church downtown, became quite ecumenical, and decided to go with them to mass. The long-awaited cold front was arriving, and the little party shivered as they puttered slowly in the Studebaker through the deserted nighttime streets to the Cathedral. Bells were ringing: the Cathedral, St. Joseph's, St. Francis Street Methodist, Canterbury Episcopal. Everyone in the Cathedral thought that Mr. Belzagui, aglow with the Chunchula spirits, had never held his sword with such military splendor as he did that night in the procession down the main aisle.

Late after mass McCorquodale stood on her balcony and savored the first quiet moment she had had in weeks. She shivered in her mantilla and watched the Christmas lights at Sam's Body Shop twinkle in the reflections on the oil slicks. A solitary drifter passed who had been scouring through downtown garbage cans in the last few weeks for aluminum cans he could cash in. He was on his way to spend the night at the nearby Rescue Mission. "What it is?!" he greeted.

"Merry Christmas, darling!" McCorquodale cried. The season was just beginning, with so many plans to fulfill.

CHAPTER 7

Improve through Improvement

The Hamburger Harbor Improvement Association was a club of five successful and witty young achievers in their thirties and early forties who met once a week at the franchise fast food establishment of Mayor Buzz Barker out on the western fringe of the city near the airport. While the clientele sat up front in an uncomfortable dining area with orange surfaces and Formica tables calculated to make them swallow and get out, the Improvement Association met in a little carpeted room in the back with soft music piped in. Barker had a bar set up in the room and they mixed their own drinks, safe from the eyes of teetotaling conservative voters.

Their motto was "Improve through Improvement," and they had a little creed that Stu Carter had written on a napkin once on a bet that he could not use the word "improve" fifty times in a 150-word paragraph. They had made Carter "Keeper of the Holy Scrolls."

Though the sessions were conducted in a spirit of droll quips and quick-witted repartee, the members worked closely together and the meetings often resulted in serious decisions and business ventures. All five men were go-getters of the New South variety, most from very country family backgrounds a generation or two back, but now hip, ambitious, going places, with it, intent on living the good life.

Hamburger Harbor had been Barker's launching pad to the halls of power in city politics. The franchise was obviously a gold mine: everyone marveled that on the salary of a city official and the proceeds of a hamburger house Barker had been able to build a posh $600,000 house near Airport Boulevard. Hamburger Harbor had the same garish building, the same sign with the logo of a hamburger impaled on an anchor towering above the road, as could be found in hundreds of other cities.

In addition, however, Barker had had the vision to cut down all the trees in an enormous area and pave a parking lot five times as big as was ever needed on even the busiest days. Enormous American flags fluttered all around the perimeters.

That vision also spilled over into city politics. County commissioners had already had the idea of moving offices out of downtown and scattering them all over the city, but Barker was the first mayor with the foresight to suggest moving city hall to the western limit of the city next door to Hamburger Harbor. It was the logical thing to do. There would be no parking problem, it was convenient to lunchtime eateries, and if the complex needed to expand there was always land in the Hamburger Harbor parking lot that might be sacrificed at a modest price. So far the city council had shown little enthusiasm for moving city hall, but it was one of the long-standing goals of Barker's administration.

Late one afternoon after Christmas (the day Aunt Odilia made gumbo with the leftover turkey, and the day Miss Alice and Miss Hattie Robinson elbowed their way through the excited mob at the Gayfer's sales to buy a vacuum cleaner at fifty percent off—imagine!), the weekly meeting of the Improvement Association opened with advertising executive Stu Carter reading one of his famous compositions. It was a short epic poem on the exploits of another member, young attorney Parker Stallings (his grandfather was Gus Stallings who had had the big haberdashery on Royal Street). Stallings was often kidded about the fact that he was the only member of the Improvement Association with social pretensions, belonging as he did to one of the more exclusive Mardi Gras mystic societies, the Infant Mystics.

When word leaked out that Stallings had been caught in an amorous escapade and narrowly escaped an irate husband, head of a local plumbers union, by jumping out of a second-story window, it had fueled excited gossip for weeks. Ce Ce Anne Stanton was merely one of a whole legion of talebearers. Of course, young lawyer scandals were a constant thing, but Carter could not resist the chance to crack a joke, even weeks after the fact.

> . . . when down around the garbage cans
> there arose such a clatter
> that the neighbors rushed out to see
> what was the matter

On and on Stu Carter's verses jingled, interrupted constantly by
guffaws so loud that the customers up front looked up in wonderment
from their bland meals. Stallings bore it heroically, trying to maintain a
weak smile, but as soon as the poem was over, the annoyed young lawyer
brought up the subject of the Colonial Acres furor that Carter, well-
known realtor Sid Wibbs, and Albert Tunney, the fifth member of the
group, were involved in.

Wibbs had made a fortune by building shoddy apartment and
condominium complexes in hitherto stable neighborhoods. They were
always the same pattern with slight variations: long blocks of buildings
with purplish bricks and cheap window fixtures. Sometimes they would
tack on a fake mansard roof facing the parking lot, a style which they
called "French Classic." Sometimes the same buildings would have half
a column stuck on the walls halfway between every two apartment doors.
That was called "Old South."

Stu Carter named the complexes and handled the advertising. The
brochures varied only slightly from "Kingsworth Manor" to "Chateau
Versailles": "Indulge yourself in the luxury of Old World charm," or
"Exclusive prestige apartments carefully planned with the young professional in mind."

The latest scandal arose when residents of an exclusive west Mobile
neighborhood learned that a rezoning request had been granted for
Colonial Acres, a complex similar to another Wibbs Realty development
that had recently been on the TV news because it had become the hangout of drug dealers and the notorious Hell's Bells motorcycle gang. The
request had been delayed repeatedly at city planning commission meetings but was passed quietly at the latest meeting when the opposing
neighborhood delegations, put off their guard by the many postpone-
ments, failed to show up. Commission members later pleaded inno-

cence, saying that they had not seen any opposition at the meeting. Wibbs had ties with the influential Greenspan Corporation, a giant development firm that had supported Buzz Barker in his campaign and had an amazing record of obtaining rezoning from the commission.

"It'll blow over," Wibbs predicted. "Shoot, you gahs know I'm just trying to serve the public and give folks a home."

Albert Tunney, a man in his forties, was, in the small world of Mobile county, married to McCorquodale's second cousin on the McCorquodale side, but she had almost no contact with him. He had only lately started to invest in Wibbs' real estate projects. His main business and chief claim to fame was his highly successful Monsieur Bidet of Alabama corporation. It had been an ingenious idea, marketing a bathroom fixture that most people had never heard of and did not know they needed.

At first it had been rough going, explaining what a bidet was, but Tunney's ads for bidets with "effervescent action" had become a familiar item in Mobile newspapers and on billboards. Always in the best of taste, they showed a stick figure sitting on a highly stylized bathroom fixture: "Hemorrhoids? Hernia? Bubble your trouble away with Monsieur Bidet of Alabama." In the last several years they had really caught on as a status symbol in affluent Sunbelt homes.

It was only after the joking had subsided that Mayor Barker brought up a subject that was to have a major influence, not only on the lives of the Improvement Association members, but on the fate of the whole city as well. The faces of the others took on a bleary-eyed seriousness when Barker began to expatiate on how the Tenn-Tom Waterway would "impact" their economic prospects. There was a chance for men with the guts to "interface with" where the development went. The truth was, up until now they had been involved in penny ante stuff. The area was becoming a part of the Sunbelt now and it was time to be a little more aggressive.

On his last trip to Houston, Barker had met a developer with ideas for Mobile, ideas of sweeping breadth. Barker had arranged for him to fly to town in the next few weeks for a little meeting that would open their eyes. "You gahs are gonna have to pick your jaws right up off that floor," Barker said. He got up to fix every member a fresh drink, passed them around, and stood at the head of the table as he proposed a little toast: "To the Houston developer!"

CHAPTER 8

The Houston Developer's Plan

When the hard freezes came in January, the Misses Robinson wrapped the banana trees in front of their house on Michigan Avenue in old sheets, and Aunt Odilia plunged all the deeper into her genealogical research.

In her morning walks past the many vacant lots on the way to the library, she often saw shivering hobos emerge from the weeds and bushes where they had spent the night. Often there were little clusters of them drinking coffee in their ragged jackets in and around the Government Street McDonald's, old men with weather-tanned faces and young men with broken eyes and long greasy hair. They never bothered her, but usually approached other men in the parking lots, or men walking on the sidewalks, for dimes and quarters. After a few days or maybe a week their faces would become familiar, then they would vanish, off to Florida or New Orleans on the busy Gulf Coast hobo route.

The vacant lots downtown, the empty store fronts, the crumbling buildings, the silent streets at night and on the weekends—all were things she seldom thought much about these days. But one morning Mr. Yorwerth, the genealogical librarian and cousin to the Thormatt florist clan, showed her a cache of old photos he had come across in a library drawer, pictures of St. Joseph Street and other downtown scenes before the First World War. Long tunnels of oaks; blocks of cast iron fences; rows of ornate Victorian houses and more sober, elegant antebellum brick houses wedged in together on little lots raised up a level high above the sidewalk; long vistas of balconies and turrets and gates, and neat concrete ledges demarcating the postage stamp yards and flower beds. All very urban, and all the pictures showed people out walking and talking on busy streets and sidewalks.

"When my grandmother first came here from Ireland, after she lived in Chicago for a year, some of the streets made her think she was back in Dublin," said Mr. Yorwerth.

Pictures of even older and poorer districts had a more tropical flavor, with front doors and tall shuttered windows often opening directly onto the sidewalk. The inevitable balconies; rows and blocks of slim cast iron columns; networks of high brick walls topped by sharp slivers of colored glass embedded in mortar. Dusty streets of oyster shells. Spanish daggers, oleanders, century plants, occasional palms in hot glaring sunlight. Corner stores and bars with wooden canopies over the sidewalk. Boys in caps and knickers sitting on porch stoops staring at the camera. A vanished pattern emerged, like a soft breath on the back of the neck, of the intimate life of city neighborhoods.

"My, my. It's a puifect shame," said Aunt Odilia, and was quiet for a while thinking about the St. Anthony Street of her childhood.

The massive destruction of so much of the old historic core in the 1950s and '60s, accomplishing what only a war might do in another country, had led to a delayed shock reaction in the public mind. In the intervening years, a totally automobilized, centerless, and anonymous new city had floated out over a huge area big enough to hold a population five times greater, and continued to gobble up more and more land westward without there being any large increase in the total population. Even among people who never thought much about such matters, or who said it was just the way things were, a cynical feeling spread, like a slow rain of ashes, that somehow things had gone wrong here and would continue that way.

Aunt Odilia, quite full of her research these days, was beginning to stress her French ancestry in conversations with Miss Alice and Miss Hattie. "Of cose," she would note as they picked through the collards at the grocery store, "I cain't say the famly hasn't chayinged over the yeuhs, but I've always felt there was that suitain French Catholic *something* about us." The eyes of the Misses Robinson would narrow, without comment, on suspect yellow leaves. Aunt Odilia began admiring the look of phrases in McCorquodale's old high school French book, and she

hilande, Dunette, fugar, Bodri … all French colonial, comme moi!

even learned two or three with the help of her friend Irene Grew, who taught French at Wright's school for girls.

In keeping with her increasingly Gallic character, Odilia decided to have her friends over for a post-Twelfth Night get-together to celebrate the start of Mardi Gras. McCorquodale had flown with H. Sloane Wolfe to Pensacola that day for an extended lunch.

Aunt Odilia served King Cake from Aroto's Bakery and coffee, and she decorated the parlor with somewhat wilted poinsettias she had bought for a dollar apiece in an after-Christmas sale at TG&Y, and boughs of pale lavender Gulf Pride azaleas, the first to bloom every year in earliest January.

Miss Hattie and Miss Alice braved the rain and sleet, as did Mr. Belzagui. Aunt Odilia held forth that afternoon on the topic of Mrs.

Victorine Lalande, an old Creole lady who lived in the little Creole cottage with aluminum windows across the street. Looking for confirmation and support in her rising French mania, Aunt Odilia had lately taken to crossing the street for prolonged chats whenever she saw Mrs. Lalande come out to get the mail or take out the garbage. A tiny, absent-minded personage with white hair, copper skin, and green eyes, she was Odilia's equal in family chauvinism. As she repeated at every opportunity, her mother was a Dedeaux from Pass Christian, while the Lalandes had been in Mobile—in antebellum days "free persons of color," though she just said "French"—since the 1750s, far back before nearly all the white Old Mobilians.

Mrs. Lalande had once owned a home on Charleston Street in the "Down the Bay" section where Mobile's main Creole neighborhood was located, and where a few individuals had still spoken the local Creole French dialect. But she moved to St. Anthony Street when the neighborhood was leveled in a Federal Urban Renewal project in the late sixties, along with the old waterfront and other districts.

The logic of the city fathers in that instance had been brilliant, but events failed to proceed according to plan. To make way for progress, five thousand residents were forced out of Down the Bay and the whole nineteenth-century neighborhood was leveled. Then when everything was in place, when a vast and empty plain stretched out south of Canal Street ready for redevelopment, no investors came forward and downtown stores started closing. Two decades later, most of the land was still vacant.

It was a subject on which Mrs. Lalande was very sensitive, and Aunt Odilia told her friends that you had to be very cautious in talking to her and confine the conversation to frozen water pipes, family history, and flowers.

"I'm telling you if you so much as mention a house that was tawn down she gets in one of those moods and stawts saying, 'Just you wait, they're gonna bring in them bulldozers up heuh, too.' I tell her, 'Sweethawt, Uiban Renewal is awl over with. Who would ever want to bother us up here on St. Anthony Stree-it?' But nobody's gotten the piece with the baby yet. Jawage, have some mo cake."

At that very moment the members of the Hamburger Harbor
Improvement Association were sitting in the back meeting room of
Hamburger Harbor staring speechless at Houston developer Ted Todd,
founder and president of Sunbelt Land Corporation. Todd had just
finished unveiling his development vision for the city. For a long
moment the members pondered the scheme, thinking how their own
industrious undertakings—the kickbacks, the buildings sold to the state
and local governments at twice the market price, the land deals—paled
into insignificance.

The members were so quiet that the customers could be heard up
front as they tried to choke down their tasteless hamburgers and soybean
milkshakes. Sid Wibbs was the first to regain his composure.

"Tear down the whole city and drain the bay?" Wibbs asked
incredulously.

"No, no, guys, you're not computing," Todd said. "Prepare it for
new quality horizons. And viableize the city only from the river to the
interstate highway. In terms of the bay, you've got to make a few
sacrifices to get the bigtime industry. We'll leave the harbor and the ship
channel, of course. I'm not prepared to reveal my clients, but let's just say
that they like the area and it's a name you know. It's a world-class
conglomerate, a company . . ." and here Todd paused significantly,
"worthy of the Tenn-Tom Waterway."

The meeting had started out very relaxed, with a glistening sally of
Barker's understated humor, so appreciated at city hall meetings. "Wibbs
is got on his red tie today, he must be steppin out amongst'em. Wibbs,
wheredju roll that bum? I might want me one, too."

"Aw, go to hell, Barker."

Similar jabs and quick retorts flashed like summer lightning, but
after several rounds of Jim Beam and Gatorade, Barker got down to
business and introduced Todd. "You gahs listen to this gah. He's got the
low-down on what's comin down."

Barker had met Todd while standing in the coat check line at the
Houston Playboy Club. When he introduced himself diffidently as Buzz

Barker, Mayor of Mobile, Todd took an immediate interest. He told Barker about some of his projects, such as a yachting marina in the Texas desert funded with Federal UDAG funds—the tourist-hungry town was to build the lake, but unfortunately ran out of money after buying up a town alderman's desert property.

Barker had been impressed by Todd's communicating skills and personable manner. After years of Dale Carnegie courses, Todd knew how to look people in the eye, call them by first name, show them he cared. Peppy and vaguely good-looking, a bit flabby but with Elvis Presley eyelashes, he was very much like a television talk show host. In the course of a long conversation, they found that they had many common interests, all of which had to do with money. Barker recognized that here was the sort of one-man think tank he had been looking for, someone who could generate conceptual sketches and feasibility studies at the drop of a hat, but let Barker call the shots.

Ted Todd patiently began to explain once again to the HHIA members the major points of his plan for the city after half of it had been cleared. There would be a crisscrossing network of superhighways to take you wherever you wanted to go in a matter of minutes; "no more waiting at traffic lights." A theme park would be built like Six Flags Over Georgia, making Mobile "the entertainment hub of the Sunbelt." And to service the huge new city spawned by the Tennessee-Tombigbee Water- way, exploding out into three states, an inconceivably vast shopping mall would be built, with parking stretching miles out into the horizon. "It'll be the state-of-the-art solution to the parking problem. I like to call it 'Supermall.'

"I guess I don't need to spell out what that signifies, Stu, Park, Sid, Al," he continued. "We calculate this area is a megagrowth high priority marketing node in terms of big bucks fiscal payload potential. And that's going to impact substantially your services infracare load. Now if you can potentialize that, and I mean hook up with it in a real sense, you can realize some very viable feedback."

Barker's four cronies stole glances at each other out of the corners of their eyes. Carter began hesitantly. "Uh, Mr. Todd . . ."

"Call me Ted, Stu."

"In terms of this mall, Ted. What are you gettin at in terms of what the real bottom line is?"

The developer looked at him intently. "Man, I tell you what, that's a real good question, Stu. Maybe it would help if I could segment it up in some bite-sized chunks."

Todd set up some sketches on an easel and began to go through them. At first glance the sketches did not look different from any other mall, low built and slung out, but a tiny group of people walking in front betrayed the gigantic scale. Theme drawings showed an Old English half-timbered Tudor mall, a pioneer log cabin mall, an adobe Mexican hacienda mall. When he came to the Williamsburg mall, with light brown brick and King Kong broken pediments and white dormer windows repeated to nightmarish infinity, they could not help expressing their admiration.

"Boy, that's architecture. Real classy!"

When Todd began to talk about the profits, all five pairs of eyes in the Hamburger Harbor Improvement Association widened and glittered.

Stallings broke the spell first: "But how're we going to get all this land? Don't you expect a little opposition?"

It would, of course, involve careful consultation with city planners, public discussion, long consideration of the pros and cons, detailed professional studies, all in the spirit of *pro bono publico*.

And it was in this spirit that Todd answered, "I'm glad you asked that question, Park, because this is where you guys come in. We're going to need a little campaign fund to persuade the right people." The meeting lasted until late into the night.

CHAPTER 9

The Premier Family of Chunchula

"City" and "country," like "day" and "night," were rigid and self-evident concepts in Mobile, as unshakable as words like "crab claw," "pecan," "mud puddle." Many who lived in the city were, according to culture, accent, and outlook, considered "country," and some in the country were known to be Mobilians. McCorquodale was "city" after having been raised by Aunt Odilia, but like so many who had passed by that narrow gate she still had connections with what she liked to refer to as her British side, "the premier family of Chunchula" in the hilly, red clay, pine-covered north of Mobile County. It was a clan devoid of vulgar ostentation. "The really old families never flaunt it, you know," McCorquodale often repeated.

It was indeed an old family. Ever since the 1820s, when Ezekial McCorquodale, the first of the line, wandered over from the Georgia coast, the McCorquodales had occupied the same land. It was characteristic of the peculiar schizophrenia of the area that they could grow their crops and brew their liquor in their piney hills for generation after generation, and yet live in a different universe from the patrician social sphere of the Wolfes and the Balleriels, or even the middle class lives of the Robinsons and the Roshfookles in Mobile.

Old Man Hiram McCorquodale was the undisputed patriarch of the clan, presiding in an old frame farmhouse with a red crystal ball on a plaster socket in the front yard facing the highway; but there were two branches of the family now. Hiram, married to Callie Clemson, had two children: the late and beloved Betty Sue, McCorquodale's mother, and McCorquodale's Uncle "Tater," who lived a few acres away on the same land in a tiny, airtight, 1970s slab house with low ceilings and dark brown brick with pink mortar. Tater, married to Trudi, had nine strapping, rifle-toting sons between the ages of fifteen and twenty-eight. They raced their pickup trucks on the county roads and were known as "the McCorquodale Boys."

Then there was the side descended from Hiram's deceased brother, Old Man Acton (Ack) McCorquodale. This, in Albert Tunney's opinion, was the prominent line. Old Man Ack's son Adlai, for example, was a Saraland city councilman and had distinguished himself as a strategist in the annexation wars that raged incessantly in the remote, twilight, hillbilly banana republic world of Mobile's northern suburbs. Adlai's lovely wife, Tammy, was prominent in the Saraland Lady Booster's Club, and the two were often pictured in the *North Mobile County News*: "Adlai and Tammy McCorquodale are back from four days in Cocoa Beach, Fla. . . . said it was 'the experience of a lifetime.'"

Albert Tunney had married Old Man Ack's daughter, Brenda, and when he made his money from the Monsieur Bidet of Alabama Corporation, they descended Highway 45 and bought a house in a familiarly pine-covered western suburb called Alpine Hills. This was the third great family migration in more than a century and a half, the second having been Betty Sue's fateful southward trek to the Mobile waterfront. In his distinguished position Tunney squirmed at the memory of Betty Sue's bar job, and considered McCorquodale a poor relation.

One afternoon McCorquodale decided to pay a visit to Chunchula in order to deliver a jar of homemade marmalade from Aunt Odilia, and also a little present of her own. Little did she suspect when she walked into the room at the rural "estate" that afternoon that Albert Tunney had been trying to get Old Man Hiram to sign a warranty deed, which he was passing off as a will, that would give Tunney possession of the McCorquodale land.

McCorquodale found that the allowance she was receiving now from Wolfe amply met her limited needs, and she decided to treat her grandparents to a priceless Art Deco martini shaker she had found by pure luck at the downtown Goodwill store. "So strict, so understated," McCorquodale thought as she admired the highly stylized water lilies and cattails wrapping around it, marred by only a few hardly noticeable dents. "They'll be ecstatic. It will go so well with the vernacular taste culture of Alabama Primitive." By that she meant her grandparents' quite unspoiled interior design motifs.

The threat to the McCorquodale land had arisen some eight months before when Old Man Hiram asked for Tunney's help in drawing up his will, which was like leaving the pot roast with a starving coyote. Hiram wanted to settle the matter quietly without worrying the family, and he knew that Tunney had connections with many lawyers. Ironically, Tunney did not want to be bothered at first, as he figured that they would get nothing more than a few dubious antiques out of it. Whenever Old Man Hiram called he had his secretary say he was out. Then, suddenly, Tunney began to press urgently to finish the will and get it signed.

How could Old Man Hiram know that Houston developer Ted Todd's plan made it imperative that Tunney raise half a million dollars almost immediately? For that amount, Todd had said, every member of the Improvement Association would have a cut of the enormous profits of their development scheme.

For Tunney it was suddenly clear what he had to do: leave aside delicate scruples, grab the McCorquodale land, and sell off as much as was necessary fast, maybe leaving Old Man Hiram with the house to live in. Later, when he was rich from the Supermall scheme, he could buy the old couple and the other relatives a farm two or three times as big.

At the very moment McCorquodale set out with the shaker, Tunney was pressing to get a document signed that would give him almost everything immediately. But that was where he had miscalculated, for Old Man Hiram was not a man to be rushed.

"Well, lookee hyar," Old Man Hiram exclaimed when he saw Tunney's pudgy figure and gray face—the thick black eyeglasses frames did it—coming through the chickens and bare raked dirt that surrounded the farmhouse. "Woman, brang us some coffee."

When Albert had stepped through the breezeway and they were both seated in rocking chairs by the fireplace, McCorquodale's grandmother, wrinkled and long-suffering, tottered back with a tray of saltine crackers, butter, and coffee. "At's a plenty," he said when she poured his cup. "Had us a raht smart a rain this week," he observed politely to Albert.

For a full hour the impatient Tunney listened as the talkative old man discussed the weather, the price of tomatoes, and the Moonies buying up property in the fishing town of Bayou la Batre. He gave a thorough report on recent crime in the whole county. Every day he scoured the newspaper and listened to the radio and TV for new incidents, and would rage about them and the Federal courts to anybody within earshot. Old Man Hiram was just getting warmed up for a visit when Tunney produced the "will" from his pocket and steered the conversation to the business at hand. Old Man Hiram made it clear that everything would go to McCorquodale's grandmother, and then on her death would be split evenly between McCorquodale and Uncle Tater.

"That's exactly what it says here," Tunney said, and produced a Flair pen for him to sign with. But to his dismay, Old Man Hiram remembered that it was time for his radio program.

Old Man Hiram was, in point of fact, famous all over the county among fans of WKKL's afternoon talk show, "Speak Out." Every day he would call in to voice his opinion on a broad range of topics, perfected during a lifetime of porch-sitting meditation. The reaction of breezy talk show host Art Kosh, an immigrant from Ohio, varied between annoyance on busy days and gratitude when no one else was calling in.

The topic of the day was crime in Mobile, Old man Hiram's specialty. "Hail, the po-lice say you cain't shoot a thief on your own propity." Old Man Hiram's voice came across hundreds of radios as a blurred screech. "But if that dude comes around hyar to Chunchula, Alabama, and starts a sneakin on my porch, ah ain't a callin ary a policeman. Ah'll pop him with that thirty-thirty . . . call the neighbors and tell em come git im . . . that dude is dead and buried . . . he's *missin persons!*"

It was twenty minutes before Art Kosh could cut him off; "Ah go shoot yourself." He was getting plenty of calls that day.

Old Man Hiram did not even notice the rudeness, and there was no changing the subject for the exasperated Tunney after that triumphant radio appearance. Old Man Hiram discoursed with blood thirst on how to stop drug pushing and assaults, thieving and mugging. It was a solution which called for massive hangings from tree limbs, a veritable Yosemite National Forest of gruesome Christmas trees. He told with equal firmness how to keep the grocery stores from injecting water into the hams. Finally, when he paused to thoughtfully pop a cracker smeared with butter and "lasses" into his snaggletooth and bewhiskered mouth, Tunney actually thrust the pen into his hand.

But it was too late, McCorquodale could be heard coming down the breezeway and Tunney had just enough time to put the deed in his coat pocket before she came walking in with the martini shaker. She could not stand Tunney. "I know I've seen you some place before," she said to her prosperous relative before dismissing his presence. "Aren't you the meter reader?"

Old Man Hiram was pleased with the shaker, even if a bit puzzled. He decided to place it on the mantle next to a stuffed rattlesnake he had killed by the smokehouse. "Well, let's see," he said, turning it around as he sampled a spoonful of marmalade. "Rightchere's a flower and yonder's some kinda tall weed. Ain't you sweet now, pretty thang, to think of your ole grampaw."

"Yes, it was quite an inspiration," she agreed. When it came out that her grandparents were not entirely certain what a martini was, she promised to pass along a few choice recipes.

Albert began the customary family sniping maneuvers McCorquodale knew so well. "I hear tell you up and quitchur job at that decorator place."

"Interior decorating was not leading to my full individuation."

"Now me and Brenda, we never been afraid a work. Brenda says unemployment ain't nothin but folks that think they're too good for a job. Did you know Brenda was sellin Lady Love cosmetics now?"

"My."

"She's tearner up. Goin to a big Lady Love convention in Atlanta next August. She can stop by with her suitcase and show you the Lady Love line if you're interested."

McCorquodale said nothing. At length Tunney picked up the

martini shaker and immediately noticed the dents. "Is this thing second hand?! Looks all chipped and gnawed and tore at to me. But I guess you saved you a lot of money."

McCorquodale could not believe her ears. "It is a *priceless* antique. I bought it at a leading downtown establishment for objets d'art."

"*Downtown*!! You couldn't pay me to go down there. Ain't nothin but bums and perverts. You're lucky you didn't get your throat cut, young lady. Brenda had to go down there the other day and it took her five minutes to park her car. Then she had to walk four blocks to the building she was goin to."

McCorquodale had to think for a moment to realize that walking represented a weird departure from ordinary life for the Tunneys.

"Suburban polyps," she said softly, toward no one in particular. She took a drag on her cigarette holder and blew out one perfect ring of smoke. "I suppose you know, Albert, that I live downtown."

"Yeah. Why in this world y'all don't get outta there is beyond me."

"It's the right side of my brain. It's very demanding."

"Well, I think they oughtta just tear it all down." He was getting piqued. "Just clean it up down there and bulldoze every bit of it." For a long moment Tunney was severely tempted to tell McCorquodale that that was just what was going to happen. Boy, would that ever get her goat. He could just imagine her foaming-at-the-mouth reaction if he spilled the beans on the Houston developer and the Supermall.

Old Man Hiram gave him a wink and tapped his coat pocket, meaning that he should keep the peace and they would talk about the will on another occasion.

All this was too much for Tunney and he stormed out.

CHAPTER 10

Miracle at the Tea

Mrs. Harmsworth Billingsley Balleriel, known to her friends simply as Rose Parkhurst Jameston Balleriel, possessed the oracular powers of a Delphic high priestess in answering the mystical question, who is, and who is not, a Mobilian? Seldom reflecting, never erring, she pronounced her judgments, sniffing out rare essences, sifting through gradations, ranking all creatures in the Great Chain of Being.

At the bottom were the invisible wraiths from the North, then came the spirits of Europe and the other continents, then those in the other Southern states. The existence of any and all could be denied at will. Inhabitants of a small circle of acceptable Southern cities were granted more or less permanent diplomatic recognition, principally Savannah, Charleston and New Orleans, plus respectable smaller places like Natchez and Selma. Her great powers of divination, however, came to the fore in discerning who was truly the most Mobilian of the *Mobilian* Mobilians in Mobile.

Not only did Mrs. Balleriel come from a long line of Mardi Gras royalty, but her husband Harmsworth had a similar background. In contrast to his wife, he was an easy-going man, well-liked and perfectly content to spend his inherited fortune in peace. Mr. Balleriel had been chosen for his impressive name to be chairman of Task Force 2000, a dynamic group of local business leaders charged with the task of preparing the city for the twenty-first century, though if the truth be known he much preferred to go dove hunting.

Mrs. Balleriel never doubted that they were "the fuist of the fuist," the most royal family in the city, as she had often told her son Ernest, now heir apparent to the throne of the Commerce National Bank. "Be proud, Uinest," she had always admonished the growing boy, "proud but not haughty. Remember, if other people were Jay-umstons or Balleriels, who would belong to the common huid?"

"How can they stand it, Mamacita?" Ernest would wonder. "Sometimes you really have to admire them, they lead lives of such quiet courage."

Another golden rule she had often inculcated had to do with discernment. "Your grindmothuh Sadie used to say—and she was a Pawkhuist!—that if you're ever confused about people, and I suitainly don't know why on uith you ever would be, then just sit down and make up an invitation list. If they're on the list, then you can be sure they're *nice*. And if they are not, well, there you have it."

Imagine if Mrs. Balleriel could have heard Aunt Odilia discoursing on the royalty of the Roshfookles and dismissing the claims of the Balleriels: "pretenduhs, usuipuhs!" But she knew nothing as yet of the obscure genealogist/coupon shopper and her niece on St. Anthony Street.

Several weeks before Mardi Gras, Mrs. Balleriel gave one of her famous teas, at which she performed the miracle of materialization and unwittingly put down an insurrection from the scheming Mrs. H. Sloane Wolfe. It was a major event of the season, comparable nearly to the Queen's luncheon. For weeks now the banner of the queens of Mardi Gras had fluttered from its flagpole beneath the oaks before Mrs. Balleriel's Government Street mansion; royal crown upon field of lozenges, purple and gold, a brave spectacle. As the excited ladies passed between two towering sabal palms and mounted the marble steps, wrapped in furs, adjusting their hats, pulling their white gloves tight, they could hear wind chimes tinkling among the Corinthian columns of the portico like temple bells.

Inside the foyer, they dropped their calling cards into the row of four silver salvers. There was one for Mrs. Balleriel and for each of the three ravishing debutante honorees: Claudia Scattergood, Elouise McFadden and Regina Hammerstein.

When the guests made their way past the reception line into a row of two great parlors and a back dining room, all connected by huge cased openings, they beheld a triumphant panorama. There were roses every-where. Roses clustered in big Chinese vases. Roses embroidered on the French dresses of the little daughters and granddaughters of Mrs. Balleriel's friends walking proudly about the rooms with Conning silver trays of hot hors d'oeuvres. Roses bursting out of the fronds of a forest of potted palm trees as though they had blossomed there. It was "Rose" Balleriel's constant theme, and she herself wore a gorgeous dress of rose pink moire taffeta matching a mountainous hat of rose tulle.

At either end of the sumptuous serving table in the dining room, the likes of Mrs. Chasuble Hedgemont and Mrs. Marmaduke LeVerne, ladies "of the fuist watuh," as Mrs. Balleriel might put it, were already pouring tea with two teapots from the Zadek silver service that had once been in the old Jameston home on Monroe Street near the river.

And yet mischief was afoot behind the roar of merry voices. There was Mrs. H. Sloane Wolfe, with that vampish gray streak in her hair and dressed to the nines, pursuing her covert strategy to take over Mrs. Balleriel's position as president of the Mobile Preservation Society. Poor Roberta Wolfe, one could almost forgive her somewhat shrill disposition and dangerous ambitions. Though blessed with wealth and a natural flair for bridge, she had had the tragic misfortune to grow up elsewhere, having moved to Mobile thirty years ago from Huntsville.

For years she had striven incessantly to make up for this fatal gaffe, determined to establish her social position by becoming the first non-native president of the influential club. Her current strategy was to lure Arlene Morganton into her sphere of influence. Mrs. Morgantan was a very prominent lady in the Preservation Society, though the other members thought she was a witch. Privately, Mrs. Balleriel was furious at her because she had torn down the nearby Morganton family mansion on Government Street a few months ago for a car wash, an act somewhat inconsistent with the goals of the Preservation Society. It was the latest bit of commercialization and demolition on what had once been the great residential grand boulevard of the city. The Balleriels were among the major hold-outs against the trend.

On top of that, Mrs. Balleriel thought Arlene Morganton had had entirely too much to say about her son Edgar being king of Mardi Gras last year, when the truly significant position was *queen*. It was a very dangerous trend. Throughout the century the "King Felixes" had never been anything more than a necessary accouterment, drones to the queen bee. As a former queen herself, Mrs. Balleriel knew better than anybody. The fact that her own son Ernest had been an outstanding exception only confirmed it.

Sensing her opportunity, Roberta Wolfe moved in and could be seen buttering up Mrs. Morganton next to the oval portrait of the antebellum railroad developer and riverboat owner, Thucydides Cicero Harmsworth.

But a major blow was dealt to this strategy when Arlene Morganton saw Mrs. Balleriel materialize a young woman out of thin air. She was Lulu Prendergrass, an old out-of-town college sorority sister—Kappa Kappa Gamma at the University of Alabama—of Ce Ce Anne Stanton's. Everyone agreed that Ce Ce Anne looked stunning.

"Y'all, don't *icek* me what I ever did before," she explained, jingling her bracelets at Lulu and a group of friends, "but I have been color-analyzed by my make-up consultant from *head to toe* and I know now that I am a 'winter.'" In the never-ending flux of Ce Ce Anne's facial expressions, her two delicately penciled eyebrows remained permanently lifted in a look of perpetual astonishment. "Will you see turquoise, will you see peach on this babe? *Don't count oin it.* I have nothing oin but my 'palette of colors.' I could *pice out* when I think of what I used to wear. Look here, *true* blue, *true* red."

"It's *just super*," Regina Hammerstein raved. She went off to mingle, but was intercepted by the ageless Mizz Rota Funderburke (née Duggins), queen in 1919. Regina was to be queen, though it was all officially secret. Mizz Rota's tiny white skull rose turtle-like above a mound of furs and fox heads. She proceeded to give Regina her perennial advice.

"Now when you're riding on that float, sweethawt, don't chunk the favors overhand like some baseball player. A *lady* always *tosses*, gently, underhand, as though she didn't know how to throw." She would not rest until the young queen-to-be practiced a few hesitant tosses right in the middle of the crowd.

Ce Ce Anne and her circle looked on ironically. Regina looked so pale and delicate in pink pearls, but Tilda O'Toole told them in a very low voice that Regina and the other honorees had been up all night at the Stratfords' bayside luau at Point Clear.

"They were chasing boys up and down the wharf with crab nets. I hear Eloise McFadden got so drunk she stumbled into the Stratfords' azalea bushes and could be heard chucking up six courses, apparently one at a time."

"Well, it just goes to show you, big azalea bushes are so practical, almost like lawn furniture. The things I've done behind them!" Ce Ce Anne's big brown eyes widened in wonder, then she let out an amused shriek. "Oh, I swear, seems like yesterday I was making my own debut. Aren't we just getting so grown up and settled? Can you believe I only went to *two* pawties last week?"

Mrs. Balleriel came up to the group, cruising majestically like a great warship visiting a friendly port. Instantly curious, Mrs. Wolfe, Mrs. Morgantan, and several other ladies moved within earshot. Ce Ce Anne quickly changed the subject. "Mizz B., Lulu is going to be here awl through Mawdi Gras. Did she tell you she's from Birmingham?"

It was a city to which Mrs. Balleriel did not extend diplomatic recognition, and she looked dubiously at the tentative mirage of the unknown girl. "Buiminghime? Yase, I've often huid of it. They tell me it's very industrial, but of cose, I wouldn't know."

"But parts of it are very pretty, you know, in the mountains and all. But since I was born there maybe I'm prejudiced."

"*Bawn* there?!" A complete out-of-towner. Mrs. Balleriel took in this staggering information, and was at a momentary loss for words. It was rather embarrassing, as though the girl had said her grandmother had been eaten that morning by a great white shark. "Well, we all have to be bawn somewhere," she smiled.

"Actually, I think it was my parents' idea. They live there. My father works there," Lulu said.

"I see. And what does your fawthuh do?" Mrs. Balleriel inquired, uninterested, mentally preparing to cast Lulu into the outer darkness.

"He owns three steel mills, and then there's that computer firm and the insurance company."

"Well!" Mrs. Balleriel paused, and seemed almost to be hesitating. "No mawss grows under *his* feet. In fact, I would venture to say we could accept him as a 'Sustainer' for the Preservation Society. We might even list his name in our newsletter, don't you think, Mawgret?" Mrs. Balleriel asked, turning to Claudia Scattergood's mother next to her.

"That sounds simply grind!" Mrs. Scattergood answered. "I think you'll *almost* feel at home here."

It was then that Ce Ce Anne uttered the incantation. "Oh, but Lulu's *practically* a *native*. Her great-inet was a Hardenberg."

Mrs. Balleriel seized Lulu's hand. "Child! It could only have been Zemma Hawdenbuig. She was a clicemate of my mothuh's at Mizz Robert's School on South Hamilton Stree-it. My mothuh was a *Pawkhuist*, you know," she added as an afterthought.

Several onlookers were so overcome that they let out a soft "Oh!" Up until then Lulu had been nearly invisible to everyone at the party.

Arlene Morganton was deeply impressed by this incident of ecto-plasmic manifestation, and lost all interest in further conversation with Roberta Wolfe. For the rest of the afternoon she tried to patch things up with Mrs. Balleriel, paying her incessant compliments.

Many a cup of tea, many a glass of sherry would be consumed at that historic event, and all would be described in breathless detail to the waiting populace the following Sunday in the *Mobile Herald-Item*. But Roberta Wolfe was completely distraught. What would she do now? She might well have given some thought, too, to her husband Sloane, captain of industry.

CHAPTER 11

Destiny at the Double Rush

Ted Todd had come to town prepared for a prolonged campaign for his development scheme, but not for anything this slow. It was like moving through a fog, a cloud of steam, a pool of molasses. So far he had only had a couple of confidential meetings with a few business and political leaders arranged by Mayor Buzz Barker and his other partners in the Hamburger Harbor Improvement Association.

What was it about these people? Here he was with a dynamite plan to drain Mobile Bay for the bigtime industry, bring in an international conglomerate, and level half the city for a shopping mall worthy of the Sunbelt, and so many of them really just seemed to want to socialize. After a few drinks they would change the subject, and they never wanted to talk about anything but their own little local world. Not only that, but they saw everything in a cloud of romanticism, and would not say what they meant. The place was badly in need of fresh blood and new ideas.

And now with Mardi Gras coming you couldn't get a thing done. To make the best of a bad situation, Todd went to the Athelstan Club Domino Ball one night less than two weeks before Mardi Gras Day hoping to meet H. Sloane Wolfe, who seemed to be one of the kingpins in town. Todd was brought as a guest by attorney Parker Stallings, the only member of Buzz Barker's group with a social in.

With a cool eye Ted Todd watched the call outs in the old Neo-Romanesque club's small ballroom overlooking Bienville Square. "Jeez, you'd think they were real queens or something," he thought as Ida Moseley was led out to the orchestra fanfares, followed by the other debutantes. All the club members were costumed in rather druid-looking long hooded robes and eye masks.

When the call outs were over, Parker Stallings went off to dance, but

Todd was ready for business and decided to go ahead and look for H. Sloane Wolfe by himself. He turned to the man next to him to ask which of the dominoes was the banker. It happened to be George Belzagui, amateur historian. He had been given an invitation and brought along by Mr. Pappadapoulos in the Savings Department, who was off dancing with his wife. Mr. Belzagui was standing by himself observing all this high society for a detailed report to Mrs. Chighizola, who would lap up every word. Already he had exchanged greetings with Miss Stanton, looking intimidatingly glamorous out of the context of the bank, and her boyfriend, that nice Mr. Ernest Balleriel. The truth was, Mr. Belzagui was feeling a bit out of his depth in such an illustrious assembly, and relieved to have someone to talk to.

"But you don't sound like a Texan," Mr. Belzagui observed after they had talked a minute, ignoring Todd's question about Wolfe. He was itching to tell an outsider about local mysteries.

"Nah, nobody's *from* Houston; I just moved there because, you know, that's where the action is." He began to list all the cities he had lived in on the West Coast and in the Northeast, but Mr. Belzagui adjusted his glasses around his magnificent flaring nose and listened with utter indifference until he could begin his speech.

"So this is your fuist Mawdi Gras. Did you know that cawnival go-uhs all the way back through the Middle Ages to ancient Roman festivals?" It was like the start of an encyclopedia article. "And although it's not actually recogni-uzd by the chuich, it does fit very meaningfully into the lituigical yeuh." Ted Todd sensed a long and truly bone-crunching discourse coming, and began to glance nervously about the ballroom where the dancers were spinning in their costumes and tailcoats and gowns to the intoxicating 1940s bubble music of Benny and the Percolators.

Meanwhile, at the other end of the ballroom, McCorquodale was moving with ease among the swank crowd. In a moment of recklessness Wolfe had arranged for her to be admitted incognito. What a stir she created in her Aztec raven costume: glittering black sharkskin cut to expose her shoulders and dip deeply to her waist in the back. A daring slit in the dress attracted all eyes, but none could recognize her in the mask of black feathers that covered her eyes and forehead, swooping to a crest behind her head.

Wolfe, mad with adventure, kept slipping away while Roberta campaigned for the presidency of the Mobile Preservation Society with some of the more influential wives. Although costumed like an anchorite, on the inside he was the King of Hearts, stealing brief dances with McCorquodale, turning away when the whistle blew to change partners, arranging to be near her when it blew again, pretending to be surprised when McCorquodale took advantage of the "double rush" to ask him to dance in her turn.

It was not until one of the interludes that Ted Todd finally managed to bolt away from Mr. Belzagui and find the prominent banker. For almost forty-five minutes Mr. Belzagui had lectured his way from Roman saturnalia to noted Lebanese-Mobilian merchants at the turn of the century, stressing first and foremost the protagonists of the late and great Belzagui's Shoeteria. From time to time Parker Stallings came to get Todd but went happily back to the effervescent sub-deb he had met when he saw Todd locked in conversation, Mr. Belzagui's eager eyes boring in on him. Todd was desperate by the time Mr. Belzagui got to the subject of Lebanese cooking.

"It's never gotten the attention it desuives, Mr. Todd. Everybody's alwayiz talking about fruitcake faw Christmas, but have you once huid them talk about Mshabbak?" Todd could not stand it any longer. "The men's room, where's the little boys' room?" he blurted and ran off.

"Yankees are so rude," Mr. Belzagui thought, though not without some satisfaction about his own good manners.

After repeated inquiries, Todd discovered the masked magnate in a corner with Roberta surrounded by a group of prominent citizens paying court as to a Byzantine emperor. Everyone was awed by the news of Wolfe's growing banking empire throughout the state. Ernest and Ce Ce Anne were just saying hello. They were making a "dream couple of the Young Set" appearance, with Eddie and Helmut at their respective homes and safely out of sight.

Wolfe was a man who could remember the days when an introduction by a third party at such affairs would have been, "Mr. Todd, this is Mr. Masker; Mr. Masker, this is Mr. Todd." The Houston developer walked right up and grabbed Wolfe's hand.

"Hi there, I'm Ted Todd of Sunbelt Land Corporation, how you doing, buddy?"

Slowly the gruff banker focused his attention on Todd, who kept on talking. "They tell me you're one of the most high profile businessmen in town. You know, I've got a really compelling concept going that you might want to log in to. Ya got a minute?"

At the words "one of," a cold north wind blew out of the eyes looking from the mask. "Maybe if you called my office Monday, Mr. Todd, it could be arranged," Wolfe said.

"*Mister*?! Hey, do I look like an old man to you? Just call me Ted. And you're Horatio, right?"

Ernest and Mrs. Wolfe recoiled in horror. No one ever *dared* call Wolfe that, the "H." of "H. Sloane Wolfe," a traditional family name which he detested. But the energetic developer had looked it up in a business directory, thinking to score a few points by coming on sincere and down-to-earth, no game-playing.

Wolfe flashed on Todd the look that could cow recalcitrant businessmen into giving thousands to the United Fund. "Son," he growled, "call me that again and your ass is grass. I'm a lawn mower, and I'm a big Yazoo." The banker stormed off followed by Roberta and his retinue.

On and on the music bubbled and the dominoes whirled about the dance floor with their ladies, but Todd avoided his cohort Stallings and brooded on how he had managed to offend this man so crucial to his development scheme.

But after several glasses of champagne he began to feel better. A drop-dead good-looking babe in a weird bird mask walked by. He had seen her come up toward him before, then stop and stare for a moment at that old bore droning on at him and turn on her heels and walk quickly away. Maybe she was interested in Todd! Plucking up his courage, he asked her to dance.

"You know, you're a pretty classy lady," he told her as Benny and the Percolators attempted a wobbly rock-and-roll number.

"Yes, how true," McCorquodale agreed, "though most people would say 'regal.'"

"I bet you're from L.A. or the Bay area."

"Well, I've spent a lot of time over the bay," McCorquodale teased.

"I knew it! Say, can you believe this scene? Think of all the money they must blow on Mardi Gras, it just doesn't compute. And what a waste of time! Think of the streets they could pave if they'd stop spending that money on parades."

"The streets are paved."

"Yeah, but they could pave more. I can't believe they hold up traffic for the parades. Why do you think this town isn't growing? People are so hung up with this, like, non-viable nonsense that they don't have time to think about progress."

McCorquodale was not charmed. It took all of her revolutionary discipline to contain herself. "You toad, you," she cried, stopping dead still. "If you could only glimpse the intellectual underpinnings of Mardi Gras, your head would spin like a top. The profound symbolism, the lore of the folk. The vital message for those at the forefront of esthetic debate. People like you don't have an ounce of postmodernism in their veins." She left him stunned on the spot as Wolfe had done.

Later, when the King of Hearts and the Aztec raven stole out onto the balcony to plan their next tryst, they discovered they had both encountered the same man. "These Sunbelt types are really too much," McCorquodale mused, "but why worry about it? They can't bother us here."

CHAPTER 12

Behind the Scenes at the Hubba Hubba

The cats were jumping and the chicks were stepping high downtown at the Hubba Hubba Club on "Joe Cain Day," the Shrove Sunday festivities. And Ce Ce Anne Stanton was flying very high indeed. She had spent the entire day there with Helmut, never remotely imagining that McCorquodale would be meeting the president and chairman of the board of the Commerce National Bank at the sleazy bar that very afternoon.

The Junior League and the Young Set were so used to seeing Ce Ce Anne and Ernest together that they would have passed out and away had they known the true state of affairs. The two had known each other since earliest kindergarten days, and for years had attended the same birthday parties given for children in their parents' circles. They became close friends at the age of thirteen when they attended the Eight O'Clock Cotillion, a series of polite dances for thirteen-year-olds who had previously taken lessons in ballroom dancing. That same year they were both in the Juvenile Mardi Gras court, and their mothers, friends from girlhood, gave a *dansant* for them the day before they were to ride in the Floral Parade. There was a huge crown of flowers on the Balleriels' dining room table, and a live band of old men playing ballroom music, which the ninety kids attending were still young enough to put up with.

Both Ce Ce Anne and Ernest rejoiced in the possession of perfect destinies, stopping at all the coveted way stations in the great parade of life. They were like dancing stone figures of the Ages of Man ascending the portal arch of a Gothic cathedral. On one side was Ce Ce Anne, starting at the bottom as a little girl serving sandwiches at the Camellia Ball, then queen of the juvenile Mardi Gras court, an adolescent in the best high school sorority, a Kappa at Alabama, Queen of Mardi Gras, the

81

Spinsters, the Thalians, the Junior League, the Maids of Mirth, and at the top of the portal in full womanhood, the Sirens. On the other side, the infant Ernest appeared at the bottom carrying a fake trumpet as a herald at the Mardi Gras coronation, then danced up the portal as juvenile king, secretary of the best high school fraternity, a Phi Delt at Sewanee, King of Mardi Gras, SCS, the Athelstan Club, the Dragons, the Order of Myths, then a young man assuming by right of primogeniture his father's position in the Carnival Association, and finally, dancing to the top of the world, the Strikers.

Ernest and Ce Ce Anne were truly soul mates on the Great Chain of Being. Old friends, yes, but deeper than that it did not go, for though they appeared at all the parties and Mardi Gras balls together, their friendship was a sort of *mariage de convenance*.

Ernest was the only one who could sympathize with, or knew of, Ce Ce Anne's attraction to Helmut. Their meeting had been so providen-

The Mardi Gras societies had no doubt pondered the coming of Postmodernism.

tial. Coming back late and oddly restless one night from a Platonic movie evening with Ernest, she had found the merchant marine sailor sleeping behind a big gardenia bush in the front yard. Apparently he had had one drink too many downtown and had wandered in the wrong direction down Government Street away from the waterfront, and strayed off into the Garden District.

It was true that Helmut didn't talk much, but as soon as she saw him Ce Ce Anne knew that the huge sailor with his crazed blue eyes, his enormous frame, his bulging pectorals and steel biceps, his long legs, long feet, long fingers, long nose, could satisfy a need deep within her. "He's *so* continental," she thought. "If *they* only knew, *they* would understand."

Ce Ce Anne watched affectionately as Helmut lined up three jiggers of straight vodka and three beer chasers on the Hubba Hubba bar. "Los geht's!" he roared, and began to toss them down.

"Oh, I have no illusions," Ce Ce Anne thought. "They're not going to be writing Helmut up in *Fortune* magazine, and I can't really see him cutting a big figure in the Young Republicans. But sooner or later Daddy will come around after I tell him. I know there'll be a place for us. A quiet life for the two of us. Maybe a small chairmanship in the Chamber for Helmut with lots of newspaper photos and not too much talking. The bank *hice* to hire him as vice president. He could be in the Country Club, a good mystic society . . . "

Helmut was yelling again, "Zerfixsakramentnochmal #_¿*!"

Ce Ce Anne continued her thought. "We could get by with a nice little bayside cottage at Point Clear near the Grand Hotel. Just twenty rooms and a couple of acres and a tennis court, with maybe a cute guest house near the wharf. I don't need much to be happy, I know I don't."

She had tried to persuade Ernest to come with Eddie to the Hubba Hubba Club that day, but Ernest would not hear of it. "You can't be cautious enough, Ce. The walls have ears. I've got my reputation to think of." Ernest could be something of a stuffed shirt sometimes in his gray pinstripe suits. "And what would H. Sloane say if he found out we're hanging out at a dive like the Hubba Hubba Club?"

Ernest went with Eddie to New Orleans instead, where he always seemed to undergo a dramatic transformation. Mimi McDermitt, a fellow Junior Leaguer, told Ce Ce Anne confidentially after Mardi Gras that she had seen Ernest dancing on a balcony on Bourbon Street. "He was dressed in a Superman suit and totally plastered," Mimi reported. "He was arm in arm with this cute blond boy in tights and this kind of San Francisco apparition with hairy legs and a black wig three feet high. The one that looked like Ernest kept kicking up his heels and screaming, 'Tear the roof off the sucker!'"

Ce Ce Anne had to think quickly. "That's ridiculous. A Superman outfit? Ernest wouldn't even go out in the back yawd without his cufflinks oin. Listen, if I were you I would lay off the *absinthe suissesse* when I went to New Awlins; you're hallucinating." Mimi decided it must have been somebody else.

McCorquodale arrived at the bar in the pink kitten costume she had worn on the decorated flatbed truck that her nine brawny cousins, the McCorquodale Boys, had driven in from Chunchula that day. They were truck float number thirty-one in the Joe Cain "people's parade." She had little satin ears sticking up from the pink hood, a tight décolleté bodice, pink stockings and high-heeled shoes, and a fluffy tail that she had wagged to the cheering crowd.

It had been an exhilarating day, but McCorquodale was preoccupied as she sat on a bar stool and peered through the smoke at the motley crowd of bar regulars, street people, drag queens, seedy middle-aged couples and groups of young people who had wandered in after the parade. "I know that Sloane is deeply committed to postmodernism," McCorquodale brooded, "but sometimes I get the feeling that he doesn't see the whole picture." She had not told the banking magnate yet what his role would be in funding her future postmodern sidewalk café.

The red-headed and enormously stacked Tonya de Luxe, ever-popular bar maid and proprietress of the Hubba Hubba Club, brought McCorquodale her usual martini. They were great friends and, in Tonya's view, professional colleagues of a sort. Tonya had a distressingly mundane tendency to view everything in terms of business and the free enterprise market economy. She ran a tight ship, but they all said that when you got to know her she had a heart of gold.

McCorquodale had discovered the Hubba Hubba Club one Saturday afternoon on an exploratory stroll downtown. She had been immediately struck by the fact that there was no sign. What were they trying to say here with this mysterious silence? Was the lack of a sign a "sign"? The show window of what had once been a store was painted completely black, and a big hole in the glass had been backed with plywood. As McCorquodale stepped closer she was nearly hit by a bucketful of soapy water flying out the front door. "How quaint," she had thought. There was an obvious stress on traditional craftsmanship here, no high tech, plastic, modern cleaning procedures.

Occasionally when she went out on a date she would take her up-and-coming young professional escorts on a slumming tour and they would top off the evening in this secret nook and view the dance acts Tonya performed on top of the bar. Later, when McCorquodale began to devote more time to esthetic theory, she had asked Tonya if she could sometimes spend the afternoons there in order to sit and meditate. "No sweat off my butt," Tonya had graciously acceded. The handful of winos and hobos who were the mainstay of the struggling bar—supplemented by high-quality consumer services Tonya sometimes performed for clients with the money—were so dazed and quiet in the afternoons that they never disturbed McCorquodale's lucubrations.

Now with Mardi Gras mobs packing the bar every night, Tonya could temporarily breathe easy about revenues, but she was always on the lookout for new ways to drum up business. McCorquodale took a sip of her drink, but before they could talk, they were interrupted by Ce Ce Anne climbing up on the bar to perform a little number she had just worked out with the band Tonya had hired for Mardi Gras. Ce Ce Anne had only danced at little do's for the Young Set and at the exclusive Santa Claus Society ball, but could she cut it in the professional world? The band struck up a heavy drum beat and the pert Junior Leaguer began to sing and swing:

I'm built for comfort,
I ain't built for speed,
But I got every thang
Any good girl need.

The crowd went wild and Helmut kept slamming his massive fist on the bar in applause.

Tonya was impressed. "Ooo wee! That's that sure nuff, low-down, nitty gritty. Where you reckon that chick learned to dance like that?"

"I wonder. She looks strangely familiar," McCorquodale said. "I think I may have seen her dance once when I was out with a member of the fleet from the navy base down in Pensacola. I was feeling very patriotic that night."

"Naw, I bet she's from one a them Biloxi bars," Tonya said, "they don't stop at nothin in them joints."

H. Sloane Wolfe, disguised in an old Order of Myths costume, walked in after Ce Ce Anne had launched into her second number, "You've Got the Papers, But I've Got the Man." It was so dark and smoky inside that the he had to pull off his neutral mask to see through the waving arms of the mob.

The bank Liaison for Commercial Loan Concepts was wagging her finger up on the bar and just finishing—"What you need girl is a complete overhaul / Your house, your body, your face and all"—when she caught sight of Wolfe. She let out a piercing scream and jumped off, but fortunately she was caught by an enthusiastic group of Spring Hill College boys.

Tonya couldn't believe it, she thought it was part of the act. "I'm tellin you *that chick is hot!!* I want her on contract." But McCorquodale saw Wolfe standing blindly at the door and went to get him.

"Sloane, Sloane," she told him back at the bar, over the roar of the crowd, "you've got to realize that as soon as the Tennessee-Tombigbee Waterway is finished, we'll be the great postmodern center of the Western Hemisphere. We've got to get ready now."

But Wolfe was not listening that day. "What the hell *is*

postmodernism?" he grumbled. The truth of the matter was that McCorquodale had not once, not a single time, gone with him to any of his secret hideaways. It was unheard of! No one had ever held this power over him.

"Little guil, say yes today. Come on up with me to the ole huntin lodge and make me a happy man."

But McCorquodale was not to be swayed. "Darling, we've discussed this before. One day, yes, but please don't rush me. You know how fragile I am."

On the other side of the bar, Ce Ce Anne was desperately trying to put off Tonya, who wanted her to sign a dancing contract, and find an escape. "You're so durn hot I'll give you the day shift," Tonya offered. "Dance all you want. Get a commission on the drinks. Do a little moppin. This is your big break, gal." Ce Ce Anne's escape came when the band struck up a New Wave number and the excited college students jumped up and started thrashing stiffly.

"Sloane, New Wave!" McCorquodale cried, and pulled the banking magnate onto the dance floor. Wolfe put his mask back on and tried to imitate the students vibrating like electrocuted chickens. He kept wishing he were somewhere else.

Ce Ce Anne saw her chance and made a run for the door, practically carrying the staggering Helmut, but all the way home she thought about what had happened. Thank *God* Wolfe had not spotted her there, but what was he doing with the stunning woman who had won the Miss Brick House contest at the SCS ball? She was dying to tell the Committee on Urban Affairs, but maybe she should wait and let the story ripen to its full savory piquancy. It needed further investigation.

CHAPTER 13

A Face In the Crowd

In the final days of Mardi Gras, Ce Ce Anne was at ground zero of events as they unfolded. Shrove Sunday, when she made her appearance at the Hubba Hubba Club, provided only a brief break in her eager tracking of the court and the most "in" of the "in."

She was there at the King's *Dansant* Saturday night following the coronation and the Mystics of Time parade—she and Ernest slipped outside to see the dragons—when the reaction broke to Lady-in-waiting Lou Ethyl Strover's train. She and Ernest sat at maid Bippy Schneidebrett's table and pretended to examine the menu, all in French and embossed in gold with the Marburg coat of arms. Young Floyd DeKoven Marburg, home from Duke, was to be king that year. Bippy filled their ears: Lou Ethyl, the debutante from Demopolis, had worn a rhinestone and appliqué train depicting the production of turpentine, source of the family money. "You're lyne!" "I swear!"

At the soonest possible opportunity, Ce Ce Anne slipped off to the king's table ("Decorated in the stag and thistle motif of his majesty's mantle . . . Covered with a handsome emerald satin cloth, a silver deer epergne . . . cascade of gloriosa rothschildana lilies, yellow hyacinth . . . tall palace candles entwined with yellow snapdragons," as the *Herald-Item* reported in their annual special section for Mardi Gras the next morning). Not only was the news about Lou Ethyl confirmed, but Ce Ce Anne learned that Elouise McFadden was not even speaking to her knight, Robbo O'Toole, since she had walked unannounced into a delicate situation involving another girl in his room at the Sheraton where the court was staying.

Ce Ce Anne was there on Monday when a small contretemps occurred at the Queen's Luncheon, *the* event of the season, that would keep people buzzing for weeks. During the merry moment when the knights came running and whooping into the hall, amusing the five hundred fashionable ladies decked out in their best suits, Billy Rushton, Claudia Scattergood's knight, flipped his tricornered hat right into the tomato aspic of the formidable Mrs. Thrush Alcott, who was not amused. "Young man, you're intoxicated," she announced. Karen Bixwell *swore* to Ce Ce Anne that he tossed off "You old buttfucker!" before staggering away from a row of dropping jaws. Ce Ce Anne, watching from another table, had heard two ladies behind her comment, "The young people are having such a good time."

Ernest was particularly satisfied with the Sunday *Herald-Item's* reporting of the royal lineage of that year's king, queen, knights, ladies, pages, heralds, and equerries. Not only were he, his mother, and father listed repeatedly, but also many of their direct and collateral antecedents. "Queen Regina's paternal grandmother, Evelyn Windenham (Mrs. Piedmont Hammerstein), was a maid in 1922 in the court of King Arthur Stewart Balleriel and Queen Penelope Gwendolyn Butt (Mrs.

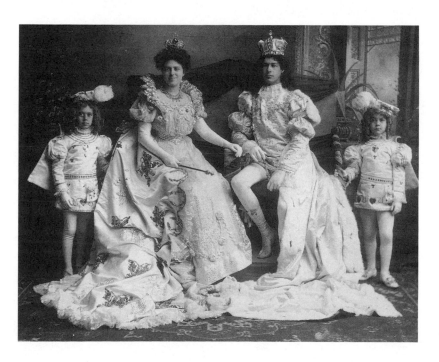

Earlier royalty established the tradition of which I am the flowering.

McCrae Stauter). Her great-great-uncle Jackson Hammerstein was king in the court of 1895, with Corinna May Jameston (Mrs. Marvin Belasco Funderburke) as his consort," and so forth and so on through parents, cousins, aunts, and uncles. And what figures Ernest and Ce Ce Anne cut on the afternoon of Fat Tuesday, dazzling the mobs on their walk from the Athelstan Club to the Knights of Revelry reception, drawing curious looks from the crowd and stupefied stares from drunk youths screaming, "Mardi Gras!" *Costume de rigueur* once again, Ernest in his tails and Ce Ce Anne in dark watered silk and sapphires. Both Helmut and Eddie were left to their own devices while the dream couple of the Young Set satisfied their social obligations.

At the KOR reception Ernest was shocked to see that several guests had slipped in wearing only black tie. This troubling lapse, together with the bumper crop of exciting scandal, impelled Ce Ce Anne, with Ernest's sage collaboration, to write a post-carnival issue of her rare but eagerly received social hotline, *Chat*. Eighty or ninety copies were Xeroxed and distributed, written in an obscure style only intelligible to the initiate, as in the following brief excerpt:

> Flash! What prominent businessman—grab your smelling salts!—has been showing a certain blond honey the sights of the town? We were told by a little bug on the wall that he likes it strictly incognito. Out of sight, babe, but not out of mind! Nothing escapes us. And you read about it first in *Chat!*
>
> Stop! Bright eyes and bushy tails at the KORs'. Claire and Bob were so punk we were all in a funk. Some changing of partners observed, "do-si-do." A number of "gentlemen" present in nothing but tuxes. Is nothing sacred? We say it's time to get tough with the dress code. If you're not going to play, don't stay!
>
> Flash! The thud of swooning matrons hitting the floor like coconuts at Wakiki Beach can still be heard all over town over the incident with King Felix in front of the Athelstan Club. It seems that blondes are very "in" this year.

Ce Ce Anne was all for writing "banker" instead of "businessman," and making up a few spicy rendezvous out of whole cloth, since mentioning the Hubba Hubba Club seemed injudicious in light of her own appearance there. She had come to the realization long ago that a slavish adherence to facts was the death knell to successful investigative reporting. But Ernest, thinking what would happen if it got back to Wolfe, put in a vehement veto.

She also considered tying the incident at the Athelstan Club—Ce Ce Anne had been so excited that she nearly fell out of the stands—more closely to the first item. And her thoughts wandered to that strange masked woman she had noticed Wolfe dancing with several times at the Athelstan Club Double Rush, the only woman wearing a mask at the ball. How outlandish, she had thought at the time, but then maybe that woman had had her reasons. Tempting connections, but Ce Ce Anne decided that premature revelations might spoil what promised to be the gossip of the year. That blond woman was still only a distant face on the horizon, but something told Ce Ce Anne that very soon a certain name she had come up with, "Margaret Constance Roshfookle," was going to be a lot better known.

What had happened was nothing less than that on Mardi Gras Day, after a succession of morning and afternoon parades, when the royal float arrived in front of the Athelstan Club for King Felix III, alias Floyd Marburg, to toast his queen, the young monarch had spotted McCorquodale in the crowd, extremely fetching as ever, and jumped down from the float to give her a kiss.

It was Aunt Odilia's idea to go watch the parades in front of the Athelstan Club that day. With Wolfe tied up, McCorquodale had planned to spend the day quietly at home refining key points of postmodern theory. Thinking of their own distinguished genealogy, and the royal days of the brilliant Camille Roshfookle, Aunt Odilia had stood in the throng and rather wistfully watched the elite crowd in the festooned stands across the street, had minutely examined the Princess Di poses of the debutantes in their silk and linen suits and broad-brimmed flowered hats, occasionally sloshing a slow cool jerk with their plastic drink cups in hand to the beat of the approaching bands. Aunt Odilia had for once discarded her stretch knit slacks and tennis shoes in favor of a discreet navy blue dress that showed up so well her beads and brooches, and she would have made a very presentable Queen Mother. McCorquodale had not prepared a costume, but after prolonged nego- tiations she talked Aunt Odilia into letting her wear her old wedding dress, with a bouquet of white camellias from the garden. The dress was rather large, and kept slipping over McCorquodale's shoulders, drawing inquiring looks from a wide radius at that display of bridal innocence.

The incident was over before anyone quite realized what was hap- pening. The crown float was approaching and the debutantes were bustling into position in the projecting royal pavilion. The young king took a swig from his plastic cup, brained a cotton candy vender with a box of crackerjacks, and was just aiming for a street light with a bean bag when he caught sight of McCorquodale and her bare shoulders. He detached his train, jumped down from the float in his crown and knee breeches, and ran up for a lingering French smack. A shocked silence and sharp exhaling of breath followed as the crowd watched aides scramble down and hustle him back onto the float. McCorquodale took a deep breath and dreamily pulled up a sleeve, then looked around at the hundreds of staring faces. She shouted "Olé!" and tossed her bouquet.

The king was able to give the somewhat jilted Queen Regina a wobbly toast with his silver goblet, and the parade continued. McCorquodale, having a commodious ego, took the whole event in stride, but Aunt Odilia was thrilled to the core. A royal omen? She talked about it all the way home and later that day when she went off for fried oysters on the bay causeway with Mr. Belzagui and the Misses Robinson, puttering away in their old car at fifteen miles an hour.

McCorquodale stayed home and sprawled out on the bed with her notes around her. In honor of the holiday, she had assigned herself the theoretical task of pondering: What was the Isle of Joy? This was the mysterious, unmapped and remote southward island "discovered" in the 1870s by T.C. DeLeon, a novelist and stager of celebrations and dreamer and Jewish enthusiast of Mardi Gras. King Felix III dwelt on the Isle of

Joy, but undertook a voyage once a year to appear before his subjects in Mobile for three days of "misrule," then set sail again at midnight of Shrove Tuesday to return to the Isle.

But where was it, McCorquodale wondered? Who lived there? What did it look like? Joyous misrule must be permanent there. Could that be something like a mirror reflection of life here? Or perhaps more accurately, was life here a mirror image of the Isle of Joy? It was strange to her that despite the annual reenactments of the arrival of the King and court by boat at the foot of Government Street, everyone seemed quite content to leave the idea in the bare outlines. But McCorquodale was going to think it through to the end and visualize the Isle. She tried to sink into a meditative calm, but outside noises kept beckoning. She kept hearing what seemed to be bands playing in the distance, hollow vibrations like approaching drums, but when she would run to the window the beat vanished into the wind and the sounds of far-off traffic.

Unable to work, she decided to go to the parade of the black Mardi Gras court and King Elexis I in the late afternoon, held on the north side

The enigma always returns, is always young. Question: What is "misrule"?

of downtown. Out of costume, wandering among teenagers and children waiting with flowered pillow cases to hold the moon pies, plastic beads, taffy kisses, and other throws from the floats, she scanned the largely black crowd looking for familiar faces. Along came a young woman she had known in her days at AAA Superior Wallcoverings, Gladys Hathaway, the purchasing agent for Azalea City Light Fixtures. She had once taken McCorquodale to the famous Order of Don Q. ball. Slowly picking her way through the admiring crowd, dressed in a long, white, satin gown, Gladys stopped to exchange delighted pecks on the cheek with McCorquodale and introduce her date, a tall man in tails. "Gracious, girl, where you been all this time?" They were going to the black court's reception afterward, had to meet some friends, could not linger. McCorquodale wandered some more after they left. Wolfe was busy with friends and family. Maybe she should have made other arrangements instead of planning to stay at home. She perceived an odd and highly unusual sensation. Was it possible that she was—no!—feeling just a bit lonely?

Cries of "Fabulous!" followed by a commotion of voices and unbelieving squeals from the onlookers attracted her attention to a little cluster of tall birds of paradise in enormous ostrich plume headdresses and sequin bathing suits approaching on skates and high heels at the next street corner, all with thick coats of makeup, and several of them sporting beards and mustaches. The costumes had been used only days before in the tableau of the highly extravagant Order of Thoth, a carnival mystic society well off the beaten track. She had seen them earlier that afternoon prancing past a block of redneck teenagers drinking beer in the back of their parked pick-up trucks, raising a cloud of whoops and yells like dust on a red clay road.

The group stopped at the corner, and out of their midst sailed a short blond boy in a Zorro outfit, his black cape aflutter. Landing on clicking tap shoes, he proceeded to execute a very credible double buck and wing. McCorquodale was spellbound to witness this abrupt vision of the coming consciousness shift, postmodern if ever there was one. Approaching closer, she recognized a young actor who had caught her eye once in a Port City Players production. Dancing out of a chorus line of cowpokes twice his size, he had executed several striking and clearly unauthorized leaps with red bandanas flying in both hands, his blond bangs flying boyishly from side to side, while the upstaged singers shot him basilisk looks. She had checked her program with interest.

It was the befeathered group's turn to be surprised, and all tap dancing ground to a halt, when out of nowhere a glamorous and poised young woman appeared, wafting cloudbanks of perfume, and proffered a gloved hand. "Excuse me, are you Mr. Edward Dooley?"

Eddie recovered from his astonishment somewhat after this imposing personage explained that she had been "exalted" by his acting and entertainment artistry. He glanced around at the surrounding circle of Babylonian temple hermaphrodites to make sure they were taking this in. It was his first fan.

"This tap dancing, Mr. Dooley. May I be frank? It thrilled me. It bore the signature of a keen mind. The click of your heels, that inspired skipping—*Oklahoma* took on new depths."

Eddie had to bite his lip to keep from breaking out into an uncontrolled smile. "I'm real serus about my work," he said suavely.

"But now tell me, darling, what is your theoretical basis?"

"Do what?"

"Your theoretical basis."

He wondered what she could be talking about. "Oh . . . there's a lots a times I like to play the field, you know?"

"Droll, but come now," McCorquodale said slyly, "give me just one hint. What did you really mean when you jumped out of the chorus line? I bet you were . . . dual-coding, weren't you?"

"Oh yeah, you can really work up a audience thataways."

"I knew it," McCorquodale cried. "So obviously polyvalent. The minute I saw it I thought how revivalist can you get? Neo-tap dancing. How very clever."

When the parade came McCorquodale caught a role of serpentine and a pretty necklace of colored glass beads with a bit of paper attached covered with Hindi writing. High school bands stopped in the street and swung their pelvises while adolescent girls screamed. McCorquodale invited Eddie to have a cocktail. His friend Bobo lent him his battered old Buick. With the radio booming full blast, they swayed and snapped their fingers in the front seat. At one point Eddie swerved onto the sidewalk rather than slow down for a group of returning parade-goers walking down the middle of Dauphin Street. Tonya's nerves were worn by the huge crowd at the Hubba Hubba Club, and she hesitated very grumpily before serving Eddie his drink.

"You eighteen? You got a driver's license?"

"Miss Thang, I done been nineteen and beyond for four whole months. I will have me a Campari and soda, with a twist if you please." He finally settled for a rum and coke.

Tonya was more conciliatory when she brought the drinks. "Thatchur little brother?" she wondered, and there *was* a certain resemblance between the two pale blond theorists.

Over the general roar McCorquodale shouted basic tidings of the postmodern imperative and the coming esthetic revolution. Eddie pictured this as something like night club appearances in Key West. They went to a restaurant for dinner, and caught the OOMs that night, the final parade of Mardi Gras. The old emblem float passed, with a very fat Folly chasing a tall and skinny Death around the broken column of Time. Wolfe had told McCorquodale he would be on float four, "Song of the Sirens," a float-long mermaid with a frozen smile nodding her head shakily as though at any moment it might roll off into the street. Bits of gold leaf on quivering papier-mâché fluttered in the light of the flares. Feeling a bit miffed at being left alone that day, relishing her anonymity and her new disciple, she watched it pass without trying to catch the attention of the maskers on the float. Eddie had forgotten to ask which float Ernest would be on. "One a them dudes up there in costumes is a acquaintance a mine, but I ain't seen a one that looks like im," he told her. A parade marshall in a glittering veiled mask and velvet cape teetered on the back of his horse, obviously drunk. He upset one of his saddlebags and a torrent of doubloons spilled onto the street. People scrambled like goldfish in a feeding frenzy.

Eddie and McCorquodale watched from the rear of the crowd, just two faces among so many. In the distance, across a parking lot, they could see approaching floats going in the other direction up a parallel street before turning. The shadow of a giant seahorse, projected by a street light, played eerily across the pink stucco facade of an antebellum town house, unreal as a stage set.

Eddie said that in the perfect Mardi Gras, all the thousands of spectators would dance the Mashed Potato and the Bossa Nova as the floats passed, changing steps according to penetrating shrills from a piccolo. McCorquodale said that a truly postmodern carnival would require blocks and blocks of maskers on balconies throwing white clouds of confetti.

"I'm going to be tied up for a while laying intellectual groundwork," she told her new disciple as they parted, "but watch and wait. When the moment comes, you will be summoned."

Part Two

CHAPTER 14

A Vote for Growth

On Ash Wednesday morning, a cold, gray rain pelted the streets. The sounds of the morning traffic reluctantly entering the business district, back to the workaday world, were muffled under the overcast skies. The flip-flop weather of the coast had changed its mind once again after days of heat and sunlight. People complained bitterly of late February temperatures in the forties. Tired of parties and commotion, they huddled inside quiet houses, or grumbled if somebody tried to start a conversation with them at the office. Old St. Joseph's Church creaked and echoed more than ever in the gloom when Aunt Odilia went to the early morning Lenten service to receive a cross of ash on her forehead. The Jesuit saints in the beautiful German stained glass windows looked brooding and mum. Father Kreismeier seemed to move miles away at the altar in a haze of blazing candlelight.

Blocks away, in a small banquet room of Le Louis XIV Restaurant, Ted Todd and Mayor Barker were wide awake and ready for a crucial conference. All through the Mardi Gras season they and their little group of cronies had been laying the groundwork, arranging confidential meetings with important business and political leaders. Their reaction to the daring development scheme for the city and the bay had been non-committal. But if Task Force 2000 endorsed the project, Barker and Todd were certain that many of the big powers in the city would fall in behind them.

At first, Harmsworth Billingsley Balleriel, chairman of Task Force 2000, had been violently opposed to having the meeting at eight a.m. following the final night of Mardi Gras. Barker did not belong to the Task Force, and realized quite clearly that in their eyes he was an upstart semi-hick and total nobody. But he knew the lay of the land only too well, and pulled all the stops to arrange it then. "Look, this Ted Todd is *big time*. He's flying to Saudi Arabia Wednesday afternoon, this is the only time he can meet you. I'd hate to have to say we didn't get this big development because the Task Force *couldn't make it*. Remember when we lost that Japanese tire factory to Galveston?"

Mr. Balleriel winced at the thought. News had spread that South American blackfish were biting off of Little Dauphin Island, and the whole Task Force had gone fishing in the Gulf on Ripley Washton's yacht on the afternoon the delegation from Tokyo stopped in town. Barker was capable of making a scandal. "Oh no, we couldn't have that," Mr. Balleriel said. "We're all for growth." And so the meeting was arranged.

Todd was jittery about facing these crucial movers and shakers. "Gee, I dunno, Buzz. When we start talking about streamlining half the city to potentialize megagrowth, they may just go, 'Hey, I have a problem with that.'" Barker just laughed.

As Barker had anticipated, the members of the Task Force were not in a mood to nit-pick as they filed into the room. Their gray and green-hung over faces, their expressions of stoic suffering, contrasted sharply with their antics only a few hours before. Fourteen of the twenty members of the Task Force belonged to the Order of Myths, had ridden floats the night before, had attended the OOM ball following the parade, and the other six, Infant Mystics, had been at the ball as guests. Most had then proceeded to Moseley Shorter's post-ball breakfast at the suite he had rented for the last four days of Mardi Gras at a downtown hotel, where up until the wee hours punch bowls of margueritas emptied like funnels, Congressman Stirling McVay did his Liberace impersonation, and Bert Eads (Mrs. Marmeduke LeVerne) did the Big Apple all around the bed piled high with fur coats.

Task Force 2000 was a select committee of the city's most dynamic business and community leaders charged with the awesome, though vague, task of "preparing Mobile for the twenty-first century." Generally that was interpreted to mean luring new business and industry into town, with an eye to the successes of other Southern cities.

No sluggards these: they were hard-headed businessmen, tireless and progressive leaders constantly on the lookout for fresh ideas and new approaches. Every effort was made to include a broad spectrum of the community. For example, not only a banker like Hearn Moseley was included, but also the owner of a grocery store chain: Moseley Shorter, his first cousin. Both old and young were on the committee, like the elder Ripley Washton and his son Ripley Junior and his nephew, young Rastor Washton. They always sat together and looked like a row of sphinxes with their big Washton noses.

By coincidence Task Force 2000 almost exactly duplicated the crew that regularly went hunting together. All of the Task Force members were part of the gang, and if they had not been so somber that morning, if they had been wearing camouflage jackets instead of business suits and had been holding paper cups of Bourbon, it could have been one of their stag parties at "Bull's Landing" or "Dead Man's Bend" or one of their other private hunting camps in the delta. The one conspicuous absence was H. Sloane Wolfe, who had been asked to serve on the Task Force but refused when he found out that his banking rival Hearn Moseley had been asked first. Wolfe had fumed for weeks, hoping that Ernest Balleriel would repeat his ranting to his father, and that it would get back to Moseley, but unfortunately Ernest was much too discreet.

Harmsworth Balleriel, president of Balleriel Stevedoring, was better known as "good old Ham Balleriel." He was made the guiding light of the Task Force because of his impressive name, his inherited fortune, and his universal popularity. How different he was from his staid son and from his formidable wife, Rose (Parkhurst Jameston B.).

"Ham" Balleriel was easygoing, always radiating good spirits with his ruddy face and the ample paunch under his belt. Sometimes, it was true, he did not seem to follow every word of the conversation, but in the flurry of handshaking and back-pounding, out-of-state visitors who dealt with him did not have much time to think about it.

But back-pounding that Ash Wednesday morning was exceedingly feeble. Rain rattled against the tall windows of the restored mansion that housed the restaurant. Several young waiters in yellow cutaway jackets

and black bow ties stood dazed in the corners of the room, their hands
behind their backs. Silence reigned, except for the clinking flatware of
Todd and Barker, eating a hearty breakfast. The others around the long
table stared at their eggs. The yolks stared back.

Mr. Balleriel's huge stomach was tossing like a ship in a hurricane. It
was so bad that he seriously wondered if he would live through the
meeting. The other members were in the same state, and when Ted Todd
began his presentation, aided by Barker, the soft fizz of Alka-Seltzer
could be heard all around the table.

Todd started out with slides showing architectural renderings of the
new city as it would look when transformed by the development. There
were visions of soaring freeways, and suburban subdivisions with miles of
neat yards stretching out to swallow up Montgomery, Slidell, and
Apalachicola. The exciting drawing showed an amusement park that
could hold five Disneyworlds. The Supermall, Todd said, would be
bigger than the Houston Galleria, but the ashen faces of the Task Force
members registered no response.

Todd decided to try to woo his audience with astounding figures
from a feasibility study which he said a Dallas consulting firm had done
for his Sunbelt Land Corporation. "Now guys, bear in mind that these
are very conservative guestimates in terms of the brass-tacks impact the
Tennessee-Tombigbee Waterway's gonna have on this strategic geocenter.
Our studies of the project planning mass show that, and we are definitely
low-balling it, that our proposal would generate $2 billion a year in sales
taxes, 600,000 jobs, and $179 billion a year in payrolls."

There was a leaden pause and Mr. Balleriel felt it incumbent on him
to say something. "Growth, gotta have growth!" he exclaimed, but the
floor of the room seemed to be rocking beneath him. Several members of
the Task Force were on the verge of falling out of their chairs, and Ripley
Washton's eyes were rolling back in their half-closed lids so that only the
whites were visible.

Todd began speaking of the miles of parking lots that would
surround the Supermall on the site of the old city. "Convenience is the
code word, guys; it'll be the end of the parking problem here. Parking

meters? Parallel park? Never! You can stop your car three miles away and, gosh, you're already there."

Mr. Balleriel's stomach gave a terrible heave, and for a moment a frightful chasm opened up before him. Would the chairman of Task Force 2000 actually throw up all over the conference table? With a Herculean effort he contained himself. "Lord have muicy!" Mr. Balleriel silently implored. "Won't he ever shut up?"

Todd smilingly began to go over the small details of the plan. The land for Supermall and the amusement park would be acquired with public funds and donated to Sunbelt Land Corporation. The City, of course, would be responsible for draining the bay. Sunbelt Land Corporation would pay no taxes on the land, and all construction would be financed with tax-exempt bonds issued by a city authority.

"Of course it won't be easy at first," Barker interjected nervously. "We may have to cut out a few of your frillier items in your city services— your garbage collection, your police force to begin with—but we've got to be ready for some sacrifices if we're gonna get the bigtime industry."

There was a refreshing lack of questions from the Task Force members. In their agony several had laid their heads on the table with their arms hanging loosely underneath. Wallace Wade Stanton's head was swinging back and forth, his mouth wide open.

Mr. Balleriel was breaking out in a cold sweat, the room was swimming before him. This time there would be no holding it back.

Barker was still talking but Mr. Balleriel pounded his gavel and cut him short. "We're all for growth here," he croaked, "free enterprise, gotta expand. All in favor of endorsing this plan . . ." Twenty choking voices said "aye," the gavel pounded, and Mr. Balleriel shoved back his chair and went running out the door to the men's room. Within half a minute all the other Task Force members had swiftly taken the same route, leaving Barker and Todd alone in the room.

Even an operator on the level of Ted Todd was at a loss for words after the exodus. The waiters began clearing the coffee cups and water glasses with badly shaking hands. Barker just grinned: "Like shootin fish in a barrel, bud."

CHAPTER 15

$\mathcal{P}$lans and $\mathcal{M}$ore $\mathcal{P}$lans

The city made a serious mistake by not hiring a public necromancer to predict which of the many grandiose schemes that were announced each year would actually come to pass. There seemed to be no way of knowing, other than by resorting to the occult.

Sometimes, after great hoopla in the news and feverish public attention, happy dreams of hotels and parks and massive federal grants would bob for years on the horizon, always just barely out of reach. Sometimes terrible nightmares of elevated expressways and warehouse developments would haunt certain neighborhoods for years, never coming true but always coming back, year after year.

And yet sometimes, after a grand announcement had spooked for ages in forgotten corners, after people had gotten so tired of it that they even stopped cracking jokes about it, it would actually be carried out.

When Task Force 2000 voted to tear down half the city for an enormous shopping mall and drain the bay for industrial expansion, Ted Todd very innocently thought that things were about to really start moving. Naturally, nothing happened. Todd had been prepared for massive public protests, demonstrations, media blitzes, but not for this wave of silence. For days after the Ash Wednesday meeting he searched in vain among the pages of the *Mobile Herald-Item* to find some mention of the epoch-making decision. He was to go through weeks of floating in limbo. "Am I dreaming?" he asked himself.

Meanwhile on St. Anthony Street, McCorquodale was drafting a master plan for the postmodern revolution of the Gulf Coast. One morning soon after Mardi Gras there was so much to do that she rose at eleven and rang Le Louis XIV to have them send over a pot of coffee with chicory and a bottle of *Chateau Petrus*. Her frequent perusal of English novels had suggested that French claret would be eminently suitable as her postmodern beverage of choice.

For a moment she watched the sun light up the crimson wine like stained glass. A mild breeze was flowing in through the open balcony door and bright sunlight sparkled in the stack of Mardi Gras beads on top of her dresser. After all the holidays, a perfectly normal morning.

She plunged into work, shifting from time to time in the satin sheets.

As we wait for the new millennium, signs of the impending postmodern consciousness shift are all about us. Yesterday at Krispy Kreme Doughnuts I noticed that Melba, the dear girl at the counter, had teased her black hair into a big bouffant do and was wearing a thick headband across her forehead.

A throwback to the sixties? Not a whit, the Charles of the Ritz "Plum Rose" lipstick, a contemporary touch, was the clue. Melba was obviously engaging in dual coding. "Look at me, I live in the sixties," her hairdo says to the unwary doughnut purchaser. But to the initiate it says, "Look darling, I'm in the eighties manipulating the Annette Funicello code." The clever girl, she feigned to know nothing about it. Does Melba read *Interview*? Must ask.

She switched to another thought, writing in fragments so that the generations of graduate students who would one day read her collected *Pensées* would have more exercise in piecing her theories together.

I see whiteness. Whiteness in the discourse of others. In the semantic babble.

Slipping of sense toward voluptuousness.

The modernists have their purism. Give me ornament. Make it binary.

Mimetic proliferation. Replete with saturated meanings.

Redundancy.

Give me the glistening syntax of the too-filled syntagm. Give me . . . a galaxy of signifiers.

McCorquodale stopped for a moment to picture how these words would look translated in one of those chic French paperbacks where you have to cut open the pages with a penknife. She attacked again with renewed gusto.

> To huddled masses and all the ships at sea, Greetings!
> We wipe the miserable dust of modernism from off our feet.
> Futurists, you have no future. International style, we spit on you.
> Functionalists, you *bore* me.
> The Winged Victory of Samothrace is more beautiful than a race car!

At last things were coming to pass. McCorquodale had long nourished a secret certainty of her own greatness, but there had been those moments of doubt in what the graduate students would probably term "the long march to the sea." She thought back to those giddy days in her senior year, those first inklings and premonitions of the coming age. The heroic blow she had struck in the name of *vin rouge ordinaire* had been sadly underheralded by certain reactionary and retarded intellects in the high school administration, but the intellectual ferment she had whipped up among French Club cadres persisted for months at small secret underground conclaves where French folksongs were sung defiantly and teacups of wine passed around. All ferment and mission faded, however, in the cold light of graduation. Her disciples had mostly gone off to college, and McCorquodale, facing financial realities, had gone off to AAA Superior Wallcoverings.

This was the period the graduate students would term, "dark night of the soul." Arriving at seven-thirty every morning to face Mrs. Clarisse Watkins's collection of Raleigh Tavern brass chandeliers, pewter pots, and other Williamsburg paraphernalia, McCorquodale had felt a certain mental bluntness setting in.

All day long Mrs. Watkins chattered to the clients about "Wong Dynasty easy chairs," "Queen Anne Empire barbecue and patio furniture," "Louisiana Plantation Regency TV/stereo entertainment centers."

There came a day when McCorquodale felt utterly adrift, having lost all intellectual bearings. At lunch time she stood and looked out the front window. The shop was located on the service road of the interstate highway. She studied the various streams of cars, the ugly proliferation of parking lots and shoddy concrete-block buildings and signs, and felt an utter inability to believe what she saw. That mediocrity could *not* be the place where she was living her life every day, where she was standing at that very moment. It was static blurring the radio program; it was distraction.

She wandered out the back door for a breath of air and fatefully saw a copy of the *Christian Science Monitor* sticking out of a garbage can. A small headline caught her eye: "London critics war over postmodern skyscraper." Unfortunately, most of the article was obliterated by tomato soup, but she had found the Path.

The next few years were spent in quiet revolutionary discipline preparing for her great mission. "Spurn delights and spend laborious days," she liked to repeat to herself. She saved money from her salary and her dates' thoughtful contributions toward the day when she would launch her quest. At times she wondered anxiously if this central thread of the age might not already be *passé* and completely out of date, as movements always seemed to drift down to south Alabama about ten years after they hit the rest of the world. But the press continued to mention various postmodern manifestations in art, film, and literature from time to time, and no other movement in particular seemed to have cropped up.

She clipped newspaper and magazine articles that referred to postmodernism, and filled notebooks with quotations. Occasionally she had tried to read some of the linguistic and semiotic books that the articles referred to, but they invariably gave her a headache. For a long time it worried her that for the most part she had no idea what the books were talking about. But finally she decided that she was missing "the pleasure of the text," and that her approach was completely wrong. Instead of trying to understand, she should simply float in the stream and pick and choose what appealed to her in a sublime eclecticism. Guided by this principle, whatever she chose, whether in books or in life, was certain to be postmodern.

Her diligent skimming and gleaning yielded isolated golden nuggets of the *Zeitgeist*, like "vertical axis," "indexical and ioconic signs," "decontextualizing," "the Babel of senses," "a relation of supplementarity whereby reading communities complete a text that is constitutively complete in itself." From these opaque shards she had wrought rich mosaics of theory.

Now these long preparations in the wilderness were about to pay off and the old excitement was back. Fame. Could she handle it? After a very slight pause, she decided that she probably could. Taking a long sip of claret, she floated off to a vision of herself sitting at a marble-top table in a fabulous old café in, where? Montparnasse? Maybe Lisbon would be suitable. She rather fancied the thought of being the great heroine of a small literature, the second Camoëns! She was a good-looking, female Fernando Pessoa, and she came here every day to write scathing and well-crafted newspaper essays about our tawdry mass culture of TV brain-washing and the lowest common denominator. Her modernist enemies would howl with indignation, but McCorquodale would not flinch. "No compromises!" she proclaimed in every piece. How starved her disciples had been for this voice in the wilderness, these earnest and promising and not at all bad-looking young men who congregated around her table. In their memoirs later they would recall the fervor, the movement, the thrill of those days, and, yes, the fun—why not?—and the companionship. The peculiar sense of being on the inside of something great whenever "Roshfookle" was around.

McCorquodale took a deep breath and sighed. A queasy feeling came to her that she would be struggling against a leaden inertia in this liberated age when everybody had an opinion on everything, and none of it even penetrated as far as their own subcutis. The modernists had had it easy! At least they had enemies who would get shocked. Ugh. She shifted thoughts consolingly to that marble-top table. There was a little glass of coffee on a saucer, a glass of cognac, a stack of beautiful, thin onionskin writing paper, and a volume of . . . she groped for a moment . . . Hugo von Hofmannsthal? Durrell? Cavafy? Maybe, Roberto Arlt, grappling with odd jobs and rooming house poverty. A painter would sit nearby and draw chic caricatures of McCorquodale writing at her table. They always seemed to have caricatures in these sidewalk café art movements. And of course they would need to edit a literary review; they always had that.

McCorquodale refilled her glass with claret and slowly took another sip. Reluctantly shifting thoughts again, she wondered whether a few lines of practical strategy might not be in order.

It is an odd thing that Umberto Eco and others do not seem to realize the significance of the fact that we have never had an avant-garde movement here before. This is the unguarded flank of modernism. Indeed, modern concepts have barely made the slightest impression here. The time is obviously ripe, rinascimento is vibrating in the air. A few well-aimed sparks from postmodern liberators, and the whole Gulf Coast will flame in the forehead of the morning sky.

Businessmen and financiers will be quick to see the economic benefits. With a cup of coffee (*un grand crème*) going for five dollars, Parisian intellectuals are languishing for a new world center of sidewalk café culture. It is quite true that Buenos Aires offers the advantage of several thousand cafés already in operation, but quick action on the part of local businessmen could grab this lucrative market.

My own sidewalk café and gallery on Conti Street will be the hemispheric epicenter. The intelligentsia of entire Latin American countries will come to sit at my tables. We'll have big film festivals and will need to launch an international postmodern literary review.

I suppose if certain key disciples can't pay for everything, we'll get the money from other Mobile businessmen. They're crazy about the arts, they'll give *millions!*

In thinking of her disciples at this juncture, her thoughts lingered rather more on H. Sloane Wolfe than on Eddie. McCorquodale pulled up the eiderdown and reflected just how to inform the crusty banker what his role would be in the postmodern movement. A loud clanging was coming from Sam's Body Shop next door. So far she had avoided making Sloane nervous with specific details, but the time was at hand for greater frankness.

Exhausted by her theoretical efforts, McCorquodale fell into a deep slumber.

CHAPTER 16

A Spat with H. Sloane Wolfe

H. Sloane Wolfe was in a very good mood the day McCorquodale decided to have her little talk with him, but the day turned out differently than both had planned.

Wolfe's quiet moves to build a statewide banking empire were rapidly gaining momentum. All around the state emissaries of the Commerce National Bank were acquiring lists of stockholders and obtaining proxies in preparation for the one grand assault, the proclamation of the Wolfe Alabama Bancorporation. Even the smallest conquests filled him with pleasure. That morning he had been delighted when Ernest Balleriel announced the fall of the Progressive Bank of Oneonta and the Boll Weevil Bank of Enterprise, two small, locally-owned institutions that had been crushed like dry pecans.

People came from every corner to pay Wolfe homage. He had been made chairman of the county Republican party's Committee for People's Politics. There were three members, the other two grassroots activists were Wallace Wade Stanton and Clemson O'Connor, president of Gulf Coast Gas Corporation. Only days before, a Republican gubernatorial candidate had made a special trip from Montgomery to seek Wolfe's favor.

Yet in all this realm of conquests, one bastion had not fallen. McCorquodale had still not gone with him to any of his hideaways, not once graced him with her favors. Behind that luscious and highly fashionable facade, Wolfe encountered a will of iron. McCorquodale had decided not to rush things, as she confided to Tonya one day at the Hubba Hubba Club: "Sloane's a doll, but I don't think he has yet glimpsed the postmodern imperative, which will require cash contributions of the most enthusiastic sort. And besides, can I be sure he wants me for myself? Call me sentimental, Tonya; I guess I'm just an idealist at heart."

They flew that afternoon in the bank helicopter to the Mermaid Inn, a seafood restaurant in Biloxi with big picture windows looking out on the beach. Over cocktails Wolfe proudly told McCorquodale about a patriotic speech he had given that week to the Rotary Club, "Free Enterprise in Alabama." "I told em it's the same old American story down here as it is all across this great country, lovely lady. Now just look at ole Sloane. I started out with only a few family connections, a little family money, and knowing everybody there was to know. But that was all, honey. I pulled myself to the top by my own bootstraps." He told her about his idea to give free ashtrays emblazoned with American flags, and Liberty Bell cups to everyone who opened a new account.

"Very inspiring," McCorquodale smiled diplomatically. "I'm sure the customers will come running." Wolfe beamed.

In this lyrical moment McCorquodale felt it was her turn to tell some of her own cherished thoughts. The colonial associations of the Liberty Bell touched on a long-held dream.

"Sloane," she whispered, voluptuously leaning toward him, "what do you think about Williamsburg? Don't you think it should be firebombed?"

Wolfe blinked a few times. "You mean that place in Virginia? Gee, I don't know, baby. Sounds a little hard-ass to me."

"Or nuked, perhaps. I figure one megaton would do the job nicely."

McCorquodale was so alluring that day that Wolfe could hardly concentrate on what she was saying. In the early spring cold she wore a padded Chinese jacket, but inside the restaurant she took it off to reveal what she called a "minimal" black top, filled to the maximum. Perhaps this was the day she would yield and fly away with him.

He produced another of the countless gifts he had presented her with in the last several months, a small jade dragon brooch, perfect for her outfit. They were in a splendid mood, and McCorquodale, eyeing the decor of the fishing nets, anchors and ship wheels, began to rhapsodize on the Mississippi Coast.

"It's so exotic here; don't you sense it, Sloane? The hot breezes from Haiti, the coffee trees nodding in Columbia just over there beyond the water?" The financial warrior felt faint when she grabbed his hand, and he involuntarily snapped the swizzle stick he had been playing with.

"I know just what you mean, sugar, I feel hot all over," he answered.

For a while McCorquodale sat watching the enormous cumulus clouds over the Gulf; fleecy, floating mountains infinitely high. One could imagine ancient craggy cities on every mass and billow where the inhabitants were staring back down at them at that very moment.

"Due south is Yucatan. Why do we always look north? That's only a fluke of history. We could just as easily be looking south here. Can't you just see a fleet of Mayans sailing into sight and landing right here on this beach to start a colony? You know people still speak Mayan. Wouldn't it be thrilling if we were all speaking Mayan?"

"I've never thought about it."

McCorquodale decided to steer the conversation more directly to the business at hand. "I knew the moment you picked me up that day in your BMW that you were a sensitive soul, Sloane, a true patron of the arts." She began to talk for the hundredth time about her postmodern café after the wrinkly waitress, in an apron and sensible white walking shoes, brought the fried shrimp.

Wolfe tried to appear intensely absorbed in everything she was saying. "You know, the next time I talk to Rotary, I'm going to tell them we really need to get going with this postmodulism business."

"You will?" McCorquodale was thrilled, and chose to ignore the slight mispronunciation.

"Sho will. But you need to give me a briefing session, little lady. I'm going to Oneonta tonight to check out the bank there. Why don't you come with me and tell me all about it. I know a real quaint place where we could stay, a Holiday Inn nestled up next to the interstate highway off ramp."

McCorquodale gave Wolfe a melting smile as she bit slowly into a shrimp. "A strenuous journey, why not discuss it now? It so happens I have a complete set of plans in my purse." She produced an architect's rendering showing the sidewalk sculptures, the balconies of the facade, and the interior courtyard with hanging gardens. "Of course, it's just the beginning, you have to start small. By the way, I've been meaning to mention it, do you think you could give me a million dollars to get the ball rolling?"

"What!?" Wolfe spluttered. "I've already given you a complete new wardrobe, and an allowance big enough to hire a new vice president!"

"I know it's not much, but I have very simple tastes," McCorquodale answered.

Wolfe grew more and more indignant. "But baby doll, it's been fo months. All we do is go places and eat. How long can a man wait?"

"Rise *above* it, darling. Think of what the Hindus did with thought control. You know, I'm sure I will feel so much more outgoing when my café is built."

"And what do I get out of it?" Wolfe demanded. "I'm a head honcho, wuiked my way to the top, one wuid from me and they all give to the United Fund, and you won't even be a little sweet with me. Who ever *huid* of such a thing? It's positively indecent."

"Let's not be so conventional," McCorquodale replied. "There's much to be said for sublimation."

"Well, I just don't know about any café on Conti Street. I think we may have to know each other *just a little bit better*," Wolfe scowled.

"Hmmm," McCorquodale parried, "after careful consideration I have decided to overlook your objections. When do we start construction?"

It was a complete deadlock. McCorquodale was piqued to the core and Wolfe pouted and sulked. They hardly exchanged a word for the rest of the meal or during the helicopter trip back to Mobile. Neither one was going to give in first.

CHAPTER 17

Silence is Golden

Ce Ce Anne knew the gossip of the year, and ever since Mardi Gras she had been dying to tell it. No one else even suspected that her boss, Wolfe, was secretly meeting a luxuriant blonde. But lately Ce Ce Anne had felt rare hesitation over the possible dangers involved of telling. How was she to explain that she had seen them at the Hubba Hubba Club? What if inquiring souls found out that Ce Ce Anne had been there with Helmut? Ce Ce Anne's jaws were aching with the effort to keep them shut, but her real ordeal by fire came when the Mardi Gras court went on trial.

Those troubles began early on the evening of Fat Tuesday when the Mardi Gras court returned to rest for a few hours in the royal chambers at the Thrifty Stop Inn on the bay causeway. No sooner had they arrived, than the august entourage decided to continue their partying on the nearby *Alabama*, a mothballed battleship on display to the public, and set sail for the legendary carnival Isle of Joy, presumably somewhere in the Caribbean. The royal party, mounted on roller skates, seized the vessel and began waving sparklers and shooting Roman candles.

The chief of police was immediately notified. In a heroic charge, all the more remarkable because there was no air cover, thirty riot police subdued the desperate terrorist debutantes and knights in hand-to-hand combat.

News of the Mardi Gras court's undoing spread over the city like a wall of flames across a dry prairie. Ce Ce Anne gnashed her teeth that she had missed everything, having gone off with Helmut late in the after-noon Mardi Gras Day for a very private celebration at home. A little shiver passed over her when she thought of those long hours of deep communion. How pure and uplifting it all had been. Helmut, with that really very delicate tattoo of two naked geisha girls flanking his navel; Helmut, so vulnerable in his brute strength.

But now Ce Ce Anne spared no effort to maintain her position as the AP service of the Young Set. She was on twenty-four hour alert. All during banking hours and late into the night she was on the telephone tracking down details to feed the other bank employees and three hundred very special intimates.

On the day of the trial, Ce Ce Anne took off work so as not to miss one phoneme of scandal. The members of the court were let off with fines and rather churlish reprimands on the part of the judge. It was the talk of the town. Ce Ce Anne was well-informed, to say the least, but investigative reporting is not quite the same thing as being an eye witness, and she was feeling very eclipsed by several who had actually been at the scene of battle. She thought longingly of the other story that would make her an instant and sole authority, eagerly sought after for weeks on end.

It was hard enough for Ce Ce Anne to keep quiet about Wolfe and that blonde when she went back to the bank after the trial, but a superhuman effort was required when she had the Junior League Committee on Urban Affairs, which she chaired, over to the 1860s Carpenter Gothic cottage in the historic Oakleigh Garden District that "Daddy" had fixed up for her.

Cars began to pull up outside under the shady tunnel formed by huge gnarled live oaks covered with little green ferns. The great girth of the trunks and low-swooping limbs gave rise to thoughts of age and grandeur. A happy blue sky and hot sunlight blinked pleasantly through the foliage, but underneath all was cool and humid, a perfectly enclosed and sheltered space. The horizon did not extend beyond one's own cozy block, and there was no particular reason to look any farther.

The purpose of the meetings was to discuss downtown revitalization. But for the last few months they had been getting a few organizational kinks out of the way before the discussion could start. A motion had been put forward last week to compile an address book so that the five members of the committee could reach each other easily without first having to look up the numbers in the telephone book. This week the first forty minutes of the meeting were devoted to specific details.

"Y'all, we've got to decide on the format of the address book, we can't just keep puttin it off," Beverly Chapen admonished, always so bright in her Malia sundress and "summer" makeup. "I mean, should they be big . . . should they be little?"

"Well, I think the address books should be big, so that when you put it with the cookbooks next to the kitchen telephone it won't clash," Ce Ce Anne offered.

Everyone considered this, hands neatly folded in their laps; it was like "Meet the Press." When Beverly offered a rebuttal, four heads turned attentively in her direction.

"Well, I think the really *big* question is, will it fit in your bedroom phone table drawer?"

When it came to a vote it was decided that the address book would be big. With that out of the way, the conversation soon turned to the scandal.

"Well, I feel as though everyone has been arrested but me," remarked Antoinette McCrae, one of the arbiters of Ce Ce Anne's circle. After a long stay in Atlanta she was very daring, and often excited days of comment by wearing metallic shoes and knickers, her hair pulled back into a tight chignon. "You know it's not very late yet, maybe if we held up a Seven-Eleven we could get written up in *Tell Tale*." That was the social column in the *Mobile Herald Item*.

"Karen Bixwell [a lady-in-waiting] still pretends to limp at all the pawties she goes to, but there couldn't be a thing wrong with her ine-kle now," said Beverly Chapen. "They say it took six soldiers to arrest her. She climbed up oin a gun turret and kept kicking them awf the sides when they came up ife-ter her."

Ce Ce Anne saw her chance to demonstrate her knowledge of the affair. "Y'all, I want you to know that Duffy Gallimard [a knight] spent the whole *night* in jail. There was this man in the cell with him, all covered with tattoos, so Duffy iced him what he was in for. 'Rape,' the man said. 'What you in for?' and Duffy told him, 'Firecrackers.'"

"Y'all, it really isn't funny," objected Binky Mastin, the only one on the committee who hadn't had her colors done by the cosmetics expert at Gayfer's Department Store, the latest fad. This theorist divided complexions and color coordination into "spring," "summer," "winter" and "fall." She could not be analyzed because she refused to go out of the house without make-up on. "Some of them have prison records now; it's serious."

"Why, you mean you cain't get in the Country Club or something?" asked Tilda O'Toole, ever pert in her navy corduroy skirts, but not always the brightest. "That would be just *gross!*"

Ce Ce Anne brought out a tray of hors d'oeuvres. Everyone present had given up Limburger cheese and canned guava shells for Lent, but fortunately that left a number of other options for the conscientious hostess. She was just warming up for more stories, when the conversation switched to the incident with King Felix in front of the Athelstan Club on Mardi Gras Day, the one subject that Ce Ce Anne wanted to avoid.

"But who *is* that woman, does anybody know her?" Beverly inquired.

"She's a blonde, but I think she's a 'winter,'" Binky ventured.

"But I mean was she a Kappa or a KD or what?" Beverly insisted.

"Well I don't know her, how could I not know her? I know everybody," Tilda interjected.

"But Tilda," Binky asked, "there're two hundred thousand people in Mobile, how could you know everybody?"

"Two hundred thousand people? But where are they?" Tilda asked.

"They're all around you, haven't you noticed?"

"Oh, *them*; you mean they live here too?" Tilda was astonished. "I've always wondered who they were; I knew they couldn't be related."

Ce Ce Anne had never perspired before in her life, but beads of sweat appeared on her powdered upper lip like tiny pearls. Could she keep it back? She had to tell *something* of what she had learned from her intelligence network.

"Carol Ortega's mother knew her inet," Ce Ce Anne began, "a Mizz Chighizola. She says she's real sweet and they've been here forevuh, and Oonah Patel's brother Peter knew her in high school. He says her name is Mawgret Constance Roshfookle and she was kind of a brain, and kind of a loner, too, even though she knew tons of people. He says she was *wild*. They say she built up a three-week waiting list of boys to chauffeur her to and from school and drive her inet to all the parish bingo games."

"Well, what about all that stuff you wrote in *Chat*?" said Antoinette. "What did you mean when you said blondes were in this year? And what was all that about some businessman seeing some chick on the side?"

For a few days after her gossip newsletter came out, Ce Ce Anne had reveled in the experience of being besieged by eager questioners, answering with a provocative, "Time will tell." But now she wondered if she had not been rash. Antoinette's own bloodhound instincts were not to be underestimated. The less she told her, the better.

"Well, you know, Antoinette, a lot of men like blondes. That thing about the businessman I'm still looking into. I think it's always good to check out your sources, don't you? And that Mawgret Constance Roshfookle, well, I just told you everything I could come up with."

The sardonic Antoinette noticed a slight reserve that was not characteristic. "But Ce Ce Ine, I bet you know more than that. I thought you'd know *awl* about it."

For a long moment Ce Ce Anne felt herself standing on the brink of a dangerous precipice. She thought how delicious the instant would be when she revealed the story of this woman and H. Sloane Wolfe. She saw in her mind's eye hundreds of people all over the city getting up from their chairs and running across the room to their telephones. The muscles of her mouth were pulling at the bones, her tongue was struggling to articulate. But what if Daddy found out about her and Helmut? The human will prevailed.

"Shuguh, you're ice-kin the wrong person," Ce Ce Anne said, not batting an eyelash. "I just never get out of the house."

Five hands raised five glasses to four pairs of color-coordinated, and one pair of classic cherry red, lips. Ice cubes clinked all around the room. They began to talk about other matters.

CHAPTER 18

War Looms on the Horizon

"Who would have guessed it? I wonder who she is?" Ernest Balleriel pondered as he stood by Wolfe's desk on the uppermost floor of the Commerce National Bank. In the back of his mind he surveyed the dramatic mountains of summery tropical clouds already floating over the harbor in the April sky. Wolfe was going over the list of new promotions, grumbling from time to time.

Ce Ce Anne had told Ernest everything. Unable to bear alone the weight of her terrible secret—which was much too newsworthy to be hoarded by one person—she had lovingly aired every detail of the encounter she had witnessed at the Hubba Hubba Club. Ernest was her only confidant, the only one who knew about her and Helmut, reliable Ernest, "earnest Ernest."

But Ernest had been terribly shocked: "Not H. Sloane, Ce Ce! You don't understand. The chief has his flings every now and then, yes, he has his little walks on the wild side. But he wouldn't be carrying on for months on end with some kept woman. That's just not his style."

Ernest had brooded about Wolfe's shocking secret life all during the weekend trip to New Orleans with Eddie. The whole drive over, Eddie kept enthusing about some artsy girl named McCorquodale he had met during Mardi Gras. Ernest wanted to confide in Eddie about the Margaret Constance woman and Wolfe, and came very close after the third bottle of ouzo at the Greek bar in the Quarter, the Athenian Lounge. Some Vietnamese drag queens were there, and they raved about Ernest's pinstripe suit. The last thing he could remember was staring at blinking lights and talking to a strapping, curly-headed Greek sailor who kept looking Ernest's natty figure up and down, then glancing over to little Eddie smiling at the bar, and winking at them both. Ernest was trying to explain why the Greek should invest in mutual funds rather than directly in stocks. "You gotta cut dow on the rithkth. Me, I doe like taking rithkth," he had slobbered. Thank *heavens* he hadn't told Eddie anything. Eddie would have blabbed it to every secretary in the bank on his first mail run Monday morning.

"Who is this Margaret Constance?" Ernest wondered. He remembered the gorgeous blonde he had seen Mardi Gras Day, and then the woman attired in crimson he had seen at the Santa Claus Society ball before Christmas. Rather like Marilyn Monroe playing Marie Antoinette in the chorus line of Radio City Music Hall.

"Well, at least he has good taste," Ernest thought. Comforting idea. Yes, even when the old guard strayed from the path in little peccadilloes, they did it in style.

Ernest studied Wolfe's face scowling over the promotion list. "Gee, you just never know," he reflected sadly. But then in the depths of his disillusionment, like Prince Bolkonsky lying on the Austrian battlefield, Ernest had one of those piercing insights that come a few times in every life. "Maybe, after all, it's our duty to maintain the appearances. Not disillusion the common herd. Mamacita would call it our burden."

He thought of his own background, so much like Wolfe's. There was the family firm, Balleriel Stevedoring. What a boon to the city. Ernest had struck out on his own to go into banking, but like a true Balleriel shot straight to the top, still in his early thirties. And the Balleriel tradition of public service. Just to think of Uncle Rothko! He gave so unstintingly of his time to the Chamber of Commerce, and helped get the first bridge built to Dauphin Island, where they happened to own a few hundred prime beachfront acres on the Gulf side.

"Yes," Ernest exulted, "H. Sloane is right to keep his secrets and keep up appearances. People expect so much from us that we can't let them see a little tarnish on the silver." The sun was shining now on the river, the clouds seemed to glow from within. . . .

"Horse shit!" Wolfe thundered.

"I beg your pardon?" said Ernest, thoroughly startled.

"A ray-uhs for Pappadapoulos in Savings? Out of the question, he just got one five yeuhs ago. Let's think of a new title for him, they always fall for that."

"How about 'Executive Senior Vice President'?" suggested Ernest, himself a "Senior Executive Senior Vice President."

"Mighty fine," Wolfe chortled, "something he can write home to the folks about." Wolfe shifted into his rough country tone. It was the first bit of humor he had shown for several weeks. He had been in a terrible mood since the sortie to Biloxi with McCorquodale.

Ernest decided to prolong the light mood with the latest good news. "H. Sloane, the Wiregrass Bank of Geneva cracked this morning. We had to lean on some of the big shareholders, but they are now proud new members of the Commerce Bancshares family."

Ernest started to go to the map of Alabama behind Wolfe's desk, but Wolfe rose and, taking the pin from Ernest's hand, personally stuck it into Geneva. He was very excited.

"Thuiteen, Uinest, do you know what that me-uns?" Ernest knew it only too well; it had been Wolfe's number on his high school football team in the 1940s. "This is the moment I've been waitin for, thuiteen banks in the chay-un."

Wolfe went to the huge window looking out on the city and the Prudential National Bank tower where his archrival was president. "Moseley, boy," he shook his fist. "You better get out your umbrella cause we gonna ray-un on you."

Next to the window there was a model of the giant pyramidal skyscraper Wolfe would build when his empire was in place. He absent-mindedly put his finger on the tip where his executive suite would be. Already the CNB's holding company, "Commerce Bancshares," had outstripped Moseley's "Magnolia Trust" in new bank acquisitions, but the real assault was yet to come with the formation of a new holding company. "Wolfe Alabama Bancorporation," Wolfe murmured. "It has a real ring to it, don't it: WolfAl!

"It's time to attack, Uinest. Ole Moseley'll be blitzen in his britches when we go public. And you know what we're gonna do then? We'll go after the big independents. The Wuiker's Bank of Jasper, Tuscaloosa,

Florence, Fuist National of Montgomery! After that we'll put the vices on the big Buimingham holding companies. Them sapsuckers," he gave a raspy laugh, "if they only knew.

"And then if we can ever get these federal paper pushers out of the way, we're goin out of stay-ut." Wolfe raised a finger solemnly. "Today Geneva, tomorrow Mississippi!"

"But H. Sloane," Ernest objected, "what if the Tenn-Tom Water-way isn't that big a deal? Are we going to generate *all* of the capital by selling shares?"

"Uinest, did you ever play football?" Wolfe asked, shifting into his wise Southern businessman tone.

"No, H. Sloane."

"Well now that's too bad, son, because football teaches you all about life. It teaches you how to go out on a limb. If you're afraid of gettin tackled, boy, you'll never go out for that pass."

Wolfe leaned forward. "Now listen here," he growled, "I'll tell you how we gonna do it. We're gonna crackback on em and we're gonna blindside em. We're gonna leg whip em and we're gonna clothesline em. We're gonna spear em and we're gonna eye gouge em. After all, WHAT ARE WE??!"

Ernest had gone to the same private boys' school, though a genera-tion later, and he knew what was expected of him. He always dreaded this scene, but you didn't say no to H. Sloane Wolfe.

"We're bulldogs!"

"And whudda we do?!"

Ernest barked out circumspectly: "We bite!"

Wolfe pounded his fist on the desk. "Write a memorandum to the boys on the platform and in the trenches all over the state. Wolfe Alabama is goin public. Uinest, this is WAW!"

CHAPTER 19

The Grand Announcement

On the day of the grand proclamation of the Wolfe Alabama Bancorporation, McCorquodale decided the time had come for bold action. She had left Wolfe bubbling on the back burner ever since Biloxi. "Let him stew for a while, he'll get tender," McCorquodale thought. She refused to come to the telephone when he began to make his penitent and ever more frequent calls. What a thunderbolt for Wolfe, then, when she appeared in the "Million Dollar Board Room" of the Commerce National Bank in the midst of the gala press conference with the air of Princess Margaret making a goodwill visit to a retirement home.

For weeks rumors of the impending announcement had circulated among the downtown eateries and the late afternoon cocktail set, causing deep tremors in the rival Prudential National Bank. In the Commerce National Bank, however, the Muzak system was playing "Victory at Sea." Eddie made a huge banner that said "Win the War!" and stretched all the way across the mailroom down in the basement.

Mr. Belzagui, always historically minded, had also risen to the occasion by creating a special coat of arms which he said represented "the bank militant." It showed a "a wolf rampant, gules, beneath an azure fess containing three fleur-de-lis, or," he enthusiastically told his friend Mr. Pappadapoulos. "Maybe when they see this up on the platfawm I'll get my fuist promotion."

As for Ce Ce Anne Stanton, she could hardly contain herself, it was like being sorority rush chairman in a bumper year. Together with some of her friends in the Marketing Department, she had even reworked an old high school sorority song, which they performed with Eddie during their coffee breaks, clapping their hands underneath their chins and swaying back and forth:

Heidi-hi! Wolfe Alabama's the best!
Heidi-hi! We're better than all the rest!
Heidi-hi! You bet we pass the test!
Heidi-hi, heidi-hi, heidi-hi!

Unfortunately, both the coat of arms and the song were squelched by the bank's advertising firm as inconsistent with the contemporary Sunbelt image they were cultivating. But the splendid press conference in the Million Dollar Board Room met the highest standards of grandeur and statecraft.

To some, the extravagant board room seemed questionable banking policy considering the bank's enormous capital outlays to expand the holding company and acquire the smaller banks. But Wolfe ordered it finished as a strategic element in his *Machtpolitik*. It had been designed in the most sophisticated local business taste by Colin Devoe, a local architect known for his pseudo-Georgian churches and offices, always with big gas lanterns and surrounded by Bradford pear trees.

Before the press conference began, the presidents of the thirteen vassal banks, who had come for the day, wandered among the CNB trustees and other top brass and ogled the oriental rugs and reproductions of English hunt scenes, the leather-bound *Great Books of the Western World* in dark oak cases. They were like captive Teutonic chieftains led back to Rome. Noting the distraction of the president of the Boaz National Bank, a plumpish man with the red bulging cheeks of a Better Boy tomato, Ce Ce Anne rushed forward to put him at his ease.

"Take it from me," she told him warmly. "You'll be *so* glide you pledged WolfAl, it's the *only* way to fly."

"I reckon you're right," he answered politely, trying to divine if this was a joke.

"Now I know some of those *Birmingham* holding companies are big, but let me tell you"; Ce Ce Anne always held her dress with one hand at the neck when she had something really serious to impart; "Birmingham is *not* cute. Now I knew a lot of girls from Birmingham up at Bama, and they were real cute, but they weren't really *cute*. People in Mobile are so much cuter."

"They seem right nice lookin," said the Boaz president hesitantly.

"For *sure!*" Ce Ce Anne's face glowed with a healthy coat of suntan make-up. Perhaps she was not up on the latest Japanese management techniques or post-industrial information age international conglomerate strategies, but she was a person with her own ideas. "And listen, this is not just *any* Mobile bank. We like to think that we've come up with a new *concept* in banking. This is where all the cute people work."

But they were interrupted by a round of speeches beginning the press conference from Wolfe, Ernest Balleriel (sporting a festive yellow tie with his so-very-appropriate sober gray suit), and other officials. They outlined the booming future awaiting Alabama, and the blue skies hovering above the Tennessee-Tombigbee Waterway. They called for other state banks to join the big happy family. But above all, they hammered home the advertising slogan of the new holding company: "At Wolfe Alabama, we're just plain folks."

McCorquodale slipped into the room and leaned against the back wall during the screening of WolfAl's television advertisements, soon to be shown all over the state. Though the Commerce National Bank would retain its name, at the insistence of certain oldtime stockholders who were cool to Wolfe's self-created apotheosis, the other thirteen banks would take the name of the holding company. The whole PR campaign was the brainstorm of advertising whiz kid Rich "Brass Tacks" O'Neill, said to have won a fortune at the county dog tracks. Like many of his best concepts, it came to him over a double scotch with one of the house shills at the dog tracks bar.

The TV spots showed heartwarming Southern scenes narrated by a pinched but caring Midwestern Standard voice. In one, the whole family was out picking blackberries. In another, Grandma came out of the kitchen carrying a lemon meringue pie. "Wolfe Ala-BEM-a . . ." the voice said, ". . . just like you."

Ce Ce Anne could feel her eyes watering, but they popped wide open when the lights came back on. In keeping with the subdued business atmosphere, McCorquodale had dressed from head to toe in what she conceived to be black Coptic nun's robes. Even her head was covered with a black wimple, leaving only her face exposed like a ripe apricot on a black napkin. Wolfe grabbed the podium, Ernest's mouth dropped open, every eye in the room turned upon her curiously. McCorquodale allowed a smile to flicker across her face like the flame on a pan of cherries jubilee. She pulled a gold case from a baggy sleeve and turned to the Boaz president next to her. "Care for a Tiparillo?" she inquired.

Wolfe watched them light their cigars with his heart in his mouth. He was crazy with jealousy, alarmed and lightheaded, all at the same time. But not until he had posed for photographs, and fabulous André champagne had been dispensed to the chatting VIPs, could he make his way back to her, as though mixing with the crowd.

"Naughty boy," McCorquodale whispered, "why didn't you tell me you were having a film festival?"

"Baby doll, you came back! So you just couldn't leave ole Sloane?"

"I don't know what it is about you. I guess I just have a soft spot for banking empires."

"And you're not still mad about those mean things I said in Biloxi?" His voice quivered with suspense.

"Water under the bridge! But remember, you mustn't rush me, Sloane. I've seen so little of the world, I need time to prepare myself for . . . certain matters." Her eyes spoke volumes.

Wolfe longed to cover her hand with smoky kisses. How could he show his gratitude? There was one way.

"Let me build you your sidewalk café, little lady. I'll get the money, just give me a little time. We're fixin to roll over the Wuiker's Bank of Jasper," he chuckled.

"Really, Sloane, it's of no importance, a mere bauble. Do you think we could start construction by Christmas?"

From across the room, Ce Ce Anne and Ernest, two radar tracking stations, watched them smile. They observed Wolfe break away to mingle with the press. What could it all mean?

CHAPTER 20

It Won't Wuik in Mobile

The Houston developer still had not grasped that what people think and what they say and what they do are not necessarily the same thing in the three-petaled lotus of Gulf Coastal reality. Indeed, since Todd got the endorsement of Task Force 2000 on Ash Wednesday, his development scheme had been more than ever in limbo. Nothing was happening.

Approaching H. Sloane Wolfe for support was out of the question since Todd's faux pas at the Athelstan Club Domino Ball. But if only he could get Wolfe's archrival, Hearn Moseley, to back him, the bulldozers would soon be rolling!

Ted Todd's delusion was naive but understandable. Only days before, Wolfe had announced enormous expansion plans for his holding company, Wolfe Alabama. In any other city a rival banker would have been desperate for a vast and profitable scheme.

Moseley's family had been in Mobile since the turn of the century, when his farmboy grandfather, Old Man Clem Moseley, made a killing in the lumber business and moved to town from Clarke County. In the following eight decades they had been almost completely assimilated with the aid of their millions. They had entered the halls of power. Socially they had risen so far that Moseley's niece, fourth-generation Ida Moseley, led the Athelstan Club ball that year (Mrs. Harmsworth Billingsley Balleriel, however, expressed the profoundest reservations to some of her friends about the rapid acceptance of these newcomers).

Hearn Moseley himself both thought and spoke like a Mobilian, even having the increasingly rare Mobile accent, which was fading out in the sea of post-World War II immigrants from upstate like a madras dye. The only trace of Moseley's origins was his inordinate liking for fried pork skins. It was something his grandmother, for all her Dresden porcelain service and fine dresses, had made and served to her dying day in her Victorian mansion on Church Street.

Though his father had continued the family lumber business, his grandfather had ordered Moseley to go into banking for the sake of diversification. Even though he never had occasion to actually make a loan, he distinguished himself in his "administrative duties," and slowly rose, like cream, to the top of the bank hierarchy. He also served along the way as the president of the Chamber of Commerce and the Alabama Bankers Association.

Yet secretly Moseley had always been intimidated by the image of his successful grandfather. He always tried to match the stern lines of Old Man Clem's face—the tough, country, empire-building decisiveness visible in the oil portrait that haunted him behind his desk—with a permanent ill-humor intended to suggest business acumen.

In setting bank policy, Moseley had established a reputation for unwavering prudence. When, for example, entrepreneurs came to him in the early sixties to get financing for Hillbrook Mall, the first large suburban shopping center, Moseley had turned them down flat, remarking, "Shopping in Mobile will alway-uhs be downtown." They had gone out of town for their financing, and the whole city moved west, but the man in the oil portrait would have been proud of his firmness.

Yet it should not be thought that Moseley was closed to new ideas. He generally got them from the thought-provoking editorials in the *Mobile Herald-Item*. They were often a bit too delicately reasoned for his taste, but he enjoyed the regular contact with the wide world of intellect and finely-wrought prose, the *mot juste* of the day.

Many people were wondering now if the long lines of black limousines Moseley had seen carrying vassal bank presidents to the Commerce National Bank, or the extensive press coverage of Wolfe's new empire would shake Prudential National Bank out of its proven course.

Todd was ushered into Moseley's office, which Moseley had installed behind the "platform" on the first floor so that he could see whether the junior officers were really working or not.

Moseley was already familiar with Ted Todd's plan from the Task

Force 2000 meeting, but Todd went back over a few of the main points, using all of the skills of persuasion he had learned from Dale Carnegie. "Of course, I'm sure you understand, Hearn, that we'll have to tear down the city at least to I-65 to parley some parking for our Supermall."

"That's progress, sir, it's time to make room," Moseley said unsmilingly. It was a felicitous phrase from the *Herald-Item*.

"I'm so glad you made that input," Todd beamed. Encouraged greatly, he pulled out a set of new drawings of industries that would be built in the bay after it was drained. "Gee, I'm really wrecked that I can't yet reveal the name of the international conglomerate that will build there, Hearn, but these pictures will give you a bird's eye mock-up of the kind of quality product we're putting out. It'll all be exempt from local taxes, of course, for goal-attainment reasons."

"Of cose. Now I do like that," Moseley said, looking at the Walt Disney vision of ten-story freeways soaring above smokestacks and refineries. But then a thought occurred to him. "But now listen here, if you fill in the bay with duit, where will I sail my yacht?"

Todd thought quickly, as though Dale himself were holding up a flash card. "It's really *great* that you brought that up, Hearn. Actually I was waiting to press release it, but our Six Flags Over Mobile will have a really quality marina in the ship channel. Just think, Hearn, what a close-up view of the coal barges when you set sail."

"Yase, a fine view. Bawges are the lifeblood of commuice. We're all for growuth at this bank!" At this light moment of espousing his favorite philosophy, Moseley decided to buzz his secretary for his favorite treat. Fried pork skins and coffee.

Todd could barely choke down the combination, but he never lost eye contact as he pulled out a handkerchief and dabbed his mouth with gusto. What would Dale have said in this situation? "I love Chinese cooking, it's so light," he ventured.

"My friend," Moseley smiled for the first time, "it's not Chinee-uhs, it's an oh-uld family recipe."

"My, how interesting. And the man in the portrait, he must have been a founding father or something."

.

Far from perceiving any irony, Moseley waved his hand diffidently, and really looked at Todd for a moment, something he rarely did with out-of-towners. After that it seemed to be a cakewalk. "They grow some real suckers in these small cities if you just know how to handle them," Todd thought. He explained that the city, as proposed by Mayor Barker, would be responsible for acquiring all the land out to the interstate beltline, demolishing all the buildings, and donating the land free to Todd's Sunbelt Land Corporation. That was where the bank came in, because the city would have to float several billion dollars' worth of general obligation bonds. "And if the Prudential National Bank handles the bonds—"

"It would produce a very handsome sum for us," Moseley finished the thought.

Everything was going so smoothly. Moseley was convinced by his figures, and even added that the city would just have to raise taxes for the next eighty or ninety years to pay for the bonds. But stronger forces than logic were at work.

Todd decided to press for a decision. "What do you say, Hearn, is the PNB going to jump in on the ground floor?"

Moseley looked very wise for a moment, and then gave his answer, the distillation of a lifetime philosophy. "Won't wuik in Mobile."

"Pardon me?"

"Won't wuik. Shopping in Mobile will alway-uhs be at the mawls. Downtown is dead and alway-uhs will be. I'm sorry but it won't wuik in Mobile."

"But, Hearn, there won't even be a downtown when we're finished. Half the city'll be gone."

"If it was that good an idea, somebody else would have tried it befo."

"But, Hearn, we're talking about billions of dollars!"

"Mr. Todd, we're making money right now. Why chay-unge? Won't wuik! Not in Mobee-ul!" Moseley could feel the portrait of Old Man Clem beaming down approval for his decision-making power.

Ted Todd tried to argue, but it was no use. Though the banker clearly liked the plan, he wouldn't budge an inch.

CHAPTER 21

The Herald-Item Takes a Stand

Even though H. Sloane Wolfe had relented on questions of funding, McCorquodale could not decide when to start the postmodern movement. "My instincts tell me that the Gulf of Mexico will soon be the hemispheric cutting edge of the avant-garde, but what if I'm just kidding myself," she would brood at weak moments. She needed a sign that the new age was about to begin, and she found it on the editorial page of the *Mobile Herald-Item*.

Late one stuffy night in April McCorquodale returned home after having cocktails with Wolfe at a remote motel bar near the Florida state line, and found a copy of the *Herald-Item* Aunt Odilia had left lying on the dining room table. McCorquodale slipped off her high heels and stood with her mink about her shoulders eating a chocolate as she leafed idly through the pages.

She came across the following indecipherable editorial. Since the newspaper had not written a single article on Ted Todd's gigantic project, almost no one in town knew about it. Actually, the forces and great minds behind the paper were quivering with excitement about the plan. It was the culmination of everything they had been pushing in the city for decades: apocalyptic bulldozing and paving, with no guarantees that anything would be built afterwards, vague dreams of industry, and elevated expressways. They loved expressways. But despite their enthusiasm, they decided it would be best not to write anything about the plan and keep the public in the dark as long as possible so that opposition groups would be slow in forming.

At length, however, some of the newspapers in other Southern cities started running incredulous articles about the proposal, and the *Herald-Item* felt forced to issue a clarion call of support. Unfortunately, nobody could make out what the editorial was about. It was a classic piece in the style of what some local wags called "the mad dog school of journalism." Even Todd himself had no idea what they were saying until it was explained to him:

Secret Conspiracy of the Big Rail Interests

The crybaby beachcomber housewives in tennis shoes who want us to believe that the Clean Water Act is not a direct vote for Fidel P. Castro will really be whimpering over this one. And do you want to know who the flakes and peacenik goofballs are so we don't have the draft?

We agree.

Thanks to an in-depth story on this issue of vital importance to Mobile, which we read in the *Atlanta Constitution*, we are ready to take a stand. Bring on this Houston developer that wants to demolish half the city. We think it's high time the obstructionists laid their wad on the table. We felt it only best not to write about it until now. Right. They'll be chomping at the bit a pretty penny till their chickens come home to roost.

You guessed it. Another secret conspiracy of the Big Rail interests, Greenpeace, and National Public Radio. These powerful Rail Barons with their Fat Cat connections in Nicaragua have a thing or two to learn. Let the liberal pinko media snivel and drool about freedom of the press while they do their massive brainwashing.

Boy, won't they be squirming on the hook at the *New York Times*, the *Washington Post*, *Tass* and *Pravda* when they read what we've got to say! Not that we don't like the idea of draining the bay. That's progress, don't think it won't. Ha! They think they're so smart. That's silly, and besides.

And in the meantime an impressive array of oil and chemical companies are twiddling their thumbs, while the snail darter paper pushers shuffle their miles of bureaucratic red tape. We ought to get down and kiss their booties to build pipelines in the bay. The so-called "Women's Movement" can just squawk.

Furthermore.

At first McCorquodale was aghast at what she had read. "Is this the handiwork of some beastly hallucinogenic drug unknown to postmodern science?" she wondered. She tried to forget about it, but even after she had gone to bed her thoughts kept returning to the boiling lines. "Whatever could it mean?"

Then all at once she sat bolt upright in the satin sheets as the full impact hit home. "But this is *marvelous*. How could I have been so obtuse? Obviously it doesn't mean anything. *IT'S DADA!*"

Neo-Dadaism at the *Herald-Item*? She had long suspected that Mobile was a hotbed of experimental thought, but never in her wildest dreams did she imagine it was so widespread. It was the portent she had been waiting for.

But then a more sinister thought occurred to her. What if there was nothing "neo" about it? What if they were real, live Dadaists? Could it be that the local modernists, after so many decades of hibernation, were now rearing their ugly heads? Her blood ran cold.

Whatever the interpretation, it was high time to act. "I must commence the movement immediately. I should have started months ago."

McCorquodale scheduled the first organizational mass meeting the following Tuesday afternoon, and, chartering a taxi, rode around nailing Xerox art New Wave posters to telephone poles all over the city. "You, too, can be postmodern . . ." they began in different-sized letters like words clipped from a magazine.

Finding the right quaint café that would combine an intimate Left Bank atmosphere with room for the standing crowd was not easy. She finally settled on Lester's Quick Stop Grill on St. Louis Street downtown. "Ah, St. Louis, did you know I would come so far?" she meditated as she prepared. She decided not to tell H. Sloane Wolfe about the event until the revolution was well under way.

Unfortunately, when the fateful day arrived the crowd was disappointingly small, but McCorquodale was undaunted. "Darlings, Robert Redford will make a film about us one day," she told her public. In all, five people came. There was businesswoman Tonya de Luxe, slightly overflowing the mold of her strapless terry cloth sundress like a plum pudding in a hot oven. Carlton Wheeler, a young buck lawyer whose uncle had been the brains behind the Stanton Steamship Corporation, had once enjoyed a few weeks of dates with McCorquodale several years back, and now that his professional income was growing he was hoping to renew the acquaintance. He had spotted McCorquodale's name on a poster and came running over in his business suit with his partner, Willis Crofton, after taking a deposition.

Finally, Eddie walked in a bit late and timidly took a place at the table with his friend Bobo, who had an orange and purple Mohawk hairdo and worked as a disc jockey at Club Fifth Avenue, the main gay discotheque downtown. McCorquodale had been disappointed not to find Eddie present when she made her recent visit to the Commerce National Bank, but mailboys do not attend press conferences. When the moment came, she decided a phone call was too banal, and sent a telegram to the bank with the time and address and a single word, "Come!" The great summons had arrived that morning. "I liked to wet my britches," he tried to tell Ce Ce Anne and Ernest during the course of the day, but their thoughts seemed to be elsewhere lately. He had slipped out of the bank without a word to Mr. Belzagui. Eddie and Bobo exchanged uneasy glances with the young lawyers, and the banquet began.

The stock menu of breaded veal cutlet, turnip greens, and sweet potatoes could not be altered, but the restaurant management allowed McCorquodale to serve her own Dom Perignon. She wore heroic white: an ermine stole, her golden hair swept up in a net of diaphanous silk marquisette. The white flesh of her daring décolletage blinked through the thinnest wisp of the same material.

After the dishes had been cleared away and the tulip glasses refilled with bubbly, she rose to read a "Manifesto of Postmodernism" over the loud conversation of a group of Orkin exterminators at the next table. "Postmodern is as postmodern does. You have to taste, breathe, touch, and microwave postmodern if you want to see the metonymic stars on a hot summer night . . ." she began. It was deeply poetic, and all five

applauded loudly when she sat down, but Carlton Wheeler ventured to
ask, "What does 'postmodern' mean?"

McCorquodale leaned back her head the better to descant.
"Postmodernism is the overripe orange of our desuetude; we perfume as
we ferment."

Everyone looked somewhat chastened as they pondered this truism.
McCorquodale took a long drag on her cigarette holder and blew the
smoke out through her nose. "Waiter, a Cointreau," she called out to
Lester at the cash register.

"But how do you know it when you see it?" Wheeler persisted.

"Darling, it's all about you. Just look out there, behold the city!"
They all stared out the plate glass window. Not a soul was to be seen in
the sun scorched parking lots up and down St. Louis Street. A Coca Cola
truck rattled past.

"Well, I hope it brings me the trucker trade," Tonya said, referring
to her latest brainstorm for Hubba Hubba prosperity. "They've been
going out to them joints on Highway 90 where the chicks get free
drinks."

"Now let's be practical," Wheeler said seriously in his deep voice,
eager to impress McCorquodale with his systematic masculine mind.
"Let's decide what we're going to do."

Eddie had not said a word, but now he saw his chance. "Say, let's us
do a big musical. We can all wear costumes, gold lamé for *days*! I'll play
one of the leads."

"How Off-Broadway can you get?!" McCorquodale exclaimed.
"Postmodern theater. An esoteric little movement that will spread
throughout South America. But of course."

And so it was decided. Tonya and Eddie would write the play, Bobo
would tape a soundtrack, Wheeler and Crofton would handle business
and PR, and McCorquodale would be the star.

CHAPTER 22

The Tip of the Iceberg

Some people liked to compare local political life with that of a small banana republic, but a more apt parallel could be drawn to the court of a senile Turkish emir in a remote malarial province specializing in the cultivation of opium poppies during the twilight days of the Ottoman Empire.

Beneath the quiet surface of normality, all the time that Aunt Odilia was quietly pursuing her genealogical research at the Mobile Public Library and the Canonical Archives, a vast web of intrigue was being spun behind the scenes around Todd's plan. And when Miss Alice and Miss Hattie Robinson came out every late spring morning to sniff the ligustrum blooming in the front yard of their house on Michigan Avenue, they never dreamed that the bush, the house, and all might soon be no more than coordinate points in the endless parking lot surrounding the Supermall, "biggest in the Sunbelt."

Indeed, the inscrutable editorial that McCorquodale saw announcing support for the plan was the merest tip of the iceberg. Even if anyone could have deciphered what the editorial was about, they could not have guessed that a power play was in progress that would decide the fate of the city.

The fact of the matter was that the plan was getting nowhere. Even the likes of Barker and Todd—Todd was forever prowling the corridors of city hall with his briefcase and bundles of drawings, a familiar sight now to city employees—had underestimated the amount of behind-the-scenes persuasion it would take.

Naturally, Todd, Barker, and the four other members of the Hamburger Harbor Improvement Association who were backing the development were careful to present well-thought-out brochures and slide shows outlining the need for, and benefits, of the project. There were maps showing how the Mobile city limits would expand into Mississippi, Florida, and Louisiana five years after the completion of the Tenn-Tom Waterway. There were visionary drawings of the Supermall and the "Six Flags Over Mobile" amusement park, "gateway to the Sunbelt."

The figures were particularly impressive: "$2 billion a year generated in sales taxes, 600,000 jobs created, $179 billion a year in payrolls" generated by the development. They were done by a Dallas consulting firm that often worked with Todd's Sunbelt Land Corporation and that no one in Mobile had ever heard of. It was actually a one-man operation; the consultant was a friend of Todd's who also ran a dating service for elderly oil barons.

Who, in the face of this cornucopia, could possibly object to tearing down half the city and draining the bay? Unfortunately, as Mayor Barker put it, drawings and figures are fine but "that don't wring the chicken's neck." In view of the flood tide of city funds that would be flowing and the bonds that would be floating, the most diverse groups were expecting a bit of extra-special consideration.

First of all, there was popular architect Colin Devoe, whose talent in designing colonial Georgian-style buildings always seemed to land him the fattest contracts. Devoe had contributed handsomely to Barker's campaign chest, and he complained bitterly to them of the destruction the development would wreak on the city's architectural heritage when he learned that a Texas architectural firm was to design the project.

Some of the local labor leaders in building and trade unions were at first delighted by the project. Draining the bay and tearing down the city would bring in jobs and money, they said. But when rumors spread that out-of-town, non-union labor might be involved, they began to pull all the stops and stand in the way of progress.

Hartwell Realty, a large firm that had recently sold Barker a large tract of land near his fast food establishment, was none too pleased to hear that realtor Sid Wibbs was one of the main backers and potential beneficiaries of the project. The normal price of the land was $85,000 an acre, yet they had sold it to Barker for only $25,000 an acre, hoping that the favor might be returned on a rainy day. Was this how he repaid their kindness? Peters and Shaker, a large engineering firm, had been promised a big part of the contract to drain the bay, but it wasn't enough, they said. Surely, they insisted, Ted Todd could make a small addition to the project for them, perhaps flooding the impoverished, black northern suburb of Prichard to create a water recreation area. They might find ways to show Barker and his associates their gratitude.

At the Greenspan Corporation, a giant local development firm, it was felt that since they had generously donated the land for Barker's expensive house near Airport Boulevard, they deserved an exclusive contract to replace all the public housing that would be destroyed for the project. Other development and construction firms, however, expressed distinct reservations to this idea.

Blackstone, Morninggate, and Pollux, a law firm very close to the county commissioners, was distressed to hear that young attorney Parker Stallings would be handling millions of dollars worth of litigation. The partners began to voice their concern that labor problems, condemnation work, leases to be drawn, and personal injury actions could cause insurmountable legal difficulties.

Both the Commerce National Bank and the Prudential National Bank had refused to help finance the project, although for reasons that had nothing to do with its merits. Finally, some local politicians were hesitant to support a project with so many unanswered and potentially disruptive questions for the city and county. For example, there was the question of where the new City Hall would go. Barker's great dream was to relocate it next door to Hamburger Harbor, but some of the others were pulling to start the new downtown near "County Commissionerville." That was what local wits called an area in west Mobile where county politicians had large holdings of property.

For a time it actually looked as though Todd's development plan was permanently stalemated. "Guys," the northern transplant told his Hamburger Harbor colleagues, "I think we're going to have to regroup."

Meanwhile, in the streets of the city, all was silence.

CHAPTER 23

Postmodern World Premiere

"Do you know what this means?" McCorquodale asked her little band of followers in the Postmodern League as they rehearsed for *Radical Chic*, the first postmodern musical held in the world. "For once we will be absolutely *au courant*; the global, maybe even *cosmic*, breaking wave of the avant-garde will be right here at the Port City Players." McCorquodale had rented the theater with the allowance she received from Wolfe. "We'll keep it a secret for now, darlings, but I'll wire Almodóvar after the opening."

Yet brilliant though the event was, it seemed for a time that it might not come together at all. Eddie and Tonya had been commissioned to write the musical, but they had distinctly different ideas of theater, and neither was sure how to make it "postmodern."

"Listen, Miss Thang," Eddie would burst out at exasperated moments, "tap dancin is *'in'*, I done read it in *After Dark*. And besides, my public expects it; they're *over* the Mae West act."

"Uh, uh, uh. I think I'll join the Peace Corps. Listen, pee wee, the music's too fast. Do you reckon I can take it off at seventy-eight RPM?" Tonya would reply. "Believe me, I've been at the entertainment business too durn long. They're here for a finger-snappin good time, slow and civilized."

They argued so much that there was barely enough time to write the play in the last two weeks, but finally, with theoretical input from McCorquodale on the death of language and subversion of the sentence, a compromise was reached.

There were parts for four characters: McCorquodale as the star, Tonya, Eddie, and the Mohawk-headed Bobo.

The two young professional members of the Postmodern League,

Carlton Wheeler and Willis Crofton, were in charge of publicity. They devoted all of their energies to persuading prominent Mobilians to allow their names to be printed on a page of the program as sponsors. The result was a three-hundred-watt list with names like "Moseley Shorter," "Mrs. Chasuble Hedgemont," "Arlene Morganton," "Mrs. Marmeduke LeVerne." It was then evident to all concerned that this was truly a high-class event.

Unfortunately, none of the prominent Mobilians actually came to see the musical, and there were only ten people in the audience when the curtain rose. There were the two attorneys, Aunt Odilia and the Misses Robinson, all three wearing chrysanthemum corsages, and George Belzagui. Helmut was on a ship to Venezuela, so Ce Ce Anne and Ernest came together.

Ernest was limping slightly in his pinstripe suit after a weekend sortie with Eddie to the New Orleans Jazz Festival. As always, New Orleans brought out a whole new side in the young businessman. Laying down for a moment the heavy responsibilities of his brilliant social position, Ernest took off his tank top, tied it around his waist, and he and Eddie climbed up poles in the Gospel Tent to swing to the fifty-voice chorus of the Greater Asia Big Zion B.C. Choir. Thank *heavens* in the very nick of time Ernest glimpsed two members of his Jaycee "Azalea Trail" Committee enter the tent carrying cans of *Dixie*. He had just enough time to drop down the pole before they saw him. His reputation was saved, but his ankles were killing him.

Ernest and Ce Ce Anne were in the mood for a festive night out, and rather curious to meet the woman Eddie had talked about so often since Mardi Gras. They watched an unknown gentleman in his forties with a thick bang of hair and pants hitched way up toward his chest enter and take a seat, then they studied their programs for a while. At the last moment H. Sloane Wolfe himself walked in and took a seat in one of the back rows. Ernest and Ce Ce Anne looked back casually to see who had just come in, and locked glances with him, petrified in position as though struck by invisible death rays. A look of immense annoyance passed over Wolfe's face and the lights went out.

Ce Ce Anne had time to whisper, "If Wolfe is here, then . . ." The curtains opened and there she was.

The one-act drama was completely devoid of plot. Off Broadway if ever there was one. It revolved around severe absurdist dialogues that McCorquodale called "language traps," designed to unmask the true meaninglessness of language with phrases like, "There is no message, get the message?" A tape of British punk bands that Bobo had made throbbed in the background.

Perhaps the news of the language crisis had not fully reached them, but the audience was strangely subdued. They only began to perk up when Tonya appeared in a hot pink bikini and was wordlessly bundled by Bobo from head to toe in Saran Wrap.

Eddie could not be prevented from working in a few vintage Port City Players dance numbers from *South Pacific*, in which his blond hair flew boyishly from side to side. And McCorquodale, in a silver body stocking, performed a classic bump and grind she had choreographed to:

> I got a little red rooster
> Too lazy to crow for day,
> I ain't had no peace in the barnyard
> Since my red rooster been away.

"Of course it's postmodern," she had told the others during rehearsals, "some things are always 'in.'"

But when the glorious spectacle was over, the patter of applause could barely be heard on stage. Ernest, eager to escape the awkward situation and horrified at the thought that Eddie might come running up to him after the show in front of Wolfe, had gone out the side door with Ce Ce Anne, who was stumbling like a sleepwalker. The discovery that Wolfe's "Margaret Constance Roshfookle" and Eddie's "McCorquodale" were one and the same, in the scowling presence of Wolfe no less, had overloaded even the tremendous capacity of her gossip computer banks. She had temporarily burnt out.

Wolfe, fearful that McCorquodale might say something compromising, had gone out the other side door. The man in the hitched-up pants went out through the front and left that door wide open. Locusts could be heard chirping from the street oaks.

Eddie stopped in mid-bow and looked around for Ernest and Ce Ce Anne. He had been looking forward to introducing them to McCorquodale. "Hey! There ain't hardly nobody here!"

The two young lawyers stood around sheepishly while Aunt Odilia and her friends, the only ones left, went up to congratulate McCorquodale.

"I decla, you're so smawt, deuh," Miss Alice said. "I didn't catch every wuid, I fall asleep sometimes you know, but it was *puifectly* lovely. I'd love to have you puhfawm fo my Pink Ladies' suikle at the Infuimry."

"Mawgret Constance was in the National Honor Society at Muiphy High School, you know," Aunt Odilia reminded everyone. "She had a puifect A-minus average."

All very sweet, but not completely what McCorquodale had in mind for a world premiere. Where were the critics? Where were the shouting crowds? Where was H. Sloane Wolfe with the roses?

"Can it be that people don't know that we have inaugurated the postmodern era here tonight?" McCorquodale asked her crestfallen followers. "Impossible! We'll give two more gala performances, and the world will ring with it."

She would not be disappointed. The one unknown spectator in the audience that night was the minister of Western Hills Baptist, "Growth Church of the Eighties." That very night he got on the phone to make a complete report on *Radical Chic* to the deacons.

CHAPTER 24

'Chic' Banned from the Stage

If it had not been for the mysterious gentleman at the premiere, *Radical Chic* might well have faded into obscurity. Only four people came to the second performance Friday night, and the cast was dreading Saturday night.

The man wearing his pants way up on his chest, they were to learn, was the Rev. Orville Tidwood, whose eight thousand-member congregation was one of the biggest Baptist churches in Alabama "and soon to be number one," as the church bulletin always noted.

It was characteristic of the perfect schizophrenia of Mobile that Western Hills could thrive in one part of the city, yet make no more impression on the "Young Set" world of Ce Ce Anne Stanton and Ernest Balleriel than an atmospheric storm on a moon of Jupiter. Even Aunt Odilia and her Baptist friends the Misses Robinson, Old Mobilians of modest families and modest means, never thought to discuss them in their daily talk of flowers, cooking and who was kin to whom.

Orville Tidwood had come to Mobile ten years before from Tuscaloosa, and had been aghast at the shocking traditions and somewhat more relaxed coastal morals of the decadent Port City. A handsome, sturdy man approaching fifty, Tidwood still had a thick mop of hair like a teenager, and a conspicuous set of strong white teeth that could grind a bag of coffee beans to "extra fine." He was a tireless organizer. He had started the church by uniting three older congregations that moved west from inner-city neighborhoods with the general tide to the suburbs.

Fresh out of seminary at Bob Jones University, Tidwood had quickly made a name for himself with his weekly inspirational Bible study TV program, "Let's Be Literal." The program relied heavily on testimonials from thick-necked athletes who always concluded with the words: "Win with Jesus, it worked for me!" In recent years church growth had been aided by a steady stream of controversies. Bottomless whirlpools of fundamentalist energy were undammed against the dog tracks, the granting of liquor licenses, gay bars, and on countless other issues. Usually nothing whatever changed as a result, but Western Hills stayed constantly in the news.

Ten years after its founding, the Western Hills complex sprawled next to the interstate highway like the Pentagon. Not a single bush or tree cluttered the grassy grounds. The sanctuary, an enormous concrete-block structure reminiscent of an airplane hangar save for the tiny pre-cast concrete spire on top, seated six thousand, but the ever-expanding long-range plans called for another twice as big. A huge banner hung above the choir loft which depicted Jesus Christ with arms uplifted exhorting, "Arise and build!" Though Tidwood lived in a modest subdivision house and received no more than an average salary, his management instincts were worthy of a president of General Motors. Western Hills was conceived as a new kind of total-service megachurch. In addition to the Youth World buildings, there was a weight room, an Olympic-sized swimming pool, an indoor track, a movie theater, bowling alley, and gym. Construction was to begin soon on a golf course and an outdoor track. The church bus fleet was so big that schedules were regularly published in the local newspapers. A huge computerized sign entitled "The Lord's Scoreboard" towered above I-65 and flashed an unceasing stream of statistics about membership and donations to passing motorists.

Reactions from the other Baptist churches in town were sometimes cool. At one end of the spectrum, Miss Hattie Robinson's old and august Government Street Baptist Church, which had changed its church covenant to allow the drinking of alcoholic beverages, regarded the Western Hills zealots as embarrassing parvenus. Members of their congregation could remember a time when Baptists were not particularly different from other denominations in town, had no reputation for militancy, and participated in Mardi Gras and the general life of the community like everyone else. At the other end of the spectrum, the tiny, rural, old-time Mt. Pisgah Baptist Church of Chunchula (to which McCorquodale's grandparents belonged) had been on the warpath ever since Western Hills conducted a bus raid on Chunchula and lured thirty teenagers, who were waiting outside for Mt. Pisgah Vacation Bible School, onto their buses and away with free Eskimo Pies and the promise of computer games.

Western Hills' biggest competitor was Midtown Baptist, an active and progressive congregation run on the same contemporary lines. For some time they had given them a run for their money, but in the last few years Midtown's membership had hardly moved beyond a plateau of only five thousand. Other, less streamlined churches, whose ambitions hardly extended beyond old-fashioned concepts, i.e. "people going to church," did not even enter the running.

Orville Tidwood stressed a wholesome Christian lifestyle that centered on eating McDonald's hamburgers and watching family-oriented shows on television. They were suspicious of downtown, never left the suburbs and the shopping centers, and regarded with horror urban events that drew large crowds drinking alcohol in public places. The congregation was far more affluent than their largely rural forebears had been, and far more attuned to the national mass culture. Increasingly, old Baptist hymns with their poignant nature imagery and stark doctrine were discarded in favor of feel-good contemporary gospel music in the gushing style of Whitney Houston hits. Christian rock groups came from all across the country to give concerts: good-looking, well-dressed young stars wielding their microphones with disarming freshness. The younger members of the congregation tended to prefer new Bible translations using contemporary catch phrases and slang. Some were simplified for easy reading.

The members were also more ideological than their ancestors had been. Sniffing survivals of ancient pagan cults all around them, they were particularly horrified by occasional Mardi Gras floats depicting ancient Greek and Roman gods. The jaded middle-aged businessmen who rode the floats would have been startled to learn that they were actually heathen votaries of Hephaestus, Zeus, and Poseidon. The church's

The modernists would turn even memory into asphalt.

efforts to entirely eliminate Mardi Gras had made no headway as yet, but during the last few years they had at least rented billboards all over town to warn, "Christians, Mardi Gras is not of God." Tidwood hoped to have more success by cultivating political ties with the city government.

Tidwood's connection was none other than Mayor Buzz Barker. Their friendship stemmed from an incident during the last municipal election when rumors swept the city that the vice squad had found Barker parked in a car one night at a local park with a young masseuse from the well-known Shady Lane Motel on Highway 90. The police never reported the incident, but Barker's popularity plummeted in the polls. Barker had previously been a backsliding Methodist, but after having a sudden religious experience he underwent a remarkably well-publicized conversion, joined Western Hills, and the solid bloc of fundamentalist votes was enough to put him over the top for another term.

It was with Barker, then, that Tidwood arranged a special meeting Saturday morning concerning McCorquodale's musical. All the deacons of Western Hills Baptist and other leading members were present.

"All these years now I've been warning about the secular humanist conspiracy and their plans for a one-world government, but to actually see those weirdoes up on the stage—man I tell you what!" Tidwood told the group. "We have reason to believe that their orders come from way out of state, maybe from abroad. Where it is, I cannot as yet say, but I suspect it's one a those California New Age groups. The humanists are here right now, more than you ever did dream, spreading their hedonist lifestyle all over town."

He handed Barker Exhibit A, a flyer promoting the play that a member of the Western Hills Youth Ministry had come across. Spotting the word "radical," he had brought it back to Tidwood.

RADICAL CHIC!! Postmodern Theater! Milestone in human history! Post-contemporary tap dancing! Thrill to over-coded entertainments that mercilessly debunk modernist lies . . .

Barker quickly scanned the page. Some little group of nuts. He tried to sound excited. "No! I didn't know people even thought things like that."

"Man, I'm here to tell you that that's just the beginnin. After they got warmed up, this big strappin red-headed woman came out practically necked and they packed her up in cellophane. And that's when a blonde came out and sang about how she misses her red rooster. I never heard such. But now listen to this, they served *wine* before the play."

"*Wine?!* What is this, Las Vegas?!" Barker slammed his fist on the desk. "We're not gonna have it here!" This was more promising. He decided to check out the cellophane act for himself.

To make sure public reaction was whipped up to a fever pitch, the Western Hills deacons called all the local radio stations with their complaints, and by noon Saturday, *Radical Chic* was on all the five-minute news spots. The top-forty disc jockeys were especially worked up. "Hey, you thought *Oh, Calcutta* would steam up your glasses, well getta load of what they're doing at the Port City Players tonight. . . ."

McCorquodale knew nothing of all this. Friday night the two young lawyers had deserted ship after the play. McCorquodale had serenely failed to hear Wheeler's frequent hints at their previous close acquaintance whenever the others were out of earshot, and treated both of them with a measured diplomatic reserve more fitting for minor spear-carriers than for great leading men. Seeing that they were not going to get anywhere with her, they said they had to go on a business trip. Undiscouraged, McCorquodale rose late Saturday morning and had the tiny cast over for an all-afternoon champagne brunch to celebrate what she confidently predicted would be a raging success that night. "The critics must have taken a slow Greyhound from New York, darlings, but they'll be there tonight, I promise you. We'll make history!"

Sure enough, the theater was packed, though the crowd was strikingly dominated by men. It was an elite audience: the entertainment committee of the Mobile Bar Association sat in the front row, and even several members of Task Force 2000 could be seen passing around a thermos full of gin and tonic. After the musical began, the vice squad and backup police encircled the theater and Barker took a seat with a good view.

What a surprise when the cast launched into the plotless and highly avant-garde assemblage of "language traps" and Neo-Dadaist happenings. The crowd looked disappointed and Buzz Barker shifted about uneasily in his chair. Yet he refused to give the signal. Even when Tonya finally appeared and the crowd broke out in a roaring cheer, Barker waved the plainclothesmen back angrily. Only when McCorquodale had come out and finished the very last bump and final grind in her silver body stocking did Barker raise his hand.

Police poured in everywhere and the crowd bolted for the doors, the Task Force 2000 members, as always, in the fore. "At last, a riot, this is just like *Rite of Spring,*" McCorquodale cried. But as the police led her out of the theater, she was all indignation: "Philistines, art will prevail!"

The front page of the Sunday *Herald-Item* showed McCorquodale smiling at the camera—shoulders back, one leg forward—in front of a police car.

CHAPTER 25

Secrets in Sin City

New Orleans was to Mobile what the Happy Hunting Grounds were to Tonto. It was a curious fact of geography that many Mobilians underwent a chemical change as soon as they hit the streets of the Crescent City. They blossomed into exotic forms like orchids in the rain forest, and would hardly have been recognized at home.

And so it was with an exultant H. Sloane Wolfe when he met McCorquodale in the bar of the French Quarter's fashionable Restaurant Jonathan during the Alabama Bankers Convention. "The Big Bankers," as they were affectionately known, met out of state as often as possible because business could be conducted so much better in places like Puerto Rico and Mexico City.

After the week's tumultuous attack from fundamentalist moral shock troops, McCorquodale was recuperating in her natural habitat: the piano player, a slender black man in a white dinner jacket with a razor-thin Prince Rainier mustache, launched into a Cole Porter medley. A young waiter balancing a packed drink tray darted among the tables of guests in elegant evening attire. Everything in the sunken Art Deco bar was silver and black and frosted glass, save for a pink heron and arching palm and crescent moon glowing down benevolently from the mirror behind them.

McCorquodale sipped her apéritif. "Ah, Herbsaint, that dear Louisiana anisette, with a breath of crushed ice and water. Just the right picker-upper after you've been battling with barbarian hordes. These peasant uprisings should be crushed ruthlessly. But now tell me, darling, how did you get me out of jail?"

Wolfe had nearly had a stroke when he saw McCorquodale's picture on the front page of the Sunday *Herald-Item*, and it was all he could do to sit through coffee with the grouchy Roberta at home before he slipped off to the phone. Wolfe was not on good terms with Mayor Barker after cold-shouldering his crony Todd, but fortunately he had made extensive contributions to the campaign chests of two county commissioners and Congressman Stirling McVay. McVay, in particular, who was running for reelection, had the highest regard for Wolfe's opinions.

"'Stuiling,' I told him, 'I read about this Miss Roshfookle in the paper this mawning, and I'm *consuined* about the precedent we're setting for the watchamacallit . . . awts in Mobile.' I thought he might just give that piss ant Bawker a call. He couldn't agree mo, and thought you should be released immediately."

"How can I thank you enough, Sloane?"

"Oh, maybe I'll think of a way."

"You know, the Huns can make life difficult for an *artiste*, such as myself, but just think how many true art lovers crowded the theater the last night. It revives my highest hopes for postmodernism."

"But baby doll, don't you think you could be a mite quieter about all this? You're gone have me in the *National Enquirer*."

"I know it's tiresome, but what can I do? I was born to international celebrity. This, of course, is just the beginning."

In the days following the Thursday night premiere and then the police raid, there had been a quiet shifting and reconnoitering on the chessboard as the various players at the Commerce National Bank tried to figure out who knew what. There was a very tense moment Friday morning when Wolfe happened to walk out into his outer office on the twenty-fifth floor, where Ernest had his desk, just as Eddie was picking up the mail on his first run. Wolfe hardly even gave him a glance. Obviously, Ernest decided, H. Sloane Wolfe could not be expected to notice a lowly mailboy, and certainly had not recognized him in the play. At Ernest's eager urging, Eddie had contacted McCorquodale and made her promise, reluctantly, not to mention to Wolfe that the bank mailboy was his co-disciple.

Later that morning Wolfe called Ernest into his office, and after a few scattered questions on bank matters, asked him out of the blue in a very deep voice, "So you and Miss Stanton go to the theater a lot, do you?"

Ernest happened to have his back turned looking at some papers. He stood transfixed for a moment, feeling two eyes burning into his shoulders, then turned around.

"Oh yes, H. Sloane, the theater, just all the time. We just adore it."

"Uh huh . . . Yeah, I like to take in a drama every once in a while myself. Any particular reason why y'all went to that particular play? Y'all know any of the actors?"

"Oh, no. We just kind of felt like going out."

"Uh huh. Left uily, did you?"

"Well, we thought it was going to be a musical comedy like the ones at the dinner theater, but it was really kind of a variety show; I mean, it wasn't like *Cats* or *Fiddler on the Roof* or anything, and they didn't have any food."

"I see." He shifted into his wise Southern businessman tone, pondering this critique. "Yase, Uinest, I see what you me-un. No, they didn't have any food. Not really." He decided that Ernest and Miss Stanton did not know anything.

As for McCorquodale, there had been troubling moments that night that she spent in the jail in a cell with Tonya, who, she discovered, snored in her sleep, when she wondered if there might not be some sinister dark force behind the ban on her play. What if Western Hills Baptist was only a front? What if it was really a secret conclave of modernists chiseling away from behind their unlikely cover? Perhaps the same ones that had written the Dadaist editorial she saw. Feverishly, she tried to imagine green-robed Cubists and Expressionists and Twelve Toners lurking in the three-hundred-voice Western Hills Baptist choir. "Oh, come on now, you're being paranoid," McCorquodale told herself. "Get a grip on yourself, woman."

The Commerce National Bank had sent a delegation of four to the New Orleans convention, including the Senior Executive Senior Vice President. Ernest had recently been honored with the additional title of Vice President for Correspondent Banking. That meant he got to handle

the reservations at the Bourbon Orleans, the limousines, and the beauty
parlor appointments for the wives. Mrs. Wolfe, sad to say, had stayed
home to host a cheese straw party for the election committee of the
Mobile Preservation Society, and was busy redoing the whole house for
the umpteenth time with a new interior decorator. Seeing his chance,
Wolfe had reserved a suite for McCorquodale at the top of the Hotel
Monteleone, a posh, old-fashioned, Thirties style place with lots of red
velvet in the lobby. It was their first overnight trip!

Wolfe was just telling about the cocktail party Wolfe Alabama held
after the convention registration, when the maitre d' came to up to them
in the bar to say that their table was ready. Wolfe was in fine form, and
looked every inch the distinguished, slightly graying banker as they
walked back, McCorquodale patting the cockatoo feathers in her side
hairbun. He was at the height of his power, and looking forward to a
night to remember, removed from prying eyes. Restaurant Jonathan was
hardly known among the bankers. Mobile seemed so far away.

But when they entered the room, Wolfe let out a dull "Huh!" There
in the corner, busy with their baked oysters, were Wingate and Cally
Kraemer, whom he had seen a few nights ago at the Country Club. There
was just enough time to back into the hall. Wolfe started to ask the
puzzled maitre d' for another room when he saw the elevator door open
and glimpsed Dr. and Mrs. Tuck Stauter in the back. He jumped behind
a huge cupid vase filled with anthuriums while McCorquodale surveyed
them coldly, statuesque and all dignity.

"We've gotta get out of here!" he told McCorquodale when they had
passed. "Let's go to Marti's." He grabbed her hand and they rushed out
to Rampart Street, stopping only to pick up her wrap.

Strolling past several sultry bars and "Dirty Dottie's" all-night
laundromat, they arrived at a restaurant that was smaller but equally
swank. They turned the corner and were just about to enter—"Sorry
about this, baby," Wolfe murmured—when down the street they heard
a blood-curdling:

"Ro-uhlllllllllll-tahd-ROLL!!!!"

Wolfe could see that it was Thurbo Newhouse of Newhouse Imports, Inc. staggering towards them down the street with several cronies. But as if that were not bad enough, they heard an answering shriek behind them.

"Roll like a WAGON WHEEL!!!" Wolfe turned around to see Marshall Hearn, a young ship chandler cousin of archrival Hearn Moseley. He was approaching with a group of young friends and shouting drunk football cheers.

"Have *muicy*. If Huin Moseley hears about us I'm done faw," Wolfe moaned. They ducked into a courtyard and crouched against a brick wall while the two groups passed. There was an abrupt hullabaloo of greetings and fiery yells that echoed in the night and slowly faded as they moved away in opposite directions. A fountain gurgled by some banana trees; a lizard crawled overhead.

When the coast was clear, they made a run for Bourbon Street. "We'll try Galatoire's," Wolfe suggested, "it's too hot around here." But on a hotel balcony directly across the street from the old restaurant, Wolfe was unsettled to see Mr. and Mrs. Chasuble Hedgemont, who had co-chaired the Opera Ball that year, doing a shimmy while a group of California bikers tossed pennies up at their feet. Wolfe shook his head. "Makin complete fools of themselves. Who would have believed it?"

A detour to Arnaud's ground to a halt when Wolfe recognized several young Junior Leaguers walking arm in arm with rosy-cheeked French naval cadets in pom-pom caps from a French ship in port. The way to Brennan's was blocked by Ripley Washton. He was standing all alone under the magnolia trees across the street beating invisible bongos. Antoine's, Moran's, Tujague's: there were familiar faces everywhere, all feeling in full fig.

"This is suitainly revolting, you cain't even have a little fling," Wolfe complained. "Why don't they do all this at ho-um?"

McCorquodale's stiletto heels were killing her. "Really, darling. I would have worn my jogging suit if I had known. Let's go to Decatur Street, I know a place where *nobody* will see us."

They passed back up Bourbon Street, heads low in the crowd. Ernest, standing on the balcony of Lafitte's with Eddie, who had caught

the Trailways bus over, was startled to see them coming and had to gag
Eddie and drag him inside to keep him from yelling to McCorquodale.

And so their gala dinner ended with them sitting at the counter of a
diner dressed to kill and eating roast beef Po-boys. The fat and tattooed
cook with a thick New Orleans "Yat" accent explained his luck at the
Fairground horse races. A hobo dozed on the last stool.

Wolfe felt deflated, but the night was still young, he told himself.
The main treat of the evening was still to come at the Hotel Monteleone.
He was in for a surprise when they got to the lobby after a romantic
carriage ride down Chartres Street.

"So sweet of you to see me back, *cheri*, but I can take the elevator
from here."

Wolfe was on the verge of tears. "But shuguh, I thought I might just
come up faw a nightcap."

"A pleasant thought, but I'm simply too tuckered. Do send the
limousine around in the morning. I have a mind to look for a new tiara.
You can tell me all about your Wakiki Luau lunch with the bankers when
we meet tomorrow night."

There was no solace for a president and chairman of the board. On
the way back to his own hotel Wolfe brooded what to make of her.
Maybe he had been misjudging McCorquodale all along. "Maybe she's
just an old-fashioned guil."

CHAPTER 26

Rutabagas and Forgotten Aristocracy

One afternoon during the week that McCorquodale was in New Orleans with H. Sloane Wolfe, Aunt Odilia and George Belzagui were invited to the home of Miss Alice and Miss Hattie Robinson. As they sat in their lawn chairs in the back yard, the Misses Robinson shelling crowder peas onto old copies of the *Alabama Baptist*, they launched into the primordial local ur-conversation of flowers, family, and the past.

"Give me Greer's for rutabagas, Delchamps' for roastin ears, and Food Wuild for tomatuhs," said Miss Hattie with the voice of firm conviction, listing her favorite grocery stores.

"And Naman's for black olives and grape lee-uvs," said Mr. Belzagui. He adjusted his professorial black glasses slyly over his stately and luxuriantly flaring Lebanese nose.

"Oh, Mr. Belzagui, you're so international. But if I could only find the real butterbeeuns. What have they done with them? Either they've improved them out of existence, aw they're just too lazy to pick em."

"Now isn't it the truth?" Aunt Odilia agreed.

The Misses Robinson went back to shelling intently. The lanky Miss Hattie had not changed her hair since it was bobbed in the 1920s: very short, "shingled" under in the back, with a well-trained "flapper" curl on either side held in place by a single bobby pin. The equally tall and thin Miss Alice, who was slightly younger, sported the Marian Marsh look of her favorite 1930s movies: marcelled waves and calf-length dresses, though with wire-rim glasses, too.

Aunt Odilia eyed the mimosas and caladiums. "What a lovely gawden y'all have; you must wuik out here constantly."

"Eggshells. It gives them backbone," Miss Hattie revealed. "I luined it when I was just a guil from Mizz Chawlotte Muitz on Madison Stree-it, three blocks from the rivuh. I would watch her digging in the flower beds by the sidewalk where you got that nice bay bree-iz."

"Was she kin to Dr. Huibet Muitz on St. Joseph Stree-it?" Mr. Belzagui wondered.

"His sister. I ro-ud by there the other day and it's nothing but a big loop where you get on the highway. I couldn't believe it."

"There isn't even a Madison Stree-it anymo," said Mr. Belzagui.

"They had a picture in the papuh of a Mawvin Muitz," Miss Alice remembered. "A fine-lookin man; it said he lives with his wife and family in Cottage Hill. He had gotten a prize from the South Alabama Pepsi Cola Distributors Association for outstanding distributing excellence."

"That was Mizz Chawlotte's grindson," said Mizz Hattie.

"Made a place for himself," Miss Alice observed.

"I guess he didn't want to study medicine like Dr. Huibert. You don't heuh much about the Muitzes anymo. What was that boy's wife's nayim?" Aunt Odilia very naturally inquired.

"Kowalik, they tell me."

"Any relation to Elsie and Etta?"

"Not that I know of."

"Hmmm. I once knew a Lois Kowalik in the thuid grayid. I believe there's a Kowalik's Auto Supply in the yellow pages."

Ignoring this delicious side path beckoning into the labyrinth of kith and kin, Miss Hattie returned to her flower beds. "The front yawd I've left just as Papa wanted it, and anyway there's not much you can do with it with all that shayid. You wouldn't believe how the oak tree-iz on the stree-it have grown in the lyest fifty yeuhs."

The house had been built when they were just young girls. Before that they had lived on St. Anthony Street down the block from Aunt Odilia.

"Well, anyway, Papa was always so modern, and when the Jaycee-iz stawted pline-ting azaleas, and the Azalea Trail came down Michigan Avenue, he had to have them too. I remember he pline-ted them all on a Saturday in June. It was the day Buitha Bolling was bitten by a mide dawg on Ohio Stree-it."

"Any kin to Fawthuh Bolling at the Chuich of the Little Flower?" asked Mr. Belzagui.

"No, her cousin rine the locker room at Littleton's Gymnasium. Well, Buitha was bitten by a mide dawg and Papa dug up all the pitosporums and pline-ted azaleas. Pride of Mobile across the front and President Clay at both cawnuhs. But the back yawd, which is private, is all my own. I get my ideas from *National Geographic*."

"Yase, I can check them out at the chuich library," said Miss Alice, the reader of the group, referring to that august Greek temple, Government Street Baptist Church.

In the cool of the late afternoon the back yard, abutting the white frame World War II garage apartment of the neighbors to the rear, was distinctly tropical. There were banana trees, and sago palms so old that their trunks were five feet high. The oleander, bottle brush, and canna lilies all had brilliant red blooms, but several clumps of oak leaf hydrangea were white. Huge Play-Doh Gulf clouds floated in the sunny blue sky, chubby white Andes, iridescent blimps.

Aunt Odilia was dressed in very snappy polka dot slacks that had grown a bit tight over the years, with her dyed black hair pulled back in a bun and long Woolworth's earrings dangling from pierced ears. She relaxed back in her lawn chair to look at the clouds and smell the gardenias. "And what is Mawgret Constance doing now?" Miss Alice inquired.

"Oh I cain't keep up withuh. She's in New Awleuns, probably meeting some nice young man, some Tulane graduate student or something over there. Mawgret Constance has always been so populuh, ever since she was in the National Honor Society at Muiphy High School. *My* talents wuh always mo faw leadership."

"Mizz Chighizola was just elected president of the Thuisday Night Sodality at St. Joseph's," Mr. Belzagui announced.

"Mawgret Constance may *look* like her mothuh's side, but she takes ife-ter my fawthuh. We were so much more social you know." She paused to allow for the appropriate confirming comments, but the Misses Robinson shelled peas fiercely. "I decla, Fawthuh knew everybody in Mobile and called them by nayim. It's true that he only wuiked as a desk cluik at the Battle House, but he always said that if it hadn't been faw his slow constitution he would have made a *wonderful* attuiney. No energy, you know. Some people are just bawn pokey."

"I still don't understand why they arrested Mawgret Constance. I didn't catch every wuid of the play, but I thought she was so smawt to be in it," said Miss Alice.

"The *nuive*!" Aunt Odilia cried, sitting up suddenly. "I'm here to say that the riffraff is running wild in the streets!" She referred to the play censors.

When Odilia got McCorquodale's call from city jail in the middle of the night and then saw the front page picture in the Sunday paper, her thoughts first turned toward purchasing a plot in Pine Crest Cemetery. She went back to bed and pulled the covers up over her head. What is more, she refused to answer the insistently ringing telephone for several hours, a form of behavior which might occur no more than once every quarter of a century.

At length, however, the ringing phone proved too tempting, and she spent all afternoon and evening talking to friends, and friends of friends, and acquaintances going back fifty years, all offering commiseration and starved for details. Aunt Odilia's initial embarrassment soon turned to thrilled enjoyment. She had become an overnight celebrity. If she was abashed in the morning, by late afternoon she was waving melodramatic sabers at McCorquodale's persecutors. So much did Odilia talk on the phone that McCorquodale only got a busy signal all day long trying to get through from the jail. When they finally let her out and she walked home, she was puzzled to find that Aunt Odilia acted rather disappointed that they had sprung her so soon.

"It was just like the time during Prohibition when they tried to arrest Joe for suiving beer at McAlpin's Pool Hall on St. Francis Stree-it," Odilia raged to her three friends. "Fotunately he got out the back doe and went to Biloxi for a month." Joe was her late husband. "Don't these people realize who they're dealing with?" She was getting excited.

"How is your resuich coming?" Miss Alice asked soothingly about

Aunt Odilia's genealogical efforts in order to distract her, ignoring a flame-throwing stare from Miss Hattie.

"I have discovered that Mizz Chighizola is descended from Chawlemayin, St. Louis, and Mary Queen of Scots," said Mr. Belzagui, the sober historian now.

"And Alexander the Grayit, don't fawget that," Aunt Odilia chimed in, calm once more.

"Didn't you say y'all arrived here in 1702?" Miss Alice persevered, though she had heard the answer many times. She had learned to suppress any skepticism she might feel on that point.

"Not only that, but we had the very fuist queen of Mawdi Graw," Aunt Odilia said.

The shadow of a little snort came from the direction of the dour Miss Hattie.

"Camille Roshfookle," continued Aunt Odilia, with one dignified hand poised on her ample bosom. A perfectly good snort had been entirely wasted on her. "Isn't that right, Jawage?"

"Pawdon?"

"I said isn't that so?"

Mr. Belzagui went blank a moment. "Roger, chief. Right on the money," he finally offered.

"They've fawgotten her, but Fawthuh always said there wasn't a lady in town mo in demand. Jawage has found documents showing that a queen was chosen in 1847 at a closed-doe meeting of the Tea Drinkers Society. Seems to have been an all-night session. Those men back then sure liked their tea. We still lack proof that that was Camille, but Jawage thinks the documents might tuin up yet, don't you Jawage?"

"Yase, by golly. Something tells me they just might," he said weakly. Something was weighing on his conscience: a certain departure from scientific method, which is to say a conjecture he had made that did not square with the factual weighing and sifting of the objective historian, which is to say a big fat lie.

"Anyway, who needs proof and documents?" Aunt Odilia wondered. "It's the inner suitainty that counts."

A whistle blew to the south. "The pulley wuiks," said Mr. Belzagui uneasily. "I guess we'd better be going."

But Aunt Odilia sat staring at the horizon, lost in thought. "It's something that can nevuh stay hidden," she mumbled.

"What on uith are you talking about?" demanded Miss Hattie.

As she answered, the approaching sunset began to tint the cloud towers in rich purple.

"The blood of the Rochefoucaulds."

CHAPTER 27

Shot Down at the Singles Bar

For weeks now Ted Todd had not been able to get the least encouragement for his development from the powers that be. One day the normally indefatigable promoter was so discouraged that he called Barker, and they agreed to meet at Edsel's, a popular singles bar in the western sprawl. As fate would have it, McCorquodale and Tonya were meeting Eddie there that very night, and would hand the two womanizers a very memorable defeat.

Barker arrived a little late after giving a talk against vice and corruption at a big meeting held at Western Hills Baptist. He had mentioned McCorquodale's revue *Radical Chic* as an example. "That's what's wrong with this country," he told them. "Five more months like this and we might as well be living on Times Square." His proposal to institute mandatory viewings of *Mary Poppins* for anyone caught walking on the sidewalks downtown after six p.m. brought him a standing ovation.

Night was just falling when Barker arrived, but the place was already filled with a motley crowd: secretaries in their office finery, college boys in cowboy outfits, middle-aged businessmen with roving glances. All showed a tendency to keep their eyes riveted on the dance floor and the other guests. Waitresses in poodle skirts and saddle Oxfords circled around a shiny Edsel parked in the middle of the floor to the beat of fifties and sixties music.

Even though Barker was ready for a little recreation after his tiring talk to the moral watchdog group, he first had to cheer up Todd about their development.

"Listen, Ted boy, I don't believe we're thinkin big enough. We've got to prime the pump, fella, and expand our base of support. We need to bring in more contractors, more labor unions, go to the state."

"How are we going to pay all these people?" Todd asked.

"You, the big time developer, are asking *me* that? Don't worry about that now, once it gets going we'll find the money. And once they sink their ole fist in that tar baby, they ain't gonna pull it out so soon. And besides, you've got the city fathers to vouch for you," Barker said piously. Both cackled. Barker took a napkin and they began making a list of groups to be "primed."

Tonya and Eddie had gotten to be great friends during the production of the musical, despite their initial disagreement over dancing styles. Eddie had wanted to see Edsel's for months, but Ernest would not take him there because he was afraid he might run into somebody he knew.

The two voluptuous knockouts got there first and made a certain impression when they strode through the door. Anticipating just a quiet night out, both had dressed very simply in matching peddle pushers and red sequin halter tops. Their hair cascaded down one side of their heads in falls, Tonya's a shining red, McCorquodale's a pale honey blond.

Seeing that Eddie hadn't arrived yet, they took a seat at a booth and looked around. All the men at the bar were staring with stunned expressions, conversations at the neighboring tables had stopped, the pool and video game players in the next room froze where they stood to look their way.

"Tonya darling, they seem frightfully preoccupied in this place. Is it my imagination or has the art of conversation atrophied in the 'modern' age? But perhaps we dazzle them."

"You durn straight. Them dudes don't see this kinda high-class trade ever day a the week."

"Well then maybe there's hope for them. To be candid, when we pulled up in the parking lot and I sensed the ambiance, I thought even that artist Christo couldn't turn these suburbs postmodern if he wrapped them in plastic sheeting."

"You know I still ain't sure I know what that means . . ."

"Happy the few who simply *are* postmodern," McCorquodale interjected.

". . . but I sure was hopin when I was in that play I could get a little PR for the Hubba. Business is rotten."

"But child, when I open my sidewalk café on Conti Street, the Hubba Hubba Club, too, will become a maelstrom of intellectual activity. You've elevated the art of scarf-dancing to dizzying heights, you know." McCorquodale ordered a Jack Daniels neat and lit up a Picayune.

The moment Tonya and McCorquodale walked in the front door, Todd and Barker forgot about their list and stared at the two lovelies like Rasputin at a hypnotists convention. Observing that their silent homage went unnoticed, Barker suggested that they walk over to McCorquodale's table. He was feeling very confident because after speaking to the church group, he had stopped at a filling station and put on a tight corset in the rest room. He had seen it advertised at the back of a supermarket tabloid among the ads for psychic healers. It gave his fortyish flabby belly a trim athletic form.

Todd quickly ran a comb through his wavy hair and thought of his long Elvis Presley eyelashes that more than made up for slightly puffy cheeks.

They swaggered over to the booth as the jukebox played "Behind Closed Doors." Tonya and McCorquodale eyed them stonily. Undaunted, Barker slid in next to McCorquodale and Todd sat on the other side and put his arm around Tonya's abundant shoulders.

"Nuh-uh! Take yer digits off the merchandise, cheeseface," Tonya admonished impressively. "Them's fragile goods."

Todd drew back prudently as McCorquodale gave him a long, hard look. "I know you. I've met you before. You're that street paver or whatever from Houston. What are you doing still in town? Shouldn't you be off some place burning rain forests or something?"

"I couldn't get you out of my mind, doll," Todd improvised gallantly.

McCorquodale thought this statement over a moment. Could these two characters have been following her?

Barker beamed a cocky smile. He considered himself a real lady killer. "Well, I know who you are, too" he told McCorquodale. "You were the star of that potboiler at the Port City Players."

"It's called experimental theater, darling. Think about it."

McCorquodale obviously did not recognize the municipal states-man who had banned her play. Barker decided it best not to clue her in, but he could not help teasing, "I bet you don't know who I am."

"Not an inkling. No doubt I could call the parole board and find out."

Todd decided to cut the preliminaries and move in for the kill. "Hey, I've got a suite at the Ramada Inn. Let's go play a game of poker. The winner picks the prize. I think I already know what I want," he chortled.

"Well ain't you just shit on a stick," said Tonya. Her smile vanished. "You're crowdin my airspace, sapsucker. I ain't a gonna ask ya twicet to clear out . . . but now lookee yonder, our gentleman friend's done arrived."

Barker and Todd nearly had heart failure as they scanned the entrance expecting to see a Heart of Dixie body-building champion approaching to crush their bones. Instead, they saw a small and very pretty tow-headed boy in white painter's pants with big loops on his hips. He had tied a long headband around his forehead that fluttered down his neck as though he had just been dancing around the maypole. When he spotted Tonya and McCorquodale he went running across the bar waving one arm.

"Check it out, chicks! Ain't this place fab! Hold me back, I may do somethin impetuous. But y'all've got *callers*. Would you care for an autograph?" the star of the Mobile stage asked the two big wheels.

It was too much for Barker that Eddie obviously did not recognize him either, and he let down his guard.

"Little man, don't you know *Mayor Buzz Barker* when you see him?" He waited for the flash of flattered confusion.

Eddie was unimpressed. "Sorry, babe, when you're in show bizz, you lose track of the local functionaries."

But McCorquodale was speechless to realize that the "head philistine of Mobile," as she had described him to Wolfe, was sitting right next to her. So this Houston character had political connections going all the way to the mayor. Were they both involved in having the police raid her play? A pattern of unseen and doubtless unsavory activity, of hidden and Neanderthal developments suggested itself. Whatever it was, it was best not to think about it. These people were beneath her notice. Without a word she stood up on the leather seat, stepped onto the table, and jumped down past Barker. Tonya did the same. A crowd began to gather around the disturbance.

Tonya slapped a majestic arm around Eddie that almost knocked the blue glitter off his nose. "Come on, stud, let's ditch these creeps and blow out of this rathole."

"I just got here!" Eddie protested, but McCorquodale grabbed his other arm and the two bombshells swished to the door practically carrying Eddie between them.

Todd stared after them longingly. "What's that little guy's secret?" he mumbled. But Barker was spooked by the crowd. Sensing the presence of cameras, he went running out the back door before anybody could take a photo.

CHAPTER 28

The Juggernaut Rolls

The whole city had slowed down for the summer, but for Todd and Barker, it was a time of frantic activity. And the four other members of the Hamburger Harbor Improvement Association were also making phone calls and paying visits night and day.

Just as Barker had told Ted Todd, their development plan was steadily coming back to life. Only this time a juggernaut of interest groups was being set in motion that the two entrepreneurs were certain could never be stopped.

As Barker had predicted, expanding their base was the key. At first it was difficult to convince the many new groups involved of the civic opportunities the plan represented, but carefully framed arguments had changed many minds. The big engineering firm of Peters and Shaker, for example, overcame its reservations and invited Barker to become a silent partner when Todd's Sunbelt Land Corporation decided to demolish vast additional neighborhoods in the southern part of town for the development and put them in charge. Since all of the bay except the ship channel would be drained and filled for industry, Sunbelt reasoned, a new artificial lake had to be created on the site of those neighborhoods to serve the need for water recreation in the area. Sixteen local trade and construction unions pledged their enthusiastic support when Barker agreed that only local labor would be used to dig the giant hole, transport the dirt and fill up the bay, and pipe the water from the vanishing bay into the newly created lake. Some six other engineering firms and ten construction companies also came on board.

The uproar over McCorquodale's postmodern play made it clearer than ever to Barker that the Western Hills Baptist Church and other similar groupings were a political resource not to be overlooked. Of course, he had been extremely pious ever since his great conversion before the last election, but now Barker realized that the amusement park planned for the site of the obsolete old downtown was blatantly pagan. Instead of "Six Flags Over Mobile," he announced, a "Six Flags Over Jesus" amusement park would be built to convey the greatest stories of the Old and New Testaments in simple images that could be readily understood by the emerging Sunbelt mind.

There would be a Mt. Sinai roller coaster, a Noah and the Ark zoo, Joshua and the Canaanites bumper cars, Roman soldier tour guides, and the tallest neon cross in the world towering over the flattened skyline. "Jericho's," a zippy night spot for adults, would serve "Wedding at Cana" grape juice and feature appearances by superstar singers from the fundamentalist TV networks that would really "bring the house down."

The centerpiece and great landmark of the amusement park would be a gigantic statue of Jesus. Preliminary sketches showed the muscular, square-jawed "masculine" Jesus lately popular in fundamentalist Sunday school books. He was depicted with shoulder-length hair and wearing a robe and sandals, but otherwise one could imagine him single-handedly managing the rigging of a forty-foot sailboat in a cigarette commercial.

Ominous rumblings had been coming from the black community as bits of news began to slowly leak out that whole inner-city neighborhoods were to be demolished, above all the old Davis Avenue district around Martin Luther King Boulevard, the traditional center of black Mobile. In days gone by the politicians and developers would simply have ignored the protests of the black leaders, and proceeded with their plans without giving a second thought as to what the black residents who were to lose their homes might think about the matter. In the last twenty years, however, blacks had obtained new power in city politics, and controlled four of the twelve seats on the city council.

A series of extremely delicate overtures were made, and Barker found that two of the black councilmen were open to negotiation. At length it was agreed that in exchange for a series of fat honorariums and shares in the Supermall project, the two councilmen would start a public disinformation campaign to create confusion and neutralize the criticisms that the other two councilmen were beginning to air at speaking occasions in the black neighborhoods.

As in the good old days of Urban Renewal, the city was going to declare the whole huge area a "blighted neighborhood." The councilmen working with Barker began to warn that the street system downtown was in danger of imminent collapse because it could not possibly meet the traffic demands which street-widening masterminds in the Alabama Highway Department had projected for the year 2075. Furthermore, they warned inner-city residents that squirrels living in the oak trees along downtown streets might soon cause a terrible rabies epidemic unless the area was cleared and sanitized. They began to foment vague rumors about fat compensations for all the property acquired by the city, and luxurious new neighborhoods and housing developments to be constructed in other parts of town.

With plans for Supermall and the other segments of the development getting bigger and bigger, Todd and Barker decided that the time had come to get out-of-town interests involved in the deal, too. The HHIA developers were beginning to worry that even with the Tenn-Tom Waterway and the—in Barker's eyes—unlimited bonding capacity of the city government, financing was getting out of hand.

Immediate support came from the legislators and city officials of friendly Birmingham, always willing to jump into the breach to assist their sister city in South Alabama. In an act of self-sacrifice they agreed to renounce half of what they felt to be Birmingham's fair share of state gas lease revenues earned from recent drilling in Mobile Bay (95 percent), so that it could be used to level Mobile. In return, Birmingham asked only that Barker coerce the Mobile legislative delegation into allowing the Mobile medical college to be closed. Both state colleges in Mobile would be transferred to Birmingham, and all other state funds to be spent in Mobile would be diverted to Birmingham for a period of ninety years.

Yet even with all of these commitments from interested parties eager to get a thumb in the pie, Barker and Todd still needed to show the hard-headed, no-nonsense traditional business leaders and other local politicians how their plan would make Mobile the industrial center of North America that they so eagerly wanted it to be.

Congressman Stirling McVay, running for reelection as a Republican, talked about industrial growth constantly, and had taken to wearing a hard-hat everywhere he went—wicked tongues said he slept in it. As for Rufus Fencepicket, president of the county commission, his great dream was to see the remains of the bay lined with oil refineries, and the teeming nightlife and limitless cultural activities of the Port City slowed down to reflect the simple upstate ways of his native Pump Hole, Alabama. Fencepicket was in the mainstream of big time political leadership, having garnered valuable experience managing the Palm Court Mobile Home Park on Highway 90 before running for office.

Barker and Todd arranged another meeting with Task Force 2000 and a cluster of politicians. The purpose was to make a secret announcement of the international conglomerate that would occupy the site of the bay after it had been drained. The twenty energetic and *bon vivant* businessmen were present whose families were among those that had steered the city through rocky shoals for the past half century.

It took some time to generate the atmosphere of breathless suspense that Barker had anticipated in the top-floor banquet room of the Intercontinental Trade Mart overlooking the harbor. During the meal all that the Task Force members wanted to talk about was a "Jubilee" the weekend before at Point Clear. (Buckets of fish, crabs, and shrimp could be scooped up when the sea life swarmed, periodically and inexplicably, into the shallow eastern shore waters of the bay.) Never once did they draw a connection with the subject being discussed at the meeting. After that, several dropped into a cozy semi-conscious trance over their bread pudding with whiskey sauce.

Barker slipped out and had the management turn the air-conditioner down to nearly freezing. Coffee was served all around. By the time Todd began his presentation, he could see his own breath and the business vanguard had perked up brightly in their leather chairs.

Todd flipped through drawing after drawing of factories and smokestacks and conveyor belts, letting curiosity build about the name of the company. At the very end, when he flipped the final sheet to reveal the company trademark, gasps resounded throughout the room: VW.

"Volkswagen, gentlemen, has pegged Mobile down as such a viable socio-urban hub that they're going to move their Brazilian works up here as soon as we upgrade the bay."

Harmsworth Balleriel had been daydreaming about a new whirlpool bath for his hunting lodge, but snapped to attention when he perceived the hush in the room. "Volkswagen?" he asked with gravity, speaking for his overwhelmed associates. "You mean *awl* we have to do is dray-in the bay and give them the land? There's nothing else we can do faw em?"

"That's just how simple it is, Ham. Except for the local tax-exemptions, tax-exempt bond issues for construction, and all drilling rights. I might add that the land will be conveyed first to Sunbelt Land Corporation, a legal technicality, you know." Todd explained that representatives from Berlin and Wolfsburg would arrive by way of Houston in the next few weeks to discuss the details.

But Barker interrupted the happy announcement with a sober warning. "Fellas, we've got to get this thing movin. It don't rain gravy but once in a man's life, and you don't wanta be caught outside holdin a fork."

CHAPTER 29

Defenders of the True Blue

Several times a week Ernest Balleriel went to his parents' mansion on Government Street for supper. The ritual was always the same at "Castle Balleriel," as he half-jokingly called it in conversations with his Young Set friends.

When Ernest arrived from the bank, he and his mother would settle in the plush Victorian furniture of the front parlor and mix themselves a Bourbon and soda from the set of crystal decanters and dispensers always ready on the marble side table. Ernest's father generally arrived somewhat later from Balleriel Stevedoring, Inc. After Mr. Balleriel had had his toddy, they would proceed through the middle parlor and two sets of double doors to the dining room, where supper was served by Weeza, the old cook.

During the rest of the week Ernest generally ate out clandestinely with Eddie or had a cold supper left behind by the maid at the bachelor town house he had recently built on a tiny subdivided front yard in Spring Hill, an old and fashionable western district. Ever mindful of the weight of family tradition, Ernest had had architect Colin Devoe, the well-known local authority on historic restoration, design a three-quarter-scale replica of the old 1830s Federal style Jameston house that had once stood on Monroe Street until it was razed for Interstate 10. There were thin shutters that could never be closed and a cast iron balcony that could never be used because the upstairs windows were sealed shut. For the downstairs the sober young businessman had chosen dark panelling and somber oil ancestor portraits in oval frames. But hidden away in the upstairs bedroom were theatrical posters of Liza Minelli, Grace Jones, and Divine that he and Eddie had bought on trips to New Orleans and Key West.

Mrs. Balleriel had found in Ernest a ready and willing pupil of the cabala of the True Mobilian. During the regular family dinners the two would consign various individuals to their place in the Great Chain of Being, interpret current events in the light of the true faith, and formulate the appropriate diplomatic policy to deal with them. Mr. Balleriel was allergic to theory of any sort and generally ignored the conversation.

Yet even though he was a recognized social authority, young Ernest was not immune to error. One evening in June, after the stuffed flounder, Ernest admitted his callow lack of judgment some time back in nearly straying from the fold of Canterbury Church Episcopal.

They had retired to the sun porch for an after-dinner drink. Mr. Balleriel wore the orange jumpsuit, size XL, of his leisure hours and sprawled back in an easy chair, his stately belly arching toward the ceiling like a capitol dome. Mrs. Balleriel sipped a green crème de menthe and shook the chains of her reading glasses sternly.

Several years before, Ce Ce Anne Stanton and her circle left the staid Canterbury Church Episcopal downtown to join the thriving St. Mark's Episcopal Church in Spring Hill. She had tried to get Ernest to do the same, saying not only that St. Mark's was *the* up and coming church for the Young Set, but was also very convenient to the Blue Parakeet Restaurant where they all had champagne brunch Sunday mornings. But Mrs. Balleriel, with her infallible sense of the social future, had prevailed upon Ernest not to leave the church the Balleriels and the Jamestons had attended for one hundred and forty years.

Now she was vindicated. Ernest reported that the Young Set was returning to Canterbury in droves. "Ce Ce Anne says she's coming back, too, she says things have gotten *entirely* out of hand at St. Mark's. There were *ripples* of concern when they first began to notice these young singles showing up at the young adults supper club that nobody knew; people who live in apartment buildings, you know. One night one of these new members said grace and made up all the words *herself.* She kept going oin and oin, upwards of *three minutes.* Everybody just kind of looked at each other while she went oin. I mean, you can go overboard in giving thanks. That night Ce talked to three of those new members who thought that the Strikers were some kind of labor union."

The Strikers were a non-parading mystic society going back to 1842. This was too much for Mrs. Balleriel.

"Horruhs! I had huid that the public schools were ignoring the basics, but that is criminal neglect."

"Things have gone from bad to worse; they're making *converts*. Young Methodist and Presbyterian executives join as soon as they get their first big promotion, even some Baptists are turning Episcopalian. You never know who you'll run into. Tithes are at an all-time high, membership is growing hand over fist."

Mrs. Balleriel was aghast. "They're coting disaster; I had no idea it had gawn so faw." She fingered her pearls in disbelief.

"And the Trendier-Than-Thous have started coming. Last spring they were holding encounter groups and sensitivity sessions with the young adults. Things got so sensitive that there were four divorces in one class. Now they're singing hymns to guitar music and 'Passing the Peace' at every service."

Mr. Balleriel raised his ruddy face indignantly from a catalogue of duck prints he meant to order for his hunting lodge. "It's gettin so a man cain't even go to chuich without some puifect stranger tryin to shake yo hand."

Ernest looked at his mother gratefully. "Thank you, Mamacita, for holding me back. I would have felt simply *out* of my element at St. Mark's." The nickname for his mother was a slight affectation left over from Ernest's seventh grade Spanish class at his military prep school. "But I suppose now the young promotees will start flocking to Canterbury," he said sadly.

"We have to carry our cross," Mrs. Balleriel concluded wisely. "Howevuh, you can hawdly blay-im them. Ife-ter all, *we* go to Canterbury."

A lull fell in the conversation. Mr. Balleriel was filling out an order form for several duck prints. The windows of the sun porch were like mirrors at night, and Ernest admired in the reflection the perfect crease of his khaki pants and the clean part of his auburn hair, as collegiate as the day he left Sewanee. "I really am quite spiffy," he thought. Mrs. Balleriel picked up a copy of the evening *Mobile Herald*.

At the bottom of the social page her attention was caught by a tiny AP story that had been cut to one paragraph. The inconspicuous headline announced, "Mobile To Be Bulldozed, Bay Filled." Several sparse sentences outlined the Houston developer's plan and the proposed Volkswagen factory on the site of the bay. Somehow some inattentive editor had let the few lines slip through the newspaper's news blackout on the project, which had continued after their inscrutable editorial.

Mrs. Balleriel perused the article casually. She read it again and then a third time.

"Hawmswuith," she called. A note of weariness entered her usual voice of authority. "I wonder if we haven't been too lenient with some of these newcomers in town. What is this all about?"

Mr. Balleriel took the paper. At first he could remember nothing about it, but then the light of recognition dawned. "Oh, yase, Buzz Bawker's deal, I think we voted for that last week."

"*Voted* faw it! I don't believe I understand. Do you realize what that me-uns? If hife the city were tawn down we would have to completely revise *Cooking Through Mobile Stree-its*." As president of the Preservation Society, Mrs. Balleriel had supervised the writing of the celebrated cookbook spotlighting the homes of prominent members.

"Gotta make some sacrifices for growth," Mr. Balleriel noted absently. He plopped the open catalogue on his stomach again as though on a lectern.

"But Hawmswuith, they would bulldoze *ouwuh* house."

Mr. Balleriel looked surprised. "Well, I hadn't thought of that."

"They couldn't possibly mean us, Mamacita y Papá," Ernest reassured them. "Think of the history behind this house. Why, this is where I gave my first coronation supper."

Ernest had been very precocious at seven. Mrs. Balleriel remembered how cute he was in his little tails that Mardi Gras, directing all the other confused little boys and girls to their place cards. Mrs. Balleriel's cheeks quivered with dignity as she made a pronouncement.

"Suitainly not. What could I have been thinking? They couldn't me-un *us*."

CHAPTER 30

Putting Charleston in its Place

The Mobile Preservation Society included one of the most remarkable battalions of ladies of the first water to be found anywhere in the city. They were firmly, though vaguely, committed to the concept of historic preservation, even if, being natives and ergo apolitical, they were not always terribly effective in that goal. Over the decades eighty percent of the city's choicest structures listed on the Historic American Buildings Survey in the 1930s had been demolished, plus huge neighborhoods. If Mobile had been able to retain what was still standing as late as 1965, it would have been famous as one of the most charming cities of the United States. But the worst had come to pass.

Occasionally the society had protested over this or that specific building, and usually lost. At least they had been able to hang on to their museum on Palmetto Street and sell pralines in the gift shop. The museum was an antebellum brick town house with cast iron balconies that had been left to them in a will.

They also held monthly meetings in the very same place that were well publicized in the *Mobile Herald-Item*. No one was pictured more often in the newspaper than Rose Parkhurst Jameston Balleriel, who had run the society with an iron hand for the last ten years.

In addition to many upper-caste members of the social glitteratti, the Preservation Society contained a large contingent of somewhat elderly ladies of respectable but modest origin who served cake and poured coffee in the background, such as Miss Hattie and Miss Alice Robinson. After that came "the new blood" of young members, usually from Ce Ce Anne and Ernest's social Young Set, who were generally held harmless in the wings.

The week after Mrs. Balleriel first became aware of efforts to demolish half the city, she was surprised to get a call from the Houston developer asking for permission to speak to the group that afternoon. For several weeks Todd had been making appearances all over town to drum up support and forestall opposition.

Permission was granted, but Mrs. Balleriel called the officers together shortly before the meeting to inform them of the change in the agenda, while Todd waited in a side room. It took some little time to clear up just whom Todd represented. Mrs. Balleriel repeated what Todd had said about working with Buzz Barker, then inquired, "But who is this Buzz Bawker puison?" When it was pointed out that he was the mayor, she asked, "Is that so? Of what city?" Stirling McVay was the only local politician with any social background. Quite naturally, she had never heard of Barker.

They took so long that a surge of impatience swept the "Opium"-scented sea of furs and smart frocks in the Paloma C. Hammerstein Memorial Meeting Room. Members launched into elaborate stories of the month's scandals that were normally not begun until after the program. A low roar shook the room. Many members began casting restless eyes at the long serving table where the refreshment committee was arranging an array of cakes, dips, canapés, and oyster concoctions in chafing dishes.

But all thoughts of a rush at the food died when the doors suddenly flew open: Mrs. Harmsworth Billingsley Balleriel!

"Her mothuh was a Pawkhuist!!" several in the crowd were heard to whisper. They stepped back in awe as she strode through, swishing a page of folded notes nonchalantly in her hand like a scepter. There were gasps at her latest ensemble, a billowy mass of summery "rose" silk, battened down with several gorgeous brooches. In her wake trailed Mrs. Chasuble Hedgemont, Mrs. Marmeduke LeVerne, and Mrs. Stallings Hammerstein IV, stepping in single file like priestesses of Isis. Todd shuffled in the rear like a self-conscious caboose.

For the Preservation Society's monthly lecture on Mobile culture, Mrs. H. Sloane Wolfe gave a talk on her expensive collection of Boehm porcelain bird sculptures. There were detailed accounts of her trips to various dealers and interior decorators around the country to buy them, lovingly detailed information on the whopping purchase prices, and a few art appreciation observations as well: "I think the blue jay looks just grind with gricecloth and Tiffany limeps." Though a native of Huntsville, Roberta Wolfe had at least acquired the Mobilian short "A."

Mrs. Balleriel listened with half-closed eyelids. She was well aware of the fact that Roberta Wolfe was after her position as president of the Preservation Society in order to make up for the irreparable faux pas of being born outside of the city. Nevertheless, when she had finished, Mrs. Balleriel rose to make some very gracious remarks of appreciation.

"I'm sure we all luined something new this ife-ternoon. Robuita Wolfe is such a sweethawt. She has been a faithful member faw so long that we almost fawget that she's *not* a native."

For the historic preservation segment of the program, Arlene Morganton, who was also not one of Mrs. Balleriel's favorites, gave a slide presentation on architectural appreciation. It demonstrated how the Morganton family had thoughtfully reused old mantles and stained glass windows from the numerous historic buildings they had demolished downtown. Mrs. Balleriel cleared her throat loudly when she came to the Morganton family mansion, recently demolished a few doors down from the Balleriels on Government Street for a car wash.

Due to the change in program, the business segment of the meeting had to be postponed, rather to everyone's relief. The building committee had proposed tearing down several insignificant structures on the museum grounds: an 1850s workman's cottage that had been built by the original owners as rental property, and also a row of 1870s cabins where the black servants for the main house had lived. The committee argued that the structures were just a bunch of old shacks and certainly did not express any kind of history that anybody was interested in. But some of those new Yankee women that had joined lately, always so literal-minded and nit-picking, had been making trouble saying that the Preservation Society should actually *preserve* them.

When Ted Todd got up to speak he was visibly nervous. Surely if anyone in the city would oppose him it would be this troupe of historically-minded and powerfully-connected ladies. He thought of Buzz Barker's advice to stick to the text, and when chatting, talk about nothing but how he admired old Southern society, the more flattering the better. Todd was not sure he would be able to think of anything to say on that topic, but since he had occasionally heard things about Charleston, he decided to use that as his frame of reference.

The logic of Todd's talk was vintage Buzz Barker. "Now if there's one thing we wouldn't want to do without your input, ladies, is change the character of your basic Old South socio-urban infrastructure. We may have to tear down every building east of I-65, but the bottom line is—and we're in a receptivity posture to any feedback—is that we don't want to impact your traditional tourist-wise Greek Revival attraction base." He outlined a new feature to his plan, a two block replica "Old Mobile" street to be constructed near the Mississippi line with cobblestones and gas lanterns.

But Ted Todd might as well have been lecturing on the use of yak butter in Outer Mongolia, for the members were getting tired of the program. There was adjusting of necklaces and examining of fingernails all over the room. When Todd was finished, he was surprised to receive a patter of applause and then see the entire audience burst from their chairs and fall upon the refreshments.

Mrs. Balleriel walked up to Todd near the rum cake as Arlene Morganton and Roberta Wolfe were telling him about their enthusiasm for his development scheme, which certainly rendered the building committee's controversy extremely moot. For once, he thought happily, he really had these people figured and eating out of his hand. Mrs. Wolfe could think of many interior decorating possibilities. Mrs. Morganton even had some suggestions for the "Old Mobile" street that would recapture the demolished city:

"Why don't you make it look like Williamsburg instead? It's so much cuter than what we've got here."

"We could be tour guides and dress up in darling colonial dresses with Dolly Madison caps," Roberta Wolfe chimed in. "And we'd have a precious gift shop with scented kine-dles and pewter dishware."

Mrs. Balleriel remained silent. Though she never thought for a moment that the development would affect her own house, she reflected grimly on the troublesome revisions she might have to make to the cookbook. Seeing her reserve, Todd remembered Barker's advice and attempted a few blundering compliments that would secure him the permanent enmity of one of the dowager empresses of Mobile society:

"It's such a thrill to be here and see all these neat ole fine Southern families. You know when I was growing up in Dayton, everybody all over town was just always talking about how you've really got some fine ones down here, just like Charleston. We used to talk about it all the time."

"Really?" Mrs. Balleriel's curiosity was piqued, even though in her eyes Ted Todd occupied a place near the chimpanzee on the Great Chain of Being. "I'm glide to hear that we set a good example. But you should say 'Chawlston is like Mobile.'" Charleston was one of the few cities to which she extended diplomatic recognition, but exact terminology was of the essence.

Todd, not noticing the thin ice, battered his Elvis Presley eyelashes. "Yeah, sure, people are always saying how Charleston has all that high society."

"Oh yase?" Mrs. Balleriel said somewhat coolly. "Is Chawlston social? I don't doubt that they have a number of prominent puisons, but . . ."

"Are you kidding? I saw this article once that said it's the ritziest place in the South."

This went rather to the quick, as it had the unfortunate implication that some people in some situations might conceivably play second fiddle.

Mrs. Balleriel could not believe the obscenity she had just heard uttered in her presence. "I *beg* yo *pawdon*," she growled in an ominous alto. Forks froze on their plates all around. Mrs. Balleriel revoked diplomatic recognition of Charleston on the spot.

"It's one thing to know a little geography, but ife-ter all, do we have any Chawlstonians in the Mawdi Graw cote? Aw they related? Who aw they? If you icek me, they're just a bit too too. Eating benne seeds, and gallivanting along those seawalls and carrying on. As faw all that Hugue-not blood, why do you think they kicked them out of Frynce in the fuist place? Obviously they were undesirables. They don't hold a *kine-dle*." This man must be stopped, she realized. An icicle smile of perfect courtesy passed over her face as she said, "Thank you so very much faw your little tawk, Mr. . . . sir. That was mawvelously infawmative."

The billowy dress drew anchor and set sail, brooches ablaze. Ted Todd was completely at a loss to explain what had just happened. He wondered what Mrs. Balleriel's possible opposition might mean to him. But Mrs. Morganton and Mrs. H. Sloane Wolfe lingered to hatch plans.

CHAPTER 31

Passing Ships in the Night

Early one evening during the midsummer thunderstorm season, a solitary figure wearing a soiled trench coat, 3-D glasses, a baseball cap, and carrying an empty Gallo burgundy gallon jug picked its way among the puddles and cockleburrs of South Royal Street. Huge claps of thunder and flashes of lightning gave an eerie monumentality to the remote waterfront scene. The smell of tar blew in from the river. A gasoline truck rumbled past and completely splattered the vagrant with muddy water.

"Goddamn!" he shouted with sexagenarian vigor. "How on uith did she think of this? The next time I'm going to say where we meet."

Many an average citizen digesting his supper in another part of the city would have been shocked, perhaps disillusioned for life, to learn that the sodden wino tottering through the rain was financial titan H. Sloane Wolfe.

At first McCorquodale had implied that Wolfe's insistence that they meet in secret was the product of a philistine mind-set. But lately, Wolfe reflected, she had come to like the idea, and showed a distressing creativity in arranging secret rendezvous at out-of-the-way places.

Wolfe's costume had arrived at the bank that afternoon in a cardboard box, together with a map and instructions to come alone (what else?) and on foot to the Frosty Stop Shore Leave Lounge.

Wolfe couldn't believe his eyes when he got to an abandoned-looking hovel with a wooden awning and posts over the sidewalk and a Coca Cola sign that dangled in the wind. "Gee minetti, they'll find us muiduhed and floatin in the rivuh."

He gritted his teeth and charged through the half-open door, little aware that a strange bedraggled female carrying a shopping bag was crouching behind a dripping oleander across the street and watching him enter.

The musty old bar was empty except for a table of the bored oriental seamen who were always wandering about downtown looking for entertainment. They looked up sullenly at the wet mogul from their card game. Wolfe set down his wine jug apologetically, then noticed McCorquodale in a dark corner gesturing to him.

She was wearing her *Heart of Darkness* outfit, with jodhpur pants and leather boots, and she flourished a long riding crop. "Sit down. Say nothing," she whispered.

"Oh come on, shuguh doll, we don't need to be *that* careful."

"Isn't this a dream? We could be in Marseilles, Lisbon, a tiny fishermen's tavern on the coast of Chile."

"Are you crazy? We could be in jail, too. How do you know about this joint?"

"Exploration, darling. I used to get around. Can you believe they only have Budweiser? One would expect something quainter." A fat, red-bearded bartender in greasy overalls plopped an open can of beer unasked in front of Wolfe, then collected on the spot. "Imagine it's absinthe," McCorquodale said when he left. "Now tell me something mysterious."

The rain pounded on the tin roof as Wolfe told his ever-attentive favorite the weekly top secrets of his banking empire. The candle that McCorquodale pulled out of her purse and lit on a saucer for added atmosphere had burned down low by the time he remembered to mention that he had been approached again by Ted Todd for the first time since their awkward encounter during the Athelstan Club Domino Ball.

"That piss ant that called me 'Horatio' wants me to stawt pushin this development of his. Said the bank could make millions from the bond issues. Wants to fill in the bay for Volkswagen and tear down the city for a shopping mall. He said he couldn't do it without my suppote."

"That doesn't sound *remotely* postmodern," McCorquodale observed scornfully. "What did you tell him?"

"I sent him packin. He said I couldn't build my skyscraper where I

want it because of a Biblical amusement pawk on the rivuh. He wanted
me to put my offices in his damn Supermall." The construction of the
soaring Wolfe Alabama Tower was to be Wolfe's small reward to himself
for an industrious career. "The bank can make millions on somethin else,
but a man in my postion needs at least sixty stories to hold his head high."

"You have a healthy self-image, Sloane. Perhaps that's the secret of
your magnetism."

The banking magnate was pleased. He cleared his throat modestly,
but put his 3-D glasses back on.

"I've gotta go. Robuita will kill me if I stay out any longer." The
more active Mrs. H. Sloane Wolfe became in the Mobile Preservation
Society, the more difficult she grew. McCorquodale insisted on staying
in order to meditate in these propitious surroundings.

The mention of the Houston developer had cast a slight shadow in
her mind. McCorquodale sensed once again a quiet scurrying in the
distance, a pattern of busy activities just barely visible out of the corner
of the eye. Of course there were always stupid developments on the
horizon; maybe this was just another one and it wouldn't amount to a
row of beans. As long as she could remember, people in town had
constantly been in an uproar over one stupidity or another. Somebody
was always chopping down a five-hundred-year-old oak, or tearing down
a block of beautiful old houses to widen a street (and then the plans
would change and the street would not be widened) or building a
highway over a French or Indian archeological site, or banning confetti
at Mardi Gras, or trying to reroute the parades into a logical square down
wide, ugly streets. Come to think of it, the worst usually *did* happen. She
thought of the orangutan mayor and that developer humanoid. They
seemed to be planning something unusually unpleasant. Oh well, Sloane
would put a stop to that. Sloane was powerful. Sloane was making great
strides in the cultivation of a postmodern consciousness. Sloane would
dash them to pieces.

Nevertheless, the pattern was very striking. Everything rare and
beautiful seemed to attract some Tartar who wanted to destroy it or
rationalize it. It was as though there were some sinister organization of

philistines all working together. Or perhaps modernists? Could such a central group really exist? No that's absurd, McCorquodale concluded. She was well aware that usually there was all too rational an explanation. Somebody was getting a kickback or a cut. She had heard of old houses being condemned as fire hazards because the pertinent bureaucrat had a silent partner in the demolition business who wanted to get the job and salvage the bricks and old timber. That was probably just the kind of thing that was happening with the Cro-Magnon developer and the mayor.

"Let's meet Friday," Wolfe said, interrupting her thoughts. He had drained his beer and was standing up. "But look here shuguh, I wanta pick the next place. Maybe Pensacola again."

"Oh all right," McCorquodale sighed, "but be creative."

The ragged female who had watched Wolfe enter had taken shelter under the canopy and was obviously surprised to see Wolfe come out so early. With no time to hide, she leaned lewdly against the wall, both hands clasped coyly on her shopping bag. Wolfe glanced at her and shuddered. "What am I doin heuh?!" He charged down the road into the storm, baseball cap pulled down low.

Wolfe would have had considerably more to say had he known that the shopping bag lady was his own employee and sole heiress to the fortune of the Stanton Steamship Corporation, Ce Ce Anne Stanton. Ce Ce Anne had had an awful time of it ever since that terrible night at the Port City Players when she realized that Wolfe's secret girlfriend was Eddie's good friend. In just a few seconds she had seen the one, big story of the decade flying away from her on little Cupid wings.

As long as it was only a question of covering up her own whereabouts in the presence of Helmut when she had seen Wolfe and McCorquodale together, there had still been some hope of finding a way to let the cat out of the bag and be the sole dispenser of inside information without getting mauled herself. But now how could she focus the gossip spotlight of the whole town on Eddie's new friend without possibly compromising Ernest in the process? How could she betray Eddie?

Nevertheless, delicate thoughts of high treason did indeed enter her mind for several days following the play. But always in the background was the awful thought that Daddy might find out about her and Helmut. And then what if the McCorquodale woman remembered seeing Ce Ce Anne dancing on top of the Hubba Hubba bar like a two-bit road whore? Ce Ce Anne's hair practically stood on end as she imagined a gossip vengeance-taking and bloodletting worthy of an Icelandic saga. All her instincts were ringing a ten-bell fire alarm. "Don't mess with the McCorquodale woman," they told her.

There was no way to tell.

In her grief Ce Ce Anne listened to enthusiastic accounts from Eddie about the blond woman and artistic goings-on. Her curiosity grew. Who was this person who produced plays that were banned by the city? In the pure, disinterested spirit of the investigative reporter, and fueled by a certain excess energy she had felt ever since Helmut had steamed away for Caracas shortly after Mardi Gras, Ce Ce Anne decided that she had to meet this McCorquodale woman and find out herself.

McCorquodale was not accustomed to showing surprise, but when the shopping bag lady dripped across the dirty wood floor and took a seat at her table, she let out a particularly big puff from her Tiparillo. The sailors gabbled loudly in Chinese when Ce Ce Anne ripped off her soggy wig and sunglasses, revealing the pert short cut of her black hair, a cut she shared with all the other members of the Junior League Committee on Urban Affairs.

"Who *are* you?"

Thunder crashed outside but McCorquodale was equal to the suspense of the moment. "*Quelle question.* I am beautiful; I am intelligent; I am here to lead us into postmodernism."

"Is that by Vidal Sassoon? I've heard of him." The fat bartender plopped down a beer.

"*Darling*, it's a complete revolution in thought and action, the shuffling off of the restrictive coils of modernity."

"Oh," Ce Ce Anne said blankly, "I didn't take that course when I was at Bama. Listen, I saw your play and it was *just precious*, but if you icek me you're going about this thing all wrong."

"I have noticed that Mobile has been slower to ignite than I expected," McCorquodale confided.

"*Sure*, now if you woint to make something work, you've got to get the 'right' people involved. *Just count oin me*, I'll get them there." She thought for a second. "I know, we'll have a do. I'll invite *everybody*."

"A 'do'? Is that something like a benefit show? Like for the March of Dimes?"

"Something in that category. I could easily organize one."

It was obviously a sign of the benign workings of fate that this person, who looked vaguely familiar, had sought her out. McCorquodale decided to listen, but was growing curious herself. "And who are you?" she asked.

"I'm Ce Ce Ine Stine-ton. I was a Kappa Kappa Gamma," she said simply.

"So what does that mean?"

"You don't *know*?" Ce Ce Anne had never been so amazed. "Sometimes you get the feeling that the world is a real big place."

Boat horns sounded forlornly as they conferred in the remote bar until early in the morning.

CHAPTER 32

McCorquodale Meets the Young Set

The Hubba Hubba Club was chosen as the naturally Bohemian setting of the postmodern "do" for what Ce Ce Anne and Ernest referred to as the "Young Set." "It will be just too grind," Ce Ce Anne predicted; "they love theme parties."

Though Ernest had in the past always been scared to be seen at the shabby bar, he insisted on bringing to bear all his formidable talent in the drawing up of invitations lists when Ce Ce Anne told him that the place was suddenly "in." But what *was* the Young Set? To hear Ernest talk, it was something like the flower of Southern youth on the playing fields of Eton.

McCorquodale intimidated him somewhat in these first encounters with her voluptuous loftiness, and he quickly grew shy about expounding his theories to her. One minute she was a million miles away, the next minute she trained a blinding floodlight of attention on him that gave him the feeling she saw to depths that he was not so very sure he wanted seen. Facing that quiet, self-possessed Mona Lisa smile, he found himself oddly garrulous, rattling on like an alarm clock.

Ce Ce Anne went through a period of similar discomfort during their initial meetings to plan the do, and could not quite decide what to make of McCorquodale. One day at the Carpenter Gothic cottage she found McCorquodale staring at her all of a sudden as though reading a wall of hieroglyphics. It was as if she had really noticed her for the first time.

"You know you really do look very familiar."

"It's a small world," Ce Ce Anne said shakily, and adjusted a little gold earbob.

"I just had this flash of you as a palace fan dancer. How very odd."

Ce Ce Anne responded nothing at all to this. Could McCorquodale possibly know Antoinette McCrae? She gritted her teeth and battened down the hatches, waiting for what was sure to come.

"I know it! The Hubba Hubba Club! You were the one strutting so very brazenly up on top of that bar. Tonya and I were quite unanimous in thinking that you must be a professional. And believe me, darling, Tonya knows."

With a heavy heart, Ce Ce Anne looked at McCorquodale, but instead of the expected expression of smug glee, she was startled to see a serious face of thoughtful appreciation that grew more and more enthusiastic. "It was sublime! I was particularly struck by a kind of polyvalent lewdness in your work. A coded reference to Gypsy Rose Lee or the early brothel days of Eva Perón, I couldn't discern quite which. Really, dear child, it was a thing of beauty!"

Ce Ce Anne was so surprised that she could not think of anything to say. She shifted around and giggled. "Why, thank you," she finally managed.

"Oh no, darling. It is I who thank *YOU!*"

Ce Ce Anne sensed that her stock had risen dramatically in the international postmodern movement. This was further confirmed when in the course of the conversation her other performance came out, her contemporary dance engagement with the Committee on Urban Affairs at the Santa Claus Society ball in December. Enjoying McCorquodale's approval was very much like lying in a hammock under a delicious tropical sun and sipping rum punches out of a pineapple. Ce Ce Anne soon found that she could chat quite uninhibitedly with her, but it must be reported that Ce Ce Anne did not brood overmuch about her acceptance as an avant-garde agitator with "not a single philistine bone in your body," as McCorquodale pronounced. Some people are destined by life always to be insiders.

Ernest took somewhat longer to find his footing, and in the interim sought an alternative audience. For hours on end he filled Tonya's ears with his theories of social life in Mobile.

"It's just something you can't describe," Ernest explained, avoiding false modesty. "We simply *are*. The Young Set does everything right. They know how to dress. They know how to act. They know me."

"Well don't that beat all." Tonya listened thoughtfully, sensing a new market. "I kinda had my heart set on gettin the trucker trade down here, but I reckon there ain't no flies on their money neither. Shoot, in my business you cain't be too picky."

By the time the steaming Saturday afternoon in July rolled around, even McCorquodale's curiosity was growing. She wondered if her years as a young businesswoman and postmodern theorist had not isolated her somewhat. "What mysterious and cosmopolitan people is this hidden away in the bosom of the city?" she wondered. "It sounds rather like Alexandria during the twenties."

She was unusually exacting in redecorating the stale, icebox, twilight interior of the hermetic bar. The broken, plywood-backed plate glass of the front window was replaced, but Tonya insisted that it be opaque violet glass so that passing motorists could not see in and "get a free eyeful." A small group of the usual winos and a mop-headed man with a flashing set of white teeth watched with interest as they took down all the nude bunny calendars and hung anti-logical Venetian blinds on the blank walls, with color Xerox renderings of plastic dolls taped to them randomly. A huge papier-mâché fossil sculpture of a semi-buried Cuisinart was placed in the middle of the floor.

For months now Tonya had been wondering what had become of that wild woman who danced on top of her bar during Mardi Gras and had been hanging out with that foreign dude, rough trade if ever she'd seen it. So that when one day in walked the girl side by side with McCorquodale to begin preparations for their do, Tonya had some difficulty believing their explanations that the chick was actually heiress to a merchant marine shipping line. "Different strokes for different folks," she would mutter skeptically, and every so often would try to talk Ce Ce Anne into signing a contract to do a bit of daytime striptease with light mopping duties.

At length, the great day of the do dawned. When the guests started arriving Eddie had the New Wave thud of *Dépêche-Mode* booming over the sound system. But instead of the expected crowd of twenty-first-century Beautiful People, McCorquodale was taken aback to see a totally familiar collection of young lawyers and young businessmen, many of them curiously pale and soft-looking, plus numerous socialites she had glimpsed over the years in Mrs. Watkins' shop, and when she had gone with her dates to parties and the balls.

A bubbling and scintillating began to swirl through the bar. Young women in snazzy party dresses who had known each other all their lives and had seen each other at dinner parties two or three nights before waved and beckoned and flew across the bar to seize an arm or a wrist. "Mary Louise!" "Hillary! It's so *super* to see you." "Corinne!" "You just look so scrumptious!"

Despite these cries of imminent epiphany and love fest, a curiously cold atmosphere pervaded. Cocked heads and tight half smiles with slightly protruding jaws suggested the facial expressions of a person who knows he is being watched, and presumably admired, but pretends that he does not. Like rival teams at a theater competition, everyone down to the last guest arrived neatly paired off with a spouse or date, and not least among the couples were Ce Ce Anne and Ernest, arm in arm, weaving and circulating brightly through their natural habitat. It was Ernest's idea to require the men to wear white summer tuxedos, and he was ecstatic at the ritzy effect.

But natty though they were, they were far from the international jet set standards of McCorquodale in her severe purple makeup on fair cheeks, pillbox hat, and flowing cape over a metallic Milanese pants ensemble. She was standing all by herself in a corner of the bar, one hand on elbow and a perfect filbert-shaped fingernail on the corner of her mouth, observing, when Ernest came up.

"Is *that* what you mean by the 'Young Set'?" McCorquodale asked, deflated.

"Yes, how does it feel to meet the uppermost skim of the crème de la crème?" said Ernest.

"Darling, I'm afraid we have our work cut out for us. How do we lead a postmodern revolt when they're not even modern yet?"

McCorquodale was getting desperate signals from Tonya, who was standing with a bottle of fabulous André champagne in hand, locked in conversation with a deeply suntanned young woman with wide vacuous eyes named Claudia Scattergood.

"Get this chick offa me, I've gotta move the liquor," Tonya whispered, and fled to pour. The radiant post-deb did not even stop talking. She was telling about the latest social phenomenon, Young Set tarot card groups.

"It's so nice because you already know everybody and you can just tune right in on the same wavelength. Lyest month we met at Ellen Stroughtovan's getaway in the Bahamas. She's so psychic."

McCorquodale had often observed that members of this upper caste social stratum always used both first name and all-important surname in referring to people in their circles, even when talking to good friends about their mutual friends—never just plain old "India" or "Chilton," but "India Sark" or "Chilton Brisbane"—and when they were talking to strangers they felt no need for any further explanation of the person indicated. But moved by a sense of mischief, she inquired, "Who is Ellen Stroughtavan?"

"Oh you know, Vivian Billingsley's husband's sistuh. Anyway, she's so inspiring. When Carol Ortega lost her emerald earrings, Ellen Stroughtovan got us to just sit down and join hineds for a moment of meditation while she laid the cards. Then right ife-ter the maid brought us our lunch, Carol Ortega found them oin her jewelry box. We just knew it had to be a sign."

Next to her McCorquodale heard a recently married young matron who was not even pregnant yet describe to the last detail the complete Feltman Brothers wardrobe she planned to buy for her firstborn through the first three years. Her interlocutor reported a "Come As Your Favorite Fantasy" party thrown by Rowen and Cynthia Hedgemont at Perdido Bay. Buffet dinner for two hundred and fifty; *Maskman Mongo and the Tabulations* in from Biloxi; and David Bixwell, Karen Bixwell's young florist cousin who looked like a boy scout and was already doing half the nice parties in town, had dotted the lawn down to the beach with tent canopies and flowery nooks. Carlotta Belasco won the first prize wishing wand costumed in fishnet stockings as a Marseilles streetwalker. "Such a cute idea. But then maybe it wasn't really a costume," McCorquodale overheard.

In another group subtle barbs were being exchanged on the merits of several private and church-sponsored twelve-year schools. "Y'all are so smawt to stawt Stewart off in the first grade at St. Mawk's, it's so much better scholastically. I don't know why we're sending Billy to Mobile Military, it's nothing but a social club." Correctly translated this comment meant, "Mobile Military is prestigious," and, "St. Mark's is for computer drudges, bookworms, and science fair winners."

A group of young men stood sipping their drinks and flexing their legs with one hand in their pocket, talking about property values on the bay and gulf, and about catamaran, sailboat and yacht outings. Tonya's redheaded and fleshy form darted everywhere, selling Long Island Tea for all she was worth.

Despite a vague foreboding, McCorquodale retired to change into her costume for the revolutionary postmodern performance art. She and Eddie had worked it out by reading back copies of Eddie's beloved *After Dark* magazine and checking out books on dance from the public library. "Girl, it's gone tear their tits off. It's beyond Isadora Duncan, beyond Baryshnikov!" Eddie rejoiced. "They'll be rippin out their hair and chunkin their babies into the ring."

But when they emerged in their broken prism costumes, bare arms and legs peeping from the hard angles jutting to a point to one side and above their heads, the conversations had reached such a shrieking pitch that no one even noticed them. The winos and the mop-headed man were holding their ears. Only a deafening blast of the Zimbabwe Zezuru drum recording was able to command the attention of the three hundred or so elite.

For a while it appeared that Eddie was right. All stared in amazement as the two prisms slung themselves around the floor. McCorquodale took soaring leaps; Eddie balanced on his back and boyishly twiddled his small feet at the ceiling.

But then a tragic error occurred. Social arbitress Antoinette McCrae mistook the performance for aerobic dancing, which she was learning at the YMCA, and, always preferring to be in the center of attention, she joined the dance. Naturally the other members of the Committee on Urban Affairs, who had imitated Antoinette in wearing Princess Di white stockings and pulling their hair back in a tight chignon, felt obliged to jump out on the floor immediately and lie on their backs for rhythmic leg-raisers. They pursed their lips in frowns of concentration.

Tonya's business acumen was beginning to have its effect. Somebody changed the tape to *Booker T. and the MGs*, and the situation deteriorated when Percy Louellen III, a burly young leader of the Chamber of Commerce, fell down and started doing the alligator. Cries of "Par-TY!" and "Do the Deke sway!" pierced the thudding drumbeat.

Tonya surveyed the scene with rare satisfaction. The cash register had been ringing all afternoon. "Man, these rich cats may be a little weird," she reflected, "but with customers like this who needs the truckers?" It was at that historic moment that Tonya de Luxe, who never gave *anything* away for free, decided to show her patrons a token of her appreciation. She jumped up on the bar and kicked and turned her ample body with short quick movements like a slap on the face. Items of lacy black clothing sailed through the air.

McCorquodale and Eddie sat down in dismay. "Eddie, darling, perhaps this is not the path to the postmodern dawn." But he was too disappointed to answer. He looked around for Ernest, but the respectable young banker had dragged Ce Ce Anne out the door when Tonya's thrashing breasts achieved full liberation before a frantic avant-garde crowd. They were not the only ones to leave. The man with the thick hair and high water pants hitched up to his chest who had been sitting among the winos also departed to make another report to Western Hills Baptist.

CHAPTER 33

Demand for Action

During the week following the postmodern do there was a chain reaction of consultation and strategy sessions in various parts of the city.

As McCorquodale and the other organizers of the experimental event were soon to learn, Orville Tidwood, minister of the Western Hills Baptist Church, had witnessed the entire evening hidden in the corner with a group of winos. He made a scandalized report to church leaders the following night.

The group knew nothing of the profound postmodern theoretical underpinnings of the event. After hearing the report, they assumed, oddly enough, that the young social elite present at the infamous bar was merely a group of crazed hedonists who would stop at nothing in their pursuit of pleasure.

The church leaders were especially outraged that McCorquodale and Tonya had performed dance numbers similar to their excesses in the drama *Radical Chic*. They made Tidwood describe again and again how Tonya had slowly discarded items of clothing unnecessary to her choreographic concept.

It so happened that this latest witches' sabbath of Secular Humanists came at a delicate moment in the growth trajectory of Western Hills Baptist. The computer statistics breakdown for last Sunday compiled by the church statistician was very discouraging. Membership transfers from other churches up only 2.9 percent over the same week last year. Accepting Jesus As Your Personal Savior up only 1.76 percent. Sunday School attendance up 0.23 percent. Tithes down 0.03 percent! They had only collected $148,664.88! And this on a Sunday when he had given a landmark sermon on the church building program, "Build, and Build Some More." At this rate how were they ever going to build the new

12,000-seat sanctuary, much less realize the long range plans for a Christian television station and a giant world-league football stadium that would serve the entire denomination nationwide, Brother Tidwood's pet dream.

To make matters worse, competition from Midtown Baptist was getting hotter. A statistics profile smuggled out of a Midtown deacons meeting showed that Midtown was making significant inroads in the young adults market, a trend that guaranteed them continued growth in tithes and the pre-adult divisions as well. It took only simple arithmetic to see that within five or six years Midtown might catch up and actually become bigger than Western Hills.

Tidwood knew that his leadership was on the line. It was up to him to find a new cause that Western Hills could champion, something that would bring moral and spiritual revival throughout the city. The alternative "The Bible is FUN! Fair" that he had organized last February as a rival event to Mardi Gras had been a dismal personal flop. The church bus fleet had succeeded in picking up only a few dozen teenagers roaming the streets, as most of the ones they approached said that their parents had told them not to accept rides from strangers. The little children at the fair started crying when they realized that there were no parades. Tidwood felt silly in his clown costume, and they had gotten minimal PR out of the event in the local media.

It was true that last week his trumpet call to the flock had successfully rallied several hundred people at city hall in order to stop a small oriental restaurant ten blocks down the street from the church from obtaining a liquor license. Staring, rather shell-shocked, at the multitudinous hosts itching to do battle, the middle-aged Vietnamese immigrant couple who ran the restaurant explained in frail English that their largely professional clientele wanted to drink wine with their meals, but this argument was easily quashed when Tidwood pointed out that the restaurant could become a breeding ground for teenage alcoholism and drunken motorcycle hoods who would threaten their congregation. Several businessmen, contractors, and bankers on the zoning board who did business with the church saw his point. Yet even though the liquor license was

clobbered in the bud by their blitz raid, Tidwood could not help feeling
that somehow the old evangelical zing was just not in it.

Could it be that Western Hills Baptist had reached a growth plateau?
Could it be quite simply that the market was saturated? For some time he
had been toying with the idea of hiring a major advertising firm and
launching a new soul-saving campaign with catchy slogans. But something told him that this new outrage committed by the blond woman
and her Secular Humanist minions could lead to a far more electrifying
crusade.

Tidwood winced as he tried to imagine what that crazy group was up
to at that very moment, that nutty, overbearing blond woman, that
tough stripper, the fruity boy and all the followers and money they
seemed to attract. He thought of all the lunatic groups he saw on TV
every night. They were probably making weird MTV videos, or suing
some town to stop them from exhibiting a manger scene at Christmas.
Then they would sue the judge for having people swear on a Bible, quite
possibly at the instructions of some sinister one-world government
movement with secret headquarters in some European city. They were
probably going through children's library books with magnifying glasses
to make sure there was no mention of the word "God" that would
supposedly violate the separation of church and state. Maybe they were
New Agers. And to think what their lifestyle must be! Those nuts must
be dealt with.

On the following Thursday, Western Hills Baptist and a whole
assortment of fundamentalist groups and conservative political action
committees jointly held a protest rally to demand action. As usual,
Mayor Barker leapt at the chance to address these religious/secular
organizations with carefully cultivated political connections.

In the wake of the shocking bacchanal, Barker proposed measures so
tough that even his stony-faced audience, which included many immigrants to Mobile from upstate, blanched at the prospect. Touching on
many chords close to the hearts of his listeners, he said that the general
moral plight of the city had sunk down to cesspool depths, "if you factor
in all the variables in terms of the real bottom line." An obvious example

was the revolting celebration of ancient pre-Christian holidays like Valentine's Day and Halloween, even in the public schools. It was a theme he allowed to lie fallow when speaking to other audiences around town. He proceeded to paint a picture of seedy downtown pleasure domes that suggested first-hand investigation.

The solution was simple: bulldoze all of the inner city. He began to tell them about the Houston developer's plan.

In contrast to the playboy image he cultivated for late-night sorties to the singles bars on Airport Boulevard, Barker wore a black business suit and combed his salt-and-pepper hair straight back in Brillcream waves.

"In terms of where you're coming from," he told them, "I don't have any problem with upgrading our image as a quality high-virtue type regional center. I know you're probably thinking, 'Gee, we've got to cost out a ballpark estimate in terms of hard-earned dollars and cents out of the taxpayer's pocketbook.' But that's like comparing apples and oranges."

Somehow from the rhetorical excelsior the audience was able to extract silver flatware of Utopian vision. It was a blend of fundamentalism and the newly-acquired suburban lifestyle of his listeners. Without downtown, Mobile, the first truly disposable city of the Sunbelt, would have no hobos, no strange people, and less sin. All the prosperous people working at the Volkswagen factory on the site of the drained bay would be able to buy wall-size television screens to watch family programming on Christian cable TV. The most fundamental right of the Sunbelt citizen, a parking place next to his destination, would be guaranteed with miles of parking lot around the proposed Supermall, and by scattering the county courthouse and other institutions over hundreds of square miles of developed area. The "Six Flags Over Jesus" amusement park to be located next to the river was the final clincher.

An awed hush spread through the crowd when Barker announced that the gigantic statue of Jesus planned for the park would actually straddle the river. Furthermore, in keeping with the "masculine Christ" concept of the artists' renderings for the project, a nationally televised golf tournament would be held for renowned golf celebrities, and the winning pro, in addition to collecting a whopping cash prize, would pose as the model for Christ. Barker drew a cheering standing ovation.

Certain Baptist and fundamentalist churches and other groups began agitating the very next day against the Hubba Hubba Club, and pulling their political strings for the gigantic development.

Meanwhile on Conti Street, the Hubba Hubba Club underwent a sudden flowering which, like nature's first green, was all too fleeting. For several days it actually appeared that the Young Set had chosen the notorious dive as *the* select hangout for people in the know.

Ce Ce Anne began advising Tonya on ways to make the Hubba Hubba "simply a dream" for a Young Set happy hour. With things booming at the Commerce National Bank, the Liaison for Commercial Loan Concepts was spending even less time doing bank work during bank hours than before.

An art show of local watercolorists was hung on the walls with discreet price tags, and plans were formulated to replace the chairs with old park benches and pews. A small snack menu was drawn up with chablis and rosé, quiche and fried cauliflower. Tonya was advised to keep her clothes on.

Unfortunately the first happy hour came the day after Western Hills Baptist began their campaign to clean up Mobile. Initially things went as Ce Ce Anne had predicted. Young executive joggers and exercise enthusiasts, as well as the old-fashioned barstool-sitting alcoholic variety of young executive, started showing up soon after five for a Bloody Mary vitamin break. Tonya might well have been just another health-conscious socialite with her rolled headband with gold intertwining, designer sweatsuit, and blood-red toenails beckoning from bare feet precariously strapped into sloping leather pumps. Soon, however, a crowd of young country dudes attracted by the sensational news stories about the previous Saturday were pulling up in their pick-up trucks ready for a good time.

The crowds did not mix. The Young Set was shocked for several days in a row by the sight of beef jerky downed with Tonya's stock of Colt 45

Malt Liquor and Champale Champagne of Bottled Ales, and they withdrew to their private parties. And the country dudes, finding no orgies, lost interest when the Hubba Hubba stopped hitting the six-thirty news. Tonya had problems targeting her market.

Finally, on St. Anthony Street, McCorquodale lay incommunicado on her bed as though floating on the ocean of sulphur in *Paradise Lost*. It was a situation where even ruby red claret could not help.

McCorquodale entertained the gravest doubts. The postmodern movement seemed to be having only slightly more success taking root in Mobile than the Hari Krishnas. "Some evil star is against me," McCorquodale reflected. "My elite Young Set cadres would require at least thirty years in consciousness-raising boot camp before I could lead them." Satin sheets soothed her senses, sleeping blinders shut out what little light filtered through the closed balcony shutters. Only the steady clanging from Sam's Body Shop next door pierced the hum of the air conditioner to remind her of the outside world.

But Eddie succeeded in visiting her bedside after Western Hills began taking to the air waves.

"Here, darling, have some claret," McCorquodale said and poured him a glass from the ever-ready bottle on the night table. "I will not partake. My salt has lost its savor; my life is in vain."

Eddie had cut short his jazz dancing lessons after work and come running straight over to tell her the news, still in his ballet tights. "Miss Thang," he panted, "the *scandal!* Ainchoo heard about it?"

"Perhaps I *will* have a glass," McCorquodale answered. "Now don't leave anything out, it's the details that really count."

"Girl, it's *you* they're talking about. The Babdis is all over the radio and TV saying as how you done sponsored a pagan riot at the Hubba Hubba Club. And they ain't even mentioned my name," Eddie added indignantly.

"That's what they said about Lord Byron, more or less," McCorquodale scoffed, but already she was feeling better. At last some reaction! "When you are an *artiste* you must be braced for the conse-quences of fame. Yet I may be forced to turn the movement over to you,

Eddie. I don't think my delicate constitution could take more disappointments after this week."

At that very moment they heard the doorbell ring and Aunt Odilia talking to somebody. Eddie ran downstairs when she called, and returned with meaning looks and a small UPS package. "The label says 'Commerce National Bank of Mobile,'" he read with keen interest.

"They're among my greatest supporters, postmodern to the fingertips. It must be from Sloane," McCorquodale observed. It was a gorgeous sapphire and diamond choker sent to show Wolfe's concern that McCorquodale had been hidden away all week.

Summoning some last reserve of strength, McCorquodale got out of bed and walked to the mirror to try it on on her graceful neck. "I sometimes wonder if I am not Anastasia or some other lost Romanov," she commented languidly, admiring the gleam of the jewels against her pale hair. "Oh well, perhaps we will continue the struggle yet. Tomorrow is another day."

CHAPTER 34

Beauty Pageant in Saraland

Albert Tunney, entrepreneurial husband of McCorquodale's second cousin on the McCorquodale side, Brenda McCorquodale Tunney, had yet to come up with five hundred thousand dollars as his ante in Barker's development monster. To raise it he would either have to take the unpleasant step of mortgaging his statewide Monsieur Bidet of Alabama Corporation, which imported 'the prestige necessity for the Sunbelt consumer of distinction,' or find some other source of liquidity.

For months now the other source dangling before him yet always out of reach was the McCorquodale land. Ever since that afternoon in January when McCorquodale interrupted them as her grandfather was about to sign a "will" that was actually a warranty deed awarding Tunney immediate possession, Tunney had always run into the same problem. In classic country fashion Old Man Hiram required at least several hours of rambling conversation about politics, the weather, and the vegetable garden before he would get down to the business at hand. Whereas Tunney, the stressed-out, go-getting Sunbelt entrepreneur, was physically incapable of sitting still and listening longer than twenty minutes. Lately he had begun to suspect that the cagey old fox was deliberately putting off signing, and was holding Tunney hostage as a captive audience to listen to his beloved and increasingly lurid and detailed fantasies about mass hangings and shootings for thieves and robbers.

Clearly, new tactics were needed. Finally that summer Tunney hit on the stratagem of the rigged 'Little Miss Marvelous' contest to obtain Old Man Hiram's crucial signature without undergoing trial by chitchat.

It should be explained at this point that in what McCorquodale called "the premier family of Chunchula," nine-year-old Velma Lynn McCorquodale occupied a very special place as the winner of some twenty-eight child beauty pageants. She was the pride of Old Man Hiram and Mammaw Callie, though actually the daughter of their nephew Adlai, the Saraland city councilman and tactician in the furious annexation wars that raged among the numerous black or very country, Anglo-Saxon metropolises, similar to Chunchula, in the wilds of north Mobile County.

Despite her accomplishments, Velma Lynn was perhaps not the sweetest little girl in Saraland. Since her mother Tammy first entered her in the world of professional beauty pageantry at age four, the steady stream of victories and occasional near misses had gone somewhat to her head. She was apt to become distinctly peevish if the remarkable shiny golden blond hair hanging down to her waist was not washed, curled, and brushed twice a day. When the other kids were giving each other Valentines in grammar school the previous February, Velma Lynn distributed autographed photos of herself reclining on a piano.

Velma Lynn never doubted when she entered that she would win the Little Miss Marvelous pageant, but she did not know just how certain it was. Tunney had been careful to conceal the fact that he had invented and paid for the entire contest. Officially the pageant was sponsored by an imaginary group called the Zeta Tau Mu Professional Manicurist Sorority of Creola. The judges were all employees of Tunney's at Monsieur Bidet who had been ordered to follow precise instructions on pain of being transferred to Birmingham, a fate worse than death.

McCorquodale came up from St. Anthony Street to see her little second cousin once removed, but walked into Chickasaw Civitan Hall rather late. She had decided she needed to relax and clear her mind after the troubling flop of her postmodern do. This pageant was just the bit of innocent diversion that she needed, an authentic occurrence of vernacular taste culture, far removed from all political machinations and the noisome rumblings of barbarian hordes sounding their Hunnish horns in the western hills. Blowing kisses to the audience of forty or so relatives of the seven contestants, the long slit in her polished silk Chinese robe blinking seductively, she took a seat next to her grandfather.

"That sweet thang done already won Miss Hospitality raht off the bat," Old Man Hiram told her loudly, working his bewhiskered jaws.

"Good stock will out! The McCorquodale blood comes through every time," she whispered back with conviction.

The talent section of the contest was already in progress, and one by one the little lovelies went through their paces. They twirled flaming batons, blew plaintive harmonicas and tubas, and wriggled lascivious imitations of popular female rock stars. When Velma Lynn's turn came, the emcee (Monsieur Bidet representative for greater Washington County) read an incredibly long list of past titles:

"Miss Christmas Star. Miss Satsuma Auditorm. Miss Prichard, Alabama, Vacation Pairdahs. Miss Black Jack 222 Home and Garden Insec Sterminator." His voice echoed solemnly on the P.A. system like flight calls at some international airport.

Velma Lynn was all frills in her short, puffy, lollipop-red dress and lacy petticoats, red shoes with white socks rolled halfway down, and huge red bow behind her head. With a sassiness beyond her years, she crooned a popular number: "Your Coffee May Have Swate and Low, But Ya Need My Sugar, Too." She skipped around the stage wagging her finger and constantly fondling her naturally curly hair. A recorded drumroll signaled the transition to the second half of her very recherché medley. With appropriate earnestness now in her starry eyes, she began reciting the books of the Bible in backwards alphabetical order while whirling a hula-hoop slowly downward from neck (Zephaniah, Zecharia, Titus, Second and First Timothy, Second and First Thessalonians . . .) to waist (Philemon) to ankles (Obadiah) and back again.

"Bless her precious heart! If that rascal ain't the smartest little jaybird!" exclaimed Mammaw Callie, wiping her eyes.

"Obviously a child genius," McCorquodale agreed. Adlai and Tammy beamed parental pride. Old Man Hiram held on to the arms of his seat.

When the poise and grace division was over the judges paused to confer. The tension was nothing if not high-voltage. Anxious mothers handed out press releases for possible Nashville talent scouts in the audience.

McCorquodale was unpleasantly surprised to see the gray, pasty face and thick black glasses of Albert Tunney entering from the rear of the auditorium wiping his face with a handkerchief, as though he had just walked in off the street. Though McCorquodale did not know the real scope of his dealings, she had always disliked him.

"Whatever you're selling we don't need it here, thank you," she said blankly when he came up to greet the family with a tense smile. "Try setting up a stand in the I-10 tunnel."

Just as he was about to reply the judges rose to announce their decision. Tunney had been thorough in his instructions. One by one, every prize went to Velma Lynn. Miss Fashionable. Miss Photogenic. Miss Talented. An angry murmur rose from the crowd; ambitious mothers of budding starlets waved their fists. "Hang em from the durn flagpole," someone yelled.

Fearing violent reprisal, the jury stopped to huddle and then awarded the Miss Personality trophy to another little girl. Velma Lynn was not pleased, and a shriek resounded when she pinched the happy winner hard on the buttock. But the eyes of the judges were on Tunney, their boss, who was furiously making the sign of the cut throat. For one terrible moment, visions of life in Birmingham passed before their eyes.

Angry crowd or no crowd, they quickly announced the top winner. "Miss Little Miss Marvelous of North Mobile County is—*Velma Lynn McCorquodale*!!!"

Catcalls rang out from the rival families, but Velma Lynn was totally unaffected. With carefully rehearsed joy she ran up on the stage to be crowned, struck numerous drooping poses for Adlai's instamatic, and grabbed a microphone for a few comments on title number twenty-nine. "You'd best believe I'll never never forget you people. This here's the happiest moment of mah ENtire second half of the summer vacation."

In the midst of the confusion Albert Tunney came running up to Old Man Hiram's row with the warranty deed.

"What's that?" McCorquodale asked.

"Top prize," Tunney answered, "an all-expenses-paid trip for Velma Lynn to Destin, Florida, for the Miss Water Wonderworld competiton. Zeta Tau Mu told me that their 'Golden Age Retirees' clause says they have to get the consent of the oldest livin relative before she can go."

"Merciful heavens, *FLORIDA!*" Old Man Hiram cried. "Gimme that wrahtin pen."

"*Not so fast,*" said McCorquodale. "We have our family image to think of. Destin, Florida, is two hours away by Greyhound bus. What kind of prize is that? Bangkok or Addis Ababa we would certainly consider, but we are not going to get down and grovel over a mess of pottage."

When Velma Lynn later threw a hysterical screaming fit, McCorquodale agreed to send her to Disney World with a small part of the allowance she was receiving from Wolfe (and with extreme reservations; Disney World was *not* postmodern). But for Albert Tunney, time was running out.

CHAPTER 35

The Chamber Checks it Out

T. Bob Maloney, Director of Interglobal Expansion for the Mobile International Chamber of Commerce, was having an exhausting morning. Not only was he instructed to call Germany that day, but he also had to line up a grueling schedule for tomorrow.

The telephone barely stopped ringing: "Hey, Jack, what you say we talk it over over breakfast at the Dew Drop Inn?" "Let me take you to lunch at Korbet's, Melvin, they make great martinis." "Let's meet for coffee and a Danish at the Tiny Diny, T.J., and I'll tell you how Mobile is going places." "Now listen, if we're gonna talk business we oughtta meet for steaks at the Pillars. Sure. No sweat, the *Chamber* will pick up the tab."

In its search for fresh talent and new ideas to prepare the area for its age of greatness, the Chamber had found T. Bob in upstate Luverne, Alabama, and promptly enticed him away from his position directing the citywide Junior Achievement Program. His natty and energetic appearance might well have been a factor: flattop, white shoes and white belt, orange polyester blazers, and cuffs on the sleeves but not on the trousers.

After growing up in Goshen, Alabama, and being trained in management skills at Boll Weevil State Junior College, T. Bob was quick to grasp the big picture of the Tennessee-Tombigbee Waterway and its significance for the Pearl of the Gulf Coast. It was T. Bob who thought up the advertising campaign, "Mobile: a city on the move," which alternated with the ineffable, "Mobile is mobile." Though wry skeptics came up with other variations such as, "Mobile: a city with suicidal tendencies."

Those naysayers! Let them doubt the coming international future; T. Bob was laying the groundwork. *They* twiddled their thumbs, but T. Bob, with his recent anti-litter campaign, had given the city a clean new image for tourists and all-important emissaries of outside industry.

While the Chamber of Commerce watched, with complete indifference, the demise of downtown and the destruction of an exquisite architectural heritage that would have drawn visitors from all across America, T. Bob worked on projects like annual football games and beauty pageants that would make Mobile a tourist Mecca. For the Chamber's monthly breakfasts, held early in the morning when their minds were clear and their hearts were pure, T. Bob chose the cosmopolitan name *Café du Port de la Mobile*, at the advice of Mrs. Irene Grew, a local high school French teacher up on colonial history.

Lately a great deal of T. Bob's time was consumed with the great development scheme to level much of the city for the Supermall. Slowly, slowly—as things progressed here—awareness of the plan was sinking into the general public consciousness, generating either helpless and fatalistic resignation, or skepticism that it would never come about.

Oddly enough, the Chamber was slow to jump on the bandwagon and months passed before T. Bob even knew of the scheme. Then word was delivered one day that Ripley Washton, president of Washton Shipbuilding, and several other members of Task Force 2000 favored the project—they thought the plan to demolish the south part of town for an artificial lake would help them dispose of some unprofitable property off of southbound Dauphin Island Parkway. Instantly T. Bob and the Chamber scurried to become ferocious advocates of the development, fully confident that the other five thousand members would also approve, though they had not been asked.

The leaders of the Chamber were especially excited about the prospect of draining the bay for industry and building a Volkswagen factory there; it was a dream come true. But as an unusual precaution T. Bob was instructed to actually call the Volkswagen headquarters in Berlin and "see just how serious they are."

Sadly, one datum the Chamber had not been furnished with was that Ted Todd's negotiations with Volkswagen were of an extremely tentative nature. In fact, Volkswagen had not even been informed that they were considering moving their Brazilian works. The huge tracts of land obtained from draining the bay were to be conveyed to Sunbelt Land Corporation, and would be divided up as they saw fit once the fiction of the Volkswagen factory was no longer necessary. The highly useful "Volkswagen card" had been the idea of Todd's "consultant" crony in Dallas, and the Volkswagen telephone number they were giving out actually belonged to the proprietor of a Berlin video game establishment the consultant had met on a gambling trip to Las Vegas. He was known only as "Willi," a glib and corpulent individual with a slick black Peter Lorre middle part and a predilection for gold chains and rabbit feet around his neck.

Though T. Bob vaguely imagined Willi ensconced in an enormous Bauhaus office suite, he had actually rented a space in a row of old brick warehouses and machine shops built directly beneath an elevated railway called the *S-bahn*. While teenage rowdies from the seedy neighborhood came to play the video games, Willi ran a seamy travel service for German men who wanted a special good time in the red light districts of Asia. Occasionally the Dallas connection brought him some oil-rich roust-abouts as customers.

T. Bob had prepared for the phone call the night before by watching *Hogan's Heroes* on TV and looking at a map to see where Germany was. When Willi answered the phone in German he decided to break the ice with a few humorous sallies. "This is the Greater Mobile *Reich* calling, is this Sergeant Schultz or Colonel Klink?" An icy silence followed. "I guess y'all don't see too much American TV, huh?"

Willi decided it had to be one of his Dallas customers. "Hallo Tex! Hey, ve got no more room on the Bangkok flight, *tut mir leid*, but I found some chicks in Manila that I tell you: wery nice."

It was T. Bob's turn to be puzzled. "This is the Mobile International Chamber of Commerce, Interglobal Division, calling Volkswagen."

With sudden panic Willi remembered he had gotten a letter from Dallas the week before outlining what he was to say if a call came from Alabama. He rifled furiously through his desk, but one of the teenagers chose that moment of all times to play a raucous German New Wave computer music number on the jukebox.

"What's that music?" T. Bob asked.

"Ve always play music in the Cherman factory system; Folksvagen is wery progressive." Willi found the letter in a desk drawer and hurriedly scanned it. He was supposed to be driving a hard bargain, Dallas instructed.

"Now vat's all this talk about pollution controls? You vant us to bring you tirty *tausend* vorkers vith that enwironment nonsense?"

"Hell, don't you worry none about that talk. Down here we don't even *have* an environment, all we got's industrial sites."

"That's vat I like to hear. But anudder ting. You unnerstand, I presume, that you are to *giff* us the land after you finish draining the bay and filling it in for us?"

"Shoot I reckon, that's the least we could do. Of course we'll give you complete tax exemptions, too." The music was over, but T. Bob could faintly hear the ringing and beeping of the video games. "What's that noise?"

"The computers, they never stop." Willi decided he had better terminate the conversation. "Vell I tell you vat, since you fellas being so nice, ve come to Mobile."

T. Bob was overwhelmed. "Gee, Mr. Willi, isn't there anything else we could do for you? Couldn't we give you the key to the city, or maybe the State Docks?"

"No, that's all, just the bay for free, *danke sehr*." A train passed over Willi's video game parlor, sending a deafening rumble over the telephone line. "That's the sound of the factory. Soon you be hearing that too!"

After the conversation T. Bob paced excitedly back and forth in his office. For a while there Volkwagen had been dangling on the line, but T. Bob and the Chamber had really reeled in that fish.

CHAPTER 36

Trouble in the Empire

From the top of the Commerce National Bank, in the celebrated Million Dollar Board Room, it was easy to imagine a great empire extending in every direction. To the north, marshes and waters led to profitable territories waiting to be subdued. To the south, the summer clouds floated out happily to tropical islands bursting with goods for enterprising Gulf ports.

But for H. Sloane Wolfe there were earthquake warning tremors and squalls on the horizon. "Of all the arts, the most difficult is the art of reigning," said the Emperor Diocletian, after twenty years of putting down revolts and holding off Goths, Vandals, Moors and Persians.

Ironically, people had never been more eager to pay Wolfe homage. At an annual reception for the foreign consuls in the port city, many expressed their admiration that a large Mobile firm—one of only four or five that had not been acquired by out-of-town concerns—had turned the tables and reestablished the city's proper relation to the hinterlands. It seemed like a harbinger of things to come. Looking at the view, the consuls could already see fleets of coal barges chugging down the Tenn-Tom Waterway.

And stretching out to greet them—the biggest parking lot in the South and "Six Flags Over Jesus" Amusement Park. Though H. Sloane Wolfe was known to be cool to the plan that would force him to move his offices into the Supermall instead of building a new skyscraper near the river, many of the honorary consuls, who were for the most part local lawyers and businessmen, sensed the exciting winds of change in the project. And the ones who disliked the idea of tearing down the entire older half of the city generally agreed, in typical local fashion, that there was nothing they could do about it anyway.

When McCorquodale heard that there was to be a consular reception at the bank, she was not to be held back. Wolfe, perhaps worn down
by his burden of care, actually agreed to let her appear in public with him,
though with the proper precautions. She was to be introduced as Mlle.
Chateau-Frontenac, a bilingual site scout for a large Canadian film
company based in Quebec. For several mornings before the reception
McCorquodale lingered late in her boudoir practicing her French. "At
last," she told herself, "the high-powered world of international diplomacy. And scintillating conversation with a group as cosmopolitan as
myself."

When the reception was well under way at the top of the bank and
foreign refreshments such as *sangría* and pizza slices spiced the conversation, McCorquodale eagerly sought out the French consul. He was Mr.
Billups, a successful insurance agent with offices on the I-65 service road.

"*Enchantée,* monsieur, quel plaisir!" McCorquodale said graciously,
taking his hand.

"*Gesundheit,*" Mr. Billups answered wittily, never at a loss for words.
He looked rather disconcerted at the fetching blond apparition in blue
satin and an ermine wrap.

"What can I do for you, little lady?"

Chapfallen to see that the French consul was just another local,
McCorquodale explained her film mission as a Montreal businesswoman.

Mr. Billips glanced nervously at her cleavage and passed his hand
over a ruddy bare scalp. "Well you don't say; sounds tip top. You know
they made *Death Ship* here. Is this going to be a horror movie or what?"

"It's a *film,* darling, not a 'movie,'" McCorquodale said somewhat
severely.

"Got a big budget? They never have any special effects in those low-
budget deals, and you can't figure out what the plot is. Those foreign
flicks get pretty artsy sometimes."

"As a matter of course, there will never be anything so primitive as
plot." After pausing to regain her calm, she added slyly, eager to make
new converts wherever possible, "It's the rapidly spreading postmodern

consciousness of this place that has brought me here. Esthetic theory is so contagious, don't you find?"

"Muicy, I wouldn't know, hon."

"I understand the movement here is in the thick of vital debate. Linear thought, for instance. Should we embrace it? Or should we lead the new age into more mythical-circular cognition. Why not spiral thought? Why not funicular polygon thought? The possibilities are legion."

"Gracious."

"I'm sure you've been receiving dispatches on *le postmodernisme* from the Quai d'Orsay. As regards your own regional revolutionary cells here, keep it non-violent is my advice. The modernists seem to have already suborned your retrograde daily news rag. You must not play into their hands with unfavorable publicity. Disciplinary actions may be necessary later for unregenerate modernists, though I should think, surely, no executions."

She was flattered to see Mr. Billups staring with a slight frown of undivided attention. "I might add that Ottawa was most estranged at the brutal political repression of the drama *Radical Chic* by the ignorant goons in your city government, and is closely monitoring all further human rights abuses. In diplomatic circles there has been talk of a trade boycott. I suppose you have no emotional ties with the expressionists or Russian constructivists or that ilk?"

"Heavens, no, I don't know any Russians."

"That is well."

At the other end of the sumptuously paneled board room, H. Sloane Wolfe, every inch the leader with his graying temples and Haspel suit, sipped a Bourbon and Coke, stared out the window and pondered his woes.

The upstate natives of the Wolfe Alabama Bancorporation were restless. Wolfe had been draining the vassal banks to maintain the CNB in the style to which he had become accustomed. The Million Dollar Board Room was a small temporary measure, but soon he looked forward to beginning construction of the "WolfAl" tower, which would symbolically rule the skyline and to hell with all that Supermall baloney.

A serious revolt had started in Wolfe's most glorious conquest, the big Magic City Bank of Birmingham. It was sad but true that neither Wolfe himself nor his board of directors owned a controlling number of shares in Wolfe Alabama, and what they did own had been seriously diluted by their acquisition wars. As long as the conquests were small country banks, that presented no problem, but Wolfe now reflected with a sinking heart that when they had acquired the Birmingham bank, they had given them a bigger block of shares than anyone else. And the Birmingham people were beginning to throw their weight around in a most unsubmissive way.

On top of that there were certain internal problems in the Commerce National Bank. The bank was staffed largely with what Ce Ce Anne in her sorority terminology called "legacies," the young or youngish scions of established families, and up until then the bank had been run with a spirit of largesse that befitted what Ce Ce Anne liked to call "the most exclusive binek in town." As the Liaison for Commercial Loan Concepts often repeated, "If they're really *cute* people, with *background*, it would be *so* tacky to ask embarrassing questions about how they're going to pay."

The figures for delinquent loans had been going into the millions lately. And then there was that incident when they lent a million in cash to the Tennessee developer in the cowboy outfit. Bank emissaries even drove it out to the airport and stuffed the green bundles into his trunks for him. "He said he was just goin to Rio de Janeiro for the weekend," Wolfe mumbled, shaking his head.

"A penny for your thoughts," McCorquodale said, surprising him from behind, alone by the windows, and holding his eyes while the other guests were deep in their conversations.

But the tender scene was interrupted when Ernest Balleriel, usually so staid, came running through the festive diplomatic gathering and nearly upset several cocktails.

"H. Sloane, they're rebelling in Opp! The directors say they want their perks back!"

"Puiks? I'll give them puiks! I'll teach em to get sassy with me!"

"They say they want to have their board meetings in San Juan again. They say they're going to vote with Birmingham!"

"That certainly isn't very nice," McCorquodale said, summing up the whole situation in one pithy phrase. "And we offered them culture, a breath of greater things. The boors."

"That's so true, shuguh," Wolfe replied. "A bunch a goddamn boors."

CHAPTER 37

$\mathcal{P}$hone $\mathcal{F}$riends and $\mathcal{S}$igns of the $\mathcal{T}$imes

Mr. Belzagui, as an amateur historian, liked to say that Mobile was a Protestant city with a Catholic foundation—fifteen percent of the population, though in the smaller city before World War II the percentage had been close to half. Catholics had been very active in city hall and the police department in those days. He and Aunt Odilia often had long conversations on the subject over a few K&B beers on Sunday afternoons at the Roshfookle residence. Mr. Belzagui would drive over as soon as he had finished counting the collection at St. Joseph's, their old downtown parish, and had had his lunch with Father Kreismeier.

Their ritual was totally unaffected by the development schemes currently rocking the city, which seemed only so much distant thunder. And the power struggles within the Wolfe Alabama Bancorporation hardly made an impression on Mr. Belzagui down in the mailroom.

What did make an impression, what was immediate, was the inexhaustible topic of Old Catholic Mobile. Mr. Belzagui, like some others, liked to assert that practically all Catholics are *ipso facto* Old Mobilians, because so many of them came by boat and they came ages ago. One can only speculate how Mrs. Harmsworth Billingsley Balleriel, an Episcopalian, would have responded to that democratic viewpoint. "Ages," in Mr. Belzagui's case, meant the 1880s when the merchant family of Maronite Catholics arrived from Lebanon.

To the innocent out-of-towner Aunt Odilia and Mr. Belzagui might have appeared rather ordinary, if colorful, people, but in fact both enjoyed an established place in the community. Aunt Odilia's late husband, Joe Chighizola, had known half Mobile in his day as bookie at McAlpin's pool hall downtown.

And only last week Archbishop O'Reilly had asked her in his brogue if her father, Alois Roshfookle, had not once worked at the old Battle House. Like seventy percent of the priests and nuns in town, the florid-faced Archbishop had come to the missionary territory of Alabama as an "FBI" (Foreign Born Irish). But quickly sensing how he must get his priorities and responsibilities in line in order to run the archdiocese, he appointed a Mobilian, Father Altdorfer at Our Lady of the Manifold Solaces, his adviser on local history. As a result, the Archbishop was able from time to time to surprise his flock with arcane knowledge about long-deceased relatives to their utter rapture and delight.

This enlightened flexibility gave him far more influence than people had, whatever their persuasion, who came to town ready to teach and reform the locals over their dead bodies. Aunt Odilia's old school chum Sophie Stanesco reported that St. Aloysius of Gonzaga Church was all torn up over a new modern priest there who did not seem to want to be very Catholic. His first act upon coming to the parish was to fire the organist of twenty years and bring in two nuns to lead the singing with a harmonica and tambourine. They always wore street clothes, and he never wore his clerical collar. He only wanted to talk about social issues, mainly things he heard on the news, and acted bored and uncomfortable with concepts like soul and spirit, or sin, redemption and salvation. If he discussed scripture at all, it was as a highly tentative text filtered through the doubts and qualifications of all the latest Biblical scholars. He publicly pooh-poohed from the pulpit the doctrine of angels and the imagery of the Book of Revelations.

With great fanfare he produced a "church mission statement" that everybody was supposed to recite at the end of mass. It was full of bureaucratic-sounding and rather harmless statements like: "St. Aloysius is called to be a dynamic and caring community" or "St. Aloysius will: be socially conscious . . . work for greater understanding . . . develop the community with the excellent strengths and talents that exist." Nobody was sure what the big deal was. But a big blow-up came when he announced that the church needed remodeling, and it came out that the side altars to the Virgin Mary and St. Aloysius were to be removed. When a protest committee of parishioners told him they wanted to keep the

Our four C's are Catholicism, coast, carnival, culture.

altars, he explained that he was building a democratic people's church that did not have its head stuck in the Middle Ages. They suggested putting it to a vote in the parish, but then he blew up and yelled that he was going to give them a progressive people's church whether they wanted it or not. Now he was using his priestly authority to force the remodeling plan through. However, many people were confidently predicting that the local practice of quiet string-pulling, rather than overt fighting, would soon have him speeding off to parts unknown on an airplane.

It was all an interesting subject of conversation, but on the whole, everyone was bewildered by these developments, and did not quite know how to fit them into the peaceful local scene. They were signs and echoes of far-off struggles slowly approaching from outside.

Mr. Belzagui had not received a single promotion after forty years of service at the Commerce National Bank, in sharp contrast to the meteoric rise of socialites like Ce Ce Anne and Ernest. But Mr. Belzagui had a whole network of old friends, including several judges and executives, in the courthouse and other banks and downtown businesses. Some of them had gone to the Catholic high school with him, McGill Institute, when it was a stately Greek Revival academy of pillars and chiseled stone friezes on Government Street, not far from the river. For years they had met for lunch once or twice a week at Walgreen's or Lester's Quick Stop Grill or other downtown eateries.

During Mardi Gras Mr. Belzagui always got an invitation to the Crewe of Columbus Ball from Mr. Ansbacher in the Savings Department—the German Catholic names were still everywhere. He always took Aunt Odilia, and when they were not dancing they were saying hello all evening. A couple of times Mr. Belzagui imbibed a little too freely and the Ansbachers had to drop them off so that he would not have to drive home. One thing he always said, Catholics sure knew how to have a good time. (The Crewe of Columbus, a local Mardi Gras mystic society, grew out of the Catholic Knights of Columbus, but then they started admitting Protestants.)

Mr. Belzagui's stuffed grape leaves were famous at the Lebanese-American dinners held every year at St. Catherine's on Spring Hill Avenue. He visited nearly every lawn party held in town, and reminisced and flirted with the widows. The great bulk of his free time was taken up with the functions of the St. Joseph Sacred Name Society, the St. Vincent de Paul Society, and the Friendly Sons of St. Patrick (he was a guest).

Among the Knights of Columbus Mr. Belzagui was considered quite a scholar. He was known for his erudite letters to the editor of the archdiocesan *Catholic Weekly*. And he had penned several learned pamphlets for the Knights on topics such as, "What Catholic Mailroom Supervisors Believe In," "Father Abram J. Ryan: Confederate Poet and Nightingale," and "The Chapeau and the Sword," an allegorical drama in ten pages explaining the KOC uniform.

Mr. Belzagui liked to boast that the KOC hall was the only place in town that served beer on Sundays, though he confided to Aunt Odilia that things got a little out of hand recently when Billy Aroto started throwing lighted firecrackers under the tables while people were trying to eat their fried fish.

Aunt Odilia was every bit as active. The shamrocks she made for the Ladies of Benevolence sold like hot cakes when Alix Lopez's little granddaughter took them to McGill for St. Patrick's Day. According to

Etta Kowalik, Alix's son drove his family from Chateaugué to Spring Hill
to go to St. Ignatius, which Frances Ebeltoft said was very much the up
and coming parish now.

Aunt Odilia spent one morning a week, wearing her best Kress's
beads, visiting mothers with newborn babies for the Legion of the
Blessed Mother. She was the very first person to report to the St. Joseph
Sodality that week that the Llewellyn baby looked exactly like his
grandfather Maurice Grew, and did they remember the time Maurice
took Irene Stumpf to the Mystics of Time ball in 1949 and got fined for
taking his mask off during the parade that night when his float passed the
corner where Irene was standing at Dauphin and Conception?

But as Aunt Odilia told Father Kreismeier and the St. Joseph
Sodality when she had them over for her noted meatballs-a-roni, her life
had sometimes been a vale of sorrows, too. After Aunt Odilia's younger
brother Red and his wife Betty Sue died in the New Orleans hurricane
party, Aunt Odilia had borne the responsibility of raising the problem
child, who was obviously too brilliant to march to the slow beat of lesser
drums.

In her teen years McCorquodale's precociousness was observed with
unease by the administration at Bishop Toolen girls' school. They had
been informed of a wild smoking party she organized at Camp Cullen,
the Catholic retreat over the bay, and there were rumors of a mixed party
at which she had demonstrated the dirty bop. Then there was that awful
day when Sister Bernard Annette caught McCorquodale wearing her
green uniform skirt half a foot too short by rolling it up at the waistband,
and when she pulled a ruler out of her wimple to measure the distance to
the knee she discovered that there were safety pins inside the skirt to
adjust it even shorter.

Aunt Odilia was so upset that she made a three day novena to St.
Anthony (a prayer after every meal) to straighten that child out. She even
sent a "flying novena" (the same prayer nine times) straight to St.
Modesta, St. Rita, St. Jean de Bréboeuf, and Our Lady of Charity for
good measure.

Aunt Odilia loved to repeat that when, after much reflection, she transferred Margaret Constance to the public high school that very next school year, she was admitted to the National Honor Society. This more than excused occasional tumults like when that silly principal suspended her for a week for some nice French Club activity she had organized. Margaret Constance was just too creative for them. What a pity she had not had the money to send her brainy niece to college, but then what college would have been on her level?

Along about the fifth K&B, Aunt Odilia and Mr. Belzagui's Sunday afternoon chats turned to the Latin mass (they missed it), the bingo games at the Church of the Blessed Sacrament (not what they used to be), and the Feast of Christ the King parades downtown, when Mr. Belzagui marched with the Knights of Columbus in full regalia (if only they could have them again!). Those were the days, but by then it was time for Mr. Belzagui to head for the KOC hall, and Aunt Odilia was facing another rigorous week of research.

Soon after the beauty pageant in Saraland, which was discussed and commented upon in great detail in Aunt Odilia's telephone circle after it was reported by McCorquodale, there arose a new topic of conversation. When Aunt Odilia, making her monthly telephone courtesy call to Old Man Hiram and Mammaw Callie, caught wind of the fact that Albert Tunney had mortgaged his bidet corporation and that the family was facing financial adversity, she soon began calling them three times a week for prolonged briefing sessions.

To say that the Tunney household suffered in silence would not be strictly accurate. Aunt Odilia, who disposed of plenty of time since McCorquodale had banned the TV from the house, relayed all details to her entire network of telephone friends: the Misses Robinson, Mr. Belzagui, Frances Ebeltoft, Irene Grew, Elsie and Etta Kowalik, Marguerite Pappas (who was in charge of the Greek salad table at the Greek festival every year at the Orthodox church), Alix Lopez, all were in on it, not to mention McCorquodale, who showed scant interest. "What do the antics of the Tunneys have to do with us?" she had wondered.

Little did it matter that Aunt Odilia was hardly even acquainted with these in-laws, and the telephone friends not at all. Albert would have been dumbfounded to learn that across town the entire church library staff at Government Street Baptist and a goodly portion of the Legion of Mary and other complete strangers were following the travails of the Tunneys like a gripping soap opera.

There were titillating details of the Tunneys' cutbacks in their west Mobile subdivision consumer lifestyle. It was said that Brenda Tunney had had to learn to cook. Instead of buying frozen pizzas and cheesecakes, she was actually chopping meat and vegetables on a cutting board and stirring things with a spoon. She was devising artful concoctions with pudding mixes, Cool Whip, and cans of mushroom soup. It was said she had started buying jars of peanut butter and boxes of crackers instead of purchasing crackers already spread in little snack packs. When Albert made Brenda put the garbage in paper grocery sacks instead of buying plastic garbage bags, she felt as though she were in Calcutta with germs attacking her from every direction, and she constantly doused the kitchen trash can with room freshener.

Opinion was divided when Albert sold the riding mower and had to push a common gasoline mower. Some felt sorry for him; others said it was good exercise. This debate was greatly amplified the week it came out that Albert had sold two of the cars, leaving them with only one. The Tunneys occasionally had to walk seven or eight blocks to the mailbox near the subdivision entrance to mail a letter, or to buy a carton of milk at the Seven Eleven. As a consequence, they sometimes met their neighbors busy in their front yards. They found out that the Malloys, a family of five who had moved here from Michigan, had been living on their right for four years, and that Mr. Monroe Hunnerwell, who had retired from Dacovich Seed Company, lived on their left. Much consulting followed as to Mr. Hunnerwell's identity, history, and antecedents, and eventually someone recalled him and was able to pinpoint the location of his childhood home in the Gritney at St. Emanuel near Canal Street, and then Aunt Odilia remembered hearing about his people and brought forth many other intriguing details.

Young Vondel Tunney had already dropped out of the University of South Alabama before the family's financial crunch, and she tended to

The Gritney was only blocks from the river and the ships.

spend most of her days watching CNN news reports on remote world events. All of the telephone network approved, almost without exception, when Albert and Brenda built a fire under that girl and she started attending cosmetology school. It was an outgrowth of her natural talent, as she loved to spend hours at a time powdering her Rubenesque young body after a hot bath, and pampering her face with skin fresheners, creamy ivory base and blush-on, and lid tone and Charles of the Ritz eye shadow, Aunt Odilia reported. She quoted Mammaw Callie and McCorquodale's Aunt Trudi, wife of Tater McCorquodale, and that cousin Adlai's wife, Tammy, sometimes caught when she answered the phone on a visit to Chunchula.

When Vondel started working two days a week as a trainee at a beauty parlor in Cottage Hill, and when her new boyfriend, a certain Jimmy Purnell as yet unidentified, could not drive her, she sometimes had to catch the bus. There was widespread concern whether this was wise for a young girl, but Marguerite Pappas maintained that it would do her a world of good to get out and fend for herself.

Everyone assumed that Tunney's bidet corporation was in some kind of trouble, and not a few asserted that it was not surprising and what was a bidet anyway? Adelaide Stoll actually went out and bought one, and reported obliquely that her husband thought it was very handy. He was widely known to have hemorrhoids.

Handy or not, there were widespread predictions that the Monsieur Bidet of Alabama Corporation would soon be going bankrupt. More signs and portents and writing on the wall, but nobody quite grasped about what.

CHAPTER 38

Fun, Profit, and Pertinent Facts Through Genealogy

Anyone who spent much time downtown would have seen Aunt Odilia on her daily peregrinations, carrying a big golf umbrella on hot summer days, or sometimes pulling a two-wheeled cart loaded with groceries from the National, down Government and Washington Avenue, then past the forlorn vacant lots of St. Anthony Street. Passing motorists closely scrutinized the combination of touched up black hair pulled back in a bun, beads, dangling red earrings to match her heavily rouged cheeks, with strikingly less formal slacks and tennis shoes.

The first stop, after early mass at St. Joseph's, was the genealogical division of the Mobile Public Library. For hours she sent the microfilm whirring. She read through year after year of nineteenth-century newspapers. She scrutinized advertisements. She constructed chronologies. She devoured thousands of names from the city directories, tax records, deeds, and census records. Whenever she found a salient fact, a tiny mother-of-pearl notebook and matching pen were slipped out of her purse.

For lunch she had a sandwich with Mrs. Ansbacher who did volunteer secretarial work for the *Catholic Weekly* on Government Street from ten till two. After lunch she continued her research at the Canonical Archives in the same building, plodding through Hamilton, Delaney, and Higginbotham's histories, going through baptisms and marriages and censuses in huge tomes from the French and Spanish periods, bound in ancient, crumbling red leather that rubbed off on the cloth gloves she wore for handling them.

With the determined expression of a GI climbing into his tank for battle, she would charge down the lists of zany names with her index finger:

Luis Duret

Domingo Dolive

St. Yago Geniez

Madame Rochon

Madame Jazuioux

Cornelius McCurtin

Jacques de la Saussaye

Pedro de Juzan

Jacob Pybunn

Savary Socier

Mathurin Ladner

Balentin Dubrocar

Madame LaBatt

But the most fragrant of them all never appeared. Aunt Odilia concluded to her dismay that the Roshfookles, or Rochefoucaulds, had what must have been a very genteel aversion to the public limelight, because references to the family were few and far between. Her father, Alois, and her grandfather Reuben, who drove the streetcar down Broad Street in his later years after Monroe Park opened, had been gentlemen of leisure with the distressing habit of sitting out on the balcony of what was now McCorquodale's room in their undershirts to read the newspaper. When she was growing up they might talk about what happened when they stopped by the oyster house after work for a beer and a plate of oysters on the half shell—sometimes they would bring home some oyster loaves from Klosky's, fried oysters on scooped out French bread and melted butter, wrapped up in paper. But they never seemed to know anything about the family history other than to say casually that the Roshfookles had once had a lot of land some place around Mobile way back before the Civil War. She simply could not fathom their indifference to this glory. How could those men be content just to live their lives from day to day?

Aunt Odilia can still taste the oyster loaves from Klosky's.

But eventually, with only herself and Margaret Constance left in the line, Aunt Odilia had gleaned a slew of exciting but mute facts. There were Roshfookles going back through the 1840s, but who were they? There was Gil de la Rochefoucauld, crew member of the French colonial ship *Renommée*, beckoning to these two lost daughters from the other side of the chasm of the 150-year missing link. But the final proof of the extreme but forgotten aristocracy of the family always seemed to hover just out of reach.

Yet there was an astonishing side result to her labors. Aunt Odilia knew practically *everything* about *everybody's* family in Mobile if they had been here longer than one generation. She knew that a certain rare and tantalizing purple fig tree that grew by the front walk of a little Victorian house in Oakdale had been planted by the mailman's great-grandfather. She knew that in the 1890s the Purdues had built their house off of Herndon Avenue on the site of the old Lopez family cemetery.

She knew that the family of Mrs. Chasuble Hedgemont, socialite friend of the distinguished Mrs. Harmsworth Billingsley Balleriel, had run a boarding house in Buckatunna, Mississippi, back before they made their money, and had not, as was generally thought, had a plantation in the Mississippi Delta. On the other hand, she knew that the ancestors of Mr. Harley, the repairman at the little air conditioner repair shop on Dauphin Island Parkway, had lived in a mansion with double galleries and silver door knockers on St. Louis Street, and they received callers in a succession of carriages on Thursdays. Wherever she looked, she saw complicated lines of connection often invisible to the persons themselves.

Listening to Aunt Odilia gossip about the lawn party at St. Catherine's last week, you would never guess that there were also other things she knew but kept quietly to herself. She knew that when they found old Mr. Pat Hammerstein, wealthy president of Hammerstein Pine and Hardwood, dead on that park bench in Bienville Square in 1909, he had not arrived there by himself. It had taken a well-known businesswoman named Sally Patton and her entire nubile staff, like so many angel hands, to discreetly remove him from a whorehouse in the red light district on St. Michael Street where he had died *in medias res*.

She knew, for example, that Mr. Pierpont Ortega, president of the Cincinnati and Mobile Railroad, had a family on Government Street, but also another one with three children by a Creole mistress conveniently Down the Bay on Savannah Street. She knew that all during the twenties Mr. Clem Moseley, lumberman and grandfather of Prudential National Bank president Hearn Moseley, maintained a Miss Stephens in a house in the working class suburb of Crichton surrounded by a ten-foot fence.

Two major sources were helpful in these additional scholarly finds. When the old Battle House closed, Aunt Odilia's father, who had retired a number of years before, secured all the registers from his old coworkers, and the former desk clerk diverted himself in his waning years by making notes and personal observations in the margins about who was seen going into what room with whom, especially during Mardi Gras.

The other source was Rosenstein Jewelry on Royal Street. Hattie and

Alice Robinson had kept the books at Rosenstein's for forty-three years. Around three-thirty Aunt Odilia would leave the Canonical Archives to go have a cup of coffee with them. Often Mr. Lev Rosenstein, who was secretly amused by asking Aunt Odilia about her weekly grocery bargains, would walk back and join them.

What Mr. Rosenstein did not know was that every day after he went back up front to the showroom to help the customers, the Misses Robinson allowed Aunt Odilia to go through the store's records back to 1897. Whenever Aunt Odilia came across a suspicious frequency in jewelry purchases, out came the mother-of-pearl notebook and the fact was jotted away. You never knew when a bit of knowledge might come in handy.

But there were no real breakthroughs in the lost history of the Roshfookles until Mr. Belzagui came across the papers of a nineteenth-century cotton factor that he said he had rescued from the safety deposit vaults next to the mailroom in the CNB basement when they flooded during the last hurricane.

This joint historical-genealogical assault had had the interesting side effect of bringing Aunt Odilia and Mr. Belzagui closer and closer together, much to the latter's satisfaction. For years he had admired the scholarly widow at Catholic functions, and had often told his friends, "That double chin of hers sure has a lot of character." But aside from occasional learned exchanges on twenties and thirties films that had played at the Crown, Crescent, and Empire theaters on Dauphin Street, and other burning points in local history, she had never shown more than a polite interest in him. Then one year at the annual Lebanese Night at St. Catherine's, after the topic of river paddle-wheelers of the nineteen-teens—the *Helen Burke*! the *Nettie Quill*!—had been thoroughly exhausted and Aunt Odilia seemed just about to make a run on the *bagalawa* and vanish out of his life for the evening, Mr. Belzagui, grasping at straws, happened to mention an old letter he had seen once concerning the Tea Drinkers Society, an antebellum parading mystic society that died out around the turn of the century after the focus of carnival in Mobile had shifted from New Year's Eve to Mardi Gras

following the Civil War. It was from the 1840s, actually written in quite
a rakish tone, and talked about a boisterous conclave of some members
of the Tea Drinkers after their annual ball into which a young woman
had been smuggled in a man's top hat and dress coat, crowned and
toasted as queen, and installed with unspecified rites of celebration.

Hardly had he sketched the contents of the letter, leaving out the
part about the smuggling, naturally, but Aunt Odilia, trembling with
excitement, started making connections with a certain antebellum Camille
Roshfookle, who grandfather Reuben used to say was "the talk of the
town" back in the cotton era. At first Aunt Odilia said *maybe* it was
Camille at that Tea Drinker gathering, but three hours later, standing on
the steps outside St. Catherine's parish hall after everybody had gone
home and all the lights were out, Aunt Odilia had decided that the letter
conclusively and indisputably suggested that Camille was the queen
described. Overwhelmed by Mrs. Chighizola's new tone of confidential-
ity, Mr. Belzagui decided that this was not an idea to be discouraged.

The letter that Mr. Belzagui had come across was written by a certain
Nathaniel Weathersby, native of Massachusetts who had moved south
while still a young spark to make his fortune in the booming cotton port.
It had actually been in an old stack of family papers that Billy Aroto
found in a desk when his grandmother Jones died. He had lent them to
Mr. Belzagui, knowing his passion for "old stuff," as he put it. When
Mrs. Chighizola started talking about the sublime Camille, Mr. Belzagui
judged it prudent to leave Billy's name out of it, and made up the bit
about the safety deposit vault, a decision that he soon recalled with
anguish. Immediately, that very week, Mrs. Chighizola began pressing
him to track down the letter. Mr. Belzagui was obliged to tell her that the
holder of the safety deposit vault, an elderly Canadian wheat farmer who
had retired to a condominium on the Gulf Shores beach in order to
escape the fierce Canadian winters, had been so traumatized by the last
hurricane, which very nearly swept away the condo with him in it, and as
it was had him cowering for several hours in waist high waters on the
second floor, that he abruptly returned to northern Saskatchewan with
all the papers of his mother's family here, of which he was the last

surviving descendent, and the bank had no way of reaching him.

With Mrs. Chighizola temporarily stalled, Mr. Belzagui felt curious to have another look at the letter, and called up Billy Aroto to see if he could borrow the old papers again. The letter was just as he had remembered it, no more no less, with no mention of names. But a cold shiver traveled up and down his spine and electric forest fires across his scalp when he happened to flip over a crumbly ledger sheet in the stack of papers.

Glued to the back was a yellowed newspaper clipping from the same era concerning an incident one night in which a young woman had been refused entrance to a local hotel as "undesirable," and when several "inebriated bachelors" lodging there rushed forward to noisily defend her, the hotel management had summoned a policeman to escort her from the premises. The words "unaccompanied female abroad at unto-ward hours" had been underlined, and above someone had written in spidery thin script, "Carrie Roshfookle." Mr. Belzagui had heard too many times—indeed, devouring with fond attention—the complete known inventory of the house of Roshfookle not to realize that this was the Carrie married to the venerable (and Gallic?) Jesse Elijah Roshfookle mentioned in the 1850 county census. His first joyful thought at the pure exciting coincidence of finding the name was to rush to Mrs. Chighizola and show her the clipping. His second thought was about what the clipping actually said. Alois and Reuben R. might have had their reasons for not talking very much about the family history.

Mr. Belzagui spent many subsequent days brooding underneath his dangling Knights of Columbus sword in the bank mailroom. The cotton factor, one supposed, had known Carrie Roshfookle, very likely in more than one sense. It was at least within the realm of possibilities that she had been the woman smuggled into the Tea Drinkers' celebration. With or without old Jesse Elijah's knowledge, she certainly seemed to have covered a lot of territory. Was "Camille" perhaps no more than a later, wistfully garbled and badly remembered or even deliberately distorted version of "Carrie"? Was "Carrie" a nickname? Old Mr. Alois Roshfookle had said that Camille had been the talk of the town one carnival. Had word gotten out about the Tea Drinkers' festivities? Had something else happened? Perhaps another year?

He wondered how Mrs. Chighizola would react if he went to her with his very unaristocratic findings. Would she, like some Persian satrap beheading the carrier of bad tidings, cut off their budding friendship then and there? With pipes and sword humming and quivering overhead to the throb of the postage machines, and a dread of the tangled webs of deceit and their unknown consequences humming inside him, Mr. Belzagui made a decision. The investigation of the real Carrie or Camille Roshfookle or la Rochefoucauld, wherever it might have lead, would go no further.

There followed several tranquil years of happy historical têtes-à-têtes and duel questing. To keep Aunt Odilia's interest at fever pitch, Mr. Belzagui occasionally threw out hints that he was on the verge of a breakthrough. So and so had said that so and so had a cache of Mystic Tea Drinker documents in his attic, or that the bank was close to tracking down the Saskatchewan wheat farmer. When he said that a bank officer had recalled that the Canadian's mother's family here in town was either Smith or Williams, that had kept Aunt Odilia busy for months on a wild goose chase through genealogical records.

Unfortunately, the moment arrived when Mrs. Chighizola's patience began to wear thin. She started putting off some of their frequent get-togethers. That was the moment when Mr. Belzagui finally started making new discoveries.

Ce Ce Anne and Eddie began to note a fierce intensity in Mr. Belzagui's corner of the mailroom. The bushy black eyebrows, the soaring vault of his Lebanese nose, the salt-and-pepper mustache, the spectacles, the glowing eyes, the olive skin furrowed in thought lines— all conveyed a somewhat prim expression of rapt concentration, bordering, perhaps, on alarm and anxiety. When they got together for their late afternoon coffee klatsches, Mr. Belzagui was so preoccupied that he hardly reacted to Ce Ce Anne's gossip briefings concerning the glittery spheres, otherwise so intensely savored by both him and Eddie. For hours at a time, Mr. Belzagui would sit brooding and frowning with pen in hand, or else scribbling away furiously, pausing only to look up words in the dictionary. They assumed that he was very close to finishing his lengthy and masterful tome, *Mailroom Regulations, Revised Edition*, and they were not contradicted in the assumption, though Ce Ce Anne was surprised to draw a total lack of response when she broached the topic of an autograph party in the bank lobby complete with wine punch.

Aunt Odilia's reserve vaporized, and she herself began to clamor for more frequent meetings, upon being informed by Mr. Belzagui that while attending the St. Pius the Tenth Elementary School Used Books Bazaar, guided perhaps by the razor-sharp instincts of the historian, perhaps by astrological rhythms and fate, he had discovered a lost diary written by the same 1840s cotton factor, Nathaniel Weathersby. Mr. Belzagui explained that he had locked up the precious document in a bank safe to protect it from antiquities robbers, that it was far too fragile to transport, and that at any event it was written in an impenetrable code in an unknown alphabet. Hence it would not be possible to show it to her at any time in the immediate future. But from time to time he read her passages that he had been able to decipher by dint of an abstruse key on the last page during spare hours snatched away from his pressing bank work. They were always frustratingly brief. "Camille seen at LaTourette's Coffee House." "Camille the toast today of the Mobile Jockey Club." It was *exactly* the life that Aunt Odilia knew that her mysterious ancestress had lead in the wealthy port. "Camille surrounded by admirers in her loge at the State Street Theatre." The only frustration, as Aunt Odilia expressed after weathering the intense emotional storms and Mogen David toasts of these troves, was that the surname never appeared which would have established once and for all the identity of the luminary in question.

It was with a sinking heart that around the time of McCorquodale's postmodern "do" Mr. Belzagui virtually dropped out of sight for an entire week, spending whole days at his desk lost in tortured thoughts. Mrs. Chighizola's thirst for Dead Sea Scrolls and Rosetta Stones was absolutely insatiable. What was all this going to lead to? He imagined muscle-bound FBI investigators in three-piece suits bursting into the bank basement to handcuff him, with Mrs. Chighizola standing behind them pointing an accusing finger. Out of the corner of his eye he saw little Edward Dooley going about his work so diligently. And that nice Miss Stanton, taking time out from her hard-working schedule to have a cup of coffee with them. What would those two think if they knew he wasn't really doing bank work at his desk? And Mrs. Chighizola's outstanding young niece, Margaret Constance. What if they knew he had a dark secret? Those innocent young people. Would they be shocked?

Despite these doubts, Mr. Belzagui manufactured new diary entries, hot off the assembly line to customer specification. He decided to kill two birds with one stone, and settle the question of both surname and royalty.

There came to pass much rejoicing on St. Anthony Street and hours of ecstatic exegesis by the two savants. "January 1, 1848. Camille Roshfookle a sight to behold. Tea Drinkers could not have chosen better. Drink to us only with thine eyes! Long live the queen!"

Could it be that Camille—yes, Roshfookle!—was the first queen of carnival, some twenty odd years before the official Mardi Gras monarchs began to be chosen, and McCorquodale her *only legitimate heir*? Aunt Odilia did not take long to answer that question. Queens such as Mrs. Harmsworth Billingsley Balleriel and her friends, had they known Aunt Odilia, would have reeled.

CHAPTER 39

As Cheap As They Come

In official city channels it was full speed ahead for Supermall and Six Flags Over Jesus. The Chamber of Commerce, Western Hills Baptist Church and allied groups, Task Force 2000—everybody was hopping on board. But during the late summer they ran into snags that threatened to put a stop to the project altogether.

Ironically, the snags were caused by the many downtown property owners who supported the project. Far from worrying that half the city would be destroyed, they were delighted at the chance to unload their property on the city government. The only problem was that their expectations were out of touch with even the bonanza possibilities offered by Buzz Barker. Ted Todd put it another way: "I've seen tightwads and I've seen skinflints, but there's no cheap this cheap."

Todd was referring to a large group of members of the progressive business and social vanguard—some were even kin to Mrs. Harmsworth Billingsley Balleriel. For months he had been taking them out to eat in restaurants all over town to discuss the city's buying their property, but at the end of a long meal they always concluded that they were not quite ready to sell yet. Once or twice in the course of a fainthearted scramble for the check, Todd thought that they were actually going to pay for the meal, but it always turned out that they were reaching for their handkerchiefs.

Todd and Barker soon realized that all the downtown property owners, watching patiently with unblinking lizard eyes, were waiting for the others to sell so that they could close the last deal and get the highest price. The more deteriorated their buildings, the more money they expected for them. And each was convinced that his or her building, no matter where it was, was the key to the project.

Difficult negotiations were under way with Irving Green, who had built up a fortune from scores of rundown shacks he rented out in the black north side of town, plus a number of after-hours drinking establishments otherwise known as "shot houses."

Todd was negotiating to buy several dilapidated one-story office buildings downtown that would, of course, be leveled, plus some adjacent lots overgrown with kudzu where Green had torn down 1840s Federal town houses with cast iron galleries so that he could sell the bricks. Todd was stunned by Green's original asking price of $3.6 million for the parcels, but when a fire gutted one of the buildings Green raised the price by $200,000. Todd shuddered to think what it would be if a hurricane came through.

Another type was Ce Ce Anne's older cousin Stanton Wade, who had inherited two 1850s row buildings on Dauphin Street he occasionally passed on trips from west Mobile to his summer home at Point Clear over the bay. During several lingering lunches at the Athelstan Club Wade told Todd how much he regretted the face of the city changing, and how he had built up a sentimental attachment for his buildings after charging them off on his income tax for years and mortgaging them twice to get cash for his mystic society fees.

Whenever there were problems in the buildings, instead of making repairs Wade had simply closed off sections until there were no tenants left but pawn shops on the first floor. Wade pointed out the historic charm, enhanced presumably by holes in the roof, and asked for one million dollars for the two of them.

Todd soon learned that since prices bore no relation to market value, a million dollars was a very fashionable figure. The owner of the old Billmont Hotel, who turned down all offers for the ruined structure, wanted a million, and the owners of numerous other downtown buildings of all shapes and sizes quoted the same price.

Todd had a theory that the formative influence on these property owners had been the 1950s television show, *The Millionaire*. For years they had been waiting for Michael Anthony to show up and hand them a check for one million dollars. "They've just now figured out that it wasn't a true story, and now they think they've gotta make up the difference," Todd told Barker one day.

"I think we've gotta massage this issue once over lightly in the economic recovery mode," the mayor answered coolly in Sunbelt newspeak. "If we can just prioritize the business with the right movers and shakers, we can start gettin on with the gettin on."

Barker decided to approach one of the richest men in town, Al Goldkopf, a purple-faced lumber and oil baron who had obtained huge holdings downtown by moving all his businesses out west and quietly buying up property from the stores and offices that moved westward in his wake.

His downtown buildings could always be recognized by the windows knocked out and the weeds growing on the roof, but for years he had forestalled criticism by circulating rumors that he was going to bequeath his opulent art collection to the city.

If he could get Goldkopf to sell, if necessary at an exorbitant price Barker reasoned, all the other property owners would do the same. But the crafty millionaire was not faintly interested. "Why should I sell?" Goldkopf said bluntly. "If you're raising the value of my property now, just think what it'll be worth after you bring Volkwagen into the bay. I always say, 'When in doubt, buy and sit.'"

Todd and Barker were on the verge of despair when the big breakthrough finally came. Prudential National Bank president Hearn Moseley overcame his delicate scruples about "government giveaway programs" and concluded a secret agreement to sell the bank's—in his view—worthless downtown trust land to the city.

Moseley was confident that he had really put one over on the entrepreneurs. The PNB trust clients were happy to dispense with the bank's questionable expertise in dynamic property management in exchange for a tidy profit.

Barker arranged to publicize the sale by having a hushed conversation about it with Todd immediately after the weekly Wednesday mayor's press conference. They made sure they were within earshot of WMOB TV's glamorous news anchorperson Tina Struthers, who lingered all alone in the press box eating her bag lunch. Everyone agreed that Tina was going places with the national news network; she had a great ability to giggle, rap, joke, and shoot the bull with her charismatic fellow journalists during the nightly newscast. At first the black-haired beauty was so engrossed in thoroughly chewing her deviled ham on rye that she ignored them totally. But after they had repeated their remarks several times in a normal tone of voice and Barker loudly cautioned, "Don't let the media get wind of this!", she looked up and slyly took notice.

The secret was all over the news that night, other downtown property owners got nervous and began to crack, and panic sales started in the older part of the city.

On a Sunday morning in early September, when McCorquodale and Aunt Odilia were savoring a breakfast of newly canned fig preserves, coffee with chicory, and a little morning *Chateau Olivier*, they were startled to see a spread of several pages in the *Mobile Herald-Item* outlining the imminent start of the Houston developer's mammoth plan with the enthusiastic front-page banner headline: "Progress Here at Last! We're Where the Action Is!!"

With an ingenious stroke of show business flare, Todd and Barker announced that when minor questions of property rights and city finances had been disposed of, the condemned half of the city would be cleared by means of a chartered firebombing which would be broadcast on national television. The front page had an artist's rendering of the city in flames while bombers circled overhead raining down Armageddon. Another page showed the future city—the immense Supermall surrounded by an endless void of asphalt parking and freeways leading into nothingness.

"Muicy, is that Mobile?" Aunt Odilia exclaimed.

"I can tell from your voice that something terribly radical is happening. What is it this time? Are the Vikings sacking monasteries?" McCorquodale walked over and studied the newspaper. Suddenly she exploded, "I don't see the Hubba Hubba Club. And where would my postmodern café fit in in *that*?"

"Child, I don't see our *house*," Aunt Odilia added.

"This simply will not do," McCorquodale said ominously. "How can I convert the city to postmodernism if there isn't even a city?"

In a way she felt almost relieved. A great philistine lunacy that had been long brewing had finally come out in the open where it could be dealt with. Really, it was all most annoying. Sitting back down, she stretched out a singularly shapely leg and straightened the seam on her caramel shade stockings with resolution.

CHAPTER 40

Bank War Rages From Within

Strange things were happening at the Commerce National Bank. The ebullient Ce Ce Anne was seen rattling her bracelets and telling some of her more subdued gossip to country bankers' wives in beehive hairdos over luncheon at the Country Club. It was said that Ernest, who never got closer to sports than the boating scenes on his bone china tea set, had been wearing blue jeans and taking groups of upstate executives to his father's hunting camp in the Delta, and there was even an unconfirmed sighting of Ernest hosting a football tailgate party at the Bryant-Denny Stadium parking lot in Tuscaloosa. Several times Mr. Belzagui was called upon to cook Lebanese delicacies served at friendly little gatherings in the Million Dollar Board Room. Even Eddie had to put on a uniform with epaulettes and stand out on St. Joseph Street to open Cadillac doors when upstate bank presidents arrived.

Had the employees of what Ce Ce Anne called "the most exclusive bank in town" experienced a sudden warm surge of heartfelt egalitarian friendliness? Had they developed a hitherto unheard-of interest in non-Mobilians? Very possibly, but perhaps other recent events at the CNB and its Wolfe Alabama Bancorporation should be examined.

The revolt that started when the directors of the Farmers and Mechanics Bank of Opp demanded their perks back had blossomed into a full-scale proxy contest that was getting worse and worse. The big Magic City Bank of Birmingham controlled thirty percent of the shares in WolfAl, almost the same amount as the CNB—Wolfe personally had very few.

To make matters worse, the Magic City shares were held in big blocs, while the CNB shares were split up among a host of small holders who had to be courted individually if the Mobile ranks were to hold the line.

Bank employees were soon amazed by a steady file of little old ladies and gentlemen never seen before who were admitted in their Sunday finery to the inaccessible CNB nerve center, i.e. Wolfe's office on the top floor. Eavesdroppers standing in the outer office could hear the fierce magnate chatting tenderly and soliciting their thoughts on banking policy.

In the scramble for proxy votes Wolfe found himself enmeshed in Todd and Barker's megadevelopment. Under pressure from Ray McDougal, one of the biggest contractors in town, Wolfe had begun to have a change of heart about the distasteful prospect of a Biblical amusement park where his sixty-story office tower was to have stood so symbolically dominant right next to the river.

Out of the two million shares in WolfAl, McDougal owned one hundred thousand, the key bloc of votes in the proxy war. McDougal's business was based mainly on building shopping centers and state highways, but he was counting on getting such a big share of the lucrative contracts to fill the bay for Volkswagen and scoop out the south of the city for an artificial lake that it would put his firm in the national big-time leagues. McDougal had told Wolfe in no uncertain terms that if Wolfe did not support Todd's plan he would vote with Birmingham in the proxy fight.

By "support" McDougal meant that Wolfe Alabama should purchase $300 million worth of city general obligation bonds. Mayor Barker thought incurring a debt would be a small price for the city to pay to get the ball rolling.

Even for a financial adventurer like H. Sloane Wolfe, buying $300 million worth of city bonds was a sobering thought. But then it occurred to him that the Commerce National Bank could purchase them and turn around and unload them on unsuspecting country correspondent banks outside the WolfAl system. That way the city might be obliterated, but the contractor would be happy, WolfAl would come out unscathed, and most importantly, Wolfe would remain head honcho.

It was soon after that that CNB employees began the lavish round of entertainment for representatives of what Wolfe privately called "the real dogs of the correspondent system." The little bank presidents in red

University of Alabama blazers who could not even make it within speaking distance of Wolfe at the Alabama Bankers Convention were showered with presents of rods and reels, hunting guns, and golf clubs, accompanied by chummy notes. They were suddenly overwhelmed with hospitality. "Y'all come on down, have some seafood and some beer, let me take you out on my yacht," Wolfe crooned long-distance to astonished ears, and sent the bank airplane up after them.

To his assistant he confided, "Uinest, we gonna pick em off like flies, one by one. Tell em they can affiliate with WolfAl."

"Are we really going to let them join, H. Sloane?" Ernest wondered.

"Are you kiddin? Any bank dumb enough to buy them bonds ain't gonna cut the mustard at Wolfe Alabama!"

One afternoon Wolfe had the president of the Cuba National Bank up to the Million Dollar Board Room for some courtly hard-sell. Wolfe bided his time and watched him ogle the oil duck paintings and try to catch his reflection in the black marble floors.

"Oscar—and I know I can call you that—you might want to hear this sittin down," Wolfe began. "I called you down here because we have high hopes for Cuba, Alabama. We think Cuba, Alabama, is gone be one of the growth spots of the Sunbelt."

The Cuban executive was so excited he nearly spilled his drink on the leather board table. "You really think so, Sloane? Durned if you don't get the wrong impression about a gah sometimes. I just never knew you were so nice."

Wolfe played with a stiletto letter-opener and smiled broadly. "Now listen here. I want the Cuba National Bank in our banking family, and I want you on the WolfAl board of directors." The single strand of hair carefully combed across Oscar's bald scalp flew loose as he sprang from his chair, but Wolfe silenced him with an upraised hand.

"No, that's not all. I want to let you in on a bond deal that's going to be the talk of the state. Something to beef up your old profits column." Wolfe sat down and began to explain Ted Todd's proposal to firebomb the city.

At the end of an hour the banker from Cuba was ready to commit in advance to taking $20 million worth of bonds off the CNB's hands whenever the deal went through. Oscar was impressed. It took, perhaps, an unspoiled mind to fully appreciate the plans for the Six Flags Over Jesus amusement park. "Wholesome family entertainment and a real quality Bible teachin concept. Cain't beat that with a stick. Maybe on down the road we can franchise it."

"Son, that's what Wolfe Alabama is aaawwlll about," Wolfe answered, shifting into fourth gear of his folksiness mode. "Our slogan says, 'Just plain folks.' It's somethin we take to heart."

They heard the door creak open and saw two sleek hands with long black fingernails grip the inside knob like claws. A mane of blond hair appeared, and then an upturned tigress face with black lipstick and white eye shadow. "Rowwwwwww," McCorquodale growled and bit the door. "Pardon me if I interrupt. I'm feeling vivacious today."

CHAPTER 41

Wolfe Must Decide

Oscar Purdue was floored by the dramatic entry, and looked her up and down. McCorquodale had come to obtain Wolfe's help in stopping the development nightmare. To match the seriousness of her purpose, she wore a severe black and white striped business suit, with black spike heels and fashionable Milanese shoulders padded formidably.

She pulled off a black silk glove and waved it in the direction of Oscar, then putting her hands on Wolfe's shoulders, stretched up and gave him a peck on the cheek, one heel winsomely raised.

Wolfe thought nervously of the twenty million dollar bond issue. He introduced her as Miss Roshfookle, a young career woman from the marketing department and also his niece, for good measure.

McCorquodale decided to be nice and play along. She took in Oscar's red blazer with the white "A" on the coat pocket. "Oh, I adore folk costumes, how charming. I should have worn my dirndl." She perched on the edge of the leather-topped meeting table, lit up a Tiparillo, and crossed her legs, causing the short skirt of the suit to slide far up her velvety thighs.

"Darling, let me tell you about the Commerce National Bank. We are not your average tedious *borné* pedestrian institution. Money is nothing to us if not used to create some subtle and inscrutable effect. I'm sure whatever your transaction . . ."

"A bond issue," Oscar volunteered.

"Oh yes, I've heard of those. Whatever. I'm sure you'll be delirious with satisfaction, darling."

Oscar looked confused, but began to praise the Biblical amusement park. "If we can just get folks ridin around on that Mount Sinai roller coaster, I do feel we can get the Bible down to kind of a sound byte level to where people can understand it in these busy times."

"That sounds like Sinai Hill to me," McCorquodale said philosophically. She did not grasp that they had been discussing the giant developments, and assumed he was talking about the "soul train" or some other pious metaphor. How delightful that they were debating ideas. Sloane was making progress. "Never lower the level, darling. Believe me, they'll climb that mountain barefoot if they really care. You know, I happen to have some experience in leading world movements and crusades and such, and my motto has always been strictly, 'Follow me!' The *real* disciples will charge though swamp and desert." She radiated an approving smile on Wolfe.

Instead of being offended, Oscar seemed inclined to linger and follow her, but Wolfe was in a cold sweat to get him out before McCorquodale could say anything else. "The yacht's waitin . . . got to get you some sun, skipper . . . try some a that deep sea fishin." Wolfe practically dragged Oscar out to the hall elevator, and soon he was zipping down twenty-five stories to meet Ernest Balleriel, who was waiting in a snappy boating outfit.

"Are you brain dead, comin in here like that?" Wolfe screeched when he returned. "You coulda cost me twenty million dollars."

"Don't be difficult. Money you can find anywhere. There are more pressing matters that demand our attention. Sloane, I fall upon the thorns of life, I bleed."

"What are you talking about?"

"I am speaking of the impending philistine destruction of the city. It is to be struck down, disembodied. Did you see last Sunday's paper?"

"No, I don't believe so." A queasy expression passed over his face. He had been dreading this moment.

"How curious. The Dadaists are running wild in the streets. People are stampeding to sell their downtown property. There is talk of condemnations. Really, one could become excited."

"Hmmm."

"Hmmm? Is that all you've got to say? Have you thought about the implications? Am I to have my sidewalk café in a horrid suburban-style

Supermall?! What would Benedetto Croce have said? At the opening, am I to welcome Fellini and Almodóvar and the literati of South America in the *parking lot*? Maybe we could get them to play 'Fly Me to the Moon' on the muzak system."

"That ain't such a bad idea. I was thinking of having it piped in here to calm down the directors." Wolfe Alabama board meetings had been rather tumultuous lately.

"The horror! Have you forgotten your most basic tenets? Contextualism, polyvalency. Vernacular taste culture. Eclecticism, revivalism."

"Don't you know it, babe."

"Sloane, dear, I know that as soon as they finish building the Tennessee-Tombigbee Waterway this will be a great metropolis, vastly cosmopolitan, capital of the hemisphere, *Weltstadt*, postmodern . . . but couldn't the Tenn-Tom get here a little sooner?"

Wolfe cleared his throat. "Well, actually, shuguh, there is somethin I'm wuikin on that'll tie right in with that." Dolefully he walked over to shut the door in order to block the shrieks that soon would be forthcoming. He trembled to think how McCorquodale would react. He began telling her about the proxy war in Wolfe Alabama. He told her he was fighting to stay at the helm. Finally, spitting it all out, he said he had decided to buy the bonds and support the project.

McCorquodale regarded him for a moment as though assessing a plate of none-too-fresh escargots. "Quisling, is this how you repay months of priceless esthetic indoctrination? You would have let the Turks into Constantinople with the doors wide open. But we've talked about all this before. You said you'd given that Houston developer his walking papers."

"I'm fightin for my life, baby. They've got me by the throat."

"They've brainwashed you, Sloane. When I see you as a Moonie, conducting mass weddings in the bank lobby, I'm not going to be surprised a bit.

"I am convinced that there is a secret conspiracy of disgruntled modernists working against me. Why else would the movement take so long to catch on here? Just look at these hordes from the western hills. To all appearances a primitive cave tribe, but you can be certain that at their sessions they're really reading LeCorbusier and Robert Moses. Their latest project is to shut down the Hubba Hubba Club. Do you suppose they don't know that a *danseuse* like Tonya de Luxe is a cultural landmark? To think what that woman can do with a pin and fourteen red balloons."

Wolfe was enormously relieved that McCorquodale was as calm as she was. He had been expecting something on the order of convulsions on the floor. "Now, don't take it so bad, punkin. It's not going to be so awful, once you get used to it. They've got some things planned that are gone be real nice." He fished around in his desk drawer for a pamphlet Roberta had given him. For weeks she had been harping on some kind of historic project near the Mississippi state line that she was cooking up with her latest interior decorator, a Mrs. Clarisse Watkins.

McCorquodale began to read the leaflet, which concerned an Old Mobile tourist village to be built in Williamsburg style under the guidance of the Mobile Preservation Society.

"Williamsburg!!" McCorquodale hissed. Wolfe frowned. Maybe he should have read that pamphlet before showing it to her.

Utterly speechless, McCorquodale studied a sketch of a three-block cobblestone street, with disproportionately small red brick Georgian buildings, fit for the Seven Dwarves, giant dormer windows, and gas lanterns strewed around promiscuously. Her eyes flew to the explanation in the cutline underneath signed by her former employer.

"The Watkins beast! Gog, Magog."

She collapsed into a chair and stared into space. The scales had fallen from her eyes, and a vision of the secret workings of reality, to which she had been so blind, passed before her. The Dadaist developer must have been shadowing her when she saw him and the mayor at that singles bar. And what kind of moral watchdog groups would be working with those two womanizers? She thought of Rev. Orville Tidwood and the green-robed choir and the countless legions of the Western Hills Baptist Church. That strange editorial in the newspaper. Mrs. Clarisse Watkins.

Huns and Mongols. They were all in on it together. Reactionary Fauves, Orphists, suburban Cubists, loathsome form-follows-function paramecia, Existentialists grinning at her. What she had said very loosely before about a conspiracy was quite true. This was some kind of secret ideological cell.

Wolfe was touched to note a rare expression of vulnerability, as if she might start crying. Even at the height of indignation and of fashion, McCorquodale retained that Daisy Mae-in-overalls curvaceousness Wolfe had glimpsed on that first hot day in November. He decided to reissue a long-standing invitation. "Now before you get all in a huff, why don't you fly with me to the bank condo in Coconut Grove, take care of some business, iron out them ole snags?"

"Cannot; my migraine, you know." McCorquodale pinched the bridge of her nose. "Until my café is built, I'm afraid the tension will not allow extended visits. I'm sure you see what I mean."

"But it's been almost a year since we met!"

McCorquodale decided to appeal to Wolfe's public-spiritedness. "Sloane, darling, where will you build the Wolfe Alabama Tower if this plan goes through?" Wolfe gazed longingly at the model of the skyscraper in the corner of the board room. Giving up his dream project had been the bitterest pill of the bank war. What was the point of building a skyscraper out in the middle of nowhere with no skyline, no cityscape, no waterfront for it to dominate? "And if you give in to this contractor now, who knows what they'll want next? Maybe *change the name* of Wolfe Alabama!"

"They'd never sink that low," Wolfe growled, but the remark had hit home. He stared out the window at the harbor. McCorquodale was at him one way, the contractor the other. Even Roberta was nagging him at home to support the development. Soon he would have to make a decision.

CHAPTER 42

Schism in the Society

When Ted Todd first presented his vision of massive demolition to the Mobile Preservation Society, Mrs. Balleriel first reacted philosophically. "Oh well, you can't save everything," she and others in the group repeated. Despite Mrs. Balleriel's instant distaste for Todd and the smoldering memory of his praise of Charleston; despite the bothersome revisions that would have to be made to the historic homes cookbook, she was calmed by one thought. In all her experience with disturbing political developments, she had found that they never affected her, Harmsworth, Ernest, their Government Street mansion, or their friends.

The first brutal shock came after the wheels were rolling and plans had been announced for the nationally televised fire-bombing display. Hitherto vague descriptions of the project were suddenly clarified. "Castle Balleriel" and every brick and blade of grass within miles would soon be acquired, leveled to the ground and paved over, they learned from enthusiastic articles in the *Mobile Herald-Item*.

Hastily Mrs. Balleriel set about organizing belated opposition, but then came the shock of the coup d'état at the hands of the strong-willed Roberta Wolfe. At long last the uphill, thirty-year struggle of the North Alabamian to become the first non-native president of the Preservation Society bore fruit. During those thirty long eternities of residence in Mobile, vampish streaks of gray emerged in her jet black hair: the attractive woman became distinguished as well. How long ago it seemed that she had swept into town, a new bride and fresh out of the University of Alabama. She had been a good-looking cheerleader who married a good-looking football player, and had naively expected to enjoy the same kind of success here. But now her entrée into Mobile society seemed just in sight. Many will sympathize with Mrs. Wolfe's human weakness. In any country, acceptance may take some little time for newcomers from distant foreign places.

Together with her friend Arlene Morganton, she whipped up enthusiasm among the members of the Preservation Society in favor of building the Williamsburg Village rather than Ted Todd's original pseudo-Old Mobile proposal. Since Barker and Todd did not know the difference anyway, they were happy to go along with it. Mrs. Wolfe had gotten her new interior decorator involved in the project, and from the word "go" Mrs. Clarisse Watkins had poured out cute and marvelous ideas. "Isn't this just the most darling thing you've ever heard of?" Roberta and Arlene had preached at every opportunity. Support for Todd's plan solidified in the Society.

A terrible split ensued among the membership like Arian versus Orthodox. There were conflicting loyalties, friendships, ties of blood and tradition. Yet as coincidence would have it, those whose homes were to be destroyed sided with Mrs. Balleriel against it, and the majority, whose homes were located safely to the west, and who were all eagerly looking forward to making the tourist village the quaint focal point of many local color articles in *Southern Living* magazine, called a special election and made Mrs. Wolfe the new president.

Mrs. Balleriel was so shaken that for three days straight she would not come out of the "crown room" next to her boudoir, except for meals. That was the oak paneled snuggery, always under lock and key, that contained the royal jewels of her previous reigns: her crown from the Leinkauf Grammar School coronation, class of 1930, various diadems from balls she had led, and, of course, the crown, train, and other sumptuous trappings from her reign as Queen of Mardi Gras, 1939. There were also crowns from both Harmsworth and Ernest's kingships, and inherited treasures and finery from both sides of the family going back to the courts of the 1870s and mystic societies as far as the 1830s, including one crown executed in Antwerp in the 1890s with genuine rubies. Memories of vanished kings, queens, knights, maids, marshalls, equerries, pages, heralds, and ladies-in-waiting haunted the room. Cut off from all noise, seated on her gilded throne from the old Battle House hotel, orb and scepter in hand—a posture which she found especially relaxing—she pondered the tackiness let loose in the world.

A dazing whirl of thoughts assaulted her. What was happening? Who were all these wild people popping up out of nowhere? Where did they come from? A cloud of horsy shrews had escaped from some remote suburban laundromat and had taken over the Preservation Society. Television gameshow hosts seemed to be swarming everywhere. Las Vegas card sharps were running the city, or maybe professional wrestlers, or rodeo cowboys. Whenever she tried to analyze more closely, her thoughts were blocked by a vision of the earth cracking open to swallow Todd and Mayor Barker amid sluggish gurglings of red hot lava. A feeling kept nagging her not to push her thoughts too far about them or the other things hovering somewhere outside.

When she began to feel dizzy, she would have the maid bring up a tray of tea on a silver platter and her favorite imported Scottish short bread. She would pour from the old antebellum Zadek silver pot, sip, munch, slip on the reading glasses that had been hanging on a gold chain down her bosom, and slowly leaf through her secret scrapbook. No one knew about it, not even in the family. Mrs. Balleriel was well aware that she had her detractors, that some people said she was, perhaps, even a bit stuffy. But what did they know? She, too, had her hobbies and her rich inner life. It was when looking at her scrapbook that she felt most relaxed, most herself, just plain "Rose."

Over the years she had slowly assembled it from occasional magazine clippings, these pictures of her colleagues, the great queens of the ages. Naturally, there was Queen Elizabeth, and the no-nonsense Queen Elizabeth I as well, a special favorite. There was Mary Queen of Scots, there were numerous czarinas. The royal houses of Holland, Norway, Sweden, etc., were given the cold shoulder, but there were several pictures of the aging Queen Victoria. The more Mrs. Balleriel's generous figure swelled to resemble hers, the more she felt she understood her. There was the imperious Empress Theodora of Byzantium from a *National Geographic* piece—oh, she was a great one!

A wicked vision came crashing through these reveries, of Roberta

Wolfe emitting a deafening fart as she stood presiding for the first time
at the next Preservation Society meeting. Time for another cup of tea.

On the last page of her scrapbook she had attached a photograph of
herself as a slim young woman standing at the banana docks on the river
where the old-time Mardi Gras coronations and other festivities used to
be held. It was taken on an occasion when she was not wearing her royal
robes, and she looked like Greta Garbo or some other thirties movie
actress with her wavy permanent and long overcoat with a very high fur
collar, both hands in her pockets. It reminded her of those pictures of
modern royalty touring hospitals and cutting ribbons dressed like ordinary citizens.

All around her the dim room, lit only by her reading lamp, was filled
with twinklings and sheens and reflections from the glass cases, manne-
quins, open chests and cabinets, and tiers of shelves lining the walls all the
way up to the lofty ceiling. Blinking, gleaming from rings, pendants,
brooches, engraved toasting cups and trays, circlets, brocade jackets, lace
jabots, puffed sleeves, collars of iridescent tracery, silver filigree. Crino-
line, cotton-backed satin, tarleton, ombre silk. Winking colors of bugle
beads, ribbons, boxfuls of aigrettes sewn on, phials worth of diamond
flitters, tiny lights and wiring, endless spindles of dentelles laboriously
stitched, fishscale net, Strass rhinestones, black jets; all beckoning with
the joy of the detail in its exact collocation, intimate and arbitrary, like
ancient mountain ranges and continental shelves frozen in place on the
earth's crust in this position and not that.

Another naughty thought flashed through the blur in Mrs. Balleriel's
mind; this time she saw Roberta Wolfe and Arlene Morganton being
stuffed into a flaming oven by devils with cloven hooves.

Something from the outside kept pushing its way toward her in the
confusion of images. She tried to focus on the events of the last few days,
on the Biblical amusement park, on the huge shopping mall. No, it
wasn't any of these things. Was it a wrecking ball crashing into their
mansion? No, but close. Then it came to her: the parking lot. A vision of
an endless plane of asphalt, perfectly level, a geometric abstraction like a
chessboard, a Martian landscape, but real. Infinite. And she was standing

on it all alone, the slim young woman in the long overcoat with the fur collar. What earthly business did she have standing on that asphalt plane?

Ernest and Mr. Balleriel were becoming frantic and were thinking about sealing off the room when she came out for a meal, but the thing that finally snapped Mrs. Balleriel out of it was a letter to the editor she saw in the *Herald-Item* criticizing the Supermall plans. It was written by Aunt Odilia.

For weeks the *Herald-Item*, foaming at the mouth, had loosed its progress-oriented thunders in favor of the Supermall/Six Flags/ Volkswagen development, and finally they outdid themselves with a stupendous, not to say rabid, editorial headlined: "Disarmniks Panned, Should Be Forthcoming." Fans of the "Mad Dog School of Journalism" agreed it was of clip and save quality. In one swoop they: 1) urged Ted Todd to demolish more of the city to create *Lebensraum* for as yet undreamt-of industrial growth; 2) called for the repeal of the 1964 Civil Rights Act and the reinstitution of slavery; and 3) denounced British Prime Minister Margaret Thatcher for allowing the export of the subversive *Masterpiece Theater* to ETV and other Cuban revolutionary organizations.

It was in response to these philippics that Aunt Odilia penned her thoughts in the classic manner of *Herald-Item* letters to the editor. Is there any thing like them? Probably not, but certain refined yet vigorous phrases betrayed the assistance of George Belzagui. His erudite style had been finely honed on the model of that doct and indelibly Mobilian novelist and Victorian bestseller, Augusta Evans Wilson:

Sirrah:

I read with "interest" your "recent" editorial, "all dark and barren as the rainy sea" (Sir Walter Scott). I needs must consider the tiny sparrow who chirrups so merrily to the "westering sun" (William Cowper) in the boughs of my little Chinaberry tree. Ah, kind friends, could we but know the coruscating flight of his twittery thoughts, should we not be as "free of strife" as "he" (Madame de Stael)?

As for that rag you call a newspaper, I wouldn't use that fish wrap

to "wipe my cat's litter box" (Che Guevara). Bomb the city will you?
What you need is a bomb, a stink bomb, so think about that. I remain
    Your respectful servant,
    Odilia Roshfookle Chighizola

When Mrs. Balleriel saw this cry from a kindred spirit, she resolved
to visit her, but was puzzled to see the St. Anthony Street address when
she looked it up in the phone book.

CHAPTER 43

Rumbling in the Great Chain of Being

It was a very bad neighborhood. Could this really be where she lived? Mrs. Balleriel pushed the buzzer in the high brick wall next door to Sam's Body Shop. She began to worry that this Mrs. Odilia Chighizola might be a drug pusher or who knows what. Her fears were allayed somewhat when the short buxom figure of Aunt Odilia appeared, not in slacks, but in beads and black silk and heavily rouged cheeks, and led her through the elephant ears and castor plants of the small courtyard formed by the house and a high brick side wall. Clouds of an unidentified perfume wafted behind to encompass Mrs. Balleriel like fumes from a mosquito truck. For a troubling moment she wondered if it could be vanilla extract.

The parlor had windows opening onto the side porch facing the courtyard, all hidden from the street by the brick front wall. Mrs. Balleriel was surprised to see a fairly proper clutter of stuffy plush Victorian chairs, brass lamps, jade and china vases, and crocheted antimacassars, though the bottles filled with wavy layers of colored sand were open to censure. There was a peculiar smell. Some kind of hippie incense? Probably an herbal sachet, she finally decided.

How mysterious, she thought again, and a tingling feeling of adventure came over her. As longtime president of the Mobile Preservation Society, Mrs. Balleriel was, of course, a militant historic preservationist, as she interpreted the term. Yet she had not taken five minutes to drive over and look at the area since before World War II. But then of course why should she? No one with any historic background lived here any more. It was just a bunch of old houses.

The district used to be called the North Side, and a lot of the Catholics still called it St. Patrick's Parish, from the church that used to stand there to serve the largely Irish neighborhood that existed further up around Beauregard Street in the nineteenth and early twentieth centuries. Others reckoned it part of the Orange Grove, a name going back to eighteenth century colonial days, when actual orange orchards grew there, though strictly speaking the Orange Grove started a little farther north around Lipscomb Street. Now it was called DeTonti Square, and was slowly languishing and crumbling into dust, despite a few law firms moving in. In the early nineteenth century it had been the most exclusive residential neighborhood, with blocks of elegant brick town houses with cast or wrought iron galleries, jammed in together on narrow little lots under huge live oaks. But when Mrs. Balleriel was a little girl the nice families had moved out. Who would have dreamed that people still lived down here?

McCorquodale was out (meeting H. Sloane Wolfe in Ocean Springs), but after Mrs. Balleriel called, Aunt Odilia had invited Mr. Belzagui to come that afternoon. He had taken off the day for the occasion, and was nearly overwhelmed by Mrs. Balleriel's celebrity presence. "You can't imagine what this me-uns to me," he said, jumping up rather too quickly from his chair when she came in. "For yeuhs I've followed every detail of yo pawties and receptions in *Tell Tale*." He was referring to the famous social column in the *Herald-Item*.

"Yase, the newspaper," she sighed, and smiled at the ceiling. A warm feeling of benevolence passed over her that she should be speaking to this simple person. "They never get enough, but I try to be patient. If they couldn't write about me every week, what on uith would they do?"

Aunt Odilia was in the kitchen preparing the coffee, and Mr. Belzagui frantically tried to think of something else to say. But Mrs. Balleriel lapsed into magnificent silence, idly twirled her ivory-rimmed spectacles dangling on the long gold chain, and meditated. The city was threatened, the bombers and bulldozers virtually ready to take off, but first she had to assign Aunt Odilia and Mr. Belzagui to their proper place on the Great Chain of Being.

Normally this invisible ritual took her only a few seconds, but she had been confused by Mrs. Chighizola's self-assurance in the midst of this seedy neighborhood. They were definitely not country, had obviously grown up in town. She had probably spent all her life in the house, maybe inherited it, so her parents, at least, had spent their lives here. That made at least one previous generation here, though perhaps the parents had been born elsewhere. A certain level of manners, a certain level of awareness, but she could see they were not related to anybody. If you saw them in the grocery store you would not know them, but if you asked around somebody would have heard of their last name. They were natives, after a fashion. "Yeomen," she decided, a private term for a lower rank on the chain.

If this judgment might sound harsh to some, to Mrs. Balleriel's mind it was quite munificent. Woe to those who had just moved to town and floated in unknown limbos beneath the lowest link of the Great Chain! "It's the facts of life, Uinest," she had often instructed the Balleriel heir when appraising people, brushing aside any other parental instruction the term might imply. "Luin it and remembuh." Aunt Odilia and Mr. Belzagui were the kind of people she might graciously recognize with a nod if they passed the Athelstan Club reviewing stand before a parade, but could she seriously work with them in this crisis?

Aunt Odilia arrived with a tray of store-bought chocolate cupcakes, reserves of Hostess Twinkies still in their plastic packs, and three assorted demitasses from her motley china collection. She looked at the tiny cups with satisfaction. Mrs. Balleriel looked at the Twinkies. That they did not disintegrate on the spot is a testimonial to modern industrial standards.

Like McCorquodale, Aunt Odilia was not easily awed, but here was the confirmation of her wildest and most megalomaniac visions of Roshfookle gentility. The audience that she had silently addressed in years of countless inner monologues was sitting right there in her parlor. Aunt Odilia's hands shook ever so slightly as she poured the coffee, and her face burned a soft red, but her voice was utterly authoritative as she began her attack, drawing on vast stores of genealogical knowledge.

"I understined yo mothuh's nayim was Pawkhuist," she began.

"Fate has been kind," Mrs. Balleriel answered with a self-effacing wave of the hand. She could already see that this Mrs. Chighizola was a brilliant conversationalist. Perhaps she *would* just sample a Twinky.

"I have been doing resuich on the nayim lately. Now tell me, is it some awfshoot of the famous Pawkhuist famly of Newpote News?"

"Suitainly not! I have been to Virginia and it is a bawbaric place. They had nevuh huid of me." Though this was said with a certain sternness, she relished the stimulating exchange of ideas.

"Now when he was a boy my grind-fawthuh, Reuben Roshfookle, knew yo great-grind-fawthuh, Mr. Theo Pawkhuist, when he was just a young man and still had his little fruit stined on Front Stree-it. He always said . . ."

"*Fruit stined*!? Could you be referring to his impote-distribution consuin?" Mrs. Balleriel was irked at this unexpected familiarity, and somewhat shaken, too. She had thought that virtually no one now remembered this shaky limb in the family tree. Horatio Alger tales of success from modest origins were not her cup of tea.

"He always said that Mr. Theo became wealthy because he was a hawd wuikuh. And his son right in the thick of everything and king of Mawdi Gras, too. Of cose . . ." she paused and very discreetly reached into her dress to pull up a recalcitrant slip strap, then started the story all her friends had heard ad infinitum, "the Roshfookles were the very *fuist* royalty, you know."

"I beg yo pawdon?"

"The Roshfookles. My maiden nayim is 'Roshfookle.'" The moment had arrived to announce their splendor to the world. She looked toward Mr. Belzagui for confirmation, but he was studying the grounds in his coffee cup with intense absorption. Divining oracles? "We were the fuist royalty."

A silence fell on the room which could have swallowed a charging gasoline truck. For a moment Mrs. Balleriel's face was as unblinking as a plaster cast, then she broke into a dazzlingly radiant and kindly smile reserved only for condemned heretics being carted to the rack.

"Mrs. Chighizola," she said at length, with immense dignity. "Do you think it might rain?"

Aunt Odilia silently produced a hand-inked invitation that Mr. Belzagui had recently discovered and had finally produced after weeks of prodding. Surprisingly, the paper looked as white as new, and the drawings were strikingly reminiscent of the style of Mr. Belzagui's sign painter friend in the Knights of Columbus, Dutch Bledsoe.

Mrs. Balleriel was quite familar with the existence of the Tea Drinkers and the other antebellum carnival mystic societies, of which only the Strikers now survived. The Jamestons had been in the

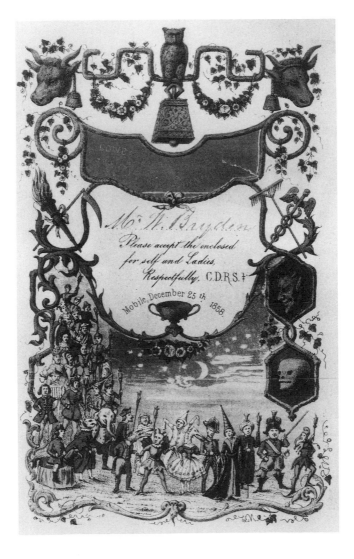

No doubt the tea drinkers were the grandest.

Cowbellions! But she had never heard of their choosing any queens.

Slowly she examined the silver crest. A beaming star set on a trickling hourglass. A stag and a bushy-tailed fox, rampant. Two smirking cherub faces. Two crossed scythes. The sun rising over the ocean. "The Determined Set of Tea Drinkers invite you to salute their Carnival Queen: Miss Camille Roshfookle. The Temperance Hall, New Year's Eve, 1847."

Suddenly the universe gaped among the marble-topped tables. The Great Chain of Being rumbled, and Aunt Odilia came flying upwards. Could there be, Mrs. Balleriel asked herself, whole new worlds of Mobile gentility she had never suspected?

What followed belongs more or less to history. During the rest of the afternoon Aunt Odilia discoursed on McCorquodale, Camille's successor. Mrs. Balleriel learned of an exceedingly demure and diligent young lady who had even made it into the National Honor Society at Murphy High School.

A subsequent meeting concerning battle plans was held the following Wednesday. It included Miss Alice and Miss Hattie Robinson. A radical manifesto was drawn up announcing that the city would secede from the state of Alabama unless the Supermall and bay-filling projects were immediately halted.

The threatened declaration of independence stressed the absolute essentials in the new city-state. Palms and Golden Rain trees would be planted at strategic points throughout the city, and Alabama Power Company would be forbidden to hack up street trees (Miss Hattie's request). The Book of the Month Club would be subscribed to for the Government Street Baptist Church library (Miss Alice). Historic plaques acknowledging the contributions of Lebanese Americans would be put up all over town (Mr. Belzagui). *All* grocery stores would give green stamps for *all* products (Aunt Odilia). All newspapers, and radio and television stations would be required to broadcast extensive society news, which had been shamefully curtailed of late (Mrs. Balleriel).

Though McCorquodale was unable to attend, Aunt Odilia introduced a plank endorsing postmodernism on her behalf.

CHAPTER 44

A Gay Old Time

As sometimes happens in the very best society, Ernest Balleriel decided to give two parties on successive evenings for two very different sets of friends. The "Secession Follies" were organized at McCorquodale's prompting to rally support for his mother's movement to have Mobile secede from the state of Alabama. Unfortunately, in an unguarded moment Ernest had told "Mamacita" that McCorquodale would be present at both gala events, and when Mrs. Balleriel's plans for a bridge party fell through, she decided to drop by unexpectedly the second evening to meet this promising new face on the social scene that Mrs. Chighizola had told her so much about.

The first party was truly stellar. The fabulous Young Set turned out practically in toto at Ernest's imitation Old Mobile town house to gobble the catered veal-Courvoisier pâté and the smoked oysters wrapped in bacon.

Regina Hammerstein revealed to a hushed audience sitting on reproduction Hepplewhite chairs that the real reason Mary Louise McCaffery's little sister wasn't making her debut was that she had gone *backpacking* through the Smoky Mountains with an apprentice electrician, taking with her only a copy of Kahlil Gibran, can you imagine? Everyone was enthusiastic about the secession idea because it just might be the way to get cute people back into Mobile politics. Ernest circulated very visibly arm in arm with Ce Ce Anne.

But how Regina Hammerstein's stories would have paled if the Friday night guests could have been present Saturday night!

In the words of Eddie, who had been absent the night before, it was "truly a gay ole time," nothing if not relaxed. Perhaps inspired by the new egalitarian tendencies at the Commerce National Bank, Ernest had invited bartenders and lawyers, auto mechanics and graduate students, architects, yard boys, bus boys, and record salesmen. The strongly male crowd showed a preference for bouncy white tennis shoes, with sweaters tied about their necks and collars nattily turned up, or else tight tank tops to show off their weight room muscles.

Ernest and Eddie were arm in arm and positively sporty in shiny gold Athelstan Club jogging shorts with matching visors. McCorquodale thought it prudent both nights to tell Wolfe she was going to the bingo games with Aunt Odilia. As for Ce Ce Anne, she appeared blissfully content with Helmut, back in port from Caracas. The brawny seaman was a great hit that night in a tuxedo with a red bow tie and cummerbund, though he acted a bit nervous at the admiring looks he got.

It was Eddie's idea to stage a little fund-raising entertainment for the secession movement. At first he had come up with rather bland, conventional fund-raising ideas their crowd had often tried: selling tickets to a high-heels-in-the-sand race at Pensacola Beach; a spaghetti dinner with Meryl Streep look-alike contest at popular Club Fifth Avenue on Joachim Street. Ernest had quickly rejected both of them on the chance that he might be seen by the wrong eyes, but Eddie finally persuaded him to allow a few carefully chosen numbers in the privacy of his Monticello-motif entrance hall.

Perhaps the greatest celebrity Eddie had engaged for the evening was "Roxanna Bardot," known by day as Wilmer Plunkett, a carpet layer much in demand. At night Wilmer switched his crew cut and baseball cap for the undulant falls of a curly red wig for performances at Club Fifth Avenue. Recently, after the city council passed an ordinance requiring female impersonators and strippers to register with the city, Roxanna had created a sensation by showing up at the mayor's press conference dressed as Nancy Reagan, and asking a speechless Buzz Barker where to sign up.

"Girl, I tell you what, you got *nerve*," Eddie told Roxanna in front of Ernest and Ce Ce Anne and Helmut. "I'd a pitched outta my high heels the minute they brought the TV cameras."

"It weren't nothin," Roxanna said. "I been applauded in Biloxi; they done give me roses in Pensacola. I just think of my image. Cold, grand, above it all, ya know?"

Eddie listened intently. "Yeah, that was me in *Oklahoma*, but people always underestimate tap dancing," he complained. "Well, I think tap dancing is *so precious*," Ce Ce Anne announced brightly, hanging onto Helmut. "I just *cried* and *cried* when Richard Chamberlain had to give it up in *The Turning Point*. Didn't Daphne Du Maurier write the book?" Like other sparkling socialites, Ce Ce Anne sometimes came out with cryptic comments.

Everyone looked puzzled, but the silence was broken when McCorquodale joined them, radiant in a slinky black sharkskin evening gown, blond hair pulled to one side and hibiscus behind her ear. She was pinning high hopes on the secession movement, and emanated energy.

Though Roxanna was certainly impressive in cowgirl boots and hat, she couldn't help complimenting McCorquodale. "Gal, you're all gal. Just flawless! You got class, honey, I bet you could perform in New Awlins. Ya been doin silicone, ainchoo?" she said, admiring McCorquodale's remarkably full and upright breasts.

"I hate to tell you darling, but I have an unfair competitive advantage," McCorquodale answered. "It's all real."

Ernest announced it was time for the show and a dazzling performance began. Everyone gathered to watch the stars come down the entrance hall stairs and perform underneath the brass chandeliers next to Ernest's Gilbert Stuart reproductions by the front door. Roxanna repeated the act that had brought down the house at Fort Whiting Auditorium last Mardi Gras during the all gay all-star Order of Thoth ball: jumping out of a huge papier-mâché hand of King Kong in a Fay Wray costume. There were cries of "Unreal!," "I ain't believin this!," "I'm wrecked!"

Several guest stars lip-synched the latest Dolly Parton, and some in the audience pretended to pass out when Miss Styx, a tall skeletal performer from Montgomery, rolled on the floor and stabbed herself with a rubber knife in a song of unrequited love. One by one, members of the audience stepped up and stuffed contributions into the stars' bras for the cause of Gulf Coast independence. It was the classic Club Fifth Avenue gesture of tipping largesse for great performances.

In the general clamor after the last act no one noticed that Mrs. Balleriel had come in until someone trained the spotlight on one of the dowager empresses of Mobile society standing darkly next to the front door in a massive chinchilla stole and tiny maroon toque.

"It's a dragon queen!" Eddie hollered admiringly, seeing her for the first time. "Y'all move y'all's butts back and give that wench some room! She's fixin to read some beads." Thinking she was part of the show, Eddie pulled out a five-dollar tip, the supreme compliment, to stuff into Mrs. Balleriel's bosom. But heaven intervened and McCorquodale pulled him back in time: "I think not, darling."

Ernest had evaporated from the scene, along with all the copies of *Christopher Street* and *Blueboy* lying about. Ce Ce Anne rushed forward to smooth things over.

"What a lot of young men," Mrs. Balleriel exclaimed as someone put on a rock album.

"Yes, it's the Washington and Lee Men's Russian Chorus, Mizz B. What a *shame* you missed the show," Ce Ce Anne said shakily, signaling for Helmut to go to the kitchen.

"Russian? I'm not sure I approve. Can you name one Russian who has a house on the spring tour of homes? Of cose not."

The guests had started dancing and Mrs. Balleriel was just putting on her spectacles to observe Roxanna hopping up and down in a frenzied New Wave jerk with Eddie when Ernest reappeared. He had changed into a pinstripe suit in record time.

"Mamacita, I'd like you to meet my latest discovery, McCorquodale Roshfookle, a natural leader. Sometimes I think she might have Balleriel blood," Ernest said, waxing reckless in his agitation.

"We do get around," McCorquodale answered, "but I rather fancy I am some wild strain of Habsburg or maybe a postmodern Anastasia."

Only a true native—in the very narrowest sense of course—would speak with such self-confidence, Mrs. Balleriel decided. If anything, Mrs. Chighizola had underestimated her abilities to participate in a secession movement. She wondered why the Russian chorus kept shrieking "Move out!" and "Whip it, whip it good!" but Ernest never gave her a chance to talk to the other guests.

CHAPTER 45

VW and the Genealogical Trump Card

Success seemed just around the corner, but Mayor Barker was getting nervous. Both he and Todd were concerned about the news of a growing movement to have Mobile secede from Alabama and the delays it might cause in the state funding they were expecting.

Despite all their frantic activity, nothing really seemed to affect the local inertia. "We've got the whole damn conurban infrastructure accessed in a receptivity posture," Todd was apt to murmur at pensive moments, "but the beat just goes on."

Yet on the surface of it, there had never been such a boom. The development bubble kept getting bigger and bigger, and the powers-that-be were not inclined to ask too many questions. Privately, of course, many business and civic leaders were sitting on the sidelines and predicting with their usual cynicism, "It'll never wuik." But they were careful to hedge their bets.

The members of Task Force 2000 had carefully reserved large tracts of land for themselves next to the Volkswagen factory to be built on the site of the bay. Barker was happy to cooperate in exchange for their support. Just so the public would not feel left out after paying to fill in he bay, Barker withheld an acre from the land sales, to be retained for a city park next to the site for the proposed Volkswagen sewage outfall line in the surviving ship channel.

In the city itself, condemnation proceedings had already started in probate court to prepare for the firebombing. The big property owners were looking forward to getting a friendly appraisal for their property and a tax-free settlement when the process went before circuit court judge Clarence "Sluggo" Madison, a man very open to suggestion. Madison himself planned to unload a long-abandoned used car lot he owned in the most desolate section of St. Louis Street on the city for $1,200,000.

Small wonder that when Barker and Todd brought over Willi Kleindorf straight from Berlin, Task Force 2000 members were ready to believe his every word as head of the Volkswagen "Western Hemisphere Expansion Office." Since Willi had been the Volkswagen contact person for the Chamber of Commerce, they gladly paid for his flight.

"Ja, ve been ready for quite some time to moof our Brazilian vorks here," Willi told a crowd of businessmen at the welcoming reception at the Commerce National Bank. "You vouldn't belieff how hot it gets down there, and vith forty *tausend* sveatty vorkers in one place . . . oof, time for a change in scenery." He was very convincing. How were they to guess that Willi had other lines of work?

H. Sloane Wolfe stared sourly at Willi's slick black Peter Lorre hairdo parted down the middle and the rabbit's foot and gold chains around his neck. In the midst of his internal bank war, he was under tremendous pressure to buy several hundred million dollars' worth of city bonds for this project; hence the bank's being chosen as the site of the reception. Wolfe was footing the bill for the party in every sense of the word. But other business titans in the group were all admiration.

"Ah now, come on, Mr. Willi," said Ripley Washton. "You folks at Volkswagen are playing the bigtime hardball. Tell us the *real* reason you're coming here."

Willi smiled nervously. There had been no time coming from the airport to go over his act with Barker and Todd. "Nope, that's it. Ve just tink dis is a real nice place. Azaleas, gumbo, industrial vaste disposal, PCB incinerator ships, you got it all."

"Well, I bet I know the reason they picked us," said Taylor Hammerstein of Hammerstein Pine and Hardwood with mischievous suspense. "The Tenn-Tom!!" There was a murmur of agreement and everyone stared at Willi, who nodded wisely. He tried frantically to think what the word could mean. Tom? Wasn't that a name? And ten of them?

Ce Ce Anne had been quietly sipping a martini and taking in the conversation for a full report to McCorquodale. But suddenly to her endless distress, she saw Helmut enter the room. The giant sailor had gotten an ear pierced that morning, and was sporting a gold earring and oiled hair pulled back tight in a little ponytail. He had on the extra-large tuxedo he had worn to Ernest's "Secession Follies" and looked like some kind of waiter. Ce Ce Anne ran behind a clump of potted palms and snatched Helmut as he walked past.

"What are you doing here?" she screeched. "I'm wearing my new 'fall' colors for 'summer' women, but this could spoil a perfect day."

"I vas bored," Helmut complained. "I vanted to see vere you vorked."

"What if the Junior League found out?! And Daddy's here! I could just *pice out*. Helmut, one day I'll introduce you, but this is not the moment, precious." She told him he could stay and watch for a while, but extracted an iron vow from Helmut to stay behind the palms. Then she returned to chat with a group of friends from the Marketing Department.

But Helmut was soon discovered by Willi Kleindorf, who was wandering about the room looking for Buzz Barker. Willi decided it would be safe to talk to the waiter. "Excuse me, can you tell me vat means 'Tenn-Tom'?"

"Beats me, man," Helmut answered, and laid a drawn-out soul handshake on him. "Giff me fife. Say, dute, vere you from?"

They discovered that they were compatriots, and in the relaxed conversation that followed, Willi told Helmut about his Far East travel service and offered to fix him up with a flight to a hot honey in Thailand for only three thousand dollars.

"No thanks, I have a girlfriend right here," Helmut said in German. "She's going to set me up with a job with her dad's ship lines." Later, when he casually repeated his conversation with the German travel agent to Ce Ce Anne, remarking what a friendly guy he was, the eyes of the "AP Service of the Young Set" got very big indeed.

That same day, on St. Anthony Street, Aunt Odilia began a massive assault on the Houston developer's plan with a series of ingeniously targeted blackmail letters. Mrs. Balleriel had furnished her a list of renegade Old Mobile names that had jumped onto the development bandwagon.

Aunt Odilia knew secrets that could reduce a social lioness to a mere heap of smoldering ashes. She arranged a stack of onion skin stationery on her desk, poured herself a glass of Mogen David, and piously turned the $1.25 St. Anthony candle she had bought at the National to the wall. Flourishing a small mother-of-pearl pen, she began a letter to the renowned Mrs. Chasuble Hedgemont, née Ruth Millet, who had been among the first to agree to sell her land holdings to the city.

Dear Mrs. Hedgemont:

I am happy to inform you that I have discovered that Estelle Millet, directress and star dancer of the Buckatunna Say-It-By-Bellygram Service, is your own blood kin and second cousin. I am sure you will agree that in these days of the shrinking American family, we must seek out and treasure all of our forgotten loved ones. You will be pleased to know that I have arranged a little family reunion, and have prepared press releases and an invitation list including many of your dearest friends to meet this talented cousin lost so long in distant Mississippi. . . .

CHAPTER 46

A Little Bit of Blackmail

After her conversation with Helmut, Ce Ce Anne racked her delightful brains for a way to break the news of the Volkwagen scam to H. Sloane Wolfe. Biceps were all very well, but she could hardly let drop that her sailor boyfriend from the German ship *Deutsche Freude* had told her about it. No, no, no. If McCorquodale told him, she would not be able to explain how she knew, and Wolfe might not believe her. No, Wolfe must hear about it indirectly, through a tidal wave of gossip. But how does one start a tidal wave? Then she had an idea.

The very next evening Ce Ce Anne convened a special session of the Junior League Committee on Urban Affairs at her Carpenter Gothic cottage. The importance of the occasion may be judged from the fact that Ce Ce Anne served her noted garbanzo bean-smoked oyster quiche, so convenient because everything came out of a can.

"You're *so* clever, Ce," said Tilda O'Toole, daintily biting so as not to spill crumbs on her navy corduroy skirt. "I've never had anything *so super* in my *entire life.*"

"But Tilda, precious, you served it last Friday at the showuh for Karen Bixwell. I gave you the recipe, shuguh," Ce Ce Anne reminded.

"Oh, I remember now," Tilda said brightly. "I had to copy it *by hand* for the caterer. I was *just exhawsted.*"

"Now listen, I really shouldn't tell y'all this," Ce Ce Anne began solemnly, "but I know y'all won't repeat it." At these words everyone sat up and Antoinette McCrae, arbiter as ever in her metallic shoes, knickers, and tight chignon hairdo, asked for another daiquiri.

As air-conditioning zephyrs whirled about them, Ce Ce Anne launched into an elaborate explanation of how, according to "reliable sources," the so-called Volkswagen executive who wanted to fill in the bay really ran a seedy travel service from Berlin to the decrepit pleasure domes of the Far East, and he was in on the deal to firebomb the city, too, and it was all a scam and they'd better act quickly. Ce Ce Anne paused for dramatic effect, but noticed that all eyes in the room were glazed over with boredom.

"Politics is so depressing," protested Binky Mastin. "I think we should think about *positive* things, don't you?"

Ce Ce Anne was stymied. How could she translate it into their language? Then she remembered that young attorney Parker Stallings was the only member of Mayor Barker's Hamburger Harbor Improvement Association with any social standing. Everyone brightened when she mentioned his name.

"Oh, Pawkuh, such a *neat* person, why didn't you say he was involved?" said Beverly Chapen. She had seen him twice in her life. Beverly had never quite recovered from belonging to one of the obscurer sororities in high school, and she was always eager to show how many cute people she knew.

"Yes, he *is* involved," Ce Ce Anne said innocently. "As I was saying, they say some of those Thai women are so accommodating. I wonder if Pawkuh has gone on any of the flights?" Silence followed.

By ten that night the slightly embellished news that Parker Stallings and the jackleg Volkswagen impostor Willi Kleindorf had been photographed by the *National Enquirer* in the upstairs rooms of a Tokyo brothel with a bevy of naked go-go dancers had rocked the metropolis.

In the half-timbered Tudor mansion of the august Mrs. Marmeduke LeVerne, a flowered Limoges cup lay smashed on the upstairs sitting room floor, spilling Constant Comment tea across the terra cotta tiles. The hand that had held the cup was still poised in the air, pinkie slightly lifted. In the other hand was a devastating blackmail letter. She was a key party among the big downtown property owners selling out to the city, and Mrs. Balleriel had placed her name near the top of the list she wrote for Aunt Odilia.

Mrs. LeVerne dabbed her eyes as she reread the letter. "On the afternoon of Fat Monday, 1946, an individual named Clyde Grunch, presently commander of Shriner's Lodge No. 221, purchased a gold-plated anklet at Rosenstein Jewelry. Can you explain why, that same night, the aforesaid Clyde Grunch was seen entering your room at the Battle House, supposedly reserved for debutante entertaining?"

How did they know? What a predicament. Such a revelation could blast her reputation. "Oh, why did I do it with a Shriner?" Mrs. LeVerne wept. "Why couldn't I have picked somebody more presentable?"

"Reserved for debutante entertaining." She had been entertaining, all right. As though appealing to an invisible jury, she recalled that at the time the good-looking, six-foot-five beer truck driver had not been a Shriner, and had entranced her with an indefinable charm during the week or so of their little fling. For several lingering minutes, her thoughts wandered away from the peril at hand as she recalled his charm.

But there was no getting around it. Oh, no one would smirk or say anything, no. But whenever they looked at her everybody would imagine her in a harem outfit, wearing a tasseled fez and riding a tiny motorcycle. And when they found out that he had given her an anklet, how tacky! Though at the time, the anklet had thrilled her for that very reason, the symbol of her little walk on the wild side, and she had worn it to the deliberate exclusion, so to speak, of everything else.

There was nothing to do but follow the instructions of the letter. She called the Trust Department of the Prudential National Bank and told them not to sell her property to the city. If necessary they would take it to court.

Fat raindrops splattered against the windows of Wolfe's office. A September hurricane, instead of striking Cuba and going up the east coast as everyone had expected, had skirted the island and plowed into the Gulf. The weathermen said it could hit anywhere from Tampa to Corpus Christi, but there would be several days of rain in any event.

Even as new developments promised to stalemate Todd and Barker's gigantic project, a conference was taking place that could seal the fate of the city. All depended on Wolfe. High, high above the harbor, he was being put under terrific pressure from contractor Ray McDougal to buy the city bonds that would help finance the project.

Wolfe thought sadly how brightly it had all started just a year ago: a small acquisition war, a few issues of stock and he was going to control a statewide empire. McDougal was waiting for an answer.

"But Ray, where's yo civic pride, podnuh? Would you want a Mobile bank to sell out to *Buimingham*?" No response. McDougal's stony face did not flinch. Wolfe decided to try another tack.

"But think of the stockholders," the financial adventurer said piously. "Don't you think $300 million in city bonds is a little risky, fella?"

"Sell them to the correspondent banks, do what you damn want," McDougal menaced, "because right now, Wolfe, *I'm* the most important person at the Commerce National Bank."

Wolfe saw it was time to bring up his real fear. "If I give in to you now, how do I know that y'all won't want any more? Why, you might even change the name of Wolfe Alabama." A slight quiver in his voice belied the casual tone.

"Well actually, Wolfe, me and some of the other stockholders've been meanin to bring that up. Don't you think 'Pilgrim's' or 'Minuteman' or 'Neo-Colonial Bancorporation' would have more charisma? Just a thought."

Wolfe sat back in his chair. A faraway blank look passed over the old football player's face as though he were watching a punted ball sail high up over the grandstands.

McDougal agreed to give Wolfe one more day to decide. From Wolfe's eyrie, the river and bay looked dark and restless. It was lonely at the top, he thought. He yearned to talk things over with McCorquodale.

CHAPTER 47

Damn the Torpedoes

That evening the TV and radio stations were full of the news that Hurricane Clotilde would strike Mobile the next night. But that did not prevent Buzz Barker, Ted Todd and their associates from having an emergency meeting at Hamburger Harbor.

Though the nationally televised firebombing was scheduled for the next week (the network was giving it a full fifteen minutes, with peppy narration to stress the upbeat aspects), Barker was beginning to wonder if they could wait that long. All day long he had been getting mysterious calls from people reneging on their agreement to sell their land to the city. And the talk about Mobile seceding from Alabama was endangering Barker's deals with the state.

But the worst news of all had reached their ears late that afternoon. Somehow it had gotten out that Willi Kleindorf was not a Volkswagen representative at all, and several deacons at Western Hills Baptist Church were said to grumbling ominously about "whoremongers."

Barker feared that the end of the development was in sight unless they took quick action. "It's past overdue for a comeback in the low-profile go-for-it recovery mode," he expostulated. Filling in the bay "for Volkswagen" was out of the question now, but they could at least save part of the plan.

His solution was ingeniously simple—firebomb the city a week early, the minute the hurricane winds died down. They would say it was done to prevent looting. After the land was cleared, the city could easily hold it for years free of charge until Todd's Sunbelt Land Corporation could put together their financial package for the Supermall. It certainly would not be the first time the city had done that for a developer.

The next morning a massive compulsory evacuation and house-to-house search began in the eastern part of the city, supposedly because of the flooding hazard. At Albert Tunney's suggestion, a fleet of bombers was quietly moved to an improvised secret air strip in Chunchula. It was the flat pasture land of the McCorquodales.

At the Commerce National Bank, H. Sloane Wolfe's thoughts were far away from the approaching hurricane. Should he give in to McDougal so that he could keep control of the Bancorporation? Should he fight it out? Would they change the name of "Wolfe Alabama" no matter what? Several times Wolfe picked up the telephone to call McDougal and capitulate, but the once steely resolution of the financial titan always faltered.

By early afternoon the bank was virtually empty. Outside, the sky was black. Gusts of rain pounded the deserted streets. A few scattered workmen rushed to nail plywood over office windows on St. Joseph Street so that they could scurry home or leave town.

Ernest Balleriel entered the silence of Wolfe's posh office to plead with him. "H. Sloane, they're evacuating, the National Guard is coming, you've got to leave!"

"I ain't budgin," Wolfe said bravely. "If the Commuice National Bank is going down, then I'm a goin down with the ship. You can repeat that for posterity when they find me lyin in the rubble," Wolfe suggested.

"Going down? I've never heard of a twenty-five-story skyscraper being blown down in a hurricane."

Wolfe was distinctly annoyed that Ernest failed to sense the heroism of the moment. "Well, who the hell asked you?" he thundered. "Go save yourself and tell em, 'He was a man among men.'"

Ernest was, in fact, getting worried about rain blowing in on his Dhurrie rugs at home. "Oh all right, I'll check on you tomorrow," he said calmly.

When the National Guard searched the building Wolfe hid in the office closet where he kept his unused weight lifting equipment, little dreaming of the fleet of bombers waiting in Chunchula. After they left, he went to the Million Dollar Board Room on the same floor for a better view of the high white waves beginning to boil across the bay. Roberta had fled that morning to her native Huntsville with several friends in the Preservation Society. Wolfe tried to call McCorquodale but the phones were out. It was getting darker outside.

"All alone," he mourned, "they've left the old bird dog to sleep out in the storm."

Wolfe had taken the precaution of sending out for provisions early that morning (an order which had filtered down to Eddie). Though he could easily have heated them downstairs in the kitchen of the employees' cafeteria, he preferred to pretend he was roughing it. He was just heating some beans over a can of Sterno on a metal tray when McCorquodale came bursting into the board room, still dripping water.

"Baby doll!"

"Sloane, darling, I've been trying to get you. Rejoice! Don't you know we're saved? Volkswagen is not coming." McCorquodale told him about the scam, carefully keeping Ce Ce Anne's name out of the story.

"Yeah, I huid all that this mawnin."

Wolfe was not as relieved as might have been expected. If the deal fell through completely, what was to keep McDougal from voting with Birmingham? "I just don't know, shuguh. If I buy them bonds they could still build the Supermall."

"Sloane, take heart. What's a little banking empire here and there? You could start anew, open a restaurant. Perhaps a postmodern gallery with a sidewalk café, to name only one possibility." Wolfe had never agreed to a definite date in funding her dream project. She shed her wet raincoat and galoshes.

After a year of good behavior imposed by McCorquodale, Wolfe always acted the perfect gentleman, but now he felt a film of grayness disappearing somewhere inside him, and a ball of fire welling up his spine. Maybe it was because of her soothing words, maybe because in her haste the fashionable bombshell had donned nothing but cut-offs and a flimsy T-shirt, now throughly wet and transparent. Clotilde was starting to moan outside, but Wolfe leaned over and spoke in a whisper, his throat gone dry. "Puddin, don't you think you know me well enough now?" Further words were not necessary.

McCorquodale sat on the leather-top conference table and lit up a Tiparillo. "I just don't know, darling, there're so many uncertainties for a working girl. If only I had my gallery."

"It's yours," Wolfe said feverishly, ready now to agree to anything. "We'll build it this winter."

"And I'll need a fitting ambiance. A city around it, for example."

Wolfe found himself suddenly not giving a damn anymore. "City? Why sho. To hell with them bonds. They can do what they damn please, I'll take it right on the chin."

She felt the warmth of his arm passing around her shoulders. He was so tall. And what strong hands.

All at once the lights went out. The winds started to roar like a never-ending freight train going faster and faster. The building trembled, the leather felt springy beneath her. It was a time for noble thoughts. In the dying sunlight she could barely descry the tossing bay. McCorquodale thought of Farragut's fleet steaming in so long ago. If a Yankee could show such nerve to take Mobile, what could she not do to save it? And besides, more than a year of revolutionary self-denial had passed. A soft moan escaped her.

She felt Wolfe's lips slowly doing field maneuvers down her neck. The heat shot through her, her iron discipline was melting.

"Baby, let's you and me have us a hurricane party," he yelled above the roar.

McCorquodale felt some troubling memory stirring. She struggled for clarity. A sheet of glass shattered somewhere. With her last clear thoughts she made up her mind. "Damn the torpedoes," she murmured, "full speed ahead!"

She put out her Tiparillo and the last spark of light vanished from the room.

CHAPTER 48

Drama and Destiny after the Storm

When daylight came and the winds of Hurricane Clotilde had died down, terrible reports were aired nationally and even internationally about the destruction of Mobile. Contradictory telephone interviews with people claiming to be eye witnesses revealed both that all the water had been blown out of the bay into the gulf, and that the bay had been completely emptied onto the city. Most alarming was the widespread but unconfirmed news that huge sections of the city had been completely leveled.

Even people in town were not sure what had happened. Mr. and Mrs. Harmsworth Billingsley Balleriel had been evacuated and spent the night crouched down in the convenient hideaway bar at Ernest's. The fright, the noise of crashing trees, and Triple Sec followed by Tia Maria proved too much, and all three leading members of polite society spent the following day in tortured slumbers.

Tonya de Luxe fled from the Hubba Hubba Club to Red Knot Rabbit Ranch, her new bouncer Tommy Jack's daytime business in Eight Mile. She spent the day after domestically baking pecan pies for neighbors with no power (they had gas!).

For Ce Ce Anne it was like old times in her old high school sorority. She, Regina Hammerstein, and Antoinette McCrae had a spend-the-night party at Carol Ortega's condo. Completely oblivious to the tempest, the four post-deb career women stayed up until the wee hours reading aloud truly delightful back issues of *Southern Living* crammed full of the cleverest new ideas: "The Decorative, Durable Sentry Palm," "Cheddar-Pimento Dip: A Fun Fiesta," "The Classic Magnolia, So Stately in Summer." They scarcely needed to raise their normal tone of voice above the sounds of extermination and *Dies Irae* outside.

With Ernest expecting his parents, Eddie stayed in a piney woods suburb on Moffat Road with his friend Bobo, the disc jockey at Club Fifth Avenue. At the height of the storm, when garage roofs were slicing through the air like flying saucers, they left the Kingview Woods Apartments and strolled and stumbled around outside in total darkness with mixed drinks in hand, were not so much as grazed by a pine cone, watched the sun rise, switched to K&B beer, and climbed over mounds of tree limbs to barbecue-hop that day throughout the surrounding subdivisions, where the residents were trying to use up all the meat in their freezers.

But where were H. Sloane Wolfe and McCorquodale? Had the Commerce National Bank gone up in flames? Had Old Mobile, pearl of the coast, vaporized under the fleet of Buzz Barker's fire bombers to make way for a Supermall?

No. Soon after the first rosy fingers of dawn appeared, the head of the great financier could be seen cautiously emerging from the main entrance of the Commerce National Bank tower on St. Joseph Street. Seeing that the coast was clear in both directions, he soon reemerged arm in arm with McCorquodale. Their clothes were were slightly rumpled, but they themselves were none the worse for wear. With calm smiles of contentment oddly out of context with the devastation around them, they slowly picked their way through the debris of Bienville Square in the direction of the Roshfookle house on St. Anthony Street.

The miraculous salvation of the city came about because of Albert Tunney's idea to secretly move the chartered bombing fleet to the extensive flat pasture land of the McCorquodales. He had managed to get the family away before the planes were towed up by desperately begging them all to come down and help him board up his house and business. He figured that by the time they got back to Chunchula they would be too busy with their own hurricane preparations to wander around the property and discover the planes. If problems did arise he would smooth things over, as he explained to his cohorts after slipping up to Chunchula later in the day shortly before the hurricane.

When the storm had passed, the developers and the pilots they had hired emerged from the cockpits in which they had sat out the storm for a last minute conference before the firebombing flight. Eleven of the heavy bombers were still upright and ready to go, but to their dismay they found that the plane in which Albert had spent the night had flipped over, knocking the McCorquodale kinsman unconscious.

It was not a good place to be lingering without an escort. After one hundred and fifty years of isolation on their land, the McCorquodales did not take kindly to strangers and trespassers.

Barker and Todd pulled Tunney out of the plane, laid him on the ground, and carefully folded his shattered glasses and put them on his chest. As they frantically cleared wind-blown pine branches and corn stalks from the planes and the impromptu runway, they suddenly noticed that nine shotguns barrels were trained on them. Old Man Hiram and his grandsons, the nine pickup truck racing McCorquodale Boys, had appeared from nowhere.

"Whutch'all done to Albert?" Old Man Hiram growled slowly. "Tell me raht quick or I'm gone pop ya with this thirty-thirty."

One of the grandsons ran over and verified that Tunney was still breathing.

Ted Todd, the great persuader from Houston, jumped in to smooth out the situation. "Hey, Albert's our buddy! Let's mellow out just one moment here."

"You ain't no friends a Albert's. You don't talk like nobody from around these parts. You got your ass in a crack, fella." Old Man Hiram, a card-carrying member of the National Rifle Association, could not believe his luck. After all these years of reading the crime reports and calling the radio talk shows and saying what he would do if he caught a thief on his own property, here was a whole passel of them, nabbed red-handed after assaulting his niece's husband. "I'm gone pop ya raht in the butt."

"Hey, give us some latitude," Barker interjected.

"You smartmouth dipshit!"

One of the grandsons fired a shotgun blast and blew away a clump of mushrooms at Barker's feet. "Jesus!" he shouted, and hopped back nimbly. "If y'all'll just let me explain, I'm sure we can arrive at a viable posture."

"What's all them planes? Y'all think you gone run drugs on my propity? I'm gone blow you away, dude."

"No sir, no. Not a thing to do with drugs. It's for official city business. Hey, just call the police and they'll tell you who I am. I'm the mayor . . ."

"I ain't callin ary a policeman so as them librel courts can letchout on parole. Y'all are some kinda smartass mafia bosses, aincha? You peaknuckle asses, you ain't diddlysquat. Nowadays they say you cain't shoot a thief on your own propity. We gone find out *raht now* if that's true." A weird gleam had appeared in Old Man Hiram's eyes. Within his mind an intense projection of the delicious pleasure of riddling them with bullets struggled with a fading awareness of the troublesome legal consequences that might follow. "Y'all gone be missin persons. Dead and buried. I been waitin a long time for this. We're gone waste you. Blow your brains out like peanut butter. You gone be Swiss cheese."

Several weeks passed before knowing rumors began to circulate about what had taken place that day. It seemed that Todd, Barker, and the pilots had spent ten hours of fast talking tied up in the barn until Albert finally came back to consciousness and spoke up for his cronies. Old Man Hiram let them escape on foot leaving the bombers behind. Weeks later, after all hopes for the development were irremediably dead, representatives of Todd's Sunbelt Land Corporation were able to quietly retrieve the planes and leave town.

The week after the hurricane, a newly confident H. Sloane Wolfe arranged a confidential meeting with contractor Ray McDougal. Now that the Volkswagen-Supermall-Six Flags Over Jesus bubble had burst, there was no need for Wolfe to buy three hundred million dollars' worth of city bonds to finance the deal. Wolfe had to find some other way to keep McDougal from voting with Birmingham in the struggle for control of Wolfe Alabama Bancorporation.

Sometimes, for financial titans, a mere stroke of the pen can work wonders. McDougal had overextended himself somewhat in his shop-

ping center developments, and found that no bank in the state would
lend him money. To tide him through the hard times, Wolfe suggested
a small ten million dollar loan with no security.

"Coach," Wolfe smiled, "your wuid is good enough for me. What's
ten million dollars among friends?" Wolfe was still basking in the
afterglow of his hurricane party with McCorquodale. "Have a cigar, prop
ya feet up, Ray." Life stretched ahead of him like a pleasant landscape
painting.

As for McCorquodale, she found that Aunt Odilia, too, had evaded
evacuation and spent the night of the storm in the old house that had
already seen so many hurricanes. During the next few days, McCorquodale
was surprised to see her aunt humming with activity and taking her meals
in her room. She seemed to be making plans.

Part Three

The Winter Social Season

O & M

POSTMODERN CAFE

...'tis folly to be wise

Debutante Sensation

The Young Set

Ernest

CeCe Anne

Eddie

Helmut

Queen of Mardi Gras

CHAPTER 49

Social Discovery of the Century

In the weeks following Hurricane Clotilde, emergency crews labored night and day to restore the most essential services. Fallen trees were bulldozed off the streets, power lines were reconnected, and Mrs. Harmsworth Billingsley Balleriel set up a committee to ensure the orderly commencement of the winter social season, so disastrously delayed by the storm.

It was decided that the annual Camellia Ball, official start of the season on Thanksgiving night, must take place at all costs only two weeks later in December if some semblance of order was to be maintained. The National Guard trucked in several loads of fabulous André champagne from California. Private airlines donated free cargo space to fly thousands of camellias from Florida greenhouses, since the local bushes had been wrecked by the storm winds. Volunteer hurricane relief work crews of Amish and Quakers, who had come down from Pennsylvania expecting to help destitute people repair roofs and rebuild houses, were set to work lettering place cards in Gothic script night and day.

Many a tender bud blossomed at the Camellia Ball, but the talk of the town the next morning and in the following months was Miss de la Rochefoucauld, social discovery of the decade, perhaps the century. Yes, McCorquodale was making her debut!

All were amazed that the house of Roshfookle, with its two remaining members, had risen so instantly to such galactic heights. Despite certain missing links in her genealogical research before the 1840s, Aunt Odilia was not slow to assert that they were descendants of ancient Creole aristocracy. They were "ninety-nine percent suitain" that they had come over in 1702 with Bienville on the *Renommée*, she told enthusiastic *Herald-Item* reporters in an exclusive interview.

In point of fact, the final documentary missing link that would have proved their French colonial origins had never surfaced. Mr. Belzagui was feeling thoroughly spooked about the artifacts and records he had already uncovered, and stubbornly refused to discover any more documents of any kind, not even a simple little French baptismal or marriage entry. But Aunt Odilia was not one to stand forever doubting on the cliff of factual Western scientific, linear thought. Making the great leap of faith, she restored their surname to its original form. Thus Margaret Constance Roshfookle became, once and for all, McCorquodale de la Rochefoucauld.

McCorquodale, it must be said, marveled that the Zeitgeist had expressed itself in this particular form, consigning her this particular group of disciples. When she had embarked on her revolutionary trek as prophetess of the great mentality shift, her thoughts had been far removed from debuts and Young Set get-togethers. But she thought it over up in her room, and as she reminded herself, "When the mountain-spoked wheel of the ages is rolling, who am I to stand in the way?" And besides, the adulation and wining and dining that began to come her way struck her as a very natural thing.

There were gasps and fainting fits throughout the city that Sunday morning when people opened the *Contemporary Living* section of the newspaper to read that McCorquodale's ancestress Camille de la Rochefoucauld had been, as it were, the first queen of carnival in New Year's festivities of the now-defunct Mystic Tea Drinkers Society in 1847. Under somewhat different circumstances, Mrs. Balleriel and some of her peers might have had a bit more to say about that assertion, and might have investigated Mr. Belzagui's documents with some vigor. But after discreetly furnishing Aunt Odilia with a list of names for her blackmail letters, Mrs. Balleriel was eager to comply with Aunt Odilia's wishes and sponsor McCorquodale's coming out.

The recipients of Aunt Odilia's blackmail letters were equally cooperative, and hastened to shower ten or fifteen teas, *dansants*, cocktail parties, and brilliant soirées a week upon the demure debutante. Throughout all the furious struggles over the land sales and Preservation Society power politics, there had, needless to say, never been an overt confrontation or direct action or direct unpleasant word of any kind among the prominent ladies involved. All bloody daggers and chain saws were kept safely out of sight, and now a picture of perfect harmony greeted the outside observer, like the unroiled surface of a mountain lake. Be that as it may, McCorquodale maintained a lofty position high up above the gory fray, and passed up no opportunities to win new converts to the postmodernism movement.

The Tudor mansion of Mrs. Marmeduke LeVerne was the site of a brunch in early December. "The buffet table was centered with a Boehm porcelain goose led by a Hummel 'Heidi the Goose Girl' carrying a basket of asters and Callicarpa berries," the *Herald-Item* reported. "During cocktails, honoree McCORQUODALE DE LA ROCHEFOUCAULD regaled guests and fellow debutantes with a brief talk on 'Semiotic Sign Systems and Metalanguage in Werner Herzog's *Aguirre, the Wrath of God.*' Eggs Florentine and a spirited match of charades followed."

At a "Jack Frost Is Here!" party thrown in her honor by "Mrs. Chasuble Hedgemont the Thuid," it was reported that McCorquodale stood out among the heather tweeds, ruffled blouses, and nubbed silk, "drawing many an 'ooh' and 'ah' in a postmodern New Romantic llama wool poncho, white silk trousers stuffed into gaucho boots, pendant jet earrings, and Brazilian peccary skin cattle whip." McCorquodale was given a lavender scented French hand-sewn pin cushion ornamented with the party theme of tiny elves peeking around icicles.

People in the know began to whisper that McCorquodale would almost certainly be chosen from all the debutantes to be Queen of Mardi Gras that season.

During the winter social season, McCorquodale rarely saw Wolfe, even though her allowance continued to arrive in the mail every week. With McCorquodale now a celebrity, Wolfe had to be careful about secret rendezvous, and bank affairs were claiming nearly all his waking time. It seemed scarcely possible and yet, just two month after the hurricane, the Wolfe Alabama Bancorporation ceased to exist.

It had taken some slick maneuvering for Wolfe to remain in the driver's seat at the Commerce National Bank after the vicious battles of the bank war. After weeks of negotiations with the Magic City National Bank of Birmingham, both sides agreed that victory was impossible in the proxy fight. Magic City consented to allow the CNB to spin off from the holding company, which to Wolfe's chagrin was renamed "BamSouth Bancorporation." For some, the end of the empire was not unwelcome. Ce Ce Anne, for one, had always worried that the people in the upstate affiliates were not quite cute enough to meet CNB standards. But for Wolfe it meant giving up little luxuries to which he had become accustomed, such as the bank yacht and the bank helicopter ("Wolflines").

There was one remaining financial adventure, however, that Wolfe refused to give up, remembering his promise to McCorquodale. In early February, a few weeks before Mardi Gras, Wolfe had McCorquodale come to his office for official bank business. As part of the Commerce National Bank's well-known program of support for the arts, Wolfe announced that an $800,000 grant would be forthcoming for the construction of her postmodern gallery and sidewalk café on Conti Street.

"Sloane, this is too much, what will the board of directors think? No, no, I can't let you do this," McCorquodale protested, and slipped the initial check for $20,000 Wolfe had given her into her purse.

"Well, they ain't fenced me in yet," Wolfe grumbled. "The Commuice National Bank is fo-square behind watchamacallit—postmodulism. I still give the orders around here . . . even if it's not quite as big as it was befo." He looked longingly at the architect's model for the sixty-story Wolfe Alabama Tower, now only a dream.

"Oh darling, there's always hope, you'll build a new empire. Think of the Tenn-Tom Waterway. Think of 'progress.'" Truly words to conjure with, but this time they had no effect on Wolfe. There was a long silence. So much had changed between them since the hurricane.

"There's been a lot of water passed under that ole bridge," Wolfe mused. "My little shuguh pie's done made good. I wonder if things will ever be the sayim?"

McCorquodale, too, was in a reflective mood. "Sometimes, on the nights of the Mardi Gras balls, when I'm stepping out of the limousine in my furs and jewels, knowing they're all waiting inside sumptuous Municipal Auditorium to toast me, bathe me in spotlights, fall at my feet, I wonder if such apotheosis is really meant for myself, a simple esthetic pioneer woman. I generally decide that it is."

Later they posed for newspaper photos—Wolfe handing McCorquodale a check while vice president Ernest Balleriel looked on— to publicize bank philanthropy. McCorquodale made Wolfe promise to come to the Mardi Gras coronation, which she hinted would be very special.

"Sloane, do you think people are *really* ready for postmodernism? I guess we'll soon know."

CHAPTER 50

Queen of Mardi Gras

Trumpets! Trumpets! Clarion calls and triumphant fanfares! When word leaked out that Eddie the mailboy was planning the ceremony, insiders knew that the coronation of Queen of Mardi Gras would be something very special that year, but they never expected anything like *this.*

Eddie had ransacked middle and high schools for trumpeters, even shipping them in from Vinegar Bend and Bay Minette, from Escambia, Conecuh, and Choctaw counties. In Renaissance doublets and blond wigs which had unfortunately arrived from New Orleans several sizes too large, they sent silvery cascades and occasional wooden blasts rippling around the magnificent dome of the Mobile Municipal Auditorium. After the first forty-five minutes of trumpet peals, the elegant crowd stared about uneasily as though expecting strange excesses.

It was a watershed in art history. As a star of the Mobile stage, Eddie had often had occasion to help in the creation of lavish stage sets, but never on such a scale.

The reverberations of the trumpets penetrated even as far as McCorquodale's dressing room, where, in a temple-like hush, the dim room lit only by the glaring lights of the dressing table mirror, the Gulf Coast Estée Lauder representative was applying the finishing touches to McCorquodale's royal make-up.

Ce Ce Anne and Ernest had just stopped by to wish McCorquodale luck. Her idea of a postmodern coronation had caught the enthusiastic imagination of the entire court, not to mention the Junior League Committee on Urban Affairs. As they understood it, the whole affair was to be very daring, though McCorquodale assured them there were the profoundest philosophical underpinnings.

It had taken McCorquodale, Eddie, and other philosophers many sessions at the Hubba Hubba Club to devise a coronation suitable for the Gulf Coast school of radical postmodernism. Wiping the dust of "purist internationalist modernism" from off their feet, they would "quote tradition and vernacular taste cultures" but add "plural coding" with "redundant clues" so that it could be read on at least two levels. In other words, it would be a classic Mardi Gras coronation just like all the others, though certain subtle signs would show people in the know that more was afoot.

"Just imagine, I've been postmodern all my life and didn't even realize it," Ce Ce Anne exclaimed, helping McCorquodale fasten her gold lace collar embossed with costume jewelry sapphires and artificial pendant baroque pearls.

"You're a natural, darling. Be a dear and light a Tiparillo for me, I must calm myself for this moment of greatness."

"Mardi Gras was never like this before," Ce Ce Anne continued. "Postmodern call-outs, postmodern tableaux. Of course," she said somewhat defensively, "even when Ernest and I were in the court, we were never really *serious* about it. I mean, we just had a good time."

"Of course not," said Ernest, spruce in white tie. "If you are a *Balleriel* and your mother was a *Jameston*, you don't need to be serious about it."

It was such a relief that after the silly distractions of politics, religion, economics and so forth during the past year, everybody could get back to the real business of life. McCorquodale took a sip of champagne. As she lifted the goblet to her lips, the cut crystal and the gems on her collar and gown cast a shifting infinity of tiny points of light on the walls and ceiling. Ce Ce Anne and Ernest experienced a sharp intake of breath and an instant of happy weightlessness, as though leaping in an unknown cave or walking on the bottom of the sea. "Honey, you look gawgeous," Ce Ce Anne sighed. With her fair complexion, McCorquodale's face looked very bright, and in spite of all the satins and trim she seemed totally fresh and unadorned.

A burst of drum rolls signaled that Felix was making his imperial

The masses delighted in the presence of postmodern royalty—ME!

entry before the glittery throng. Ernest and Ce Ce Anne went to take their seats, and the make-up lady left, too. McCaffery ("Skip") Hardenberg, first cousin of Ce Ce Anne's friend Mary Louise McCaffery and hope of the Mobile business community, was King Felix III that year. Young McCaffery had made quite a name for himself as a junior at the University of Virginia for his trick of whipping down his pants and mooning unsuspecting pedestrians and bystanders at fraternity parties and university functions.

Alone in her dressing room, McCorquodale mused on the events of the year that had led to this pinnacle, this *non plus ultra*. She thought of that hot day in November, the silver BMW of H. Sloane Wolfe pulling to the side of the road, the Miss Brick House contest at the Santa Claus Society ball, the banning of her play by the Goths, the conspiracies of the modernists and the decisive action she had taken with Wolfe during hurricane Clotilde to stop them from leveling the city. "It was the least I could do," McCorquodale said aloud with self-effacing nobility.

She could hear the ladies-in-waiting being announced, the time was drawing nigh. Eddie burst into the room, black tails and blond bangs flying. "Miss Thang, you could pour me out of a spoon. I'm gonna swoon, I feel it comin."

"Never get nervous, darling, what would your public think? The age cries out for its great tap dancer."

Eddie bit his lower lip in pleasure.

Several attendants arrived to attach McCorquodale's train. She rose. From the auditorium they could hear the announcement: "Empress of beauty and joy, image of love, ruler of our hearts."

"McCorquodale, do ya think this-here is really the beginnin?" Eddie asked. "Is tonight the night we really go postmodern?"

McCorquodale paused at the door. The trumpets were blowing for her. "Take a note," she said. Eddie whipped out a pencil and pad.

"Thanks—if I may say so—to my humble efforts, we are now at the cutting edge of the present, *axis mundi*. Tell my people there is no turning back, for the eyes of the world are upon us." And she was gone.

Eddie's subtle use of postmodern plural-coding soon revealed to even the most unobservant of McCorquodale's subjects that there were unfathomed meanings in the "traditional" ceremony. A nervous Carnival Association had banned the massive use of soap bubbles, but Eddie managed to slip in a few surprises.

Preceded by standard bearers and nymphs scattering rose petals,

Queen McCorquodale rode through the auditorium in an Italian Renaissance float drawn by eighty semi-nude Egyptian slaves being lashed savagely with ostrich plume scourges. The hundred-foot train, stretching from her shoulders to far behind the float and carried by a virtual Children's Crusade of young pages, was strewn with fleurs-de-lis executed in brilliant paillettes, marquisette rhinestones, and cabuchon costume emeralds, symbolizing their colonial forebear, Gil de la Rochefoucauld.

Everyone thought it was such a shame that the king's mother fainted when the procession stopped at their table for McCorquodale's salutation. Aunt Odilia, however, had insisted on dressing as the Queen Mother, and waved her own scepter when McCorquodale rose on her float and bowed to her. Mr. Belzagui, Miss Hattie and Miss Alice Robinson, Father Kreismeier of St. Joseph's, and Tonya de Luxe— busting out, so to speak, in a deep-cut crimson gown—were all there.

White-bearded Old Man Hiram McCorquodale, Aunt Trudi and Uncle Tater, and the nine McCorquodale Boys, long arms sticking out of their tail coat sleeves, had come down from Chunchula, and they let out Rebel yells when the float pulled away from the table.

H. Sloane Wolfe, gruff mogul though he be, was misty-eyed as he sat with Roberta near none other than Mr. and Mrs. Harmsworth Billingsley Balleriel, Mr. and Mrs. Sturtevant Washton Belasco, Mr. and Mrs. Marmeduke LeVerne, Mr. and Mrs. Wallace Wade Stanton, Mr. and Mrs. Thurbo Newhouse, Dr. and Mrs. Tucker Batré Stauter, Mr. and Mrs. Montego Cronenburg Scattergood Funderburke, Jr., Mr and Mrs. Chauncey Bixwell Duggins Sark III, Mr. and Mrs. Pierpont Windenham Ortega IV, Ernest and Ce Ce Anne and ranks of others of the very first water. As Mr. Belzagui later reported to the Knights of Columbus, it was first class all the way.

When the moment came for Felix Imperator to crown her, McCorquodale made a shocking departure from tradition. Remembering her predecessors Charlemagne and Napoleon Bonaparte, she seized the crown from the somewhat tipsy king's hand and crowned herself.

From a tiny hole in the stage sets behind the thrones, Eddie watched every shimmering step of the proceedings. "I wonder what it's like to be a queen," he said wistfully. "I guess I won't never know."

THE EPILOGUE

Café on Conti

McCorquodale's postmodern gallery and chic sidewalk café on Conti Street, "Chez la Reine," was finished only four months after the coronation. It was one of the first great monuments of Gulf Coast postmodernism, a revival Federal style brick building with a cast iron balcony over the sidewalk tables and floor-length windows ironically outlined in slender red and blue neon lights. A marquee announced avant-garde events.

There was an Albanian film festival at the opening in July that drew rave reviews in Tirana and two lines in *Interview* magazine. Telegrams in Spanish arrived from Almodóvar and Antonio Banderas conveying their regrets. They caused a tremendous sensation, and were framed and hung near the door. Droves of art lovers from the State Docks and the Pensacola navy base regularly showed up whenever McCorquodale and Tonya de Luxe appeared on the gallery stage to perform conceptualist skits with minimalist attire and bursting gold balloons.

Also, after McCorquodale's debut the entire Young Set began to hang out at Chez la Reine to see and be seen, another sign of the passion for esoteric art that had taken the city by storm. McCorquodale was pleased that they dressed, talked, and acted exactly as they had before, because it showed that the region had leaped directly from the nineteenth century into the twenty-first without succumbing to dangerous modernist influences.

Chez la Reine became so popular and so crowded that the fashionable clientele spilled over into the Hubba Hubba Club only a block away. Tonya redecorated with hanging ferns and started serving garbanzo bean-smoked oyster quiche, and there was even talk that Task Force 2000 might start meeting there. Yet even with her economic future assured, Tonya never stopped longing for the elusive trucker trade.

"Them business cats'll keep you in pork and beans arraht, but now you getchoo a good trucker on pay day and you've got steak on the table sure nuff."

After his attempt to defraud and firebomb the city, it might be supposed that some citizens would have wanted to look into Buzz Barker's role in the Volkswagen bubble, but the seasons worked in his favor. Everybody was mad, and everybody kept saying somebody should do something. But fortunately for Barker, the only time of year when people on the coast had any initiative was in November and December, after the first breath of cold weather and before the Mardi Gras season really cranked up after Christmas. Fall that year was taken up with hurricane recovery efforts and rebuilding, the spring was filled with festivities and Queen McCorquodale's coronation. Then the summer steams were approaching, and elderly black ladies could already be seen carrying brightly colored umbrellas to block out the sun as they walked around town. Nobody had the energy to start a big investigation.

Both Barker and Ted Todd hotfooted it out of town in the confusion after the hurricane, but an interesting television interview took place when Barker sneaked back a few days later to retrieve a few valuables from his house. WMOB TV had had his house staked out, and when Barker emerged with his arms loaded with sacks and suitcases, glamorous newswoman Tina Strothers was waiting with the TV cameras rolling. News of the attempted early firebombing had spread everywhere, and Tina wanted to know what his thoughts had been about the stragglers who missed being evacuated and who would presumably have been incinerated in the fire storm. "Buzz, have you got any problem with that?"

"No, Tina, I feel real good about things," he smiled, as relaxed, poised and confident as an anorexic or compulsive gambler spilling his guts on a TV talk show. "You know everybody makes mistakes. Hey, I did, too. A breakdown in judgment definitely transpired. I'll be the first to say it."

"I guess you feel a lot of stress right now, admitting it and all."

"I think I've grown from the experience."

"Catch you later, Buzz!"

"You bet, Tina."

Yet despite this display of good vibrations and positive karma, Barker judged it prudent to forget about carrying more things out of the house, and jump in the car and leave town before another interview with the police could follow. For months rumors circulated that they had surfaced in Yucatan and were attempting a big political and economic comeback. They were hoping to demolish thousand-year-old Mayan temples as dangerous "satanic cult sites," then sell the carvings on the international antiquities market. But the Protestant fundamentalist groups that Barker always counted on for support, though spreading quickly, were not big enough yet in Mexico. Later rumors had it that they opened a hamburger franchise in Costa Rica after Barker secretly sold his Hamburger Harbor outlet in Mobile. Anyway, the whole subject soon lost its appeal as a cocktail party topic.

With Buzz Barker gone and their link to city hall taken away, the Western Hills Baptist Church stopped their campaign to shut down the Hubba Hubba Club. Rev. Orville Tidwood felt thoroughly disgusted with the Secular Humanist conspiracy that had so obviously taken over the town, and in private with the deacons he began to wonder if there was any future for their congregation here. Midtown Baptist Church contin- ued to show vigorous growth trends, and a crushing blow to Western Hills morale came when Midtown Baptist announced plans to construct a gigantic new complex on the interstate highway directly across from Western Hills' own giant megacomplex. The moment had arrived for a final slug-out of the titans.

A terrible silence emanated from Western Hills. Months passed without a single protest against a liquor license or the dog races. Onlookers trembled to think of the tornadoes of energy building up within those concrete block walls. Rumors circulated that they had been buying giant computers and flying in market analysts from Houston and Miami. The smaller Baptist and fundamentalist churches in town braced themselves, while Midtown hurriedly began construction on their new site.

The onslaught came Fourth of July weekend and was first reported by startled motorists on I-10, who at first glance assumed it was some kind of military maneuver. Within hours practically everyone within a radius of two hundred miles had heard about the launching of the bus fleet. This time it was bigger than anything they had ever seen, swollen with new vans and scenicruisers, a yellow armada, and every vehicle had a flashy logo painted on the sides: "New Life Church: WE'RE #1!"

The bus fleet came to a halt for a groundbreaking ceremony at the new territory the church had quietly purchased flanking the interstate highway at the Mississippi-Alabama state line. It was a daring idea that confirmed Tidwood's management skills once and for all. Deciding that the city of Mobile and surrounding county were too small to support a truly great congregation and his long range building program, Tidwood had resolved to build a new *mega*-megacomplex for what would be the first four-state congregation in the country, linked by their swift transportation network all the way from Slidell, Louisiana, to Fort Walton Beach, Florida. Their marketers had advised them to change the name to something more upbeat, with connotations of self improvement, and to drop restrictive labels like "Baptist" and "Western Hills." It was generally conceded that Midtown was never going to top all that.

After the defeat of the Supermall, the old downtown neighborhood around the Rochefoucauld house began to experience a gradual revival, in large part because of a key new construction that aroused much favorable comment. Sam's body shop was purchased and torn down and an opulent new town house (the Neo-Georgian esthetic did not please McCorquodale's critical sensibilities, but she managed to keep polite silence) was built next door to Aunt Odilia. It was the home of Ce Ce Anne Stanton, now Mrs. Helmut Kugelhopf.

It all came out in April after the coronation. For weeks practically the whole city was entertained by rumors about the uproar in the Stanton household and the tantrums thrown by magnate Wallace Wade Stanton. But in the end there was a tremendous wedding at Canterbury Church Episcopal and a reception for fifteen hundred on board the merchant ship *Deutsche Freude*, at which Helmut, following some lucrative arrangements with the German shipping company and the distribution of silence money to the crew, was presented as the captain.

Soon Helmut was able to make use of his seafaring experience as a respectable young executive in the Stanton Steamship Corporation, with his own office, secretary, and dart board. He was often pictured in the *Herald-Item* shaking hands at conferences on industrial development. The Mobile International Chamber of Commerce even made Helmut chairman of their Committee on Environmental Protection, and as the brawny seaman hardly spoke coherent English, he was able to do the job to their complete satisfaction.

After his humiliating experiences, Albert Tunney gave up trying to steal the McCorquodale farm in Chunchula and generally made himself as invisible as possible, in fact leaving town for eight months. Old Man Hiram and the McCorquodale Boys, however, began to use the newly painted and refurbished Rochefoucauld house as an elegant pied-à-terre when they came to town for the Saturday night wrestling matches. The tumultuous events of the past year had brought the clan closer together than ever. Sometimes, after a successful evening's entertainment, Old Man Hiram and his grandsons could be heard shooting their guns at magnolia limbs in the courtyard, but fortunately for Aunt Odilia and Ce Ce Anne's peace of mind, they spent most of their time on the up-country estate.

When Ce Ce Anne married, the break-up of the Dream Couple of the Young Set fueled much excited conversation, but everyone marveled that she and Ernest Balleriel seemed to remain on perfectly good terms after the wedding. Ernest soon started appearing at all the Mardi Gras balls and other social occasions with Ce Ce Anne's friend, Carol Ortega.

And his rendezvous with Eddie could be somewhat more open, because after staging McCorquodale's impressive coronation, and thanks to Ernest's influence and McCorquodale's indicating to H. Sloane Wolfe that Eddie deserved special attention as a member of the postmodern inner fold, Eddie was promoted to a very presentable job in Commercial Loan Concepts. Soon he and Ce Ce Anne were putting on the most sought-after coffee breaks in downtown Mobile. Indeed, Eddie began to find investment banking so satisfying a career that he decided that he would not mind so much if talent scouts for the Key West piano bars did not discover him quite yet, at least not for the next year or so.

Mysterious were the ways of the Commerce National Bank. For forty years George Belzagui languished quite forgotten in the mailroom. But suddenly he flew upwards to a big desk in the lobby "behind the brass rail," an ideal place for him to give out friendly advice on Lebanese cooking to bank customers. One factor may possibly have been his marriage to the newly prominent Mrs. Odilia de la Rochefoucauld Chighizola.

What an event! His excellency archbishop O'Reilly wore his miter to perform the nuptials for the two sexagenarians, and Mr. Belzagui's friends in the Knights of Columbus turned out at the Cathedral with enough swords and capes to put Westminster Abbey in the shade. As a result of Aunt Odilia's vast genealogical research, McCorquodale's reign became a kind of "new dispensation." Aunt Odilia, who knew everything about everybody, revealed that going back to the 1800s and beyond, nearly everyone in the city was in some way related to everybody else, which greatly expanded the ranks of society. And there was no doubt that in future generations, when the oaks had grown along the suburban roads in West Mobile, the descendants of the new arrivals would talk for hours on end tracing their lineage back to McCorquodale's reign for the benefit of non-natives, who, perhaps, would have been content with considerably less information.

No one was affected more by the "new dispensation" than the once-sour Roberta Wolfe. For over thirty years she had had to live with the terrible curse of being born out of town. But life took on new meaning as a result of a five-minute chat with Aunt Odilia at the coronation. Inquiring, very naturally, as to the maiden names of Roberta's maternal great-grandmothers, one of whom was a Longstreet, Aunt Odilia recalled a conversation back in 1952 in which she had heard that a vanished family of Longstreets had been related to the Billingsleys. A foray into the public library's genealogical archives revealed that Roberta's *great*-great-grandmother had been a Billingsley and grew up in a big Creole cottage on Theatre Street on one of the lots where old Fort Condé was demolished. Roberta was Old Mobile!

Rose Parkhurst Jameston Balleriel, it must be said, was not entirely thrilled about this newfound cousin of her husband's. But since Roberta yielded her position as president of the Preservation Society back to Mrs. Balleriel, Mrs. B. reluctantly conceded her a somewhat higher place on the Great Chain of Being.

Roberta's whole personality changed. She took to wearing red peddle pushers and breaking out into peals of laughter for no apparent reason. No one was more astonished than Wolfe. He began to have quick glimpses of that good-looking Bama cheerleader he had married that he thought had vanished long ago. Throughout that dizzying year with McCorquodale leading up to the coronation, Wolfe's activities had been as opaque as an Order of Myths tableau. Roberta had been too busy with the Preservation Society to ask questions, and now a genuine reconciliation took place. In August just the two of them went on a cruise to the fjords of Norway, which resulted in a very edifying slide presentation at the Preservation Society's September meeting.

And yet there was no one like McCorquodale. Sometimes on rainy evenings Wolfe would grow nostalgic and sit all alone in the corner at one of McCorquodale's sidewalk tables for hours on end. On these occasions McCorquodale always told the bartender to make it a double bourbon and Coke, and would go sit with the financial titan and talk very rapidly about avant-garde affairs and the latest gallery openings in Buenos Aires and Montreal.

Numerous hopeful developments took place which demonstrated that the postmodern consciousness shift was having its effect. The Tennessee-Tombigbee Waterway opened that summer, following years of construction by the Federal government, and a modest increase in port activity was registered, though not quite the stampede of construction and factory openings and progress that had been anticipated. McCorquodale noted that the local modernists seemed to have dropped quite out of sight, and were obviously cowering in their lairs, their conspiracies crushed and thwarted. A special election was called and an enlightened new mayor was elected—Wolfe was on his campaign committee—who rushed to proclaim a citywide "Postmodernism Week."

In point of fact, McCorquodale would have preferred an old-fashioned absolute monarchy with herself as head of state. She graciously contrived to live with unchangeable political facts, but set a new precedent by actively maintaining a royal presence in the public eye far past the carnival season. Unfortunately, the young Felix Imperator had had to return to college so as not to miss the regular fraternity parties crucial to his education, but McCorquodale was more than equal to the task all by herself, touring schools, shooting the start gun for the Azalea Trail marathon run, awarding the prizes at the Deep Sea Fishing Rodeo, to mention only a few instances of progressive rule. The flash bulbs popped and local TV cameras rolled when, wearing a glamorous tiara, she hosted a midsummer reception at Chez la Reine for King Elexis I and queen and the entire black Mardi Gras court, a gathering of monarchs that would have left the international gossip press agog if only they had caught scent of the story.

But McCorquodale began to feel a certain restiveness as the new winter social season approached and passed and another Mardi Gras went by with the selection of a new king and queen. Despite the months of pomp and circumstance, despite the nightly crowd packing her café, at quiet and unguarded moments she kept hearing hollow vibrations in the distance, as of drums. It was as though she caught some pattern out of the corner of her eye that disappeared when she looked more closely.

On sunny days she would sit for hours and watch the shifting mountains of Gulf clouds with their infinite shadows and bulges. Sometimes she would borrow Wolfe's BMW and drive alone to the beach, where she would sit on the sand and stare toward the south. Seagulls circled and turned. Snazzy new condominiums were going up all up and down the beach in the wake of destruction from the last hurricane. But when she shut her eyelids to a narrow crack she found she could eliminate all annoying distraction and see only empty shores and a delicious flash of hot light on the green seas that made her feel dizzy and weightless.

Refining this vision back in her room, sipping claret and preserving all for posterity in her annals, she saw aquamarine tropical waters, crystal clear to tremendous depths where schools of scarlet and indigo minnows flimmered and shivered. She was sailing past a white city descending from mountain slopes, and bending palms waved in an orange sunset.

For those who knew her well, it was not so very surprising when McCorquodale announced that duty dictated an extended tour of Rio, Montevideo, and other South American ports to last perhaps a year, perhaps longer. She would be contacting leading lights of Latin postmodernism, and laying the groundwork for a truly Pan-American movement. Pending her return, management of the café would be left to the capable stewardship of Tonya. To be sure, before making these announcements, McCorquodale was careful to calculate that artistic activities, and perhaps more to the point, liquor sales, would provide a more than adequate monthly income for her peregrinations. Even esthetic missionaries must keep one foot on the ground.

A small but devoted crowd of old-time disciples and new followers turned out at the State Docks to watch her walk up a red carpet to the *Deutsche Freude*, back in port and bound out for Brazil with a load of coal and scrap metal. McCorquodale looked like just another commoner in a pure silk Diane von Furstenberg hooded cloak. In an impromptu ceremony, she insisted on smashing a bottle of *Moet et Chandon* against the hull, stretching out a hand for balance so that an impressive row of jeweled rings sparkled in the sunlight. She had always wanted to christen a ship, and although the seasoned vessel had seen many a port since the virginal times of its maiden voyage, she decided to at least christen the voyage. Anyway the crowd was drooping and dizzy in the steam cloud heat of a late august dog day afternoon, their damp clothes were clinging, and they were in no mood to be pedantic. They clapped resolutely.

Ce Ce Anne started to cry and had to dab her eyes. "Oh honey, I could *pice out*. We were havin just the grindest time, we wish you'd stay right heuh."

"Quite naturally," McCorquodale answered, grabbing a microphone so that her selfless words could be heard more clearly. "But believe me, darlings, 'tis a far, far better thing I do." It was a very opportune introduction to a little speech she had prepared, but all this time black thunderclouds had been blowing in from the southeast, covering the sky. A spectacular flash of lightning against this dark backdrop caused everyone's jaws to drop. McCorquodale, standing with her back to the coming storm, wondered for a moment if the emotional trauma of her departure was causing an outbreak of mass hysteria in her audience, but after a long interval came an ear-splitting crash of thunder. Everybody ran for shelter.

There was a smell of rain on the sluggish breeze. Whole webs of lightning bolts flashed somewhere to the northeast over the river delta, followed after a pause by long rolls of crackling thunder. The faint wind from the bay abruptly changed to a steady gust and turned very cool, blowing away the heat with incredible speed.

"Thank Godfrey," said Eddie. He and McCorquodale had run under a metal awning propped up by two-by-fours over stacks of chains and oil drums. They had a perfect view. In her many musings, McCorquodale had sometimes discoursed on the elements that make up the ideal whole of the one true and perfect subtropical thunderstorm. Eddie was fascinated to see the storm following the exact steps.

The low ceiling of purplish black across the sky was now closing in on them. As the light changed, the windows of several skyscrapers and the gilded domes and crosses of the twin cathedral towers suddenly caught the sun and flared white and gold. Then the sun was covered and it seemed night was falling. Then came an exhilarating putrid smell, as if some last window had been opened, like a whiff of the paper mills and burning rubber and the oily water around the docks. A few fat raindrops splattered around them.

"Wow!"

The rain came down in solid sheets.

It promised to last forty days and forty nights, but in fact was over in ten minutes. Soon the sun was out blazing again and the rainwater began to evaporate. Two customs agents appeared and took McCorquodale off for some last-minute checking and form-filling. When she came back half an hour later, the water had run off and the sun had evaporated all but a few scattered puddles among gleaming white oyster shells. After all the tempest and commotion, it was as though nothing at all had ever happened.

The little crowd had regrouped, but the boat horn was sounding urgently. A group of seamen grabbed McCorquodale's trunks and suitcases, and she had no choice but to follow them up the gangplank. Eddie distributed white handkerchiefs, and everybody started waving them, even Wolfe. McCorquodale tried to salvage some of her speech as they loosed the moorings and the boat started to move. "They say Rio is a regular petri dish of postmodern culture," she shouted down to them. "A land of opportunity." Another horn blast drowned her out. She pulled a scarf out of her purse and waved it frantically, flustered and excited.

"Y'all, I'll be back! Be ready!"

Gleanings from the *Cahiers* of Margaret Constance de la Rochefoucauld

Down in Mobile they're all crazy, because the Gulf Coast is the kingdom of monkeys, the land of clowns, ghosts and musicians, and Mobile is sweet lunacy's county seat . . .

. . . And anyway Mobile is certainly a kind of island . . .

. . . But I felt that this house-party was *tellement spéciale*; I had almost a sense of embarcation for Cythera.

— Eugene Walter, *The Untidy Pilgrim*, 1953

"Endless genealogies" could be made of many city families, some noble, some bourgeois.

— Peter J. Hamilton, *Colonial Mobile*, 1897

Never choose the saltmines when tea in the orangery will do just as well.

— McC. de la R.

Fun is worth any amount of preparation.

— Dr. S. Willoughby

To make a railroad round the world available to all mankind is equivalent to grading the whole surface of the planet.

— Thoreau

The ideal land is small, its people very few . . .
Where people die and die again
But never emigrate . . .
Their meat is sweet; their clothes adorned,
Their homes at peace, their customs charm.
And neighbor lands are juxtaposed
So each may hear the barking dogs,
The crowing cocks across the way;
Where folks grow old and folks will die
And never once exchange a call.

—Lao Tzu

Never too big! Never too much!

—The Order of Thoth

Heaven is a balcony on a parade route.

—Edward Dooley

When everybody is brunched and cocktailed to the gills, throw a good theme party.

—Ce Ce Anne Stanton

If one doesn't use teabags, never watches the Oscar ceremonies, never drinks coffee out of a styrofoam cup, and never reads polls or the bestseller list, one can't go too far astray.

—McC. de la R.

The first duty of a responsible citizen is to be uninformed about the issues.

—McC. de la R.

The stained house fronts put on human shapes and looked at me.

—Dickens, *Bleak House*

Gulf Calendar:

Winter
An odor of fried sausage lingering in freezing air.
Clumps of mistletoe in bare pecan limbs.

Spring
Patches of narcissus bloom in cold fog in vacant lots by the bay,
last spoor of old gardens where houses once stood.

Summer
Bright light through slats of shutters.
Cool plaster walls, polished surfaces.
Mirrors and starched white tablecloths.
Mirage rooms flash, where
Muslin sheers billow playfully in whisps of air.
After an afternoon cloudburst, the sky is livid.
The sidewalk is crimson and glowing
With crepe myrtle petals,
In readiness for bare feet.

Fall
Hundreds of yellow butterflies perch in a tallow tree.
Seagulls circling in a parking lot.

—McC. de la R.

Jennie fell in love with Mobile, with misty mornings in winter, with rainy evenings at six when traffic was a jam around the square, with the bells of the Cathedral orating the hours deeply over the sounds of the traffic.

. . . She loved the old buildings and houses, and loved naming over the thousand variations of subtle color in the old bricks. Henna, rose, terra cotta, clay, mauve, ox blood, dark crimson, grey, Naples yellow, burnt sienna, Cassel earth, sepia, Etruscan, dubonnet.

... She loved the glimpses of back alleys with vines and trees and high walls, and clothes drying, and people sitting on the upstairs galleries reading or on downstairs galleries shelling butterbeans.

... It was the time of afternoon when four-o-clocks open; the scent filled her with a great sadness ... she wept to see a town pillaged by those who should have been her lovers.

—Eugene Walter, *Jennie the Watercress Girl,* 1946

Gumbos suitable for a royal barge:

Snail
Escargots languedociens, spinach, pine nuts, gruyère cheese, anchovy, a hint of grated orange rind, nutmeg. Dark roux the color of chicory coffee.

Fowl
Sparrows, squab, truffles, okra, tarragon, mushrooms.

Game
Venison, boar, madeira, juniper berries, thickened with blood. A brown roux the color of roast pecans. Sprinkled with chopped chives, paprika, fresh filé powder from Mon Louis Island. Served over wild rice.

Dessert
Hammond strawberries, cinnamon, cloves, allspice, Chateau d'Yquen, Framboise brandy. An orange roux of sweet potato flour and butter. Served over rice pudding.

—McC. de la R.

NOTES ON AND SOURCES OF PHOTOGRAPHS

Photographs appearing in this book have a McCorquodale reality and a historical reality. Mobile's tradition of New Year's Eve carnival/ Mardi Gras, complete with parades, balls, and secret mystic societies, goes back to 1831 and is well documented in local museums and archives.

Page 22: The shuttered back galleries and wing of an antebellum brick house on State Street. Courtesy of the S. Blake McNeely Collection, University of South Alabama Archives.

Page 59: A prominent Creole family of Mobile in the 1940s. Courtesy of the University of South Alabama Archives.

Page 82: Tableau of a Mardi Gras mystic society for women in Mobile in the 1930s. Courtesy of the Erik Overbey Collection, University of South Alabama Archives.

Page 89: The Mardi Gras royalty, with pages, 1907. Courtesy of the Erik Overbey Collection, University of South Alabama Archives.

Page 93: Felix, Emperor of Mirth, arriving from the Isle of Joy for Mardi Gras, ca 1920. Courtesy of the Erik Overbey Collection, University of South Alabama Archives.

Page 149: (Top) A row of shotgun houses in a black Mobile neighborhood, 1937. Courtesy of the Library of Congress; Arthur Rothstein/FSA photo. (Bottom) German immigrants at their store on Beauregard Street and the black residents with whom they lived and worked. Beauregard Street was the beginning of the largely Irish Orange Grove. The "Mobile Lager Beer" sign is a testament to the large German population and the local breweries, ca. 1890s. Courtesy of the University of South Alabama Archives.

Page 222: For decades, Roman Catholic Archbishop Thomas J. Toolen, third row center, was a Mobile leader. He is in procession here from the diocesan mansion on Government Street, shown in the rear, to the Cathedral. Late 1930s. Courtesy of the S. Blake McNeely Collection, University of South Alabama Archives.

Page 227: A house in the Gritney on the south side of Mobile around Canal Street and the river, before World War I. This working class neighborhood is now a network of entrance and exit ramps for the interstate highway. Courtesy of the University of South Alabama Archives.

Page 231: Lignos Brothers Grocery on Government Street. Run by Greeks, it was known for its olives, salamis, cheeses, dried cod, and other imported delicacies. Photo ca. 1930; now destroyed. Courtesy of the S. Blake McNeely Collection, University of South Alabama Collection.

Page 263: An invitation to a Christmas ball held by the Cowbellion de Rakin Society in 1858, then in their twenty-seventh year. The Cowbellions—at one point so wealthy they ordered their costumes from the Paris Opera House—were the first carnival society of the Gulf Coast, and originated the custom of balls and parades which spread to New Orleans. Courtesy of the Mobile Public Library, Local History and Genealogy Division.

Page 296: A Mardi Gras ball at the Battle House Hotel, 1950s. Thigpen Photography.

Page 311: Downtown seen from the Mobile River with the old waterfront, which was destroyed in the sixties in a Federal Urban Renewal project. This photo was taken by S. Blake McNeely for his book, *Bits of Charm in Old Mobile*, 1946. Already, half a century ago, he felt compelled to write in his dedication of the book: "To my sons, Basil, Blake, and Robert, who have come along too late to see and enjoy all the glories of Old Mobile." Courtesy of the S. Blake McNeely Collection, University of South Alabama Archives.

FRANKLIN DAUGHERTY, a native of Mobile, Alabama, is a graduate of Duke, Tulane, and Yale universities, and also studied German literature in Munich and Berlin. He has taught English to foreign students at Loyola University of New Orleans, and now teaches at the University of South Alabama. He has spent many years overseas, having taught in Saudi Arabia, Japan, Egypt, and Argentina. An inveterate traveler, he has been in many other countries as well. He enjoys studying languages — German, French, Spanish, Arabic, Anglo-Saxon — and their literatures. With the same enthusiasm, he has observed the culture of the Gulf South, working for three years as a waiter in the French Quarter of New Orleans, and for four years as a journalist in Mobile. He has published in several magazines and the anthology *Mobile Bay Times*.